CRY OF THE CURLEW

Peter Watt

CORGI BOOKS

CRY OF THE CURLEW
A CORGI BOOK : 0 552 14794 X

First publication in Great Britain

PRINTING HISTORY
Corgi edition published 2000

3 5 7 9 10 8 6 4

Copyright © Peter Watt 1999

Set in 11/12pt Sabon by
Falcon Oast Graphic Art.

Corgi Books are published by Transworld Publishers,
61–63 Uxbridge Road, London W5 5SA,
a division of The Random House Group Ltd,
in Australia by Random House Australia (Pty) Ltd,
20 Alfred Street, Milsons Point, Sydney, NSW 2061, Australia,
in New Zealand by Random House New Zealand Ltd,
18 Poland Road, Glenfield, Auckland 10, New Zealand
and in South Africa by Random House (Pty) Ltd,
Endulini, 5a Jubilee Road, Parktown 2193, South Africa.

Printed and bound in Great Britain by
Mackays of Chatham PLC, Chatham, Kent.

For Duckie and her daughters

ACKNOWLEDGEMENTS

I am indebted to three mates from Cairns whose contributions must be acknowledged. They are Brian Simpson who took me to the rivers and rainforests of Far North Queensland. Len Evans who I had the fortune to work with in the Aboriginal communities of the Gulf Country. In those days we were forced to live on fresh barramundi and mud crabs because we could not afford meat pies. And Phil Murphy who had the knack of producing historical answers to even the most obscure matters raised in my research.

Publication of a novel is not done alone. As such, I would like to acknowledge Tony Williams, my agent, whose patience has finally been rewarded. Brian Cook, whose appraisal of the manuscript was the catalyst. Cate Paterson and Madonna Duffy, whose ideas and editing helped shape the final draft of the novel. And the wonderful staff at Pan Macmillan whom I have had the pleasure to work with.

Finally, a thank you to the Spirit of the Gulf Country whose power stole my soul forever. May that be a warning to any tourist who should stray away from the European luxuries of Australia's coastal regions onto those beautiful sweeping plains of endless horizons. You too may learn what the Aboriginal people have known for thousands of years – that the Earth has a real spirit.

Colony of Queensland
1859 ~ 1868

Kilometres
0   100 200 300 400 500

Torres Strait
Islands

CAPE
YORK

Gulf
of
Carpentaria

RIVER OF
GOLD

Palmer River

Coral Sea

Burketown

BURKESLAND

Townsville

Port Denison

Q u e e n s l a n d

Fitzroy River

Rockhampton

CHANNEL
COUNTRY

GLEN VIEW

Tambo

Toowoomba

Brisbane River

Brisbane
Town

He crouches, and buries his face on his knees,
And hides in the dark of his hair;
For he cannot look up to the storm-smitten
*   trees,*
Or think of the loneliness there –
Of the loss and the loneliness there.

'The Last of His Tribe', Henry Kendall

PROLOGUE

This is my place of Dreaming.

I am Wallarie of the Nerambura clan of the Darambal people.

In your whitefella time I am almost one hundred years old and, although I am blind, I know I am sitting in the red dust under the bumbil tree where the elders used to sit and tell the stories of the Dreaming.

Although I am blind I can see the Dreaming, and I know the ancestor spirits up in the skies have spoken to me in many places I have travelled. You see me as a very old man whose body bears the scars of my tribal initiation . . . and the scars of the whitefellas' bullets.

You ask me did I know the bushranger Tom Duffy . . . Ah! He and I were brothers and he taught me the killing ways of the white man.

How many whitefellas did I kill? (A long silence.)

Do I believe that the ancestor spirits have power over the living world? And now you ask me about the curse although you do not believe in the Dreaming.

I will tell you a story about two whitefella families who believed in the ancestor spirits. One family was called Macintosh and the other family was called Duffy. They were young when I was young and the story started here a long time ago when the black crows came to pick out the eyes of my people.

It is a long story and it started when the other black crows came on police horses before the sun rose over the brigalow scrub. (A long silence.)

I remember that day and I will tell you the story.

THE
DISPERSAL

1862

1

Piccaninny dawn was behind the troop of eight horsemen as they rode in silence out of the fading bloom of the false light. Horses snorted and men shivered as a hint of the rising sun gave a touch of warmth to the cool night air.

Soon the sun would rise over the endless sea of tough and stunted brigalow scrub and the dark blue of the horsemen's uniforms would become visible in the early morning shadows of the vast and ancient inland plain. The rising sun would be a soft kiss on the faces of the two white men who rode with their Aboriginal police troopers. By mid-morning the soft kiss would turn into a savage bite, blistering their paler skins.

Sergeant Henry James rode at the rear of the troop of mounted police. His knee ached, so he rubbed at the old war injury with his free hand. It had been the cool of the long night that had brought on the dull and persistent throb to the once badly damaged leg. He knew the hot sun would help ease the pain, but the sun was still a good hour away and so, too, was the Aboriginal camp they were about to descend on with carbine and sword.

17

He slipped his boot from the stirrup and slowly stretched the aching limb. Corporal Gideon twisted in the saddle as the column plodded forward in silence.

'Leg baal?' he hissed to the big bearded sergeant as Henry winced, bending his leg to slip his boot in the stirrup.

'Yeah ... Leg baal. Always bloody bad out here,' he grumbled.

Corporal Gideon made a sympathetic clucking sound as he turned to regain sight of the horseman in front of him. Sar'nt Henry was a tough man. But he was also fair. Sar'nt Henry always stuck up for the Aboriginal police troopers of the patrol against the white devil, Lieutenant Mort.

The Aboriginal troopers of the patrol knew that the sergeant and the boss did not like each other. They had often heard the raised voices of the sergeant and lieutenant locked in confrontation. Mostly their heated words were over the welfare of themselves and their families back at the police barracks outside of Rockhampton Town. The heated clashes penetrated the bark and slab walls of the lieutenant's office to reach the troopers who strained ears to listen and they would hear the Mahmy – the term used by the Aboriginal troopers to address a white officer – threatening the big sergeant with disciplinary action. But the Mahmy was astute enough not to carry out his threats against his second-in-command as he knew full well the efficiency of the troop rested on the popular sergeant's shoulders.

Henry tested his leg in the stirrup. The stretching had taken away some of the stiffness and he sighed with pleasure for the relief. Eight long years of constant pain had plagued his life since he had received the wound, which had indirectly brought him to be three hundred miles – and two weeks west of Rockhampton – to this harsh and lonely place on the Australian frontier.

His worst nightmare, as a soldier of Queen Victoria's army to the Crimean peninsula, was realised on the banks of the Tchernaya River near a little town called Inkerman. The formidable Russian soldiers had poured out of the nearby port city of Sebastopol; a thunder of Russian cavalry drowned by the awful crash of Russian artillery. And behind the wall of shrieking lead and thundering hooves, the grim-faced Russians had advanced to swamp the English army.

On a misty and bitterly cold morning, the nineteen-year-old soldier fell screaming as a shrapnel ball from the Russian guns opened his leg from thigh to knee. The initial searing and awful agony was long gone, but it had left him a legacy of a lifetime of suffering.

Discharged because of the permanent damage to his leg, he was left alone with his pain and a bleak future in England. He took stock of his life. Before he had enlisted, he had worked on his family's smallholding in Yorkshire. He knew farming as well as he knew soldiering and the distant colonies of Australia offered land to those willing to work hard. The former soldier was prepared for work and with his meagre savings from the army – and a loan from an older brother – Henry took passage to the far shores of Moreton Bay.

When he limped from the gangway of the

migrant ship onto the banks of the Brisbane River he knew he would never be returning to England. Unlike many of his fellow passengers, he immediately fell in love with the vitality of the frontier town. Everything around him exuded a newness; the town itself, with its bark and pit-sawn timber buildings, was in such stark contrast to the cold stone houses of England. The very fact the town was built of timber and tin implied a state of flux, holding a promise of bigger and better things to come.

But it was the native-born colonialists themselves that impressed him most as he limped along the dusty and wagon-rutted streets of Brisbane Town. They were taller, stronger and healthier than the pallid and malnourished inhabitants of England's smog-choked industrial cities. He was also awed by the fierce and proud bearing of the bearded, wild young men who recklessly galloped their mounts at breakneck speed past the lumbering teams of ox drays laden with supplies for the far-flung homesteads of the settlers on the frontier. The colonial centaurs wore brightly coloured shirts as vivid as the parakeets that flew in whirling clouds overhead and they wore riding breeches tucked into knee-length boots, with big revolvers strapped at their waists in holsters or slipped behind wide leather belts. On their heads they wore curious broad-brimmed hats made from the plaited leaves of the cabbage tree.

He had stepped off the migrant ship in the year 1856 and three years later the Colony of Queensland was given its independence from New South Wales. Brisbane Town, on the banks of the

Brisbane River, was declared the capital of the new colony. A colony encompassing half a million square miles of yet to be explored territory stretching to the lush tropical islands of the north and islands where cannibals and head hunters still roamed the Torres Strait in their long war canoes, as they had for centuries before the white man came with the flags of Portugal, Holland, France and England fluttering from the mastheads of their ships. The colony stretched west over the coastal spine of rugged mountains covered in tropical rainforest. Where the rainforests of the mountains ceased, grass and scrub plains extended further west into sand and gibber stone deserts seemingly without end. A land of limitless horizons.

While in Brisbane, Henry learned of a position with the Native Mounted Police as barracks sergeant and he was able to convince the commanding officer that, despite his war injury, he was more than capable of filling the position. The commanding officer was convinced when Henry demonstrated his ability to ride and handle horses – a legacy of growing up on an English farm – and he was appointed to Lieutenant Morrison Mort's troop.

From their first meeting, the new barracks sergeant and the commanding officer of the troop took an instant dislike to each other. For Henry it was his commanding officer's martinet behaviour. Henry might have found a rationale in the new officer's petty bureaucratic manner if he had been born an Englishman, but he was colonial-born, and Henry avoided Mort whenever possible as he felt distinctly uneasy in his presence. Despite the man's handsome and dashing appearance, his pale blue eyes held a madness that was terrifying in its intensity. More than the madness were the occasional flashes of a creature, less than animal, staring up from the burning pits of hell.

Henry shuddered superstitiously at the recollection of the madness. He had seen that same smouldering insanity in those cold blue eyes the evening before, when the officer had briefed the police troop and the shepherds who accompanied the squatter Donald Macintosh and his son Angus. Henry also knew the Aboriginal troopers instinctively sensed the madness as they stood warily away from the *white debil* while Mort had scratched lines and circles in the red earth with the point of the infantry sword, marking a crude map which had outlined a creek and a range of low and broken hills to the west of a meandering string of water holes.

'We are here,' he had droned to the gathered party of men who stood – or squatted – in a semi-circle around the sketch, etched in the crumbling dry earth. 'The nigger camp is here.' He jabbed with the sharp tip of the sword to indicate a place between the creek and the hills and he had then turned to the broad-shouldered Scottish squatter.

'That is where you last knew of their whereabouts, I believe, Mister Macintosh?'

Donald nodded.

Donald Macintosh was an impressive man and his son, Angus, who stood beside him, was a replica of his imposing father. Both men had long, dark, bushy beards with a touch of red streaks through them. Donald – at fifty-five – had the physique of a man half his age. His face above the beard was tanned by the years he had spent under the Australian sun and he wore the same work dress as his shepherds; moleskin trousers tucked into knee-length boots, a flannel shirt of bright red. A brace of Tranter pistols tucked behind a wide leather belt around his waist set him apart from his men who carried rifled muskets. A casual observer would never have guessed that the burly and rustic-looking Scot was the patriarch of a family whose wealth rivalled that of the richest in any of Britain's far-flung colonies. Land, shipping and merchandise formed the basis for the extensive financial interests of the Macintosh family. With the purchase of the Glen View pastoral lease, they were now adding sheep and wool to swell the coffers of the family's considerable fortune.

'Angus says he saw them gathering there last week,' Donald scowled. 'It's their traditional camping ground this time of the year and it's not likely they will be anywhere else.'

Mort sketched a line with the point of the sword in the red soil map to the east of the camp and continued, 'My troopers will form up here . . . 'Bout a mile from the niggers' camp. I suggest that you circle the camp tonight, Mister Macintosh, with your party, and take up a position . . . here!' The sword tip came to rest between the creek and the range of low hills. 'My guess is that when we go after the niggers they will break and make their way towards the high ground as they will no doubt run from us. All going well, they'll run straight into you and your men,' he concluded with grim satisfaction for the lethal simplicity of his plan.

'Are there any questions on what we are doing to-morrow?' He scanned the ring of men around the dirt map.

'What about the gins and piccaninnies?' Henry asked when Mort's eyes met his. 'Mister Jackson always ordered they be spared in a dispersal.'

The police lieutenant's eyes narrowed as his expression barely concealed his contempt for the question. 'This is a dispersal, Sergeant James,' he replied. 'You leave the gins and piccaninnies and they will breed their treacherous kind to become a nuisance in the future. Mister Macintosh has not called on us to have us come back to do this all over again. No . . . we do the job once, and we do it efficiently . . . I *will* allow the troopers to dally with the nigger women that they might take alive . . . But you will ensure that the problem of the gins' disposal is met before we leave. Does that answer your question, Sergeant James?'

Henry nodded and stared down at the lines and circles on the ground which were now becoming vague patterns in the dust as the hot sun slowly sank in the west.

Before the sun set that evening, Donald Macintosh and the party of seven shepherds rode out of the police camp to take up a position to the west of the unsuspecting tribespeople. Neither European nor Aboriginal could imagine the terrible consequences the following day would bring to all their lives. Consequences that would stretch far beyond their time to haunt the living of both cultures. Even of those yet unborn.

Mort had ordered that no camp fires be lit and it

had been a long night for Henry as the dark chill seeped through his body and gnawed at his damaged leg, while the mournful cry of the curlews deep in the brigalow scrub had also kept him awake. Although he knew the eerie cries came from a small ground-living bird, there was still something haunting in the sad wailing cry. Like the cries of the dead – which they were, according to Corporal Gideon. Henry could almost believe the trooper's story as he lay shivering under a coarse blanket. First one curlew would cry out – then be joined by many others. The chorus of wailing like the pitiful cries of souls doomed to eternal damnation in hell.

'Corporal Gideon!'

The whispered command from Mort was passed down the line of horsemen until it reached the tall and wiry police trooper who spurred his mount past the column of Aboriginal troopers to stop beside the Mahmy.

'Yessa, Mahmy?'

'I want you to go ahead and confirm the presence of the enemy on the creek.'

Gideon frowned. The white debil used words he did not understand – like confirm! Mort saw his perplexed expression and swore as he thrust his face belligerently at him.

'Damned ignorant charcoal!' he snarled. 'I want you to go and see if your nigger brothers are at the camp on the creek. Then I want you to come back and tell me. Do you understand that much?'

'I savvy,' the trooper replied with a carefully controlled edge of anger as he reined away and was quickly swallowed by the scrub.

Gideon was unerring in his ability to guide his mount silently through the dry scrub of the brigalow but he rode cautiously as he approached the creek line. The police corporal had a grudging respect for the tribesmen of central Queensland who, given the tactical terrain of thick scrub and rocky hills, were men to stand and fight. The white man dared not pursue the warriors into the scrub because their mounted mobility and European firepower were negated by the terrain, and the lethal accuracy of the long hardwood spear hurled at close range had taken more than one foolish settler who had underestimated the tribesmen on their own ground.

The Aboriginal warriors of Queensland had quickly learnt to exploit the tactical weaknesses of the white invaders. Only Gideon and his fellow Aboriginal police troopers were any match for the skills of the painted black warriors in the close-quarter fighting of the thick bush and rocky hills.

Founded by the flamboyant and hard-drinking bushman Frederick 'Filibuster' Walker in 1848, the Native Mounted Police had come from the remnants of the southern tribes of the Riverina district of New South Wales. Gideon had been recruited from the banks of the Murrumbidgee River by Frederick Walker himself. He had been selected for his superb physical condition and ability to learn the killing ways of the white man.

Gideon had no qualms about killing his fellow Aboriginals because the Queensland tribesmen were as alien to him as the white man. His own world was a thousand miles south on the banks of the Murrumbidgee where he had another name. One that had been granted to him on his traditional initiation into manhood. But it was a secret name that he could not tell the white man for fear of tribal punishment. So they had given him one of theirs – Gideon – and told him it was a sacred name of an ancient warrior. His natural leadership qualities had quickly earned the respect of his European officers and he was soon promoted to the rank of corporal.

Gideon's acute hearing first alerted him to the camp as he guided his mount cautiously through the scrub. He'd picked up early morning sounds of old men coughing from the smoke of rekindled cooking fires, babies crying as they sought the first suckling of the dawn and the yelp of a dog as it received a kick for its furtive attempt to snatch a meaty bone from beside a smouldering fire.

He slid from his mount and crept forward with the stealth of a hunter and, as he edged his way towards the camp, he thumbed back the hammers of the double-barrelled carbine and carefully scanned the disappearing darkness for any signs of his enemy. He was once again the warrior and alert to the most minute sounds of the bush. But this time his enemy was a tribe he had never known before.

Through dark eyes he observed the peaceful camp come to life. The Nerambura were not aware of his presence on the other side of the water holes.

2

The warbled sweet notes of the magpie in the brigalow scrub was the first thing young Tom Duffy heard when a big and bearded Irishman kicked at his bare feet. Tom woke reluctantly with a groan and pulled the blanket over his head.

'We won't be reachin' Tambo this week', Patrick Duffy growled down at his son, who attempted to retrieve the fragments of a shattered dream steeped in carnal pleasures, 'if you don't give Billy a hand.'

'Yeah, Da,' Tom replied truculently. 'I'm getting up now.'

The sweet aroma of damper loaf and strong sugared tea from the crackling breakfast fire a few yards away drifted across to Tom who still lay under the heavily laden bullock dray. He yawned and hauled himself to his feet while his father growled a greeting as he trudged past the Aboriginal teamster Old Billy squatting beside the fire.

Patrick Duffy's life had been lived in two worlds: that of his birthplace of Ireland where he had opposed – sometimes with force of arms – the British occupation, and in the Australian colonies continuing his struggle against the English Crown at the Eureka Stockade. Now he lived far from the memories of those struggles to build something for his children . . . For the memory of his beloved Elizabeth who had died of fever on the sea voyage to the Australian colonies and was buried at sea.

Billy was the last of his clan as the white man's sickness had killed most of his people. And where the epidemics had failed to decimate them, the arsenic-laced flour left by the squatters beside the water holes had finished off the handful of survivors. He had watched helplessly the agonised death from poisoned flour of his wife and children so many years earlier, and afterwards had wandered aimlessly among the giant river gums that guarded the billabongs of the mighty waterway that meandered across the flat plains between two colonies.

Eventually his wanderings had brought him to a white settlement called Corowa. He had stayed on the fringes of the town where Patrick found him begging for food and rum. He gave the old Aboriginal a job because he needed the skills of a natural bushman. But more than that, the Irish teamster gave him respect and together they had seen fire and flood. Common adversity and an acceptance of each other's spirits had cemented the friendship between the two men.

They had shared camp fires and discussed the meaning of their two worlds. The white man was like no other the old Aboriginal had known and now the turning of the dray wheel measured the moments of his existence.

As Patrick Duffy walked away from the

Aboriginal teamster squatting by the camp fire, he was unaware that a strange and terrible portent had appeared in their lives. One that only Billy recognised all too clearly.

Tom scratched at his beard. He itched from the dust of the track and thought about the creek Billy said was only a few miles to the west. The evening before he had watched the swirling cloud of tiny finches fly overhead and carefully noted the direction the birds had taken. They knew that the birds' flight was towards a source of water, and a plentiful supply of water meant a chance to wash away the cloying sweat-caked dust of the track from his body and beard.

He paused in his scratchings. Billy was rocking on his haunches beside the fire and crooning an eerie sound. Tom instinctively knew what it meant and a chill ran through him like an icy river.

'Da!' he called to his father who was un-shackling the leg hobbles from the bullocks while they stood still with bovine patience.

'What is it?' his father answered as he straightened and gave the lead bullock, Mars, an affectionate pat on its broad forehead.

'I think you should come over here,' Tom replied with an edge of panic in his voice. 'I think something is wrong with Billy.' In all his twenty-one years on earth, Tom had never felt more fear than he now experienced. The crooning chant was a weird and alien sound as if at one with the shadow world between night and day, and the young teamster fervently wished he would stop his wailing.

'Billy, you old pagan, you're scaring the bejesus

out of us,' Patrick chided as he strode towards the man crouching and rocking with his head in his hands. 'What in the name of Saint Patrick are you going on about?'

Billy did not answer but continued to chant and stare across Patrick's shoulder to where he could see the Messenger watching him with the smug knowledge of what was to happen. The same Messenger had been foretold in his vision during the silent hours of the night. How could he tell his friend of the terrible vision that had come to him in the dark? Nearby, a crow with shiny black feathers perched on the eucalypt tree beside the hobbled bullocks.

Patrick noticed the old man's stare fixed on a point beyond his shoulder and turned to see the raven-like bird perched in the tall tree watching them with beady evil eyes, seemingly alive with malice. A superstitious shudder ran through the big man's frame.

'A bloody crow,' he growled. 'You've got yourself into a state over a bloody crow.' He tried to sound annoyed but secretly he had a great respect for the old Aboriginal's unexplainable insights. The same strange powers had been strong in Elizabeth, his wife, and now in his daughter, Kate.

He searched around for a rock. Unable to find one, he wrenched a tuft of dry grass attached to a clod which he hurled at the crow. The clod fell short and the bird remained unperturbed by the angry Irishman's efforts to scare it away. It would leave in its own time.

Then the crow spread its wings and caught the morning's first rays with a spectacular shimmering

31

flash of green light. It gave a long, lazy cawing call to Billy. The crow had spoken to him, but in a way the white man could not hear, nor understand. And the ominous words that the crow spirit spoke had been plain and simple. They were in a place of death!

Corporal Gideon returned from his reconnaissance as silently as he had left.

Sergeant James joined Lieutenant Mort who glanced impatiently at the sun creeping above the scrub. Time was running out for the troop if they were to be successful in catching the tribe unawares before the men left to join hunts and the women scattered to dig for yams.

'How many?' Mort asked the scout.

'Big fella camp, Mahmy. Many blackfella . . . from here to here,' he replied, spreading his arms in a wide arc, and Mort turned to his second in command for an interpretation.

'Probably around fifty,' he mused as he leant forward in the saddle. 'Seems like a clan gathering rather than the whole tribe. What side are the young bucks sleeping on?'

The Aboriginal corporal waved with his hand and replied, 'Away from the water, Sar'nt Henry. Young blackfella toward the bush on the other side.'

From his answer Henry knew that the single men, who would compose the bulk of the warriors, were sleeping in a rough form of an outer defence perimeter, while the unmarried girls, old people and children slept in designated areas within the defensive arc.

32

'Can horses cross the creek?' Mort asked anxiously and Gideon's face broke into a genial smile.

'My word, Mahmy,' he replied. 'Water . . . this deep.' They watched the Aboriginal corporal lean from his mount to indicate the water only came as far as the belly of his horse and Mort breathed a sigh of relief. Fortune was still on his side.

'Corporal Gideon,' Mort said, sliding his infantry sword from its leather scabbard hanging at his waist. 'You will take the centre and guide the attack. I will be just behind you.' He then turned to his sergeant. 'Sergeant James, you will form the men line abreast. When we get to the nigger camp I want you to stay with the horses while the boys go in after the darkies on foot.'

Henry wheeled his mount away and trotted back to the waiting troops. He was pleased that he was not required to pursue the survivors. On more than one occasion he had witnessed the savage ferocity of the mounted troopers as they cut down the near helpless Aboriginals in the mopping-up phase of a dispersal.

He relayed the order and the mounted troopers formed the single rank with precise ease. They were superb horsemen and Henry could not help but feel a flush of pride as the hours of tedious practice on the parade ground was manifested in the way men and horses responded calmly and professionally to the order.

'Ready carbines!'

The black troopers propped musket butts against thighs, cocked the hammers of their carbines, and awaited the next order. The expressions on their dark faces were studies in alertness and anticipation as their horses tossed heads and snorted as they too sensed the imminent charge being transmitted in the tense action of their riders.

'Walk!'

The mounted troopers moved forward in an orderly line. Small shrubs bent on the broad chests of the police mounts, and then were crushed under hoof. Tiny bush birds fled from the thickets in alarm as the strange beasts advanced like an unstoppable monster. After a few minutes, the police corporal turned to his commanding officer to hiss, 'Here, Mahmy!' They were within striking distance of the Nerambura camp and Mort spurred his mount through the line to take up a position at the front of the rank where he raised his sword which caught a flash of early morning sunshine bursting with an explosion of white fire along its length.

'Charge!'

He brought the sword down and leaning forward in the strirrups the troopers gave a whoop as horses exploded into a furious gallop with heads outstretched and nostrils flaring while the big mounts vied with each other in a race to be first across the creek and into the camp. The ripple of horsemen became a tidal wave on its way to swamp the unsuspecting and peaceful Nerambura clan of the Darambal people. And like a tidal wave it surged forward bringing indiscriminate death to all in its path.

At first the strange rumbling sound was like that of the summer storms before the time of the heavy rains. The dogs of the camp sniffed suspiciously at the air, at the unfamiliar scent, and trotted stiff legged with tails erect to the edge of the camp where they began a furious barking. Babies began to wail as the rising fear from their mothers was transmitted to them. No-one thought of running as the sound paralysed them with the fear of the unknown. Then the sound became visible and even more terrible than the Nerambura could ever have imagined.

The horsemen burst upon them splashing across the creek to crash through the flimsy gunyahs and scatter the cooking fires in showers of orange cinders. The blasts of the carbines came as a single shattering volley, and the heavy lead shot flung men, women and children, torn and bleeding, into the dust of the earth where they were trampled under the hooves of the frenzied horses.

The dogs were first to scatter, barking their defiance against the strange four-footed beasts as they sought refuge in the surrounding bush. Mothers snatched at babies, warriors for spears and nullas but the troopers were upon them before they could fight or flee. Many of their terrified cries were strangled short by a second volley from the muskets as lead shot found easy targets of yielding flesh and bone. When the carbines were emptied, they were wielded like clubs to crush skulls and snap necks. It did not matter whom they killed. Such was the speed and surprise of the attack that the warriors did not have an opportunity to effectively arm and resist and, like the wiser women and dogs, they chose the course of fleeing the terrible killing ground.

In the melee of killing, Mort caught sight of a toddler. The divine madness was upon him. The child stood paralysed with a wide-eyed expression of wonder and fear of the strange creature that had come into his world. He raised his chubby fists to his eyes to block out the sight that had caused him so much anguish as it thundered towards him. The sword took the little boy through his tiny chest and the momentum of the galloping horse lifted him bodily from the ground.

With an expert flick of his wrist, Mort released the toddler from the point of the sword and had a fleeting glimpse over his shoulder of the little body tumbling like a rag doll in the dust with blood pumping in short, bright spurts from a ruptured artery.

With a whoop of exhilaration for his first kill of the day, he searched with feverish eyes for another victim. A young woman or an unarmed warrior was his preference. But only the old and infirm remained amidst the carnage of the camp. Too slow to escape the troopers, they died with their hands over their heads in futile attempts to ward off the boots and carbine butts of the black policemen. Those able to find strength to resist their petrifying fear had now fled into the surrounding scrub. Mothers carried babies or dragged toddlers while the men desperately attempted to rally, to resist the troopers pursuing them, but they were scattered by the volleys of shot poured into their ranks by the troopers who had quickly and expertly reloaded.

Henry snatched up his reins as the troopers slid from their mounts. The black police quickly shed their uniforms which only impeded them in the thick tangle of scrub. Naked, except for forage caps and ammunition bandoliers slung across chests, they plunged into the bush in pursuit of their helpless quarry, skilfully reloading their carbines on the move . . . Bite the end off the paper cartridge, pour powder down the barrel, paper cartridge as a wad, lead ball, ram home with ram-rod swivel fixed to end of barrel, percussion caps on nipples of musket . . . gun primed and loaded.

An eerie and unnatural silence descended around Sergeant Henry James, broken only by the crackle and hiss of the fires swirling clouds of grey white smoke into the morning air. Scattered screams of terror, popping sounds of muskets and excited yells from the stalking troopers drifted from the scrub to intrude on the silence.

Later the crows would flock to pick at the feast left in the wake of the troopers' murderous charge. At night the dingoes would scavenge as they snarled and fought with each other over the corpses. And finally the goanna would come to tear at the rotting flesh with its sharp teeth and dagger-like claws. But, for now, the buzzing of the myriad flies formed the vanguard of the scavengers as they settled on the dead and dying.

With his revolver drawn, Henry searched warily about the devastated campsite because these were not people who gave up their lives without a fight. He brushed away from his face a cloud of flies which rose from the corpse of an old Aboriginal man whose head had been crushed by the leather boot of a trooper and whose opaque lifeless eyes stared blankly at the cloudless sky above.

As the police sergeant picked his way cautiously through the scattered bodies, he surveyed the devastation in the camp. Stone slabs, grooved for grinding seed for flour, lay scattered and broken among discarded spears, shields and boomerangs. A carcass of a wallaby lay black and hairless by a cooking fire and a gunyah, toppled by the impact of horse and rider, had collapsed into a nearby fire where it burned with a sweet and pungent scent from the oils in the timber framework. Henry had long steeled himself against such sights . . . they were the way of the frontier. Despite this, he knew that the day would leave a heavy debt on his soul.

He stepped over the dead Aboriginal and advanced cautiously towards the muddy creek. When he was near, he heard a sound he prayed would not be what he knew it was. The moaning was long and pitiful.

He scanned the creek and saw a young woman sitting in the shallow water in a tangle of her own entrails, which trailed away like pale blue sausages. In her agony, she was barely aware of the white man approaching her and it was only in the last second of her life that she looked up with pain-filled eyes into the face of her executioner.

The recoil of the blast from the revolver caused the gun to buck in the sergeant's hand and the conical bullet tore through the girl's forehead. It was not the first time that he had used the gun to end the lives of the critically wounded. Nor would it be the last.

The girl seemed to shrink as the bullet exploded in her brain and she slumped sideways turning the water crimson around her head. Her blood swirled away on the gentle eddy of the slow-moving creek and carried his words written in red to eventually stain the earth when the water was gone.

'Poor, bloody myall,' Henry choked as he turned and walked away from her. 'Just a fucking girl!'

Wallarie trembled uncontrollably as the sergeant moved away from the dead girl. The line of troopers had passed by him and had not seen the young Aboriginal warrior crouching terrified in the scrub where he had watched with helpless horror the slaughter of his people. Why had he not used his spears in an attempt to stop the killing? His haunted question begged an answer and the answer came to him in cold and practical terms. How could he be expected to face such an irresistible onslaught of men and beasts?

The young warrior tried to control his fear as he crouched and tugged frantically at his beard. He fought his terror with the courage of a man who had lived through the shock of a lightning strike from the bowels of a raging storm. But soon the uncontrollable trembling of the frightened man became the tremor of an enraged warrior who knew that he would exact a toll on the killers of his people. He would use every skill he had – as warrior and hunter – to revenge his clan.

He watched warily the big white man limping among the bodies of his people: rolling each one over with his boot with the pistol pointed as he did so. Wallarie gripped his spears with a calm certainty, but the white man appeared alert and dangerous as he moved from one body to the next.

Although he was within range of the spear, there

was thick bush between them that could easily deflect the weapon in flight and Wallarie knew that his option of closing with the white man across open ground was not a good one. The killers of his people carried a weapon that had the ability to kill with the sound of thunder. No, instead he would stalk the black crows who would not expect an attack from behind, as they would be too pre-occupied in chasing his people who were fleeing for the comparative safety of the nearby hills.

He slipped deep into the bush away from the ground that he knew he would never visit again. It had become a place of spirits where only the dead should roam. A place where the dead could hear the whispers of the ancient warriors reaching to them from their graves on the sacred hill.

The young warrior did not know that he too was hearing the voices of the long-dead Darambal warriors calling to him down the corridors of time. But their words would come to him only when he had despaired of surviving the day.

Henry, unaware that he had been under observation from the warrior, continued with his grisly task of shooting the critically wounded Nerambura. He counted his blessings that, apart from the girl in the creek, he could only find three others alive.

When he was satisfied that the only surviving creatures were the flies, he slumped with his back against a coolabah tree where he wiped tears from his eyes with the back of a gunpowder-stained hand. The powder stung but his tears felt good. Killing warriors was one thing . . . killing women and children another.

The fires of burning gunyahs crackled and the smoke swirled on the early morning breeze to drift wraith-like in the azure sky. There would be times later in his life when the smell of burning eucalyptus would bring back the bitter memories of the dispersals. Eucalyptus was the scent that he had first associated with his new home, but now burning eucalyptus was the smell of death.

A solitary crow cawed in the distance while Henry waited alone for the troopers to return. He cried softly for the dead girl in the creek and he cried for the loss of his soul. But no man would ever see him cry. Grief was a personal thing that he shared with the Nerambura dead who now surrounded him with their accusing silence.

3

In the predawn, Donald Macintosh and his party had silently saddled their horses, snatched a breakfast of cold damper washed down with water from their canteens, and to the fading cries of the curlews and the creaking of saddle leather, picked their way to the sacred hill of the Nerambura people.

There they waited slouched in saddles, brushing away the swarms of flies that bothered man and beast as the sun rose in the clear skies.

Donald's thoughts were not on the ambush but on the long dry season that had stubbornly persisted. The destructive tornado-like swirls of dust on the plains were more and more frequent, and they came as choking masses of red dust twisting and spiralling into the cloudless skies, tearing the bark roofs from the outbuildings of the homestead. The summer rains had come and gone the previous year without delivering the promise of a good drenching for the parched plains, and the last remaining water was quickly disappearing from the water holes.

For all his wealth and power, he had no control

over nature. But he was able to console himself that he could do something about one problem affecting the future financial success of his property. He could drive off the Children of Ham who competed with his flocks for the precious last sources of water.

He gazed down the line of horsemen to his son who had taken up a position at the far end. When their eyes met, Angus flashed him a smile and the young squatter felt a rush of admiration for his father who seemed so calm, as if he were waiting for the start of a grouse shoot and not the slaughter of the Aboriginals who lived on Glen View. He envied his father's apparent calmness because he could not feel the same peace. Something, somewhere watched him. Something with no form but as real as the dust and heat of the ancient land. A sickening wave of nausea over-whelmed Angus and he swooned. Donald noticed his son slump in his saddle and could see that he was pale and distressed.

'Are you feeling unwell, lad?' he called down the line with paternal concern. Angus could hear his father's voice call to him, as if he were speaking from a long way down a tunnel, and he recovered momentarily.

'It's nothing, I am well,' he reassured him. 'Just a touch of the sun.' But he knew it was not the sun that had made him feel the dread whose form was as real as the nausea that had almost swept him from the saddle.

The Cave ... White warrior searching for his prey ...

The image shimmered in his fevered mind like

the sun-parched plains at midday and he desperately attempted to shrug the disturbingly persistent idea from his thoughts. But the image persisted as a haze before his eyes.

The white stick-like warrior stalking him with spear poised for the killing thrust . . .

A week earlier Angus had met the white warrior of the cave when he and two of his shepherds had stumbled on the sacred place of the Nerambura. They had gone in search of missing sheep in a small range of ancient hills on Glen View and stumbled into a cavern partially concealed under a massive rock overhang.

'Jesus! What is it? What is this bloody place?' One of the shepherds had sworn as they gazed with superstitious awe at the sweeping panorama of ochre paintings on the cavern walls. A depiction of life and death. And even beyond death! Of ancient hunts of creatures long extinct and stick-like men with spears. The shepherds had exchanged apprehensive glances. The primitive place was somehow frightening and the ancient paintings seemed to have a life of their own.

Angus had noticed the frightened exchange between his men and sneered contemptuously at their unspoken fears. The eerie majesty of the cavern had made him think of being inside a primitive cathedral – albeit a heathen place of worship – and it was apparent that his companions did not want to remain in this obviously sacred place of the Darambal people.

A hushed and brooding silence had warned him that he was trespassing. But he was, after all, the heir to a sprawling Anglo-Scottish empire and, as such, he should not be cowed by primitive icons.

He had slid a broad-bladed knife from the side of his boot and approached the ancient paintings where he had singled out an ochre depiction of a white stick-like warrior poised in the act of holding a spear above his head. How long ago the ancient artist had painted the hunter was beyond estimation. The shepherds watched nervously as he scraped slash marks through the white figure.

'I don't think you should be doin' that, Mister Macintosh,' Jack scowled, shuffling his feet. 'It could bring us bad luck.'

'You're right, Jack. It *will* bring bad luck . . . for the darkies . . . not us,' Angus sneered as he had slid the knife into his boot and stepped back from his desecration to gaze upon the panorama of paintings. 'When we get the chance we are coming back with powder . . . and blasting the overhang down.'

Satisfied that he had made his point, he led his men from the ancient cave to a world where one could feel the wind and hear the reassuring natural sounds of the bush. Inside the vast area of the overhang, none of those things had seemed to exist. There had been only an overpowering and brooding force that was frightening in its inexplicable existence.

Stones and pebbles showered down on the line of horsemen and the shepherds, tense with the waiting, jumped in fright. Muskets and pistols swung to face the threat from the rear as horses skittered under their riders.

'What are ye, mon?' Donald taunted. 'Sassenach

women to be frightened by a wee, furry beastie.' The shepherds flashed sheepish grins at their tough boss as they watched the small rock wallaby bounding up the slope behind them.

Donald shook his head. He only ever lapsed into the Scots' version of English when he was joking – or very angry – as he felt the Anglo-Scots' dialect had more purity in expressing a point at these times.

He glanced anxiously at his son to see his re-action to the false alarm. His son's bearded face gave him the predatory look of a hawk and Donald felt a swell of paternal pride for the young man who would some day inherit the Macintosh empire from him. He was still reflecting on this when the distant and violent sounds of the dispersal drifted to the waiting men.

The horses' ears pricked and the shepherds stirred from the drowsiness that had returned to them after the false alarm. They became alert and fidgeted nervously with their muskets and revolvers. 'Be ready, lads,' Donald growled quietly down his line of horsemen. 'Won't be long before we see the darkies.'

But it was a long twenty minutes before the first of the fleeing Nerambura stumbled blindly into the ambush and Angus Macintosh killed his first man.

The young warrior burst from the scrub dragging his shield and spears. So intent had he been to avoid the pursuing troopers that the thought of reaching the comparative safety of the hills had distracted him and the naked warrior came to a gasping halt only ten paces from Angus.

'Look out, Mister Macintosh ... he's got a spear,' a shepherd called unnecessarily to Angus who was as aware of the man as the warrior was of him. There was a terrified and cornered look in the man's smoky eyes as he realised the trap that he had stumbled into and he desperately brought back his arm to hurl the barbed spear at the horsemen blocking his escape. But he was off balance for the throw and Angus reacted quickly, thrusting his pistol at the warrior and snapping off four rapid shots. The first two rounds went wild but the second two struck the man in the chest and his spear clattered harmlessly to the ground as he was thrown backwards by the impacts of the lead balls smashing into him.

'Good shot, Mister Macintosh!' One of the shepherds congratulated as Angus stared at the body and wondered at the ease of taking a life. He felt no remorse. After all, it was well known that the black people did not have souls. So it was not a case of killing a fellow human. It was really no different to being on a kangaroo hunt, except that this quarry had the potential to be more dangerous.

He flashed a broad smile acknowledging the praise, and twisted in his saddle to see how his father had reacted to his first kill. He caught a nod from the tough squatter and felt a rush of elation. *Now he was truly a man!*

'There's more acomin'!'

The shouted warning snapped him out of his self-congratulatory elation as more Nerambura survivors stumbled, panting and sweating, into the killing grounds.

A young boy staggered to the line of mounted shepherds and came to a sudden, wide-eyed halt. Lead shot flailed his puny body and he crumpled in the dust as blood oozed from the many puncture wounds inflicted by the bullets.

'Don't all go after the same target,' Donald roared. 'Powder and shot cost me good money, you bloody fools! You're wasting ball. You could have run that one down.'

The shepherds normally listened to their boss but they were excited by the sport and ignored him until an exhausted huddle of survivors burst from the trees. Less of a volley met the screaming Nerambura as they ducked and dodged between the startled horsemen and ran towards the slopes of the hill.

'Leave 'em – more coming,' Donald shouted as he levelled his pistol on a woman carrying a child at her breast. The gun bucked in his hand and he grunted with satisfaction to see that his bullet had passed through the bawling baby to also hit the mother. She toppled and the baby flew from her arms. Two for the price of one, he thought with grim satisfaction.

Now the shepherds were more careful selecting their targets and the dead and dying – men, women and children – were piled in untidy bloody heaps in the killing ground as the murderous gunfire cut them down. Only the young and more nubile Aboriginal girls were spared. The shepherds rode them down and dispatched them with kicks and clubbing from the butts of their muskets.

The slaughter continued furiously – and then spasmodically – until no more of the Nerambura survivors emerged from the scrub.

Angus was not even aware of how many times he had fired and reloaded his pistol. At one stage he was caught in the act of reloading the pistol when a young girl tried to dodge past him. He had pulled down on the reins of his prancing mount to turn and knock her down but she ran like a frightened hare until the horse caught up to her. With a savage kick from his boot, Angus dropped her to the ground where she tumbled and came groggily to her hands and knees in the dust.

He had tried to trample her but the horse would not cooperate. It was not in the animal's nature to kill a human. Angus stared angrily down at her and he was acutely aware of how inviting her nubile body appeared as she lay face down in the dust. His anger dissipated as he contemplated the pleasure she would provide when the dispersal was complete and he kicked his mount forward and trotted it back to the line of horsemen.

Smoke curled from gunbarrels too hot to be touched and everywhere the naked black bodies of the Nerambura lay shattered in the powdery red dust. The shepherds' ears rang with the silence which was broken only by the pathetic moaning of the wounded who attempted to drag themselves away.

It was a glorious day for Angus and it was further improved by the thought of what was yet to come. A sense of supreme and savage power had overwhelmed him. Never had there been a sport invented as satisfying as killing darkies! English fox hunting paled in comparison with this Australian pastime.

Donald slid stiffly from his mount and was

grateful to be out of the saddle. He stretched his aching back and wiped sweat from his brow with the back of his shirt sleeve. 'Give me your gun, Jack,' he said as he reached out for the shepherd's long-barrelled musket.

'It's not loaded, boss,' the puzzled man replied as he leaned forward in the saddle to pass the gun.

'Just give me the gun,' Donald grumbled irritably as he took the musket from the shepherd and walked casually over to an old woman who moaned in her terrible pain. She tried to drag herself away from the terrifying spectre of the white man striding towards her.

The squatter raised the butt of the musket over his head. She screamed as he brought the carbine down and with a sickening crunch, the brass butt plate cut short her cry. Grunting, Donald raised the butt again and smashed it down on the woman's already crushed face. The second blow had been unnecessary as the woman was already dead.

'Finish the rest off the same way. Don't go wasting shot on the wounded,' he said as he handed the blood-spattered musket back to the stunned shepherd. 'And make sure you don't leave any of the gins alive when you are finished with them.'

The men nodded. The cold and brutal manner in which their boss had dispatched the old gin had impressed the shepherds. He was truly a man to be feared and respected.

They dismounted and went eagerly about the work of slaughtering those who were not of immediate interest to them. Only wounded women and young girls were spared temporarily for the pleasure they would bring, and those spared screamed and rolled their eyes in terror as they watched the white men go among the wounded Nerambura with their muskets. The terrible crunch of shattering skulls was mixed with the grunting of the shepherds' exertions as they brought death to the helpless wounded.

Angus returned to the young girl who he could see had attempted to crawl towards the hill. Blood caked her long hair as she lay on her stomach whimpering in her despair and he rolled her over with his boot.

With just a small twinge of guilt he searched about for his father. Killing darkies was one thing, but coupling with them was another. He was relieved to see his father walking into the bush with one of the Aboriginal troopers who had emerged from the scrub naked and gleaming with sweat.

The girl groaned at the young squatter's feet and shivered with uncontrollable fear. Her bladder voided when she looked up at the white man standing over her and the ammoniac scent of her urine excited Angus. With a savage leer, he grabbed her by a twist of her hair. She screamed her despair but her cry was lost in the sounds of her doomed sisters now in the hands of the shepherds.

4

Patrick Duffy leant against a fire-blackened tree.

The distant sounds of the dispersal had ceased.

'All finished, boss,' Billy said with a sad sigh. 'All blackfella finished and gone.'

Patrick shook his head. 'Poor bloody bastards,' he muttered sadly. 'Probably come across what's left of them before sundown.' He turned to walk back to the dray.

Tom greeted his father with a questioning look.

'It's all over for the poor buggers.' Patrick answered the question and swigged from a water canteen which left a bloody taste in his mouth. 'May as well get back on the track and get the team down to the creek,' he said as he shaded his eyes and gazed in the direction of the sun now high over the scrub. 'It's going to be another bastard of a day.'

Patrick glanced at Billy who still had the look of a man sentenced to die and he placed his big hand gently on the old Aboriginal's shoulder. 'It's done, Billy,' he said gently. 'What you saw in your dreams is done. Whoever ... squatter or trooper ... has finished their bloody work, and we are all right.'

But Billy was not convinced. In his vision an Aboriginal warrior had come to him with blood on his face and so far the warrior had not appeared to them this day.

'No, boss,' he replied stubbornly. 'This place *baal* . . . No good we go to the water . . . Better we go along next place.'

The Irishman sighed. He respected Billy's convictions, but they were low on water and the big beasts' heads lolled the way they did when they were thirsty. 'We have to get to the water before sundown, Billy,' he pleaded, with a note of exasperation for the doggedness of his old friend's convictions. 'You can see the bullocks need to drink or they will go down. It's either the water now or we are going to end up with six dead bullocks. And I'm not about to pull the bloody dray.'

'No boss. The debil is here,' Billy stubbornly reiterated and stared down at the ground. 'He will get us if we go up for water.' Although he did not like arguing with the big Irishman, he knew this time he must if they were to remain alive.

Patrick let out the air from his lungs with an audible sound of frustration and he knew that he would have to think of a compromise to settle his friend's fears. 'What if you and I take a look up ahead? We can leave Tom with the team and go on a bit to see if things have settled down,' he suggested hopefully. 'If you think we should turn around and come back, I promise you that's what we will do. What do you think about that?'

Billy appeared deep in thought as he recalled flashes of the vision. Had he not seen the lead bullock, Mars, standing in a pool of blood? Then this must mean that the death would come to wherever the team was. Maybe they could find a way to get through the evil place and come back to lead the team through safely. The feeling of dread was not as strong where they were now. That was it! If they located the place of the dispersal they could steer around it. And out of the spirit haunted places.

He looked up into the grey eyes of the taller man with his hand on his shoulder. 'All right, boss,' he replied. 'We have a look around . . . then come back.'

Patrick was visibly relieved at his decision. 'Good fella, Billy. You will see that everything will be all right.'

Despite his boss's assurance, Billy still had a nagging feeling that everything was not going to be all right. He was not able to fully persuade himself that the vision had been more of a warning than an actual prediction of future events.

Patrick turned to his son who stood by the dray. 'Stick with the dray until we get back. We should be here by midday.' But Tom was uneasy about his father's decision to split the party.

'Why not leave Billy here and I'll go with you?' he offered, but his father shook his head.

'Billy knows the bush better than you and I put together. We won't be too long away,' he said to reassure his son. 'Billy knows the bush and *you* know the bullocks,' he added as a means of justifying his decision. Tom did not reply because his father always made the right decisions.

For some reason he had a sudden urge to say

something to his father as he watched them stride into the bush but it was an urge without rational basis so he kept his thoughts to himself. His father was not a man who expressed love easily in words but he was strong in showing it in his actions.

After a couple of minutes, the sparse timbers of the bush came together to hide the two men from him. Other than the jangle of the cowbells dangling from the necks of the bullocks, there was no sound in the bush. The young teamster shrugged his broad shoulders. He would say something when his father returned.

He returned to the dray and sat leaning against the big spoked wheel.

The sun was warm and the silence of the bush first lulled him into a fitful doze where strange and disturbing thoughts, incomprehensible in their own right, came to him in his troubled sleep.

The girl lay face down in the hollow and with the cold detachment of a butcher, Angus slit her throat as he straddled her. He could still feel the warmth of her bare bottom against his exposed groin as he wiped his blood-soaked hands on her back, before rising stiffly to his feet to adjust his trousers with a grunt of satisfaction.

He did feel a little regret for killing her as she might have provided some entertainment on the trip back to the homestead, but the explosive sexual climax had left the young squatter devoid of passion. In its place had come a dispassionate emptiness and the girl had no other reason for her existence other than the short-lived pleasure she gave him.

'Want some black velvet, boss?' Monkey called to Angus as he strode towards a group of shepherds huddled around a young girl. The shepherd, known as Monkey because of his simian resemblance, sat at the head of a girl barely older than a child, with his boots on her shoulders as he stretched her arms over her head. Two other shepherds held the girl's legs apart while a fourth grunted with bestial pleasure as he entered her tiny body. His pale and naked buttocks rose and fell rhythmically above the girl who alternately screamed and sobbed as the white man entered her.

'No thanks, Monkey, I might ruin her for you,' Angus replied with a wide grin and the shepherds, holding the near dead girl child, laughed with delight at their young boss's retort.

The shepherd ravishing the girl gave a final grunt as his back arched and he spent himself inside her and his place was soon taken by Monkey. Unlike Angus, they were not particular about their privacy nor about sharing what they had.

The use of the term 'boss' by Monkey had not been lost on Angus. Prior to the dispersal, he had always been 'Mister Macintosh'. But now the tough shepherds had used the term they normally reserved for men they respected as employers. And the title was not lost on Donald who had overheard Monkey's offer.

'You did well today, Angus,' he said to his son with a note of pride. 'The men will follow you without question,' he added as he surveyed the killing ground and the shepherds, busy with their prize. 'This sort of thing is good for bringing men together.' But his mood suddenly changed.

Angus followed his father's angry gaze to a shepherd known as Old Jimmy and he saw the look of disgust and disapproval in his father's eyes. Old Jimmy had claimed a terrified and trembling boy, who had miraculously survived the slaughter, for his own pleasure. The sodomised boy under him sobbed and bucked from the pain of the violation. But the young Aboriginal's resistance only excited the wiry shepherd to greater exertions. Old Jimmy's eyes were glazed and rolled back in their sockets, like those of a stallion covering a mare, while he drooled like an imbecile.

'Damned sodomite!' Donald exploded. 'I want him gone when we get back. His act is an abomination in the eyes of Jehovah.' Angus nodded, but secretly he did not agree with his father. After all, he thought mildly, was not sodomy practised in some of England's best boys' schools.

'I thought I might ride back to the darkies' camp and pick up some of their things before the troopers destroy everything,' he said casually, thinking that his statement might take his father's attention away from Jimmy. 'Some of the spears and nullas will look good on the wall of the library back in Sydney,' Angus added. 'Kind of battle trophies, I suppose.'

Donald nodded. 'Before you go, make sure the men leave the gins alive for the troopers. I promised Corporal Gideon they could have them before we leave here. But make sure you put down that darkie piccaninny after Jimmy is finished. I don't want the Queen's men perverted by his sodomite ways. Bad enough they need to mount the gins, let alone darkie boys.'

Angus casually checked his pistol and walked away from his father. Donald could hear the whining protest of Old Jimmy, interrupted in his pleasures, and then the blast of Angus's revolver. His son had carried out his task efficiently and without fuss. Yes, Donald thought contentedly, some day the Mackintosh empire would be in good hands.

Wallarie had followed the sounds of death; the screams of the dying and the terrible explosions that were like the old trees splitting and crashing to the ground in the silence of the night.

As the noise of the slaughter advanced towards the rise, he had hoped that some of the clan might reach its safety. But his hopes were shattered by the volley of the shepherds' guns that drifted to him from the lower reaches of the sacred hill. Hope turned to impotent rage until the distant drumbeat sound of a galloping horse caught his attention.

The young warrior merged with the blackened trunk of a tree and became one with the tree spirit as the rider appeared briefly within range of his spear, but he was moving too fast for an accurate strike. The rider seemed intent on pursuing something – or someone. Then Wallarie saw what the man was chasing. Mondo – youngest sister to his mother.

The girl was only one moon from being initiated into the secret rites of the women and after her initiation she would have been the wife of the elder of the clan, Kana. But Kana was dead! Wallarie had seen him fall at the creek. A mysterious hole had appeared in his back, and the elder had toppled forward never to move again.

Mondo was young and agile. Her lithe and naked body twisted and turned as she swerved to avoid the pursuing horseman who was uttering unmistakable sounds of frustrated rage as she dodged his attempts to bring her down. He wheeled his mount to cut across the path of the nimble girl. She ducked and twisted avoiding his ruse to block her flight towards the edge of the clearing of tall dry grass. She was wisely trying to reach the thicker scrub where the horseman would have trouble pursuing her.

The spear shaft lay balanced and poised in harmony with that of the warrior's intent. If only Mondo would make a break towards him he might be able to get a clear and close throw at the pursuer . . . or at least his animal. Forced from the horse, the white man would be on equal ground with him and he could then close with his enemy and effectively use the deadly nulla.

Wallarie watched the chase being played out in the clearing and he could see that his kinswoman was weakening. The series of twists and turns had sapped her reserves of strength and her young body was pushed to the extreme limits of exhaustion. She was now surviving on pure fear and spiritual strength alone.

In one last act of desperation she made a sprint towards the grey scrub on the furthermost side of the clearing and Wallarie hissed his disappointment. She was running to her death. Unwittingly, she had turned away from the warrior waiting with the spear for her pursuer.

* * *

Mort gave a victorious shout as he galloped after her. He had her!

The broad chest of his horse slammed into the slight figure and flung her tumbling into the dry grass where she attempted to rise, but the breath was gone from her lungs. Mort reined his mount to a halt and his boot caught her a savage kick in the ribs. At the same instant, Mort had claimed his prize, Wallarie's attention had shifted to an unexpected threat that had suddenly materialised in the scrub near him. The young Aboriginal warrior saw Angus Macintosh before Angus saw him and, with the speed of a striking taipan snake, Wallarie whirled to confront the startled horseman whose mount shied and reared at the sudden appearance of the black warrior stepping into its path. Angus's attention had been so fixed on the chase of the black girl and its outcome that he had failed to see the dark shape until it was too late.

With a cry of despair the young squatter vainly tried to bring his frightened horse under control. But the mount would not respond to his frantic attempts to rein it out of danger and the highly strung thoroughbred crabbed sideways, resisting him. An irrational fleeting thought of a cave painting flashed through Angus's mind as Wallarie's spear hissed with blurring and lethal speed across the short distance between them.

With a scream that ended in a pain-racked grunt, the heir to the Macintosh empire toppled from his saddle and crashed into the hard sun-baked earth. The spear shaft snapped with a pistol-like crack as he hit the ground leaving the tail of the broken spear protruding from his chest.

He lay on his back grasping frantically at the shaft while the pain came as an overwhelming sensation. But more than the pain was the certain thought that he was dying and he was only vaguely aware that his mount was galloping away to leave him alone with the warrior who had speared him.

Mort had instantly forgotten the young girl at his feet when the young squatter's agonised screams drove all thoughts of her slow and painful demise from his twisted mind. With a chilling clarity, he realised his vulnerability to an attack from the black warriors should the mad gallop of Angus's horse threaten to cause his own mount to bolt.

He desperately scrambled for the reins of his horse which had sensed the panic of the riderless animal galloping towards them. Its nostrils flared and it swung away from the police officer.

Who had cried out? Mort did not know but the sound was unmistakably that of a dying man. He hauled himself frantically into the saddle and grappled for his revolver. From his vantage point high on his horse, he had a momentary glimpse of a dark shadow disappearing into the scrub. He fired wildly at it until he had emptied his pistol.

'Help me! God help me!'

The sobbing cry for help chilled Mort as his imagination ran riot. At the edge of the clearing just inside the line of scrub, he could see the young squatter writhing on the ground, clutching futilely at the spear in his chest. How many more of the black savages were around him? Mort cursed himself for allowing the girl to lure him away from his troops. Were the black warriors waiting for him to

61

go to the aid of the dying man, then spear him? Every shadow took on a sinister shape in the scrub and he knew that his best chance of survival was to stay in the centre of the clearing and out of range of the deadly spears.

He closed his mind to the agonised cries for help and with trembling hands reloaded his cap and ball pistol. Powder in, wad in, ball in, ram home with lever under the barrel, percussion caps on the nipples. The litany of loading the pistol was his sole thought of survival. 'Shut up, you fool,' he screamed hysterically across the clearing. 'No one can help you. Shut up and die like a man.'

But Angus did not hear the terrified and cowardly advice from the police officer as he was already dead. Wallarie's slender and primitive wooden spear had taken the life of the man who was to inherit a financial empire that spanned two continents and encompassed the most modern technology the European world had to offer.

So preoccupied had Mort been with his own survival that he had not noticed the Aboriginal girl slip away into the sparse cover of the scrub. Mondo had found a second reserve of strength to run, and she did not stop running until her body and spirit led her exhausted into the silence of the bush, where she collapsed and lay in a stupor. Although her fear persisted, something in her head told her that she was safe. It was like a voice coming from a long time ago.

Wallarie had heard the crack of shots as he fled from the dying squatter and one of the sounds had reached out to stab him. It was like the sting of a giant wasp, he thought, as he gasped and stumbled from the impact.

With a groan he slumped to the ground and examined the wound above his hip as a more intense pain came over him in agonising waves. He had seen the same wounds, from the invisible spears of the black troopers and white devils, on the bodies of his own people.

He plucked at a clump of grass to plug the wound and groaned from the searing raw nerve ends that came into contact with the prickly grass. The bleeding did not stop and the pain continued. He knew that he must get away.

He regained his feet and stumbled blindly forward. Deep in his spirit he knew he was already a dead man and it was only a matter of time before the black crows would find him. He was beyond covering his tracks that were leading him back to his Dreaming.

5

Billy froze and stood as still as the breathless hot air of the scrublands. 'Blackfella ... blackfella over here, boss,' he hissed as he covered the unconscious warrior with his old Baker rifle.

'Dead?' Patrick asked Billy, who had not taken his eyes from Wallarie.

'No, boss, this blackfella alive,' he replied through his teeth. 'But mebbe not long.'

The Irishman squatted beside the naked warrior and could see where the bullet had entered and exited through the man's side leaving an ugly purple swelling. The bleeding had ceased but the man had lost a lot of blood. Patrick wiped his hand over the freshest of the bleeding and examined its colour. Had the blood been a coffee colour then it might have indicated a stomach wound and such a wound usually eventuated in a slow and painful death. The blood was a bright red colour.

The Aboriginal man was in the prime of his life. His body glistened with sweat which ran in rivulets along the contours of his muscled chest where he had many raised welt-like scars indicating that he had a respected standing among his people.

Patrick reached for his water canteen and pressed it against the unconscious man's mouth. Wallarie stirred as the water trickled through his parched lips and his eyes flickered, then snapped open with alarm at the terrifying sight hovering over him. Had he met a ghost in the other world of the Dreaming?

Behind the white man he could see the less than friendly face of an old Aboriginal dressed in the manner of the whites.

'Take it easy, old fella,' the white man said kindly and, although Wallarie did not understand the words, the man's soothing voice had the tone of a mother with a child.

'We should leave this blackfella. No good we should help him,' Billy said fearfully as he cast about the scrub for signs of lurking tribesmen. 'This blackfella bring us bad luck, boss.' Patrick ignored his warning.

'The poor bastard's been shot and left to die like some dog, Billy,' he said as he encouraged Wallarie to drink slowly from the canteen. 'There's probably a good chance he won't last. But he may as well have a drink before he leaves this world. And I do not think he is in any condition to be a threat to us.'

Despite the Irishman's opinion on the wounded Aboriginal warrior's physical state, Billy kept the rifle trained on him. He did not trust the blacks of central Queensland whom he considered treacherous and cunning, particularly one that was wounded, who could react like the big plains kangaroo. When it was cornered, it would fight to the death.

Wallarie felt the cooling water slake the terrible thirst that had tortured his body and he groaned as he sat up. The white man helped him and his touch was gentle, but still Wallarie felt fear rising in his chest. Why would a white man help him when all the others had slaughtered his people? His dark eyes flicked from the white man to the black man. Then back to the black man where he saw both fear and hostility reflected in the old Aboriginal's eyes.

'You savvy this myall's lingo, Billy?' Patrick asked as he replaced the cap on the water canteen.

'No, boss. This blackfella a bloody savage,' Billy spat with disgust. If the man was not of his own people then he was inferior, in Billy's opinion. But he was also the warrior of his vision.

'No matter,' Patrick grunted as he helped Wallarie to his feet. 'We will get him back to the dray and see if he comes good. But I don't think it looks very good for him.'

'Bloody waste of time,' Billy grumbled. 'Bugger will die and his spirit will hang round us.'

The Irishman ignored his friend's ungracious attitude as he helped Wallarie take teetering steps, and Billy followed, grumbling with a surliness that he very rarely displayed. They had taken only a few steps when his attention suddenly shifted from contemplating the warrior to the faint sound in his head. Not a whisper on the wind but a tangible sound in the bush.

'Horses! Horses comin'!' Billy warned quietly and Patrick felt an unexpected and ominous knot twist in his stomach.

'Coming this way?' he asked tensely. The old

66

Aboriginal teamster remained facing the west.

'Comin' this way, boss,' he replied quietly. 'Plenty horses.'

Patrick instinctively thought of the revolver at his hip. He did not know exactly why he felt the need to be armed when to all intents and purposes the men approaching were no doubt white men or black police. His reasoning told him the horsemen were coming for the wounded Aboriginal. He felt a shiver run through the body of the young black man leaning on his shoulder as he too could hear the horses approaching. Wounded and alone, up against impossible odds, the warrior would have no hope.

The Irishman remembered a time when he had been in a similar situation. It was the Eureka Stockade all over again. How the police and some of the soldiers had massacred the wounded and those who surrendered foolishly believing in British justice. He knew exactly what the position of the wounded Aboriginal would be when the horsemen arrived, and he also knew what he must do.

Corporal Gideon had not needed to dismount to follow the warrior's tracks as he could see from the footprints that the man they hunted was near collapse and had not attempted to cover his trail.

Behind the Aboriginal corporal rode Mort, Donald Macintosh and his party of shepherds – less two – who were preparing the squatter's son's body for transportation back to the Glen View homestead for burial.

They rode into a clearing where the appearance

of the big bearded Irishman and the old Aboriginal came as a surprise to all in the mounted party. But more was the shock and anger at seeing them helping the wounded warrior as they might a white man.

Mort raised his hand, bringing the riders to a halt. 'I see, sir, that you have caught the man we have been tracking,' he said, addressing Patrick who stood supporting the warrior. Wallarie glared at the police officer with barely concealed hate and Patrick could feel his shiver turn into a trembling of despair.

'We haven't caught him, Lieutenant,' he replied with an almost casual indifference to the police officer's statement. 'We were trying to help the poor bastard. Seems your lot have been up to your old tricks, dispersing his people. Would I be right, Lieutenant?'

Mort did not answer immediately. He did not like the Irishman's attitude and he sat astride his mount, eyeing him with contempt. The man was aiding a killer, and he did not have to justify himself under the circumstances. He cleared his throat.

'I would advise you strongly to step aside from that murdering nigger and allow me to take him as a prisoner. I order this in the Queen's name, Mister . . . ?'

'Patrick Duffy. And I have no intention of handing this man over to you . . . Not here, anyway,' he replied as he stared at the uniformed policeman. There was something about the man. Something about the eyes that glared at him with undisguised hostility. 'Not out here where he wouldn't last five minutes with that bunch of cut-throats riding with you.'

Mort was dumbfounded. It was unthinkable that any white man on the frontier would oppose the Queen's lawful representative bringing to justice a killer – let alone a nigger!

Donald also viewed the Irishman's insolence with disbelief. He was not about to have any damned Irishman stand between him and vengeance for his son's brutal murder. 'Stand aside, Mister Duffy,' he said softly, but with the venom of cold fury, 'or I will shoot you down. Step aside from that murdering darkie now!'

Patrick saw the gun in the squatter's hand levelled at him, and from the corner of his eye he glimpsed Billy bring his rifle to bear on the squatter. With a swift and almost casual gesture he brought his own Colt up and levelled it at Mort before the shepherds could react. 'That may be. But I promise you, Mister, that we will both be dead before I hit the ground. And most probably the Lieutenant here as well,' Patrick said, calmly addressing Donald without taking his eyes from Mort who could see in the Irishman's expression that he meant exactly what he said. He had watched, with a kind of morbid and paralysing fascination, the big Irishman's arm rising to point the pistol directly at his chest and, although the gun was heavy, there was no sign of trembling in his hand.

Neither did Donald doubt the Irish teamster's resolve and he had a sudden grudging respect for the man who stood facing them. But this did not diminish his anger or hatred. Now the Irishman and his darkie had placed themselves squarely with the black killer. 'You realise, Mister Duffy, that you have just committed a serious crime. You are aiding a darkie who is wanted for murder,' Donald said. 'A cold-blooded killer of my son. You can probably understand that under the circumstances I could have you shot down as you stand. If you look to my men you will see that they all have their guns on you . . . and the darkie with you. Under the circumstances we are fully entitled to use any force necessary to take appropriate action in removing the darkie bastard from you.' The Scottish squatter's voice was cold and calm as he prudently lowered his pistol and he held no doubt that the old Aboriginal pointing the ancient but lethal Baker rifle at him would shoot him down.

Patrick fully understood that what the squatter said was true in all respects, but he also realised that he had pushed himself into a very tiny and exposed corner. He was once again confronting the might of the British Empire. But this time there was no quarter, no retreat. It had been the sight of Mort's uniform that had reinforced his resolve to give the Aboriginal some chance and he fully realised that he was now laying his and Billy's lives on the line for a wounded black man he had only known for a few minutes.

Patrick's mouth felt uncomfortably dry and the gun he held on the police officer was very heavy in his hand. He tried to lick his dry lips. 'Under the circumstances I will concede what you say has a lot of merit,' he said. 'So I will make a deal with you . . .'

'No deals, Mister Duffy,' Mort snapped. 'As a representative of Her Majesty, I do not make deals with criminals.'

'I said I would make a deal. I think you should find it satisfactory to yourself . . . and the Queen,' Patrick continued patiently. 'I will let this myall go. But you will give him a fair chance to run as I have no doubts that otherwise you will gun him down here without recourse to Her Majesty's justice. Just like I saw your kind do at the Ballarat diggings in '54. We will give him half an hour to get away and then I will lower my gun. I see that you have a trooper with you who is, no doubt, more than able to track a wounded man. You have more to gain than lose by the deal.'

'You were at the Eureka Stockade?' Mort asked with veiled interest.

'I was that,' Patrick replied softly.

'Then you and I may have met before,' he mused as he eyed the Irishman more closely. The fact that the captured rebels who had stood trial in Melbourne were acquitted, and treated as heroes by the thousands who rallied outside the court-house, would forever rankle with him. A travesty of British justice that condoned rebellion and treason. Worst of all for the embittered Victorian policeman had been the sight of the tumultuous reception received by the giant American Negro, John Josephs, who had been the first of the rebels to be acquitted. The crowd of rebel sympathisers had gone wild and carried the Negro triumphantly on their shoulders around Melbourne's streets . . . *A nigger!*

Mort had been a sergeant in the Victorian Mounted Police and he had walked away from that day swearing he would not forget the court's failure to mete out justice. And now one of the

Irish rebels stood a few feet from him with a gun levelled at his chest. Half an hour was not a long time to wait, he thought with seething hatred. Especially when he had been waiting eight years for a chance to even scores. He realised that all attention was focused on him for a decision.

'Your offer sounds reasonable, Mister Duffy,' Mort finally replied. 'But you realise that you will have to honour the deal when the half hour is gone. I will require you to throw down your arms. Or we cannot go ahead with what you propose.'

Patrick stared into the pale blue eyes of the police officer and saw something there that disturbed him. Was there a madness? Or was it merely his imagination stretched thin with the situation at hand? Half an hour was not much time for a badly wounded man to evade his hunters, especially when they were on horseback and had the services of an Aboriginal tracker. But that was better than nothing – and nothing he had plenty of! So the lieutenant would take him prisoner, but it was doubtful if any conviction would be recorded when the facts of what had happened out here were revealed to the court. The government was not keen on having the true nature of dispersals advertised.

Outnumbered and out-gunned, he had little alternative. 'Sounds fair enough, Lieutenant,' he replied. 'You have my word I will surrender to you as soon as the half hour is up.' Patrick turned to Billy, who had not taken his eyes off the squatter. 'See if you can tell the myall here to get going.'

Billy nodded but he did not take his attention from the squatter, while he used words that were common along the Aboriginal trade routes between the many scattered tribes. Wallarie understood the word *run* and Patrick shoved him in the back to reinforce Billy's order.

Wallarie was hesitant at first. He was confused by the events unfolding around him. But he did realise that the white man had somehow used sorcery to keep the men who would kill him at bay.

He broke into a stumbling run for the sanctuary of the scrub while Donald watched the departing warrior with hate and vengeance-filled eyes. He had accepted the deal without comment as he knew he had little choice, but he also knew that half an hour would not get the wounded man very far. And then he would have the man's hide – literally! Yes, he would have the murdering black bastard's skin peeled from his living body while he screamed in his heathen language for mercy. There would be no mercy ... just a lingering death marked by extreme pain.

'Pray that we catch him, Mister Duffy,' the squatter said quietly, 'or I promise you that I will peg the skin of your darkie on my wall.'

Patrick glared at the squatter. 'If you make threats like that, Mister, I promise you that you will have to kill me first, and a lot of men have tried over the years without much success.'

Mort removed a silver fob watch from his jacket and flipped open the cover. 'It is now eight o'clock, Mister Duffy,' he said softly. 'I will tell you when the half hour is up.'

The sun rose high above the scrub and brought

sweat and flies to torment the men and horses waiting below.

Although Patrick's arm ached from the effort of holding up the heavy pistol, he did not waver and he kept the gun levelled at the police officer's chest. After a while, he brought his elbow down to rest his arm but the gun remained pointed unerringly at the police officer who sat staring impassively at him. No words passed between any of the waiting men and the half hour ticked slowly away. The time marked the passage as an iota in the measure of history.

After a time Mort took the fob watch from his pocket and with a lazy smile reminiscent of some predatory animal, he broke the silence. 'Time is up, Mister Duffy,' he said. 'I believe we have a deal.' Reluctantly Patrick lowered the pistol to his side. 'I place you under arrest for obstructing the Queen's justice,' Mort intoned, 'and for giving assistance to a felon. You will be transported in chains back to Rockhampton where you will appear before a police magistrate to answer the charges. The irons, Corporal Gideon,' he snapped at the police trooper, who had dismounted from his horse.

With the heavy manacles dangling at his side, Gideon walked towards Patrick while Billy kept his rifle levelled at the squatter and glanced questioningly across at his boss.

'Put down the gun, Billy,' Patrick said in a tired voice. 'I have to honour the deal.'

Billy handed his rifle to a shepherd who had also dismounted. He smiled disarmingly at Billy before slamming the butt of his rifle into his face. Billy felt his nose crush under the unexpected blow and stumbled backwards from the impact, but refused to let himself be felled. Blood spurted in an explosive shower over the smiling shepherd.

'No nigger points a gun at Mister Macintosh, you black bastard,' the shepherd spat with savage fury. 'Remember that, you heathen darkie.' Patrick spun on the shepherd with his fists clenched but froze.

'Don't take another step, Mister Duffy,' Mort's threat was backed by the pistol in his hand, 'or I will put a bullet in your nigger friend.'

The Irishman glared at the police officer. 'Anything happens to Billy and you will answer to me personally – Queen's officer or not!' he snarled with his fists clenched by his side as Gideon applied the heavy chains to his wrists. Mort sneered at the man now helpless in the shackles.

'Your fate is in my hands, you Irish bastard. And I suggest you remember that well for the time being.' He scanned the clearing until he found what he was looking for. 'Corporal Gideon, secure Mister Duffy and his nigger to that tree over there,' he said, pointing to a tall gum which stood out as a stranger among the smaller and stunted brigalow scrub trees.

Gideon led Patrick to the tree where he secured his arms around the trunk. The corporal felt uneasy. He sensed that something was wrong. But he feared the white officer too much to question his intentions.

Billy was similarly manacled to the tree and the two men faced each other. Billy saw Patrick's expression of concern for him. 'I'm all right, boss,' he said with a weak grin to reassure his friend.

But he knew he was not all right. Nor was Patrick. He sensed that he was saying goodbye to the white man who had befriended him these many years past. Soon Patrick would go to his heaven and meet Jesus. Patrick had told him of the white man's heaven and how Jesus had once been a carpenter in a land far away, in a time long ago. Billy knew carpenters were people who built the towns where white men lived, places which denied the pleasures of the wandering life of the teamster and the tribesman and he would shake his head sadly for Patrick's afterlife. Surely the white man's heaven was no place for a bullocky. Was it that Patrick would have to live with the carpenter Jesus and build towns? Better that he join him beyond the Dreaming where they could again roam free along the tracks they knew so well and together hear the sweet song of the butcher bird in the early morning. Or see the eagle on outstretched wings soaring high in the azure sky. Maybe Jesus would let Patrick come with him beyond the Dreaming! . . . If he was as good a boss as Patrick said.

When the two men were secured to the tree, Mort dismissed Gideon.

'I want you to track that murdering nigger for Mister Macintosh. And after you have found him, you can go to Glen View where you can rejoin the troop.' Gideon nodded. He felt even more uneasy about the situation. There were things happening that were not right and he wondered if he should tell Sar'nt Henry about the white man and the old Aboriginal. But this was impossible when he was ordered to track the wounded Nerambura warrior with Mister Macintosh.

Donald sidled his horse over to Mort. Both men were a distance from Gideon and the shepherds who waited eagerly to resume the hunt. 'I expect you have everything under control here, Lieutenant Mort,' he said quietly. 'I do not take kindly to anyone coming between me and my rights to avenge the death of my son. You understand what I am saying?'

Mort stared across at his two prisoners. 'I understand, Mister Macintosh. And I am sure justice will take its course here today,' he replied quietly.

'Good,' the squatter grunted as he wheeled his mount away. 'Make sure justice is done.'

Mort watched the squatter's party follow Corporal Gideon and ride after the wounded Nerambura warrior. He waited for only a few minutes until he could no longer see or hear the departing horsemen, then he dismounted and strode across to Patrick and Billy manacled to the gum tree. He was grinning with the fixed expression of divine madness as he approached his helpless captives with the infantry sword trailing in his hand.

It was then that Patrick knew that he and Billy would not live to see the sun set and he prayed silently that Tom would not be found. For if he were found, he would surely share the same fate.

6

The smoke rose as a grey column into a pale blue sky, and spread like the broad canopy of a rain tree. The black troopers gathered the last of the implements that had marked the life of the Nerambura clan. Stone-grinding dishes were smashed and dilly bags were thrown onto the bonfire along with shields, spears, boomerangs and nullas. They were subdued in their tasks. The place was *baal*! The killing ground was taboo to the living. Nightfall would return the spirits of the slaughtered and the Aboriginal troopers feared their awesome powers.

Sergeant Henry James looked into the rising flames fuelled by the gathered pile of wooden weapons and tools and stared with a spiritual numbness at the flames that carried the spirits of the weapons into the heavens. His soul was crippled. Or was it that the work of the dispersals had killed his soul?

'Finished, Sar'nt Henry. Boys all finished.'

Trooper Mudgee stood at Henry's elbow and his words seemed to come from a faraway place, interrupting Henry's brooding thoughts.

'All right, Trooper Mudgee,' Henry replied with little enthusiasm in his voice. 'Get the boys together and set up camp along the creek a bit. Make sure they get their uniforms and you can start a fire so we can eat. I'll wait for Mister Mort here and tell him where you are camped. I'm putting you in charge for the moment and I will give you a thrashing with the cat if the boys play up. You understand me?'

The trooper's nervous grin acknowledged the threat as he hurried away to relay the orders to the others with appropriate and embellished warnings. The thought of an overdue meal spurred the hungry troopers into gathering up discarded uniforms and leading their horses along the bank of the creek to a new camp site. Henry watched his men depart, chattering in their own dialect and jostling each other like excited schoolboys on an outing.

When they were out of sight, he walked away from the bonfire to the edge of the creek where he sat down on the grassy bank above the body of the girl he had shot through the head. She now lay with her long black hair trailing away in the muddy waters. As he sat and stared with vacant eyes at the dead girl, Mort rode into the deserted camp.

'Have the men returned from the hill, Sergeant James?' he asked.

'Yes, sir,' Henry replied as he walked away from the creek. Mort did not dismount. 'All but Corporal Gideon.'

'I know where Corporal Gideon is,' Mort said from astride his horse. 'He's with Mister

Macintosh tracking a nigger. The one that murdered Angus Macintosh.'

Henry was startled by the news of Angus Macintosh's death. 'What happened?'

'Speared. Damned nigger we missed in the dispersal ambushed him. Young Angus didn't have a chance and unfortunately I was not in a position to save him. But it appears that one of my shots wounded the nigger responsible.'

Henry shook his head. 'Very sad for Mister Macintosh. I suppose he will need us to help him bring the man in.'

Mort brushed from his face a cloud of flies that rose from the body of a nearby child. 'No,' he replied. 'He has Corporal Gideon and his own men. That should be sufficient to hunt down one badly wounded nigger. We will have our meal and leave. Our job is done,' he said irritably.

'Very good, sir,' Henry replied. 'The boys are up the creek preparing a meal now. Should be ready by the time we reach them.'

Trooper Mudgee, at the head of the column, brought it to a halt. Mort and Henry rode up to where Trooper Mudgee sat, surveying the bullock team yoked to the dray. Henry commented in his puzzlement, 'There appears to be no one around.'

Mort shifted uneasily in his saddle. 'I think I know where the men are who came from this team,' he said, feigning sadness in his lie. 'I found a couple of men up the track who appeared to have been speared by the niggers. Poor beggars.'

Henry was surprised at his commanding officer's

oversight and said, 'You didn't mention this before, sir!'

Mort did not look at the sergeant when he spoke. 'No . . . I was including their murders in my report when we got back to the barracks. You would have known the details then, Sergeant James.' And he continued to stare at the big bullocks, yoked to the centre pole of the dray. He felt sick in the stomach as he had not expected to stumble across the bullock team. The discovery was just bad luck. 'I was a bit upset about the death of Mister Macintosh and forgot to tell you,' he added, by way of making his 'oversight' sound reasonable. But the damned bullocks and dray stood before him as a silent witness of the existence of the two men he had murdered. The question remained of what he was to do about the evidence.

Trooper Mudgee dismounted and examined the footprints around the dray. 'Bin t'ree men here, Mahmy,' he said, as he crouched to peer at the signs in the earth. 'One man is blackfella.' Mort felt a knife twisting in his stomach – *three!* The Irishman had not mentioned the existence of any other white man before he died. Who – and where – was the third man?

'You sure there were three men here?' Henry asked the police trooper.

'Yes, Sar'nt Henry . . . one old blackfella,' he answered confidently. 'One old white man. And a young whitefella. T'ree men.'

'You said you found two bodies, sir,' Henry quizzed his commander. 'From what Trooper Mudgee says, there must be a third man out there.'

Mort pulled a face. 'Yes, two bodies,' he snapped. 'My guess is that the third man, whoever he was, has also been speared by the niggers. It's highly unlikely he is still alive.' He was not inviting any further investigation surrounding the events pertaining to the deserted bullock team.

'Don't you think we should start a search for him?' Henry persisted as he scanned the surrounding bush. 'He might still be alive.'

Mort turned on his sergeant and his irritability became anger. 'I make the decisions here Sergeant – not you – and I say we are wasting our time searching for a man who, in all probability, is dead.'

'We could at least give him a Christian burial if we find him . . . sir.' The English sergeant's words had an edge that did not go unnoticed by Mort.

'The best we can do right now, Sergeant, is destroy the dray and kill the bullocks. Thus we will deny any darkie survivors the supplies. And, as soon as we meet up with Mister Macintosh, I will bring to his attention the matter of the third man. I am sure that his shepherds are better placed to make a search of Glen View. They know the area better than you or I.'

'Sir, I . . .'

'If I were you, Sergeant, I would keep my mouth shut,' Mort snarled. 'Before you say something I might construe as insubordinate. I do not wish to put you on report but I will . . . if you persist with your questioning of my decisions.'

Henry seethed with anger. Years in the Queen's uniform had conditioned him to obey orders no matter how distasteful. But the idea of leaving a white man alone in the bush was against all the unwritten laws of the frontier. His commanding officer's behaviour was extremely erratic. But he knew that there was little he could do as a sergeant. Any complaint by a subordinate of his superior was not tolerated in the colonial constabulary.

Valuable stores went up in flames as the troopers torched the dray. Police carbines cracked and the big bullocks bellowed and died in their yokes. The final bullock to go was the leader, which did not die immediately. Mars bellowed and slumped to his knees before toppling onto his side.

When the police had finished their task, they rode away and a single black crow landed on the grass beside Mars. In two hops it was next to the big bullock's head where it plucked out the sightless eyes. Then it flew away.

'Baal blackfella gone, Mista Macintosh. No more tracks. Blackfella all gone.' Donald stared hard at Gideon who stood nervously beside his mount among the dead Nerambura at the base of the hills.

'Gone!' he snapped angrily. It was incredible that a badly wounded darkie could just disappear as if into thin air. Corporal Gideon had assured them they were almost on top of the murdering savage and now, suddenly, he makes a statement that the man's tracks have simply disappeared off the face of the earth.

Donald could feel a rage boiling up inside him. There was something about the whole affair of losing the trail that worried him, something about the manner of the police trooper who seemed very nervous – even evasive – as if he were lying about the disappearance of the myall. But the man had no reason to lie, Donald mused, as he stared at the big police trooper. After all, he had been more than eager to hunt the man down. At least until now.

But Gideon had not lost the trail. He had no trouble tracking the wounded Nerambura warrior and even now knew where he was. He had lied to the squatter about losing the tracks and had gambled on the fact that the white man and his shepherds did not have his expert skills in reading the ground for a trail. From the puzzlement he saw in their faces, he knew he was right and the squatter had to accept what he said. 'Me think blackfella probably die anyway, Mista Macintosh, no worries,' he ventured to the squatter whose face was now a mask of fury. 'Mebbe some day find baal blackfella and skin 'im.'

Donald shifted angrily in his saddle to stare up at the hill and felt cheated of personally revenging the death of his eldest son. Corporal Gideon was probably right, he thought. His chances of surviving the wound were slim. 'All right ... We will return to Glen View,' he finally said. 'Corporal Gideon, you are free to join your troop and my regards to Mister Mort for your help.'

Gideon nodded and shuffled, embarrassed at the squatter's undeserved thanks, and he watched as the man and his shepherds disappeared into the bush. He turned to give the hill one last look and his gaze came to settle on the shadow of a rock overhang now being swallowed by the sun. The Darambal warrior was up there. Gideon knew that the wounded man was even now watching him.

He shivered superstitiously and tore his eyes from the overhang. Yes, he thought uneasily, the Darambal man was in a place where no man should go un-invited. It was a sacred place of the Darambal people, but also a place to be respected by all men – black or white.

The white men had not felt the force as he had felt its overpowering presence and they had been deaf to the voice that shouted from the heart of the hill. An angry voice that had called on him to stop and go back. It was as if he had hit an invisible wall at the foot of the sacred hill, beyond which he could see the tracks of a man protected by a spirit with a power he had never experienced before in his life. And he knew that the wounded man would not die this day. It was as if he had been chosen for something . . . Something beyond understanding.

Gideon spurred his mount into a gallop to rejoin his troop. Some places no man should go!

SILENT
ECHOES IN
THE DARK

7

The harbour breezes puffed across the shimmering expanse of blue water. White sails unfurled on the little sailing boats as they skipped the tips of the gentle waves mocking the inactivity of the big ships at anchor in the coves and inlets of the southern shore of Sydney harbour. The big sailing ships lined the wharves and shore where they appeared as a forest of tall and slender masts naked of the sailcloth that gave them the means to cross the world's oceans. Many of the stately ships now had funnels among their masts and others had huge round paddlewheels that protruded from their once graceful lines. For this was a time of transition between wind and steam on the oceans of the world.

The young man perched at the edge of a sandstone ledge gazed over the magnificent harbour. From high above the expanse of blue water, his thoughts roamed across the myriad of possibilities that the vantage point gave him to record the tranquil beauty of the harbour. A sketchbook dangled in one hand and a pencil in the other and beside him lay a leather satchel case which held his sketches.

It was a hot day and his shirt sleeves had been rolled up to reveal biceps that rippled with the latent strength of a fighter. His face was clean shaven and the summer sun was leaving a reddish impression on his normally fair skin while his thick mop of brown curling hair touched the collar of his starched white shirt which clung to a broad and muscled chest.

The twenty-one-year-old son of the teamster, Patrick Duffy, had been born in Ireland. But the land of his birth was now a sad and fading memory. Sadder was the distant sorrow of losing his mother to the fever that plagued the immigrant ship bound for the colony of Victoria from Ireland. A haunting memory of a terrible grief-stricken morning when the shroud-wrapped body was committed to the dark waters of the southern ocean. His mother's final existence was marked by a transient splash in the cold seas and the land of his childhood was now a place haunted by the spirit of a soft and gentle woman who had sung to him in the night. For Michael Duffy, the beautiful harbour he now gazed across defined his new world.

Behind him stood his cousin Daniel, who might have passed as a brother had it not been for the difference in their physiques. Michael was broad shouldered whereas Daniel was lean and slightly stooped. Both men were of the same age and had grown up together, gone to school together and were, often enough, in trouble together. Michael was usually the instigator as he had learnt at an early age how to use his size and strength to settle disputes in the tough Irish-dominated streets of Redfern.

And it was Michael Duffy's face that told the story of his fights. A small scar intersected his eyebrow over the right eye and his nose was slightly awry on a face women found appealing. But beyond his violently acquired badges of manhood were the grey eyes and slow smile. At times the eyes could be soft with a dreamy and faraway look. At other times hard with the appearance of a deep and cold sea. His smile and deep resonant voice charmed men as much as they charmed women and there was an aura about him that made women feel protected and men trust his word. He was not consciously aware of the strong effect he had on those around him. He was a young man preoccupied with dreams of fame as a great artist. But the considerable reputation he enjoyed as one of Sydney's best bare-knuckle fighters was also a reality of his life.

Daniel stole a glance at the sketch Michael had shaded with a soft graphite pencil. It was a landscape sketch of the flora that covered Sydney harbour's foreshores; spear-like stems rising up from squat tussocks, the spiky cone-like flowers of the banksia bush.

'I thought you might sketch the harbour,' he said in a bored voice. 'The plants here aren't exactly an artist's delight.' Daniel would have preferred to be promenading on the Manly Corso appreciating the pretty young ladies who walked in pairs coyly pretending not to notice the admiring stares of the young men who watched them. Michael glanced up from his sketch at his cousin who stood at his elbow with his coat slung over his shoulder.

'Ahh . . . But there is a beauty in the bush,

Danny boy,' he drawled. 'You have to understand that this is not Europe. The beauty here is unique.'

'How would you know that, Mick? You haven't been to Europe.'

Michael nodded. 'Well . . . That may it be,' he replied with a frown, 'but I have seen paintings of European landscapes. And it's obvious they have different light and shadow. The Europeans have a certain dullness about their landscapes. We have a contrast in the vitality I can bring to my paintings with the brilliant light and colour we have here,' he explained.

Daniel shook his head and smiled. His cousin was himself a strange contrast of light and dark; a powerful physical entity and yet, a gentle and intelligent spirit. 'Yes, well, speaking about light, I think we are about to lose ours. If that storm catches us up here.' Daniel noted the heavy clouds gathering as an ominous billowing wall of boiling purple-black over the stunted scrub of the distant headland that was Sydney's harbour gateway.

Michael marvelled at the depth of hues of the storm rolling in from the south. But his cousin was right, Sydney's summer storms were welcome, so long as you were not caught in the open. They brought cool relief to the city, washing away the refuse of the streets that harboured the seasonal epidemics of cholera and yellow fever, cleaning the air of the sickening smells of tanneries, and blowing off the coal smog of the factories for a short and pleasant time. He slipped his sketchbook into the satchel and slung the strap over his shoulder as he stood and wiped the dry moss from his trousers.

* * *

They made their way to a track leading down to Manly Village which had established its popularity as the place for day trippers to escape the rapidly expanding urban sprawl of Sydney. To reach Manly from the southern shore entailed a ferry trip which was all part of the holiday experience of visiting the pretty village which bordered both the majestic Pacific Ocean and the waters of the tranquil harbour. The steam ferry crossed the harbour from south to north and when the passengers reached Manly they could promenade along The Corso, take in a picnic in the nearby bush, pick succulent oysters from the rocks or walk on the yellow sand beaches that were buffeted by the Pacific's majestic breakers.

By the time the two young men had reached The Corso, the storm was a low and black blanket stretched over Sydney. Michael was tempted to stop at the Steyne Hotel for a shot of rum but his less impulsive cousin warned him that the ferry would depart at 5.45 p.m. from the wharf. If they missed the ferry, they would be late getting back to the Erin Hotel and have to answer to Francis Duffy for their tardiness.

This was not a comforting thought to either as Sunday was the only day both men had away from work and they did not want to lose their day of rest by disobeying Daniel's father. Frank Duffy had set the rules on when they should be home. His wife, Bridget, would serve a roast dinner late that evening and all were expected to be at the table when grace was said.

They walked the short distance to the jetty which was crowded with day trippers eager to catch the ferry before the storm broke. Men dressed in tight-fitting trousers, waistcoats and tall stovepipe hats carried picnic baskets for the ladies whom they escorted. The ladies wore their best crinoline dresses, wide colourful headwear and carried parasols.

The storm rolling in from the south added another dimension to the end of the day. The excited and nervous laughter of the ladies, the deeper and raucous voices of men who had imbibed port, claret or sherry on the picnic added to the festive feeling of the late afternoon. Couples and families, single men and chaperoned ladies waited with an underlying tension for the imminent fury of the Southerly Buster to unleash itself over a parched city.

The thunder and lightning were almost simultaneous, promising that the heavy and pelting rains were not far away and the waiting day trippers cast nervous glances to the south. A deep and violent boom of thunder overhead caused the jetty to vibrate as if it had been hit with a giant sledgehammer and Michael suddenly felt his biceps gripped with such a force that he had a fleeting thought that he had been hit by lightning!

'*Oh!*' The gasp that accompanied the pain in his arm was not his and he turned to see the profile of a very beautiful and pale face with mouth agape revealing a perfect set of ivory white teeth. The beautiful young woman stared up at the boiling sky, which was lashed by jagged tridents of light, and when she turned her head her eyes, wide with fright, looked directly into his. They were emerald green and a faint memory of Ireland's grassy fields on a summer's day flashed through Michael's mind. They were the most beautiful eyes he had ever seen. In stark contrast to her milky white complexion was her long raven hair which was pulled down and tightly parted. Although she was a head shorter than he, this made her tall by most standards for a woman.

'May the angels protect you,' he said softly to her as he gazed into her eyes with an exploring frankness. He did not know why he had used the phrase he had so often heard his Aunt Bridget utter. It just seemed appropriate for the situation.

'Oh . . . I am sorry. I must have hurt you.' The young woman apologised as she released her grip on his arm and he wished she had not.

'You didn't hurt me,' he lied. 'I was rather flattered that you chose my arm in your moment of distress.' He continued to gaze into her eyes and she blushed with a giddiness when she looked into the gentle grey eyes of the stranger.

There was a strange contrast of savagery and gentleness in the rugged features and she had a momentary remembrance of how hard his muscled arm had been under the pressure of her fingers. She was also acutely aware that his presence seemed to cause an exquisite tingling in her stomach. Or was the exquisite, tingling feeling wickedly lower?

'Fi, are you feeling well?' A young woman's voice broke the spell between them.

'Yes, Penelope . . . I . . . I was just frightened by the thunder,' she answered, without taking her eyes from his face. Michael resented the intrusion of the second woman although she was equally as beautiful and around the same age as the girl with the raven hair.

Fiona realised self-consciously that she was standing very close to the tall young man and stepped away from him. Side by side the two women were a striking contrast; Penelope had hair the colour of spun gold and a smattering of freckles over her nose. Her large eyes were a deep sapphire blue set against high cheekbones and she exuded a noticeable blatant sensuality. He could see that both young women were dressed in the finest of flowing muslin.

His appraisal was met with a frank expression from Penelope reflecting an unabashed exposition of sexual attraction. 'If you would like I can stay with you,' he said in a lame attempt to engage the company of Fiona for just a while longer. 'Until the ferry arrives.' She smiled in a way that he could see that she wanted to accept his invitation.

'Your offer is very courteous but I think I should be with my cousin,' she replied hesitantly. 'But thank you for the offer, Mister . . . ?'

'My name is Michael. Michael Duffy, Miss . . . ?'

'. . . Macintosh. Fiona Macintosh. And this is my cousin, Miss Penelope White,' she answered formally. Penelope smiled and nodded her head slightly as recognition of the introduction then turned her attention to Fiona.

'Fi, we must join Granville. He is waiting for us at the end of the pier.' She turned to the young Irishman. 'If you will excuse us, Mister Duffy. I must say, however, that I am grateful for the assistance you rendered my cousin.' With a parting and polite smile, Penelope took Fiona's elbow and guided her through the crowd.

Michael watched them walk side by side down the jetty. They were certainly a striking pair of young ladies, he thought, without taking his eyes off Fiona and was rewarded to see her turn once and glance back at him. He flashed her a beaming smile and felt a little foolish. Maybe he was leering more than smiling, he thought. Like the drunken patrons of the Erin at the voluptuous barmaids Frank Duffy tended to employ.

Daniel had observed the exchange between Michael and Fiona and although it had been fleeting, he was perceptive enough to notice their mutual attraction. Michael had been so enamoured by the beautiful young woman that he had failed to introduce him to the young ladies and Daniel felt a little annoyed at his cousin's oversight.

'She must be the most beautiful girl in the whole world, Dan,' Michael said with a boyish tone of awe in his voice.

'Shut your mouth, Mick. Or you will drown when the rain comes,' his cousin growled lightly. 'Beautiful she is,' he mused as he watched the two young women walking together, 'but I think she is not in our class. From the look of her I would say she is one of those ladies born to wealth. Probably the daughter of some big Sydney merchant or landowner.'

'How do you know that, Danny boy?' Michael challenged quietly. 'She might be the child of a publican . . . Or working people like ourselves.'

Daniel pulled a pained expression at his naive optimism. 'You only have to look at the way she is dressed, her accent. Her whole appearance says

97

gentry,' he said, shaking his head. 'That's how I know. Best you forget her.'

But Michael was not convinced that the beautiful young woman was unobtainable. So she might be high born but she was still a woman and he knew she had been attracted as much to him as he was to her. 'Some day I am going to marry her, Daniel,' he said quietly. 'You watch and see.'

Daniel groaned and rolled his eyes to the sky. 'Michael, Michael, Michael . . . It cannot happen.'

'Yes it can, Daniel. You just watch,' he answered with quiet determination and his grey eyes were set with the hardness of gun metal. It would not be easy! But he was sure that he and the girl with the green eyes would meet again. And how would this happen? He had already formulated a plan.

Fiona giggled as she walked away. Although it was a childish thing to do, the tension of the moment needed release. 'Isn't he magnificent, Penny,' she said. 'He is like a Greek god.'

Penelope had to agree, but she did not want to encourage her cousin in her admiration for the handsome young man. 'He certainly is handsome, in a rough sort of Irish way, I grant you that,' she grudgingly admitted. But there was no future in allowing one's feelings to be drawn by such a man, Penelope thought, as her cousin prattled on with the deep sigh of a young woman in love for the very first time.

'Oh . . . You should have seen those eyes of his,' Fiona sighed. 'So gentle.' Penelope had seen those eyes, the broad shoulders and the slim waist and was duly impressed. Yes, she thought. He was like a Greek god. And she found herself imagining his hard body pressed against her own naked flesh in a sweating carnal and erotic embrace.

The thought caused her to shudder with a sensual fantasy. But she felt lust where Fiona imagined a romantic interlude. Penelope had no illusions about a man like Michael Duffy. He was extremely dangerous to women and, from his slightly scarred face, dangerous to men. Yes, she would have given much to have him naked in her bed and at her mercy. But that was unlikely as the young Irishman was not a man of their social circles. He was just another handsome Paddy from the wrong side of Sydney.

'I feared that I may have lost you two ladies,' Granville White said as he took Fiona's elbow and guided her to the end of the jetty. Granville's attention to Fiona was more than attentive. It had a touch of possessiveness about it. He held a cane picnic basket and spoke with an unmistakable educated English accent which was not surprising as he had lived all but two years of his life in England, managing the considerable family estates there. He was three years older than his sister, Penelope, and had the physical appearance of being 'aristocratic'; pale, with a thin face and delicate hands. His eyes were blue like those of his sister and his prematurely thinning hair was a brown colour.

Ladies in the upper circles of Sydney's gentry found him very attractive, not only for his wealth, but also his genteel style. He had impeccable social manners and was what was termed a 'true gentleman' in colonial society.

'I was frightened by the thunder,' Fiona said. 'But a gentleman came to my assistance to save me.' Granville considered her explanation rather extravagant.

'And who was this gentleman who *saved* you?' he asked sarcastically. 'Someone we know?' He was peeved at the way she had lavished the praise on her 'saviour'. A gentleman did not show his emotions which were the property of the common working-class Irish.

'No, he is no one we have met before. It was that young gentleman standing over there,' she said, turning her head to glance in Michael's direction, and Granville followed her gaze to where a tall and broad-shouldered man stood. It was obvious that he was the one she referred to as he was intently watching her. Michael flashed her a smile when she caught his eye and she looked away shyly.

'I am afraid the man is no gentleman by his appearances,' Granville sniffed dismissively. 'Probably one of those uncouth Irish navvies.'

'He is *certainly* Irish,' Penelope said with a hint of mischief in her voice. 'But he is not uncouth. In fact, he is rather charming from what I have briefly known of him. I would even dare to say, a very attractive man.' Granville glowered at his sister as he did not expect her to contradict his views. But it was obvious that the stranger had a certain charm about him that had infatuated both women.

'The Irish are a brutish people loyal only to their church,' he said with just an edge of anger. 'You only have to read about their drunken

100

brawling on their Saint Patrick's Days to see how low their intelligence levels are. They are like those savage apes from Africa.' His obvious bias against the Irish was fuelled by his desire to put down a man whom the two women found attractive. It was not natural that women born to a higher social class should be attracted by something almost animal-like in a man. Genteel ladies did not harbour carnal desires as men naturally did.

'I think you should keep your voice down, dear brother,' Penelope said, mocking him. 'Or that Irish brute might hear you and give you a thrashing.' He bristled, but did not reply to his sister's taunt. Instead he turned to glare at the Irishman and both men locked eyes.

Michael wondered who the elegantly dressed man with Fiona was. There was no mistaking the murderous look he was giving him. He sized him up and dismissed him as no threat.

The storm broke as a rumbling growl followed by the hiss of cold raindrops on the hot surface of the jetty. The *Phantom* steamed into view around Middle Head and its timely arrival promised salvation from the pelting rain.

The rain lashed the usually placid blue waters into a sheet of cold grey. When the ferry steered into the main channel, it rolled and rose in the heavy swell that rushed in from the Pacific Ocean through the twin heads that guarded the harbour against the full might of the ocean's power.

Under the canopy stretched over the ferry's main deck, Michael and Daniel stood watching the foreshore of Manly disappear as the ferry rounded Middle Harbour and both men shivered when the wind blew a fine mist of spray under the canopy. They had been drenched to the skin waiting to board the ferry and the temperature had dropped dramatically with the arrival of the rain.

Further under the shelter, Michael propped himself against a support pole to sketch in his art book, and when he had completed the drawing he shoved his way through the close-packed passengers. Daniel had an idea where he was going. He rolled his eyes and groaned. He was up to some crazy scheme of his own making and was only going to make a fool of himself.

'Miss Macintosh, I have something for you.'

Fiona was startled by the voice at her shoulder and felt her heart seeming to miss a beat. 'Oh! Mister Duffy – it's you!' she exclaimed.

'I thought you might like this as a memory of today's outing,' Michael said, as he pressed the sketch into her hand. 'But I'm afraid it does not capture the beauty which is naturally yours.' There were some wrinkles in the paper where water had splashed on it but the sketch remained reasonably intact. She glanced down and caught her breath with an audible sigh. It was a remarkable portrait of herself before the rain had drenched her and, in the sketch, fluttered tiny angels and the words, 'May the Angels Protect You – Forever.' She considered the Irishman's gesture as the most romantic thing that had ever happened to her in all her seventeen years and gazed up into the face of the big man standing close enough for her to feel his body heat.

'Penny! Look at what Mister Duffy has drawn,' she said and her cousin could not help but admire the portraiture.

'It's very good, Mister Duffy. Are you an artist?' she asked.

He shook his head. 'I wish I were . . . But I have a lot to learn,' he answered modestly. 'I hope one day to go to Europe and be enrolled in one of the great art schools.'

'I think they might learn from you . . . if this is any example of what you can do,' Penelope said graciously and was now very impressed by Michael Duffy who, she had originally presumed, was merely just another handsome young working-class man. But she had noted that he had an educated lilt in his voice, and the sketch Fiona clasped in her hands demonstrated his creative talent. Penelope sensed that he was an interesting juxtaposition of the creative and destructive.

'What do you think of Mister Duffy's portrait of Fiona?' Penelope said, turning with a wicked smile to her brother and added, 'Very good for someone as you previously described to us.' Granville shifted uncomfortably at his sister's dangerous reference to his inflammatory opinions of the Irish race and fervently prayed that she would not go further.

Michael had noticed the tense exchange between the two. There was something deep and unresolved between them, he thought.

'It has some merit,' Granville conceded reluctantly.

'I am sorry, Mister Duffy,' Penelope apologised. 'I have not introduced my brother Granville to you

. . . Granville, this is Mister Michael Duffy.'
Neither man offered to shake hands as it was
tacitly agreed that each disliked the other.

'Do you work in town, Mister Duffy?' Penelope
asked. 'From your manners I might presume you
are employed as a clerk with a solicitor . . . or
similar.'

Michael laughed softly at her interpretation of
his social status. He had noticed that she was the
more assertive of the two women and had an air of
self-assurance about her to the point of being
brazen.

'Very flattering, Miss White . . . but no,' he
replied politely. 'However, my cousin, Daniel, is
undertaking his articles with a firm in town. I
work for my uncle at the Erin Hotel in Redfern.'

'Well, I would never have guessed you were
employed in *that* kind of work, Mister Duffy,' she
commented. 'Not with your obvious artistic
talent.'

'*That* kind of work, Miss White, enjoys a lot of
patronage in Sydney,' he replied in a manner which
left her in no doubt that he had been insulted by
her demeaning statement. 'I would daresay that
some of Sydney's finest imbibe from time to time.
As a matter of fact, they might even get falling
down drunk,' he added with a facetious smile.
Penelope blushed. He was so damned sure of
himself.

'I did not mean to infer your work was not
important.' The words tumbled from her mouth.
'And I humbly apologise if you took offence.'

Michael smiled. 'I know what you meant, Miss
White,' he replied. 'But I accept your apology.'

104

Penelope felt a surge of fury. He had made her do something she had never done before. He, a mere working-class man, had made her apologise. Some day, Mister Duffy, I am going to force you to submit to my will. And I don't care how long it takes.

'I think I should return to Daniel, my cousin,' he said, as he noted with some satisfaction that he had caused Penelope to flush with anger. Ah but the gentry could lose their composure as easily as the working class. 'I hope I may be fortunate enough to meet both you ladies again in the near future,' he added, catching a frank and admiring glance from Fiona.

'Sydney is rather a large town,' Penlope retorted coolly, still smarting from her apology. 'It is not likely we would see you again.'

Michael stared her directly in the eyes before answering. 'Two of its most beautiful ladies stand out in the largest of crowds,' he said, holding her angry stare.

'Sir, you are being impudent,' Granville flared. 'You should take back what you have just said. Immediately. And apologise to the ladies for your impudence.'

The Irishman burst into a deep laugh that rolled over them. 'The truth need never be retracted,' he said as he turned to stare at Granville. But there was no sign of merriment in the eyes to accompany the laughter. Just a deadly cold greyness that chilled Granville. Fiona unwittingly broke the tension between the two men.

'I must give you back this drawing, Mister Duffy,' she said, as she pushed the paper towards him. 'It is too beautiful for me to keep.'

'The portrait is yours, Miss Macintosh,' he countered gently. 'You can do whatever you like with it . . . except return it to me.' She was aware that he had pressed a note into her hand as palms had touched and instinctively knew that the passing of the paper was a secret between them.

'Thank you, Mister Duffy,' she said coyly as she wrapped her fingers around the note. 'I will always keep this wonderful gift to remember my meeting with the man who saved me from the thunder . . . If not the rain.'

He flashed her a knowing smile as he bade good afternoon, then turned on his heel to make his way to the rear of the ferry.

He was smiling as happily as a schoolboy who had been given the day off lessons as he pushed his way through the mass of wet bodies to reach Daniel.

'I gather you made a further acquaintance with your young lady, boyo?' Daniel asked his grinning cousin.

'That I did, Danny boy . . . that I did,' Michael replied with a sigh. Daniel frowned as he turned to stare at the pounding rain on the harbour waters. Nothing good could come of such an impossible affair, he thought sadly.

Both men watched in silence as the southern foreshore of Sydney harbour slid past the port side of the ferry and the paddlewheels churned the grey sea into a white wake trailing behind them. Michael was lost in thoughts of the anticipated rendezvous he had proposed in his note to Fiona and his wiser cousin brooded on the stupidity of even contemplating any form of courtship with the young woman. Sure and Michael might be better educated by the good Jesuit fathers of Saint Ignatius School as any gentleman in the colony, but he lacked the considerable means to support such a quest for the young lady's hand. He was a young man rich in dreams – but poor in money. The Duffy estate was of moderate comfort but far from the unimaginable wealth of those whose class the beautiful woman appeared to be from. No, Michael was in for a big fall, when he confronted the fact that there could be no future between himself and Miss Fiona Macintosh.

The rain eased as the *Phantom* approached the clippers and sailing ships moored to the wharves busy with the commerce of the colony's trade. And, as the ferry churned past the residences of the colonial elite dominating the heights east of the Quay, Michael stared over the water at the most imposing mansion of all – the Macintosh mansion. A magnificent home with beautiful gardens that spilled down to the harbour's edge rivalling the homes of those of the other colonial aristocracy, the Wentworths of Vaucluse and the Macleays of Elizabeth Bay.

Fiona also gazed up at her home but she did not see the beautiful gardens or imposing structure of the house. She only saw a lonely place of restrictive confinement and little laughter. The house was not her home. It was the house of Enid Macintosh – her mother. A house where her mother ruled over the Macintosh financial empire as an iron fist inside a velvet glove, as she ruled the house of servants and her own children in the same manner.

If only Father had chosen to remain in Sydney and not go to Queensland to manage Glen View personally, she thought wistfully. But he loved the land more than he loved the company of his family.

She sighed and made a silent wish that her oldest brother Angus would soon take over the management of Glen View. Then her father might return to Sydney to spend more time with his family.

A cold breeze whipped up a salty spray, splashing Fiona. She shivered and in the chill was an echo of something strange and dreadful. She suddenly felt faint and swooned. Penelope noticed and inquired if she was ill but Fiona gave a reassuring answer that her corsets were just a little tight. The restrictive corsets had a bad habit of cutting the blood supply causing young ladies to faint on occasion. The explanation seemed to satisfy her cousin's concern for her welfare.

8

All was not well at the Erin Hotel.

Michael and Daniel exchanged questioning glances as they hung their rain-soaked coats on wooden pegs on the back of the battered kitchen door. The loud and booming voice of Francis Duffy echoed down the narrow hallway from the hotel's dining room and his angry tirade was occasionally interrupted by the softer and more reasonable tones of Bridget, his wife.

Max Braun, the cellarman, slopped at gravy on a tin plate with a chunk of fresh bread as he sat at the kitchen table. He grunted a welcome to the two young men as he wiped away remnants of spilt gravy from his chin with the back of a gnarled hand and was seemingly oblivious to the angry scene taking place in the dining room.

The big German was an imposing figure. A former sailor from Hamburg, he was Michael's height and somewhere in the huge frame was muscle that had long disappeared behind bulging fat as an inevitable result of Bridget's excellent and copious meals. His head, which was a mishmash of scar tissue, seemed to be connected to his shoulders, such was the thickness of his bull-like neck.

'What's happening, Uncle Max?' Michael asked, as he stood in front of the wood stove to warm his hands. 'Why is Uncle Frank angry?' Steam rose off his shirt, filling the kitchen which was only just big enough to hold a table and six chairs crammed uncomfortably close to the stove.

'*Schlechte. Neuigkeiten,*' Max answered in his native tongue then switched to English although he knew Michael spoke German well enough. 'Best you stay away from Mister Duffy.' He gave a loud belch before scraping his chair away from the table and heaving his big frame to his feet. '*Die kleine Katie ist geschwangert,*' he added coarsely to describe Michael's sister's delicate condition.

Michael felt his face drain of blood. Katie pregnant! She was only sixteen . . . and unmarried! 'Who . . . who is the father, Max?' he asked and blurted, 'It's that bastard O'Keefe.'

Max nodded.

'Ya. I vill break his neck . . . the no goot svine-hund.'

Michael knew that his threat was not idle. The big German was prepared to kill the defiler of his beloved Katie as he had a special fondness for both Michael and Kathleen Duffy. To him they were his adopted children. A special link with their father, the big Irishman Patrick Duffy, who had saved his life that terrible day of the Eureka massacre. And over the years both Michael and Katie had grown to adopt him as their 'uncle'.

'You won't have to break his neck, Uncle Max,' Michael said quietly as he clenched his fists. 'I will.

110

But just enough so that he will still be well enough to marry Katie.'

Max nodded. 'She is your sister. Und it is vight you do this . . . For her honour, mein friend.'

Despite Max's warning to steer clear of Francis Duffy in his anger, Michael and Daniel entered the lion's den. The dining room was not a large or elaborate room. The few tables in the small room were pushed close together to economise space. The first impression that struck the visitor to the dining room was the pleasant odour of wax that wafted off the highly polished floor and big cedar sideboard adorned with neat rows of cruet sets. Expensive Irish linen and the cutlery for the morning breakfast covered the table tops. The Erin Hotel enjoyed a reputation for some of the finest accommodation money could buy for travellers visiting Sydney. And part of the attraction was the high quality of the meals served in the dining room and the main bar.

A large candelabra on the centre table flickered as the door was opened and the two young men stepped as unobtrusively as possible into the room. The table with the candelabra was central to the three people already gathered in the room, each of whose faces reflected different expressions of emotion caught in the candles' soft light. Bridget Duffy sat showing concern while her husband's face expressed a black anger and Katie's look was that of defiance, as she stood behind her aunt, gripping the back of Bridget's chair. Kate had a strong face that would mature from girlish pretty to womanly beautiful as the years passed in her life. It was a face framed by lustrous and wavy

111

dark hair that spilled over her shoulders almost to her waist. Like Michael, she had expressive grey eyes capable of speaking her thoughts. Michael had never thought of her as an attractive girl – as brothers are prone not to do – but he knew other men found her striking.

A short silence fell as the three around the table turned to view the two young men. 'Max told us the news,' Michael said.

'Did he tell you who the father is?' Francis Duffy thundered. 'Did Max tell you about Kevin O'Keefe being the father?'

'I guessed as much, Uncle Frank,' Michael answered calmly. 'Who else could it be?'

'Oh! And you are all so sure Kevin O'Keefe is the father of my child,' Kate flared. The men carrying on as if she were not even in the room with them. 'I don't remember anyone asking me who the father is. It might be the Chinese market gardener down the road for all you men know.'

Her furious outburst caused all the men in the room to blanch. With horror all three men stared at her and she smiled wickedly now that she had their attention. 'I will put your minds at rest. Kevin *is* the father of the child that I carry.'

But this was not a consolation to Francis Duffy as the Chinese market gardener who delivered vegetables to the hotel might be a preferred husband to the son of convict parents. The fact that O'Keefe's parents had been Irish convicts, even if they were of the True Faith, did not compensate for their lowly social status in the colony. There was an ingrained snobbery among freeborn colonialists and immigrants about such matters. It was Frank Duffy who raised the painful and socially embarrassing issue.

'Katie, you know O'Keefe is of convict stock,' he said. 'How could you allow yourself to get . . . umm . . . with child to him. You could have had the choice of marrying any young Irishman in Sydney. Any young man from a good freeborn family.'

Her bitter laugh echoed in the near empty dining room. 'Have you ever thought that possibly I might love Kevin O'Keefe himself? That I care little for what his parents were. Not that it should matter, anyway. Some of the wealthiest and most respectable citizens in the colony were once convicts, Uncle Francis. Does anyone hold that against them? What if the British had caught my father in Ireland for his activities? What if they had transported him as a convict? Would that make me or Michael any different?'

Francis coughed behind his hand. Yes, Patrick had come close to being caught on many occasions. What Kate said was true. But it was hard for the Irish publican to shake the bias against those of convict blood. And yet many of the good customers of the Erin were themselves men who could show the scars of the cat on their backs and tell stories of lashings that took so much meat that the guards' dogs had feasted on the bloody flesh at the base of the cruel triangle. They were good men all the same.

He felt his anger dissolving when he stared across at his wife holding Kate's hand protectively in hers. He knew full well that his wife had sided with her niece from the beginning and there was

113

little a man could do against one woman's opinion, let alone two. 'Is O'Keefe going to marry you?' he asked gruffly.

Kate could see from her uncle's demeanour that he had conceded defeat but she also knew that he would have to bluster for the family's honour in lieu of her father, absent somewhere on the Queensland frontier. It was the way of men, to fume and bluster on matters that had no real concern to them, other than a stupid male thing about honour.

'I don't know,' she answered quietly. 'He does not know about my condition.'

'Jesus, Mary and . . . !' Michael checked his blasphemous outburst.

'*Michael!*'

'Ah, sorry, Aunt Bridget,' he apologised meekly before continuing. 'O'Keefe got you this way and he doesn't know! Katie, do you know what sort of man O'Keefe is? Do you really know?'

'I have heard talk, Michael. But I also know Kevin is a good man who just needs a woman to love and look after him. He will change when we are wed,' she answered without rancour at her brother's well-intentioned if not tactful question.

Oh yes, she had heard the stories about Kevin O'Keefe, but they were only stories spread by jealous women he had scorned.

Kevin had come to work for her Uncle Frank a year earlier. She vividly remembered the first time he had stood framed in the doorway of the kitchen with his cap in his hand and his flashing eyes, and the way his slow warm smile settled on her. She thought she would faint. Kate knew from that instant that he was the man born to love her as she would him and as the months went by she found herself finding excuses to be around him at the hotel. He could make her laugh with his easy charm and make her feel special with his gentle words. In many ways Kevin reminded her of Michael: tough, gentle and handsome.

Soon she could do nothing but daydream about being in his arms. She had vague swirling thoughts about love that began to focus on the power of his body. And then one day she found herself in the cellar of the hotel alone with Kevin. He was stripped to the waist hauling the heavy wooden kegs and was not aware she stood watching him. She remembered so well the way the muscles rippled in his shoulders and arms as he strained to lift the kegs. He turned and his eyes met hers – he wanted her and it was only a reflection of her own desire. They moved closer together and stood facing each other until with gentle, lulling words he began to undress her. His power was mesmerising. She let him do what he wanted, for she wanted his touch.

The pleasure was all that she could have imagined and when it was over Kevin confessed his love for her. The visits to the cellar became frequent and their lovemaking, snatched amongst the big wooden kegs, exquisite. She had felt their love sealed forever in the sharing of their bodies, and now even more so by God's gift they had created together.

Michael's father had warned him that Kate was her mother's daughter – headstrong and stubborn. Michael also knew that his mother had defied all the rules of her society to elope with a wild young Catholic rebel and bear him two sons and a daughter.

Patrick Duffy and Elizabeth Fitzgerald had been an unlikely pair; she, the daughter of a Protestant landowner who was descended from French nobility, and he, the son of an educated Catholic Irishman who reared his sons on the bitter and bloody ideas of rebellion. Was not history repeating itself with Kate's decision to marry a man not socially acceptable to the Duffy clan?

But Patrick Duffy had been a man with a noble cause, whereas O'Keefe was flawed. His only cause was the pursuit of women and gambling. It was not hard to like O'Keefe who had natural charm and a quick wit. He was also a man who could use his fists which Michael respected about him. He might have a reputation as a womaniser but he was also a man's man.

The regular patrons of the Erin had often discussed the possibility of an organised bare-knuckle bout between the two men. They were matched in size and weight and both had reputations as the best bare-knuckle fighters around Sydney's Irish areas.

'Well, I suppose the matter is settled then,' Frank said, as he fumbled in his vest pocket for his old briar pipe. 'I suppose we will have to get a letter to Pat and Tom up in Queensland. Pat will be pleased to hear that he is soon to be a grandfather,' he could not help adding. 'Even if it is the son of a convict father.'

'He will not be the son of a convict father, Francis, and you very well know that,' Bridget snapped angrily. 'Kevin O'Keefe is as freeborn as any Duffy. And Kate's child will be a freeborn Australian.'

'An Irishman,' he rebutted. 'The boy will be born an Irishman. His father is Irish and so is Kate.'

Daniel smiled. 'Mother is right, Da,' he said. 'Kate's child will be an Australian. Kevin was born in New South Wales and so will be Kate's child.' Francis frowned at his son's statement of nationality. To him, Ireland was 'home' and this new country was just an extension of Ireland.

'You are both wrong,' Kate said, cutting across the two men's discussion on birthright. 'My child will be a Queenslander.'

'What!' Frank gasped and she serenely sailed on, 'As soon as Kevin and I are married, I intend to journey to Queensland to start a business there with the money Da has set aside for me.'

Her second startling revelation, following the first concerning her pregnancy, caused even Bridget to stare at her aghast. Queensland! The new colony was a land of savage natives and little civilisation. Had not the explorer, Mister Kennedy, been speared to death by the savages? Did not the German explorer, Mister Leichhardt, disappear with his expedition in the wilderness of that terrible place? Not to mention the ill-fated Messrs Burke and Wills' expedition. No, the Queensland colony was no place for a pregnant young woman who had known only the civilised comforts of Sydney. And besides, Kevin O'Keefe was no bushman. He was city-born and raised. She shuddered at the thought of Kate on the frontier. She had given her support – albeit reluctantly – to her proposed marriage, but this was a different matter altogether.

'Katie, you cannot go to that terrible place in your condition. It's unthinkable,' she said quietly but firmly.

'Other women follow their men, Aunt Bridget. Why shouldn't I?'

'Because in this case, O'Keefe would be following his woman,' Michael interjected cynically. 'It's a rather unusual situation.'

Kate did not see the situation in the same light as her brother. Kevin was a strong and healthy man who could adapt to the new way of life she had in mind for them and it did not cross her mind that it was *she* who was making decisions usually made by a man. 'I don't expect Kevin will be out in the bush,' she said confidently. 'I have plans to start a hotel that will be the best in the new colony. That means we will be in a town and not in the bush.'

'Kevin is not a publican,' Francis noted. 'He has no real experience in running a hotel.'

'I will teach him,' Kate replied defensively. 'Growing up here, I have learnt a lot from you. I know how you keep books and how you manage a bar and I probably know more than Daniel and Michael put together.'

Francis had to admit she was right as Daniel had never shown much interest in the hotel. His ambitions were in law and Michael had aspirations to be an artist. 'Have you thought that a man might object to being taught a trade by a woman, Kate?' the publican parried. 'That he might feel your knowledge ... ah ... a bit

118

intimidating to a man such as himself?'

'Sure and Kevin might think this,' she answered carefully. 'But I know he will learn. And be as good a publican as any in the new colony. He is smart. And he has a way about him that would make our hotel the most popular in Queensland.'

Frank Duffy sighed. The young woman's eyes blazed with the enthusiasm reminiscent of her father and, had she been raised in Ireland, he had no doubt that she would have been harassing the redcoats beside her father.

'You know your father gave me control over your share of the money that he left in trust for you and Michael,' he said. 'But it was intended for when you turned twenty-one. You are only sixteen, Kate.'

'And soon to be a wife and mother, Uncle Francis. I can write to Da. And I know he will agree to release my share to me when I explain what it is for. Or you can make the decision as he said you could in his absence. Either way . . . I am going. And I am going to have the best hotel in Queensland. And that is that,' she said, folding her arms across the swell of her breasts and staring defiantly at her uncle.

My God! She looks so much like Elizabeth when she was determined, Frank thought. And like Elizabeth, she would not back down. Only Patrick had been able to change Elizabeth's mind with his beguiling ways. But not all the time. 'I will write to Patrick and see what he thinks, Kate,' he said, in a last effort to change her mind. 'You know it will take time for any mail to reach him. The last we heard from him was that they were picking up

119

supplies from some place called Rockhampton. He wrote that they would be a long time on the track and it may be months before I get a reply.'

'I am planning to have a place Da and Tom can live in when they are not on the track, Uncle Francis. That means I need the money now because time is wasting just waiting for his permission. I am determined my child will be born in Queensland.'

Exasperated by her stubbornness, the burly Irish publican snapped, 'Why is it so important that your child be born in Queensland?'

'Because I want my father to hold his first grandchild when he or she is born,' she replied softly. 'I want to show Da the happiness of the moment. To give him something he has lost since Mother was taken from us. It's important to me.'

Bridget understood her niece's motivations. Kate had always adored the man who was both stranger and idolised father to her. She had grown up with the memories of a big gentle man who cried with joy at the sight of his little girl on his rare visits to Sydney and the bond between father and daughter was special. Just like the bond between mother and son. Bridget had hoped to hold her niece's child, but she also understood why Kate wanted to be near her father. 'I think you should make the decision to give Kate the money now, Francis,' Bridget finalised. 'I know that is what Patrick would do under the circumstances.'

Francis Duffy stared at his wife. He had expected her to be on his side in stopping their niece from risking her life on a frontier so far away from their loving protection. 'You realise Kate could be speared by a wild blackfella,' he said despairingly. 'That she and her baby could be lost forever up there in the bush, Bridget. Do you wish to condone that risk?'

Bridget knew that her husband was right, but he did not understand the deeper meanings of life as only a woman could. Some things transcended even the risk of a potentially short life on the frontier. 'Kate has already said that she does not intend to go bush, but set up a hotel in one of the new towns,' she countered quietly. 'I am sure she and Kevin will be perfectly safe. I am also sure there are people who can look out for her up there.'

Francis tapped his briar pipe distractedly against his leg before answering. 'God preserve us from the day women ever get into politics. Though that is not likely,' he sighed, resigned to defeat. 'Kate, you can have the money.'

She rushed at her uncle giving him a crashing hug as her words tumbled over each other. 'Thank you, Uncle Frank . . . Aunt Bridget,' she babbled. 'I will have the best hotel in Queensland and I know you will be proud. You can come and stay with Kevin and myself. Da says the climate is wonderful and balmy in the colony and . . .'

'Yes, yes. I know,' Frank said gruffly, trying not to catch his niece's contagious excitement. 'But just remember you always have a home here with us if you ever need to come back for one reason or another. Now all we have to do is find Mister O'Keefe and tell him he is going to be a husband, father and publican in that order,' he said between her crushing hugs. 'And tell him that all this is going to happen a thousand miles from here in a place where even explorers get lost,' he continued with a mournful sigh.

Michael was next in line for a hug. Then Bridget, and finally Daniel, as Kate's tears of joy splashed each one in turn.

'Does anyone know where Mister O'Keefe is tonight?' Frank asked quietly. 'I think he should be here to ask my permission to marry Kate.'

Michael frowned. 'I think I know where he is, Uncle Frank. Dan and I will go and fetch him.' Daniel raised his eyebrows to ask where. Michael saw his questioning expression and drew his cousin out of hearing of Kate who was babbling excitedly to Bridget about wedding plans.

'O'Keefe goes to the Hero of Waterloo on Sunday nights.'

Daniel recoiled as if confronted by a deadly snake.

'You aren't suggesting we go over to The Rocks on a Sunday night,' he said horrified. 'You have to be a lunatic to suggest going there at any time.'

'We will take Max with us,' Michael replied and Daniel shook his head sadly. The Rocks! Better they just cut their own throats and die at home! But Michael was going and he knew he must dutifully follow. Max accompanying them was at least some consolation. He sighed like his father. The Rocks!

9

Electric blue flashes of lightning lit the three people on the sandstone verandah as the storm rumbled and rolled across the inky darkness of the harbour below. A cool breeze off the waters came to break the sweltering air and play with the loose strands of Enid's hair as she sat in a cane chair on the verandah.

One year short of her forty-fifth year, Enid Macintosh was still a beautiful woman and it was not hard to see where Fiona had inherited her fine features. Enid sat in one of the cane chairs that were left on the wide verandah so that guests could admire the sweeping views of the harbour which was now becoming invisible under the cloud-covered night sky. Only the little blinking lights on the sterns of the fishing dories marked a place in the oily black waters of the harbour to indicate its presence. The fishermen would be netting for the abundant and delicious fish, she thought idly, as she held a china cup and sipped delicately the hot coffee laced with sweet cream. She luxuriated in the refreshing breeze that wafted the fresh scents of the garden renewed by the rain. It was good to be out of the house where the air was stagnant and muggy with summer dampness.

David Macintosh stood beside his mother's chair and sipped a sauterne from a crystal goblet. The sauterne was a local wine from the Macarthur vineyards at the Camden Estate outside of Sydney and he mused that it had a fruity flavour comparable to any of the French wines he had known in his student days at Oxford.

Enid's son was very much like his cousin, Granville White, in physical appearance except that he was not prematurely losing his hair as Granville was. David was twenty-two years of age and had only recently returned to Australia after graduating from England's hallowed Oxford University with a Bachelor's in the classics.

He had returned somewhat reluctantly as life in the cloistered halls of Oxford had suited his scholarly disposition. He was in every way a stark contrast to his tough and pragmatic older brother, Angus. David was more than happy to see Angus inherit the running of the Macintosh enterprises. For now he was content to bide his time in Sydney, sipping excellent local wine, and plan a foray on the virtues of the many beautiful young ladies of colonial society.

Granville stood with his back to Enid and David and was deep in thought about what he was to propose to them as he swilled an imported Portuguese madeira and puffed on an expensive Cuban cigar. Although preoccupied, he could still taste the rich flavours of the meal served at the Macintosh table that evening.

The dinner had had an interesting and delicate

balance of European spices with local produce. First course had been a kangaroo tail soup served steaming hot with redcurrant jelly and a dash of port to lift the strong flavour. Then a freshly caught whole baked snapper was served smothered with an oyster sauce as the next course. The third selection on the menu was a pigeon pie in a thick and delicious gravy of red wine and vegetables. A choice of local sauterne or imported burgundy accompanied the meal. The final course was apple in a delicate pie crust with thick, yellow cream topping. Needless to say there was much left over from the dinner and the remains of the pigeon pie would be served cold for next day's lunch.

The three contemplated their private thoughts and enjoyed the cooler air of the verandah until Enid broke the silence.

'I could not help but noticing Fiona was very quiet at the table tonight, Granville,' she said. 'Did something happen on your picnic at Manly Village today?'

Granville took a large swig from the madeira before answering. 'She was accosted by a damned Irish lout just before we boarded the *Phantom* for the trip home.'

'What do you mean "accosted"?' Enid asked. 'Was she hurt in any way?'

'No, not physically hurt,' he replied as he ashed the cigar in the rose garden below. 'More upset by the man's loutish behaviour.'

David joined the conversation. He was five years older than his sister but they had been closer than he had ever been with his older brother, Angus. 'What do you mean by his behaviour?'

he asked. 'How did he upset my sister?'

Granville shifted uncomfortably. 'He, ah, pressed his unwanted attentions on Fiona and Penelope.'

'Did he in any way insult the ladies?' David asked, showing fraternal concern. 'Or was he just talking to them?'

'He was talking to them,' Granville answered reluctantly. 'But he was damned impudent! Some kind of Irish oaf who works in a hotel in Redfern, from what I could gather. Damned ungentlemanly behaviour on his part in the way he approached the ladies.'

David grinned and was relieved to hear that there was really nothing in the incident to warrant concern. 'So. He was rather handsome and charming, I gather,' David concluded.

Granville gave his cousin a puzzled look. 'How can you make that inference?'

'I make that inference, Cousin Granville,' David answered still grinning, 'because my sister had the look of a young lovesick girl who had just met her Sir Lancelot. I could see it written all over her face all through this evening's meal.'

Granville scowled. 'And you think that is good? That she be infatuated by some popish Irishman from the lower classes?'

David shook his head. 'I do not condone any such relationship,' he replied. 'But it is not likely she will ever see the man again, if what you say about his pedigree is correct. And it does not hurt a young woman to be flattered by the attentions of *any* young man. Knowing my sister as I do, I doubt she would have tolerated a man who did not act

126

like a true gentleman. So Fiona will moon around for a little while until the next charming Lancelot comes along. Probably some squatter's son. Or an eligible regimental officer at the next spring ball.'

Granville could see the sense in what he said but still felt a touch uneasy. She was to be his wife one day – naturally, with Donald Macintosh's permission – as such a marriage would help bind the vast fortunes of the Macintosh family closer to that of the Whites' considerable estates. The Whites had always been the relatively poor relations to their cousins, the Macintoshes. But through Enid's marriage to Donald they had increased their estates substantially.

'I suppose you are right, David,' Granville said as a closing remark on Fiona's brief infatuation. 'What I would like to do now is put forward a proposal that is guaranteed to make us a lot of money . . . the subject I touched on before dinner.'

Enid delicately placed her cup on the saucer in her lap. 'Ah, yes, cotton-growing and black labour,' she said. 'A rather interesting proposition. I suppose you need Mister Macintosh's assistance in the proposal?' Enid always referred to her husband in the third person formal when she discussed business, even with family.

'Yes. I would need, at the least, the use of the *Osprey* for what I would propose,' Granville replied eagerly. 'And the purchase or lease of further land on the Queensland coast.'

David filled his wineglass from a crystal decanter. 'The *Osprey*. Where is she being used now?' he asked as he placed the stopper in the decanter.

'She's being used on the run between Sydney and Brisbane,' Granville answered quickly. 'She isn't being used directly in Macintosh business at the moment, so she can be spared.'

David knew of the ship. She was a barque designed for short hauls along the New South Wales and Queensland coast. But she was also capable of longer hauls between the Pacific Islands.

'And you want control of her to transport indentured black labour?' he asked as he swirled the clear wine, catching the shimmer of the faint light from the dining room candles behind them in the crystal goblet. 'Darkies from the Pacific Islands to work in cotton fields in Queensland. In the first place, Granville, I would counter that the Americans have cotton-growing sewn up and that they will be back into the business as soon as they resolve their differences.'

Granville had known this argument might arise. 'The war will drag on for a long time,' he parried. 'And in that time we will be able to grab control of the market. And keep it!'

'What makes you so sure the war will go on for a long time?' Enid asked. She was a careful woman in her business dealings and never made a decision unless she could see clear precedents for guaranteed success. Granville turned his attention to his aunt because it was she who held the power in the absence of Donald Macintosh to make the major business decisions.

'I have been reading a lot in regard to the war lately,' he replied in a carefully measured delivery. 'And I have discussed the matter with officers from Victoria Barracks who have been following the

128

war closely. Although most sympathise with the Confederate States, they admit that they are worried by the North's capacity to replenish its war stocks from its rather substantial factories.'

'From what I have read, it appears the Confederacy has that Yankee, Abe Lincoln, on the run,' David interjected with a hint of his Southern sympathies. 'Industrial strength or not, the Confederates will win. And there is also a chance that Mister Palmerston might bring Britain into the war on the Confederates' side which will certainly give them the logistics they need. *And* break the Northern blockade to boot. Britain certainly has the navy capable of giving the Yankees a bloody nose.'

Granville shook his head. 'I doubt if Britain will get involved in the American war. I am sure Mister Palmerston's advisers have reminded him about the past disasters she has suffered at the Yankees' hands. And then there is the question of slavery. The English public's abhorrence of slavery will not tolerate siding with a nation committed to keeping it. No, Britain will not rally to the Confederacy and I doubt if she will give any support to Mister Lincoln's government either.'

'What about the Confederate victories?' David persisted. 'That must count for something with Palmerston and the cotton millers in Britain. They are desperately short of cotton because of the Yankee blockade.'

'What my military advisers tell me is that the Confederates are winning battles but are not able to adequately replace their losses in men and material,' Granville continued doggedly. 'It's only a matter of time before the North wears them down. I suppose you could say it is a contest between Northern money and material against Southern guts and dash. I am afraid for the South that guts and dash will not be enough. So, in the end, all that will happen is a long war, prolonged by the South's lack of a sound commissary system.'

Enid had listened carefully to her nephew explain the strategic implications of the American Secessionist War and was impressed by his depth of analysis in the matters concerning logistics.

'Is there any other crop we might be able to fall back on if the cotton enterprise falls through?' she asked quietly.

Granville smiled triumphantly. 'Yes. Sugar!' he answered.

'Sugar. Yes, I believe sugar grows in warm climates from what Mister Macintosh has written to me.' Enid mused as she delicately sipped at her coffee. 'Queensland has such a climate as may be conducive to sugar-growing.'

Granville had another card up his sleeve he had not yet played and he now threw it on the table. 'The Queensland legislature has just passed a Coolie Act that opens the way for black labour,' he said. 'I've heard around the Australian Club that Robert Towns is going to use Pacific Islanders as indentured labourers for his property near Brisbane, instead of Indian workers. Towns is no fool, and I think we should get in on the same deal.'

The mention of the shrewd and wealthy Northumbrian shipowner and merchant impressed Enid. Captain Robert Towns was well known as a businessman who rarely made a mistake in his dealings, and if Towns had decided to use Pacific Islanders as indentured labourers then there must be substance in her nephew's proposal.

Enid placed her cup carefully on a small cane table from which she took a Chinese fan and flipped it open. With the storm almost gone, the air was becoming humid and unpleasant again. She stared into the depths of the harbour as she waved the fan slowly, contemplating all that her nephew had outlined and, although she had the authority to decide on Granville's proposal, she would have preferred her husband to be in Sydney to make the decision. But Donald was more interested in establishing the Glen View lease and had become besotted with the idea of carving out a pastoral empire to rival any in the colonies. She could not understand her husband's love of the harsh land he described in glowing terms as a new Eden and the idea of being with Donald on the frontier had no appeal whatsoever to her.

'The *Osprey* is at your disposal,' she said with a slow wave of her fan. 'And the venture is under your control.'

Granville smiled triumphantly and with a single gulp downed the last of the madeira in his goblet. Now all he had to do was win Fiona in marriage and he would be another step closer to a full partnership in the Macintosh business interests.

'You will always be glad you made the right decision, Aunt Enid,' he said jubilantly. 'In a few years the enterprise will be a major jewel in the business. That I promise you both.'

'There is one thing I failed to mention,' she said,

eyeing him shrewdly. 'You have total control of the running of the enterprise, but David will review the operation from time to time on my behalf. And David will allocate all finances.'

Granville ceased smiling. If David controlled the purse strings then he really controlled the whole venture. The damned Macintoshes gave nothing away! And his aunt, once a White herself, had become a true Macintosh. But he did not allow himself to display his bitter disappointment. Instead, he flashed a broad smile of his seeming pleasure at having his cousin as his de facto boss.

From the harbour they could hear the clanking of a channel buoy and the sounds of fishermen calling across the water to each other. The storm was almost gone and the cruciform constellation of the Southern Cross reigned supreme in the southern sky.

As Granville completed his deal, Penelope and Fiona were chatting in the drawing room where flickering candles cast a soft glowing backdrop to a conversation that was inevitably about Michael Duffy.

'You cannot seriously entertain any thought of meeting the man,' Penelope cautioned her cousin. 'He's nothing more than a common labourer.' Fiona stared at the crumpled sheet of sketchpad paper in her lap. 'Meet me at Hyde Park next Sunday afternoon. I will find you.'

'He may be a common labourer, as you call him, Penelope, but he has the manners of a gentleman,' she retorted defensively. 'And besides, what harm is there in just meeting him?'

Penelope frowned because her cousin was not as worldly wise as she in the ways of men and she did not feel Fiona was really ready to discover what she herself knew intimately of men's natures. It was time to be frank.

'Men want more than idle chatter,' Penelope said bluntly. 'A man's intention is to seduce you to his bed. And I fear that Mister Duffy, as charming as he is, has that intention. You must know that anything more between you is impossible. Although the very thought of him does have *that* appeal,' she added wistfully as she imagined what it would be like to be under the Irishman's muscled body.

'Penny! Sometimes you are shocking,' Fiona said with a nervous giggle. She knew her cousin had experienced the illicit pleasures, never spoken of, except between close friends. And they were more like sisters than cousins in their relationship.

Penelope smiled. Although she was only two years older than her cousin she was two hundred years more experienced when it came to men. 'Fi, trust me when I say you are no match for that man,' she said quietly. 'He has *that* look about him.'

'What do you mean by *that look*?' Fiona queried.

'It is in the eyes . . . the voice,' Penelope said as she stared into the flame of the flickering candle. 'The way a man stands like a proud stallion among the brood mares.'

Fiona blushed as she had a vivid image of her father's big roan stallion mounting a mare to service her. It was a savage and arousing sight that had caused her to imagine, long after the event, things that disturbed her and which she tried to put from her mind with feelings of guilt. The images were definitely erotic, but disturbing, and she found tht she was squeezing her knees together as the imagery took form in her mind. *A desire to be totally filled by the giant organ of the stallion*. Penelope continued to philosophise on the ways of men.

'It is the way of his arrogance. And you, Fi, are like the lamb before the lion – helpless.' Fiona could understand what her cousin was saying. Yes, she felt a certain amount of helplessness when she gazed into those grey eyes. An actual weakness in her body. *Like the stallion servicing the mare . . .*

'I intend to meet Michael Duffy regardless of what you say,' Fiona replied with a hint of defiance. 'But I assure you I will be fully in control of my feelings.'

Penelope smiled at her naive belief that she could control her deepest passions and leaned forward to grasp Fiona's hands in her own. 'Always remember what you have just said. Always control men, because they are easily controlled by strong women. I have learnt that much. Oh! they bluster and carry on like peacocks but a woman's body is something they will fight for. When you know that, *then* you will always be in control of all else that follows.' The flickering candlelight caught the intensity of Penelope's plea on her face. Then her hands fell reluctantly from the grasp and slid down Fiona's lap before she drew away from her cousin.

'What was it like the first time?' Fiona asked quietly. Although she knew from intimate discussions between them on previous occasions that Penelope had slept with many men and – it was rumoured – with women, Fiona had never inquired into the physical description of the act. The whispered stories circulating in the drawing rooms and parlours of Sydney's colonial mansions alluding to her cousin's unnatural acts with other women, Fiona dismissed as malicious fabrications. And yet they held a fascination she found disturbingly arousing. How was it that a woman could pleasure another?

'The first time?' Penelope's face clouded as she echoed bitterly her cousin's question. 'The first time is something I would rather forget.'

'I am sorry I asked,' Fiona hurried. 'I did not mean to cause you any distress.'

But Penelope continued to speak as if disembodied from the pain of the first time. 'After the first time, with other men it was nice. No, not nice. Nice is a word that does not describe the feelings. It was ... it is ... all-consuming. Like an explosion in the body and mind at the same time. An explosion of wonderfully wicked pleasures while the men grunt like animals and, for a while, all that is forbidden ... except in your mind ... happens. You become part of a secret world and can be anything or anywhere. And for the moment you really are. I cannot describe it in any other way.'

Fiona listened in rapt silence to her cousin's description of the act called love. But it sounded more like something else. It was partly as she imagined – a metaphysical experience – but at the same time strangely distant from what she had expected. The thought of Michael as half-man half-stallion crept into the dark rooms of her mind again and she felt the delicious thrill of the forbidden.

The candles suddenly flared and both women glanced in the direction of the entrance to the drawing room.

'I thought you might have the gaslight on, ladies,' Granville slurred. 'You could not possibly see anything in this gloom.' His entrance into the room had become an intrusion resented by both women. But it was the bitter look from Penelope that Fiona noticed most as she had never seen her cousin look at her brother in that manner before.

'I think the candles are much preferable to the gaslight on Sunday evenings,' Fiona said defensively. 'They are so . . . romantic.'

Granville swayed on his feet as he stood in the doorway, and he had a strange expression on his face that was somewhere between happiness and regret. But when he adjusted his eyes to the candlelight, his expression altered and, when he stared at Fiona, it took on the expression of a horse dealer appraising the worth of a good brood mare.

'I hope your talk with Aunt Enid and David was satisfactory,' Penelope said conversationally to her brother. She knew of his plans to broach the subject of the *Osprey* as he had discussed the project with her the previous week over breakfast in the house that they shared.

'Yes, quite satisfactory,' he lied. 'Aunt Enid has agreed to the setting up of the Queensland properties . . . and my use of the *Osprey* to get them under way,' he said, as he walked unsteadily into the drawing room to stand between the two women.

'Good,' Penelope replied.

'I shall bid you both good night,' Fiona said, as

she stood and brushed down her long satin dress. 'I will see you in the morning at breakfast.' They acknowledged her departure and remained silent until they could hear her footsteps on the stairway to the second floor of the mansion.

Granville slumped into the chair that Fiona had vacated and stared into the flame of a candle with his chin tucked in his hands. Penelope could read her brother's brooding mood.

'It did not go well at all,' she stated simply.

'No, it did not,' he answered bitterly without looking at her. 'David has ultimate control over the whole project. The damned Macintoshes never give anything away.' Granville had meticulously planned the whole enterprise. He had dined at his own expense with the regimental officers from Victoria Barracks, spent long hours speaking to men with experience in cotton- and sugar-growing and met with the less than savoury characters of the waterfront to inquire into the types of ships needed for transporting black cargo. Men who had once transported slaves to the New World from Africa. Now it was all taken from him by his aunt and her weak son.

'I am sure you will get around David and Enid in time, Granville,' his sister said sympathetically. 'Knowing your skills at manipulation as I do.' He glanced at his sister questioningly as he could sense that she was angry towards him over something. But he was not in the mood to inquire what it was.

'In time,' he mused as he stared into the flame of a candle. 'David is not the problem. Enid is the real problem. David lacks her knowledge of the Macintosh companies. He would have preferred to remain in England and spend his life at Oxford reading Aristotle or the like. He's never been cut out for work in the business and is nothing like his father . . . or brother. I don't know why they didn't leave him in England.'

'Because he is Enid's son,' Penelope said simply.

'So is Angus,' Granville replied and was surprised at his sister's statement of blatantly obvious fact concerning David's parentage.

'You don't understand what I mean,' Penelope said enigmatically. 'Do you, Granville?'

He shifted his gaze from his sister back to the candles. 'I think you should elaborate.'

'David has always been Enid's,' Penelope said. 'While Angus belonged to Donald. It has always been that way. Enid wants David beside her because she sees him as a male extension of herself.'

Granville snorted at his sister's perception. 'You really have some strange ideas about people, dear sister. An extension of herself! You know, you sound ridiculous when you say things like that.'

'I might sound ridiculous to you, dear brother,' she retorted, 'but any fool can see that Enid dotes on David. She always has. I am not saying she doesn't love Angus, but it is in David she sees herself. He is her guarantee of immortality.'

'So where does Fiona fit into all this? Who does she belong to?' Granville asked, leaning forward in his chair with just a touch of respect in his tone for his sister's observations. Yes, he had seen Enid's doting ways around David.

'Molly O'Rourke.'

'Molly O'Rourke!' he exploded. 'But Molly

O'Rourke is nothing but an old drunken Irish nanny. Molly O'Rourke is nothing more than a paid servant.'

'A paid servant she may be,' Penelope replied in a measured tone. 'But Fiona is closer to Molly than to her own mother. It has always been Molly who saw Fiona through her worst and best times. It has always been Molly Fiona goes to when she has something important in her life. You see, Granville, you might be good at business dealings but you do not know very much about women . . . and how we think,' she answered astutely.

'I will keep your advice in mind,' he said as he turned to stare into the flickering candlelight. For now there was much to think about, including how he would win Fiona as his wife. But then he had Penelope as an ally to help him in that matter. And as much as she might detest him, he knew her weaknesses and he was not beyond exploiting anyone in his obsessive ambition to have total control of what he desired.

10

Daniel's unease at entering the infamous Rocks area was highlighted by the lonely sound of their footsteps echoing eerily in the Argyle Cut. This was not a place to be caught out alone. He hurried to catch up with Max and Michael.

The rain had gone and in its wake the narrow lanes and alleys had an unhealthy sheen, like the sweat on a fevered body. The Rocks had been left behind the city's growth to die a slow and obscene death, providing a rotting corpse to fester the maggots of crime. Gangs of cut-throat thugs flourished in the decay and ruled the streets by violent means, and haggard prostitutes of all ages plied their profession in the cramped hovels and back alleys, while street urchin pickpockets gained acceptance into The Rocks' older and more vicious underworld ranks through their apprenticeships.

Unscrupulous publicans adulterated gut-rotting grog with substances such as sulphuric acid, and they worked in tandem with the press-gangs to shanghai drunken customers to crew the ships that sailed and steamed for all parts of the world. Despite – or because of – its evil reputation, the area attracted sailors from ships anchored and moored in the nearby coves who came for the cheap grog, easy women and a place to doss.

As they hurried through The Rocks, Daniel could smell the poverty of the area; the pungent and unpleasant aroma of cooking cabbage, human refuse and the natural decay of the neglected streets. The rain might have washed away the blood, urine and vomit from the narrow streets into the waters of the nearby harbour, but the lingering scent remained, hanging heavily in the stagnant and humid night air. He was acutely aware of the distant clanking of anchor chains and creaking of timber of the big ships waiting for cargoes of wool and grain. They were strangely normal and comforting sounds in contrast to the despairing wail of a baby neglected by its prostitute mother, and its wailing was drowned by the profane and hysterical screams of a madwoman raging obscenities into the night. Sounds that seemed to echo out of the bottom of hell itself.

He could not help but think they were in some surreal version of hell. But for Max Braun, the sights, sounds and smells were familiar and varied little from the many waterfronts he had known as a sailor. They could have been in Hamburg or in San Francisco's notorious red-light district. Daniel did not know whether the eventual sight of the Hero of Waterloo Hotel was welcome or not, as he knew that inside the confines of the popular hotel was concentrated the human face of vice and viciousness.

Max was first to enter the hotel built on the corner

of two streets. His bull-like frame forced a way through the close-packed patrons. Daniel and Michael followed in his wake as they were assailed by the acrid, thick smoke of cheap tobacco, vomit and the unpleasant stench of unwashed and profusely sweating bodies.

Kevin O'Keefe saw the three men make their entry as he stood leaning against a wall with his arm around a young prostitute with sad old eyes. She might have been twelve and her grime-smudged face could have been pretty, except for the scabs around her lips and a blackened eye from a beating she had suffered at the hands of a drunken customer the night before. Her long greasy hair hung limply around her face and she clung to O'Keefe, desperate to have him share her flea- and lice-infested palliasse for the night – at a price.

'Ahh, gentlemen,' O'Keefe slurred. 'It's so good to see you all here in my Sunday retreat.' The girl eyed Michael with a mixture of curiosity and mercenary calculation. He was certainly handsome, she thought, as she tossed her head to help hide the bruises. 'Michael, Max and Danny meet . . . damn! I don't know her name,' O'Keefe said, pushing the girl in Michael's direction. 'Anyway, meet this little lady who wants to befriend me for the night.'

The girl flashed a coy smile at Michael who ignored her. Nor did he smile at O'Keefe's weak attempt at humorous reference to the girl's status as a friend. Kevin O'Keefe was big and handsome with flashing eyes that always seemed to be laughing. Traces of a brogue still existed, a legacy of

142

growing up with Irish parents. Like Michael's accent, it had the touch of the Cockney about it, and visitors from the Old Country had often commented on this strange new accent emerging among the Australian colonials.

'We've come to take you back to the Erin,' Michael said in a loud voice to be heard over the raucous and drunken laughter around them. 'There is a serious matter we have to talk about . . . in private.'

O'Keefe's eyes narrowed as he glanced sharply at Michael. Then he shifted his attention to Max and Daniel. 'What serious matter, young Michael?' he asked suspiciously, as he sensed trouble if the three had ventured into The Rocks to fetch him.

'Not something we can talk about here. Something I want to talk about elsewhere,' Michael replied, as he pushed away an old and toothless whore who had attempted to attach herself to the handsome young Irishman. Daniel prayed she would not settle on him next as she looked capable of inflicting physical pain in return for rejection.

O'Keefe swigged from the tin mug. 'Can't go yet. Have to stand Jack Horton a round,' he finally replied. 'Jack is not someone you stand up if you want to keep friends in these parts.'

As if on cue, a bull-necked man, slightly shorter than Michael but much broader in the body, growled, 'Yer not be plannin' to go just now, O'Keefe, would ye?'

Michael could smell the putrid stench of rotting meat at his shoulder and tactfully stepped aside to give the man space. O'Keefe had hoped that

Horton might not have noticed the entry of the trio but they had stood out for the fact of their sobriety.

'I am afraid I have been summoned by young Michael Duffy here for a meeting of sorts ... at the Erin,' he replied apologetically to Horton.

'Michael Duffy?' Horton registered a hint of recognition on his badly scarred face that vividly reflected a life of physical violence.

'Michael Duffy. The great man 'imself from the Erin! I've 'eard about you, pretty boy,' he said with a sneer, as he pushed his face up to Michael's. ''Eard yer some kind of fighter. But yer don' look much to me, pretty boy,' he challenged, with his unblinking yellowed eyes.

'My friend, would you like to talk to me?' Max said quietly, but with a menace that could not be mistaken for a request as he stepped protectively between them. Horton felt the sharp tip of the small knife prick his belly through the dirty jacket he wore and he turned to face the ice-cold smile of the German. Their eyes locked and Horton recognised a man equal to himself in the ability to inflict pain and death.

O'Keefe realised the deadly situation developing, as Horton was not a man to back down, and he did not want Michael or Daniel caught up in what might become a bloodbath in the hotel. If Kate found out that he had allowed the situation to turn into a brawl she might never speak to him again. He was fully aware of how much she idolised her brother.

'Jack, I'll tell you what,' O'Keefe said reasonably. 'You take what's-her-name here for the night, my compliments, and we will call it square. How does that sound to you?'

Horton made a quick appraisal of the girl clinging to O'Keefe. She was young and he liked them young. He liked to make them scream, to make them beg for mercy, before he took them. 'I'll take the girl an' you can leave with the pretty boy an' his friends,' he said, licking his lips with anticipation. The young girl instinctively shrank away from the man whose reputation for inflicting sadistic pain was well known in The Rocks. Horton was relieved to have an excuse as a way out of the confrontation. He knew the German was a man like himself and thus capable of slitting his belly with the short knife. Accepting the offer was not backing down. Just a bargain between mates.

O'Keefe pushed the girl towards Horton who grabbed her by the throat and kissed her roughly on her broken lips as he groped with his hand at the tattered and grimy dress she wore. Tears streamed from the young girl's eyes as she tried to find her strangled voice to plead for mercy, but no words could come. He held her and lifted the hem of the dress as his hand slid up the inside of her thigh, and he chuckled with pleasure when he felt the girl stiffen as his stubby fingers entered her. She gasped with pain at the rough probing of the sausage-like fingers and tried desperately to struggle free, but his bear-like strength pinned her helplessly.

'True love,' O'Keefe said lightly as he placed his hand on Michael's chest. He knew that any rash move by him to help the girl might be his last as Horton also carried a knife, and he could see that

145

the man was watching Michael from the corner of his eye, anticipating his reaction.

'The girl . . .' Michael attempted to protest, but Max cut him short.

'Not vorth dying for, my friend,' he muttered as they pushed their way to the hotel's entrance.

'Hey! Pretty boy!' Horton shouted as they departed. 'Next time I meet yer, we will see 'ow good yer are. Before I kill yer,' and he turned his attention to Max. 'And you, cabbage eater, I will kill you if you get in my way,' he snarled. Max ignored him. A lot of men had threatened him over the years. Most of them were dead. Michael heard the threat directed at him and felt an ominous chill. Men like Horton did not make idle threats and he reminded himself to stay away from The Rocks in future.

They left the hotel and Daniel breathed an audible sigh of relief. Now all they had to do was get back to the Erin where the patrons preferred fists rather than knives to settle arguments. They hailed a horse-drawn tram in Pitt Street which took them most of the way to Redfern.

The four men sat in silence for the journey and O'Keefe searched his own thoughts for reasons that might bring the three men into The Rocks on a Sunday night to fetch him, and he had a vague and disturbing thought that it might have something to do with Kate. Had Kate gone to her brother and told him that he, Kevin O'Keefe, had forced himself on her? Forced himself on her! Why, she had practically seduced him in the cellar beneath the hotel's main bar.

When they left the tram at the top of Pitt Street

they trudged in silence to the Erin where Max pushed O'Keefe roughly to the back of the hotel.

They stood facing him under a jaundiced yellow light cast by the gas lamp of the street outside the yard. Deep shadows covered the spaces between empty wooden crates stacked neatly awaiting collection, and something about the silence from the three men and the atmosphere in the tiny cluttered yard warned O'Keefe all was not well. His survival instincts were soon realised when he saw Michael slip off his coat and hand it to Daniel. He balanced himself warily in a fighter's stance. So this was it. But why?

'You know I like you well enough, O'Keefe,' Michael said casually, as he circled him with his fists raised in the traditional bare-knuckle fighter's posture. 'So this is not personal. Well, that is not completely true. This is personal,' he added, as O'Keefe licked his lips and raised his hands to defend himself.

'I don't know what this is all about, Mick,' he replied as he eyed Michael's defence for an opening. 'But you are making a big mistake.'

Michael's first punch came blindingly fast and caught O'Keefe's ear with a sting that caused him to swear and retaliate with a wild swing of his own. 'Bejesus, Michael. That had a bit of ginger in it,' he said with a snarling grin as he unleashed a one-two-three barrage at Michael's head. Two of his punches connected and Michael grunted in pain, but he was not slow in returning the barrage as he sought the opening that, for a split second, O'Keefe had left after hitting him. One of his punches slammed into O'Keefe's face, bursting his nose with an audible crack. Blood sprayed over both fighters and spattered Daniel, who tripped over a wooden crate in his haste to get out of the way of the two slogging at each other with blows heavy enough to drop lesser men.

In his haste to escape, he dropped Michael's coat which tangled itself around O'Keefe's feet, causing him to lose his balance. Michael took advantage by slamming three hard punches into him. The blows caught him face, belly, face. O'Keefe toppled, cursing whatever had hold of his feet, and he slammed into a high wooden paling fence which gave way with a splintering crash.

Michael danced back from his fallen adversary with his fists raised for another telling barrage as O'Keefe lifted himself groggily from the muddy ground. He could taste blood in his mouth as a red haze drifted before his eyes and he was not sure whether he had been tripped or had fallen of his own accord.

'Jesus, Michael,' he groaned as he spat the blood from his mouth. 'What in hell is this all over?'

'Are you going to marry my sister, O'Keefe? Or does Max get a go at you after I'm finished?' Michael answered between gasps for air as he danced around O'Keefe. The punches had taken all his strength and he was hoping his opponent would not rise in a hurry.

'Katie!' O'Keefe exclaimed. 'Why would Katie want to marry me?' Michael did not answer as he was not satisfied that his sister's honour had been properly defended, and when O'Keefe finally regained his feet, shaking off the coat from around his ankles, he circled Michael warily. The red haze was gone from his vision and he was once again a fighter who had a healthy respect for his opponent's style.

He feinted with a left hook but Michael had anticipated what was coming and had stepped inside his defence, snapping a stinging punch to his broken nose. The telling blow was rewarded with a grunt of pain from O'Keefe.

The pain enraged him and, with a bellow like a bull, he waded into Michael with a flurry of hammering blows that forced him back against the stack of wooden crates. Michael felt his lip split as his back went up against them and he desperately fought back to fend off the blows.

The fight deteriorated into a slogging match between the grunting and panting men. Max yelled advice but Michael was too busy fighting to stay on his feet to heed him, and the finer points of bare-knuckle boxing advice were lost in the haze and pain of the battle.

Exhausted from the furious exchange of punches, both men mutually separated to circle each other. Blood from Michael's split lip splashed down the front of his once starched shirt which was now crumpled and stained.

'Why would Katie want to marry me, you bog Irish bastard?' O'Keefe panted as he jabbed at Michael's face with a short left.

'Because she is going to have your kid,' Michael hissed back as he unleashed a left and a right to O'Keefe's face, who unwisely dropped his fists and stared at his future brother-in-law in amazement. 'And she wants you as her husband.'

Kevin had never really considered marriage to

149

Kate as he knew Frank Duffy's low opinion of his convict parentage. Now Michael was saying he had to marry Kate because she was expecting their child!

Michael saw the opening when O'Keefe dropped his hands and instinctively capitalised on the other man's mistake. A single blow sent O'Keefe crashing into the ground. He sat up groggily rubbing his jaw. The red haze was back, but this time it was full of swirling black spots.

'Are you saying all this is about me marrying Katie?' he groaned.

Michael kept his fists up waiting for his opponent to rise to his feet. 'That . . . and a matter of honour,' he panted. 'For what you have done to my sister, O'Keefe.'

Kevin tried to grin but his face hurt too much. It was a strange way to become a member of the family! But it was no less than he expected from the likes of the Duffys.

'Well, then, I suppose it's my duty to stand you all a drink to celebrate the occasion,' he said, extending his hand in a gesture of peace. 'If you will only help me up. I am sure old Frank will let me buy a bottle of the best.' Michael eyed the outstretched hand with suspicion.

'Ja, Mikey. O'Keefe can buy us a drink,' Max said as he retrieved Michael's coat, now equally as tattered as the two fighters' faces.

Michael dropped his fists and took the offered hand of his soon-to-be brother-in-law and heaved him to his feet.

O'Keefe placed an arm around Michael's shoulders. 'I could have beaten you,' he said with a grimace, spitting blood on the ground. 'If you hadn't told me about Katie. Except Katie would never have forgiven me for hurting her precious brother.'

Michael returned the grin. 'No chance of that,' he replied. 'No one beats a Duffy. Especially an O'Keefe.'

They laughed as they shook hands and Daniel breathed his second audible sigh of relief for the night.

But his relief was cut short when the kitchen door was flung open and all four men cringed at the sight of the woman standing with her hands on her hips in the doorway. There was a fire in the beautiful eyes and they instinctively winced at what they knew was coming. They were like guilty schoolboys caught stealing apples from an orchard.

'Michael Duffy! Daniel Duffy! And you . . . Uncle Max! What have you done to Kevin?'

Michael attempted to protest. '*Us*, look at . . .' He stopped short as the withering glare of his sister came to rest on him. The grey eyes softened noticeably when she saw the amount of blood on his face. But just as suddenly the coldness returned to her eyes.

'What am I going to tell Aunt Bridget?' she snapped. 'You know she hates you fighting, Michael.'

'*Me* fighting!' her brother protested. 'What about . . . ?' Her withering glare cut him short again and he knew that his protests were futile. He hung his head like a little boy. What could you do when a sister gets angry with you?

Daniel foolishly decided that he should try legal logic about the merits of natural justice employed to defend a sister's honour. But as soon as he opened his mouth he only brought himself to her attention, and he wisely decided that it was best to save his legal logic for reprieving men from the gallows. It would be easier than reasoning with Kate Duffy when she was in this kind of mood.

Sheepishly all four men followed Kate into the kitchen where she poured hot water into an enamel bowl from the big kettle that remained permanently simmering at the edge of the stove. She fetched clean rags from a kitchen cupboard as Michael and Kevin sat at the table side by side, waiting meekly for her nursing skills to be applied to their battered faces.

Max and Daniel made a tactful retreat from the kitchen, leaving the angry young woman alone with the two battered fighters as she dabbed at Kevin's bleeding nose.

'You will have to hold the cloth underneath until the bleeding stops,' she said gently. But when she dabbed at her brother's split lip with a clean cloth she was not so soft and gave him another of her withering looks.

He took away the blood-soaked rag from his swollen and bleeding lip. 'Kevin says he wants to marry you, Katie,' he said and hoped that his statement of the marriage proposal might soften his sister. 'Told me out in the backyard himself.'

She paused as she washed and wrung out a blood-soaked cloth in the enamel basin. 'Kevin will ask me when he is ready,' she answered. 'I don't think it is the concern of brothers, uncles or cousins, to be the first to know. And it's not as if I am prepared to marry the first man who asks me for my hand.'

Confused, Michael shut up to dab at his lip, and he noticed that her eyes said silently, 'Leave us'. He nodded his understanding and, as he closed the kitchen door quietly behind him, he was able to catch Kevin's mumbled proposal. 'Kate Duffy, will you honour me by becoming my wife?' Michael did not have to hear his sister's reply because he knew what it would be.

He smiled and winced as he dabbed at his bleeding lip and mused on the profound differences between men and women. How was it that his sister had no sympathy for a matter of honour that was inevitable under the circumstances? He sighed and shook his head at the eternal mystery of life. Ah, but they were wondrous and mysterious creatures, despite all their vagaries.

11

The seagulls rose as a squalling white cloud over the yellow low sands of Manly beach. Michael Duffy watched the birds float on a gentle breeze before they descended again on the dismembered carcass of a cuttlefish. He scooped up a scalloped shell and tossed it at the squabbling seabirds but the shell fell short.

'Leave them alone, Michael,' Fiona gently scolded. 'They are doing you no harm.'

The barefooted Irishman stood in the break of the wave's wash that ebbed and retreated hissing back to the ocean. His trouser legs were rolled just below his knees and his shoes strung around his neck by the laces. Fiona had also removed her shoes and she carried them in one hand. She also carried a colourful parasol as the late afternoon breeze plucked at the long filmy material of the white cotton dress she wore. The sea had soaked the hem because she had not been fast enough to avoid one of the big breakers rushing ashore when she had played the timeless game of daring the ocean to catch her with its watery fingers. She would shriek with delight and fearful anticipation as the sea rushed up the hard-packed sand towards her. Then she would dance away nimbly to avoid its clutches. Once or twice the ocean had won the dare.

Michael had scooped her up into his arms when an extra-large wave threatened to swamp her. When the wave broke around his knees and rushed back to the ocean, he had gently placed her on the beach with his arm around her slim waist. Oh, if only the day could go on forever, she wished. The moment was perfect. The serene beauty of the summer's day as the sun's bite had gone in the late afternoon, and the gentle presence of Michael. But the nicest thing of all was that they were finally alone to share the intimacy, just as they had been alone the first time after their initial meeting on the Manly jetty. In the weeks following their first rendezvous at Hyde Park, they had always been accompanied by either Molly O'Rourke or Penelope. Both chaperones conspired with Fiona to keep the meetings with Michael from the rest of her family. Especially from her mother.

Although they agreed to be involved in her secret meetings, both chaperones had their own personal reasons for never letting the couple out of their sight. For Molly, her motivation was driven by maternal concerns. Fiona was as dear to her as if she were her own daughter, and she knew well enough, after seventeen years of rearing her, that she would not be able to talk her out of a meeting with Michael Duffy. To try to do so would only cause the young woman to find another way of meeting the man she was so obviously infatuated with, and chaperoning was the best alternative to allowing the young woman any practical opportunity to be seduced by the charming Irishman. But even Molly could not help but fall under his charm.

Such men Molly had known as a young girl in Ireland. Big handsome lads who could sing with the sadness of lament for Ireland's persecution and bring tears to her eyes while making her laugh with their funny stories. But such men had stood against the British and died for their beliefs. Ah, she had been young and beautiful herself in those days! And not the shell of a woman bent in the bitterness of her lost innocence. A loss of innocence at the hands of the Royal Marines who had stripped and raped her in the hold of a convict ship bound for New South Wales, and a lifetime of service to the Macintosh family where devotion to the children was viewed as little more than paid service by Enid Macintosh.

She knew well why Fiona found Michael overpowering in his attractiveness. He was a raw and unbridled spirit. But she also knew that there were social differences that could never be bridged. At least not in her lifetime. She must let the infatuation take its course, and Fiona would eventually realise who she was, and leave the young Irishman. When that day came, as it must, she would be there to comfort her as she always had in the past.

Penelope's reasons for chaperoning her cousin were not as altruistic as Molly's. Her motivations were selfish, even spiteful. She did not want her cousin to have something she desired. But there was an even deeper desire that she tried to deny to herself. One which persisted in her constant and passionate yearnings to be with her in every sense.

Like Molly, she accompanied Fiona to ensure that, in subtle ways, her cousin was denied opportunities to be alone with the Irishman.

Thus the excursions to Hyde Park to listen to the Regimental Band perform, the trips into Sydney for the late evening markets with their bustle and brashness and the occasional visits to the newly opened Sydney Library under the everwatchful eyes of Molly or Penelope. As wonderful as those times had been, they were not conducive to the couple's sharing of confidential thoughts or intimate caresses.

After such frustrating outings, Fiona would return home to spend a restless night in her bed where strange and erotic thoughts haunted her. She was disturbed by the exquisite – almost physically aching – effects of the vivid images, and her distress caused her to confide to her more worldly wise cousin what she was experiencing.

Penelope had smiled mysteriously when she broached the subject and told her she suspected that every woman born, at one time or another, escaped into the privacy of her imagination. It was a place where she could be seduced by her private and erotic images without fear of judgement or guilt and Penelope reminded Fiona of what she had meant by ... *being anyone* ... *or anywhere*. There were no taboos in those private places of the mind and she explained how she could go about relieving the agonising tension such images evoked when she was alone in her bed.

Fiona was both shocked and fascinated by her cousin's explicit description of what she should do. But that very night she explored the depth of her sensuality and, alone in the night, her thoughts drifted to Michael.

She lifted the end of the long nightdress and tentatively slid her hand down to rest between her legs. But instead of an image of Michael, she imagined a black stallion – nostrils flaring and eyes rolling – proudly displaying its distended maleness. She tried to block the image but it persisted. She felt her heart pounding and was vaguely aware that she was wet and swollen where her fingers rested. The stallion was somehow Michael! And she the helpless mare. Or was she herself?

The black stallion's eyes rolled back as it mounted her. She felt her back arch as the powerful animal serviced her with brutal thrusts of its huge organ and she gasped, surrendering to the animal's domination of her body. She imagined the stallion filling her with its seed and shuddered violently. She was not aware that she had cried out just before she felt the sublime darkness overwhelm her. It was like some small insight into death, she vaguely thought, as she lay back against the pillows and time ceased to be of any consequence. If only the moment could go on forever. The entity of the black stallion was very gentle as it nuzzled between her legs with its soft tongue lapping her.

Her opportunity to be alone with Michael had come indirectly through an invitation from Sir John Merle and his wife, Lady Susanna. Their offer for her to visit their estate at Penrith had arrived earlier in the week and Enid had wholeheartedly given her permission for Fiona to stay with them. Sir John had financial interests in the

Macintosh companies and was a close friend of the family. His sprawling property was renowned for its magnificent gardens and many eligible young men were often weekend guests at the estate. Enid knew Sir John and Lady Susanna were especially fond of Fiona as they had no children of their own, and they had watched the pretty young daughter of their friend and business colleague grow into a beautiful young woman.

Fiona knew that her mother planned to be at their cottage in the Blue Mountains, which were a popular retreat for Sydney's wealthy during the hot sweltering months of summer. The cooler mountain breezes carried the scent of eucalyptus and flowering gums – and not the stench of Sydney's primitive sewerage system – to the delicate noses of the colonial gentry.

Fiona had not confided in Molly what she had planned as she knew that her old Irish nanny would not approve of her being alone with Michael for the day – let alone a night. But she did confide in Penelope, who reluctantly agreed to help establish an alibi for her temporary absence from Sir John's estate.

As she watched Michael walking ahead of her with his coat thrown casually over his shoulder, she was acutely aware of the power in the movement of his body; the broad shoulders that tapered to a slim waist, the flat buttocks and muscles that rippled along his arms like steel cords when he had lifted her so easily from the sand.

The stallion . . .

The realisation of what she was imagining

shocked her. But then, what had she expected might be the outcome of all her planning anyway? She smiled when he turned and walked back to her. But her smile had a sad edge.

'Sure and you could not be thinking sad thoughts, Miss Macintosh,' he said in a mocking but gentle voice. 'On such an evening, God is at rest and the angels are playing in the waves out there,' he said, gesturing towards the lazy roll of the sea. 'And what would you be thinking to cause such melancholy?'

'Oh, nothing of great importance. Well . . . yes,' she said hesitantly. 'I was thinking that this day will end. I was thinking how different everything seems on this beach, when there is just you and me together. Now there is nothing between us. Not family, nor who I am . . . who you are.'

He stood very close to her and reached down to take her hand in his.

'Who am I, Fiona? Who do you think I am?' he asked quietly, and her eyes were moist with tears as her troubled thoughts welled.

'I don't know. I have only known you for such a short time,' she answered, trying to avoid looking into his eyes. She did not want him to see her distress as her hand slipped from his. He turned to gaze at the ocean which had become an oily grey, tinged with a golden sheen as the sun slowly disappeared behind the mountains.

'I have a few regrets in life,' he sighed. 'I regret that I did not join my father and brother in Queensland last year and see the harshness and beauty of this land as they have. But I do not regret meeting you. I suppose I know there is little chance of a life together here in a society that has rules for people like we Irish . . . and a place for who you are,' he said as he turned to face her. 'I told Daniel that some day I was going to marry you. But I know that was said on impulse. Ahh . . . but it's a foolishness that bedevils Duffy men . . .' His voice trailed away and he fell silent for a moment. 'You don't have to tell me what is troubling you because I think I know.'

'Do you?' she whispered as she fought back the tears. 'Do you know what I am thinking? Or are you making assumptions, Mister Duffy?' she said defiantly. He could see the set look on her face and he realised that this was the first time that he had seen her angry. There had been times that he had seen flashes of something troubling her which were never far from the surface.

'I think you want to tell me', he answered quietly, 'that you and I cannot meet after this day.'

'Yes, you are right. I do not think we should meet again.' She fell into a short silence. 'I do not know why I wanted to see you this day. I think that I am too frightened to let myself admit what I want . . . and I know I am confusing you. Penelope and Molly tell me I confuse men all the time.'

He reached out and cupped her chin in his hand as he gently forced her to look at him. 'You are saying that you love me,' he said sadly. 'But once we leave here, everything changes. You become Miss Fiona Macintosh and I . . . I go back to being just another Irishman. Yes, I know the rules of your society. But there are other societies where you and I could be equal . . . where you and I could be together.'

Fiona shook her head sadly. 'I do not think such a place exists, Michael.'

'America,' he exclaimed. 'That's where we could go. Your English system is dead there. In America, we would be accepted for who we are. Not who we were.'

She was frightened. America was so alien. The people were rough and rude, and devoid of the elegance that the class system bestowed on society. The Americans were lost children, brawling with each other in a bloody civil war.

She felt a sudden coldness and recognised the fear of what she could lose if she loved Michael. But when it came down to hard choices, she knew that she did not want to give up the security and comforts of her way of life for anything – or anyone!

'What are you going to do, Michael, if you go to America?' she asked in a frightened voice. 'Did you not say that you wanted to go to Europe to learn to paint? What would you do in America?'

He frowned, as he had not previously thought about emigrating. 'I don't know,' he replied. 'All I know is that we would be together and start a life where . . .' his voice tapered off as he realised how frightened she appeared at his suggestion. 'Damn! Sure and it was not such a good idea. I will think of something else,' he continued and her eyes expressed relief at his shift in ideas. At the same time she felt guilt at her own denial for the man she thought she loved and his mooted suggestion for her to give up all she had known for an uncertain future had tested her and she had failed. At least the realisation of what she was – rather than who she was as a woman – had become clear in her own thoughts. Penelope has been right! Michael was truly a dangerous man around women.

Now she was faced with a decision that she had tried to deny to herself. Would she give herself to him? For her, the issues of not seeing Michael in the future, or living for the moment, were in a turbulent conflict with each other.

She made her decision. 'Michael, I think we should go back to the cottage,' she said lightly, as she took his hand in hers. 'Cribbs will have made us supper and I do not want him to be disappointed by not availing ourselves of his undoubtedly fine efforts.'

The young Irishman shook his head and folded his big hand around her delicate fingers. What man could know the intricate workings of the female mind?

The sandstone beach cottage was as fine as any good home Michael knew in Sydney. It had well-kept gardens and a high timber verandah.

At the top of a broad set of steps facing the sea, they were met by a wizened old man who had once been a convict. His skin was as leathery as the broad belt about his waist and he was stooped with arthritis. Fiona had bribed Cribbs with a good supply of gin to remain silent concerning her presence at the cottage, and the gin had also purchased a prepared supper and the old caretaker's absence for the night. He was more than happy to accept the opportunity to go fishing.

'Good even'n, Miss Macintosh.' He greeted her and carefully ignored Michael. It was his way of showing he could be discreet. 'I left yer supper in the kitchen. Nuthin' fancy, but all fresh. Trapped 'em meself yesterday.'

'Thank you, Cribbs. I appreciate your thoughtfulness,' she replied graciously, and the old man beamed happily. He liked the young mistress, whom he had known since she was a child when he had carved her tiny horses from driftwood. But he eyed Michael suspiciously and decided that he did not like him as the young man did not have the appearance of a gentleman. His face had scars that were reminiscent of a man who knew the meaner streets of Sydney and not the town's more genteel parlours. Why Miss Macintosh was with such a man mystified him as she was more than worthy of the company of the colony's finest gentlemen.

'If'n there be nuthin' else, I'd be seein' to the nets, Miss Macintosh,' he said before hobbling away.

Michael had remained silent as he sensed the animosity towards him. Fiona waited until Cribbs was out of sight before she took Michael's hand and led him up the broad steps and into the cottage.

Inside, he was duly impressed by the subtle display of vast wealth the Macintosh cottage held. The internal timbers were of dark cedar brought down by Macintosh ships from the northern rainforests of the colony and the furniture was the best money could buy. The Persian carpets had been imported from the Holy Land and there were even one or two expensive vases from the land of the Chinese.

The polished timber floor echoed their footsteps

as he followed Fiona down a hall that led into a sitting room with a commanding view of the ocean. If this is what she called a cottage, what would a house be like, Michael thought.

'My brother, David, is going to stay at the cottage for a while when he returns from visiting Queensland. I think he will be bringing young ladies here,' Fiona said with a conspiratorial giggle.

Michael scanned the room, admiring the decor. 'Is that a common occurrence?' he asked, as Fiona sat on a settee decorated with a floral pattern. She brushed down the cotton dress she wore.

'Granville says my brother is quite a ladies' man,' she answered, with a sisterly note of pride. 'He says David was almost expelled from Oxford for having a lady visit him in his rooms after hours. It caused quite a scandal. But they excused him in the end because they said that they expected no better from a colonial.' She reached up and drew Michael down beside her on the settee.

'I didn't know your brother was in Queensland,' he said, by way of small talk. He had an impulsive desire to explore her body with his hands and mouth.

'David left before Christmas to see Father about land purchases,' she explained. 'He really did not have to go. But he has not seen Father or Angus for over five years and he thought that he should spend Christmas with them since they were unable to join us this year. We expect him to be returning next month when he and Father have finished their business. Father has plans to extend our properties in Queensland and stock them with cattle because he feels that the land is more suited to cattle than sheep. Angus will manage Glen View while Father sets up a new run.'

Michael had learned a lot about the Macintosh family. Fiona had spoken about them at length when they had met on their first secret rendezvous. He'd formed the impression that they were not a close family. At least not in the sense that the Duffy clan were. So the wealthy paid a price for what they had, he thought as he listened to the young woman bemoan the fact that business took precedence over a family reunion. He also knew from the way she spoke of her family that she was closest to three people: her brother David, Molly the Irish nanny, and Penelope her cousin. Although he had never met David, he felt that the man did not sound as pompous as Granville White whom he had instinctively disliked for his arrogant and foppish manner.

'I hope David enjoyed his Christmas up north with your father and brother,' he said wistfully. 'My father and my brother were supposed to come down to Sydney to spend Christmas with us. But we have heard nothing from them since October when we received their last letter. Da said they would make one delivery out to some place called Tambo and then return to Rockhampton.'

She squeezed his hand gently and said, 'I am sure nothing has happened to them. Daddy says in his letters that they have a lot of rain this time of year and that often they are cut off from the coast for weeks. But you have said that your father and brother are teamsters, so they should not starve with all the supplies they undoubtedly have should they have been cut off.'

166

Michael stared at the cedar-panelled wall opposite the settee and, despite her attempt to reassure him, he had a deep fear that could not be consoled. Something was very wrong and he had the terrible feeling that he would never see his father again. He also knew that his uncle Frank felt the same way.

'I should see what Cribbs has prepared for our supper,' Fiona said as she leapt up from the settee. 'He can be a wonderful cook when he sets his mind to it and I can smell something delicious in the kitchen. I had some special things delivered on Friday for Cribbs to use in the cooking. Oh!' she exclaimed with a sudden and terrible realisation. 'I only hope he did not drink the port I had delivered.' But her fear was quickly realised when she went to the kitchen. Cribbs *had* drunk the port intended for a pigeon casserole. So instead, he had roasted two wild ducks that he had trapped on a nearby lagoon and he'd fervently hoped that his culinary expertise in preparing the game birds would appease Fiona in lieu of the missing port.

Fiona discovered the switch and was extremely annoyed. But less annoyed when she saw the feast the old man had prepared. He had certainly earned a bottle of port for his efforts.

The table was laid with fine silver and candelabra in the dining room and the delicious aroma of roasted wild duck wafted through the cottage.

Michael lit the candles and Fiona told him to wait while she brought the food to him. The day spent in Manly Village and on the beach had made him ravenous, and she served the supper with an exaggerated flourish; roasted wild duck stuffed with rock oysters (an imaginative and delicious touch by Cribbs), green minted peas, straw potatoes and spiced peaches. Next to Michael's plate she set a crystal goblet of the Macintoshes' finest burgundy wine imported from France.

'You are a fine cook, Miss Macintosh. And as fine a wench as I have seen in any good hotel,' he said laughing as he sliced a portion of rich dark meat from the crisp breast of the roast duck. 'I think we should go to America and you could open a restaurant.'

'You know I really did not prepare this wonderful supper,' she said with a frown. 'And it is not exactly restaurant cuisine.'

He gazed through the candle's soft light at Fiona who sat and sipped delicately on her wine. 'You mean you eat like this all the time?' he said, with a hint of awe for the rich and imaginative variety the meal presented.

'Michael. Do you know . . . you sound like some kind of peasant when you say things like that. Of course we eat like this,' she answered with a small note of haughty disdain for his less than urbane question.

'Yes, well for me it's a long way from corned beef, cabbage and potatoes. Or pickled pork,' he answered as he loaded his fork with succulent oysters dripping with their own gravy. 'This is the kind of meal we starving Irish only dream about.'

'You *really are* a peasant type,' she said in a way that made him pause and glance up at her from his meal. There had been a hint of arrogance in her comment he did not like.

'*Us* peasant types keep this kind of food on your

plate, Miss Macintosh. But I think you know that,' he said, and he felt uneasy at the tense atmosphere that had crept into the room between them. It was like some evil spirit haunting the cottage.

'You sound annoyed, Michael,' she flared, with a touch of Macintosh haughtiness. 'I do not think your cricitism of how we earn our wealth is warranted.'

'Maybe it's because without your clothes, or without your money, you are no different to any of the other women I know,' he growled.

She flushed with anger and glared at him. How dare this man speak to her as if she had anything in common with the other women he knew. Penelope was right in trying to dissuade her from seeing him. She had been infatuated with him like a schoolgirl in love with her music teacher, and now that they were finally alone she was seeing him for what he truly was. Despite his peasant upbringing though, he was a damned desirable man.

They remained uncomfortably silent for the rest of the meal. Fiona picked at her food and wished she had been less haughty in her manner towards Michael, who tucked heartily into his own meal. She could not understand how he could eat when she herself was upset. Although he was disturbed by the tension between them, the roast duck tasted too good to be wasted, and when he had finished eating he wiped his mouth with a linen napkin.

'Thank you for the meal, Miss Macintosh,' he said formally, as he stood and walked across the room towards the door. 'I hope all goes well for you in the future.'

'Where are you going?' she asked in a strained voice. She had not expected him to just suddenly depart. The realisation that her hold over him was very tenuous stunned her. Could he not see that she was practically sacrificing her noble body to him? It had not occurred to her that a working-class Irishman was capable of dismissing her. She was, after all, the daughter of the powerful and renowned Donald Macintosh.

'I'm not sure,' he said with a shrug of his broad shoulders. 'Maybe the Steyne for the night.'

'You cannot leave me alone here, Michael,' she pleaded in her panic. 'Something might happen to me.'

'If it's any consolation to you,' he said bitterly, 'it was I who forced my attentions on you. But I realise how right you have been about the situation. We have no future together in this country. Maybe if you had considered the Americas, we might have had a chance. But I know the idea was a foolish and stupid impulse of mine.'

She stared at him. The wine was taking effect as it flowed through her body, and she felt that same hot feeling that she had known alone in her bed when the images of the black stallion had come to her. There had to be a first time for every woman. And she wanted that first time to be with him. She did not know if she was using him or was in love with him. All she knew was the ache to be held in his arms and feel his sweet breath on her cheek. A feeling which had never been so strong as at the present moment. Had denial of her love for him been the reason for her haughtiness towards him? Had she tried to play a game . . . as Penelope might . . . to dominate him?

'No, Michael,' she whispered. 'You only think you have all the control. Have you ever considered that I might want you as much as you want me?'

She rose from her chair and went to him and placed the palm of her hand on his cheek. Her hand felt soft and warm against his skin and he stiffened. The woman was confusing him! One moment she was arrogant and aloof. The next, soft and gentle.

'Right now, all I know is that I want you,' he said quietly, as he placed his hand over hers. 'I want you like I have never wanted anything else in the world.'

She tilted her face to him and her lips parted, inviting him to taste the sweetness of her desire, and he covered her mouth with his kiss. It was at first soft – then demanding – and she could feel his body relax and fold into hers. Nothing else mattered between them for this moment in time.

She was vaguely aware that he had lifted her in his arms as he had when they were on the beach. She slipped her arm around his neck and curled into his chest. With little effort, he carried her across the room to drop her gently on a counterpaned double bed in the cottage's master bedroom.

'Wait,' she said in a husky voice, as she knelt on the bed and began to undress. She removed the long white cotton dress, under which she wore a tight-fitting corset under a camisole bodice and a knee-length chemise. The cumbersome clothes fell to the floor one by one. Finally she knelt on the bed, wearing only her pantaloons which were divided at the crotch.

She did not feel embarrassed, as she had thought she might. Instead, she knelt near naked before him because it felt so natural. She reached out to draw him to her on the bed and he reached out to embrace her, sliding his hand up the inside of her thigh where his fingers found yielding flesh at the top of the pantaloons. She gasped and closed her eyes, absorbing the animal feelings that his touch triggered in her mind and body. And she thrust her hips towards him, moaning with pleasure as his fingers gently entered her. Whatever lingering doubts she might have had about giving herself to him were gone. All that mattered was that this bed had become their universe, and this time exclusive to their lives.

The sharp physical pain she had initially experienced was soon forgotten as Michael caressed her body and soul with soft kisses and gentle, murmured words. The kisses all over her body were in places she had only imagined in her wildest and most erotic dreams while his hard body pinned her helpless in its embrace.

Their lovemaking continued throughout the night. At first it was passionate with the violence of mutual lust. But it soon became a tender expression of love and the experience was all Penelope had said. Fiona had gone to places without limit, experienced sensations explosive and sensual. And Michael had journeyed with her as a loving guide to those secret places in her mind.

The distant swish of the ocean breaking against the shore was as regular as a heartbeat. It was like a lullaby that finally soothed the two lovers into a deep and dreamless sleep in the early hours of the morning.

Fiona lay naked beside Michael in the time before dawn and gazed with wonder at his sleeping body. His soft snoring, a legacy of his nose broken in a fight, was itself a pleasant and reassuring sound of a man.

She touched his face with her fingers as lightly as a butterfly's kiss and traced the outline of the hard muscle contours of his arm. She felt content and fulfilled in a way she had never known. But she was also frightened.

Slowly and reluctantly, she took her hand away from his arm and stared past him into the glow of the golden light that was creeping across the floor. It was a warning that the time had passed between them and with the new day she would have to leave him, probably forever. The joy and wonder of their lovemaking was now replaced by a sadness for what was to come.

She eased her naked body away from Michael and lay on her back staring at the ceiling. It was a dark place not yet touched by the sun, which was rising over a serene and crystal ocean. Dawn was upon them with its silence, a time where the soul was free to converse with the conscious mind.

She was not aware that sleep was returning to claim her. Nor was she aware of a disturbing voice that seemed to call from the depths of a desolate place as she twitched in the drifting world of half sleep. It was an eerie sound, like the voice of lost souls from far, far away. It was a lonely sound, a mournful cry in the depths of the early morning. There were whispers in the room that she could not hear.

The urgent rapping on the front door of the cottage woke Michael.

'Fiona. Open the door. It's me, Penelope. I must see you at once!'

Fiona snapped from her troubled sleep and dragged herself into a sitting position as her long raven hair fell across her face. Exhausted, she slipped from the bed and groggily pulled on the dress she had left on the floor. It clung to her body in a way that accentuated the curves of her hips and breasts.

Michael cast her a questioning look as she dressed. Puzzled, she shook her head before she padded across the bedroom floor. He waited until she had left the room before hastily dressing.

When Fiona opened the door to her cousin, she knew immediately that something was terribly wrong. It was clear in the anguished expression on Penelope's face.

'Penelope! What are you doing here?' she asked as she closed the door behind them. 'I thought you were up in the mountains with Mother and Granville.'

'We were,' her cousin answered as she glanced around the living room. 'But David has returned early from Queensland and they are all in Sydney waiting for you to come home.' She reached out and grasped Fiona by the arms. 'There is something I cannot tell you here. Something that I think you should be told by your mother. Or David. Go and dress properly and we will return to Sydney on the next ferry. I have your mother's carriage waiting for us at the Quay.' Fiona stared at her cousin with a sick feeling in her stomach.

'Does Mother know about Michael?' she asked in a voice weak with fear, but Penelope shook her head.

'I don't think she is sure about Michael,' she lied. 'But she does know you were not at Sir John's place last night. She asked Molly about where you might be, but she said she did not know. However, that is not why I have come to fetch you home,' she added quickly to divert Fiona's questions.

'What is it, Penny? Is it about Father?' Fiona gasped and was terrified at her cousin's possible response to her question. Had her father been stricken with one of those fevers so prevalent in the north of Australia? Had there been an accident?

'No, your father is as well as can be under the circumstances,' Penelope answered evasively. 'But I would rather you did not ask me any more questions here ... or on the journey back to Sydney. Please accept what I say as any questions you have will be answered as soon as we are home.' Fiona nodded and turned to the bedroom as Michael appeared in the doorway.

'Good morning, Miss White,' he said politely.

Penelope's expression hardened at his appearance. 'Good morning, Mister Duffy,' she replied curtly. 'I dare say you are well.'

She fell silent and looked away from him until Fiona was out of the room, when she said, 'I believe you had a father in Queensland. And that your father's name was Patrick?'

Michael stared at the young woman's face now etched with a stony bitterness and he suddenly felt uneasy. She had used the past tense to ask about his father. Why? And it was something to do with the question she'd asked. So inappropriate to the moment.

'Yes, my father is Patrick Duffy. How did you know my father's name, may I ask?'

'I suppose Fiona must have told me your father's name at some stage,' she replied. 'If I could just ask one more question? Was there anyone else beside the Aboriginal called Billy with your father on the trip to Tambo?' The hardness in her face was also in her voice.

'Yes, my brother, Tom. But I don't remember ever mentioning Old Billy to Fiona,' he answered and his uneasiness became outright fear. 'You are asking questions as if you know something of my father.'

Her reply was a cold and arrogant smile.

'You know something about my father,' he growled. 'And I want you to tell me. Your questions were not made as part of polite conversation.'

'I do not have to do anything of the sort, Mister Duffy,' she spat venomously. 'Especially to the son of a man who would give help to the murderer of a white man.'

Michael was lost to what she was saying, but her words had stung him to react. He took three long steps across the room to grip her by the shoulders and shook her as he roared, 'What are you talking about? Damn you! What are you talking about?'

'*Michael!*'

Fiona's voice cut across the room and Michael released his grip on Penelope who stepped back and said bluntly, 'Your father, Mister Duffy, is dead. And so probably is your brother. They were speared by the blacks on Glen View in November.'

Michael's face drained and his shoulders slumped.

'Oh, I almost forgot. The blacks speared Old Billy . . . as you call him . . . as well,' she added viciously and turned calmly to her cousin. 'Come, Fiona. I am sure Mister Duffy will find his way home,' she said, and she was satisfied at the pain she had inflicted on him. Such is the wrath, Mister Duffy, for anyone who would dare take what was rightfully the property of a White, she thought, with a savage sense of victory over him.

She held out her hand to Fiona. 'Come, Fiona. We must go immediately.'

Fiona responded to her cousin's command like a sleepwalker. The events that had unfolded in the living room had shocked her into an almost comatose state. Deep in the now forgotten memories of her pleasure was an echo of a nightmare she could not remember.

12

Although Enid Macintosh wore the traditional black of mourning, she still radiated an elegance that accentuated her dignified beauty. She was composed and in control of her grief when her daughter entered the large and dark library with Penelope.

Enid did not greet her daughter, but merely nodded her head to recognise her existence. Fiona immediately sensed a hostility in her mother's set expression and returned the formal nod. When she glanced at her brother, David, who stood beside his mother, she saw only grief in his face.

Across the room, Granville stood with his hands behind his back and stared out of a full-length window at the gardener who was trimming a hedge that bordered the gravel driveway. The sombre atmosphere of the room was something tangible and stifling.

Fiona stood at the centre of the library where she had most of her memories of her estranged father. The library walls were covered in bookcases along which, behind glass doors, were the books that he had collected over the years; journals of explorers, farming almanacs, atlases and books on religious philosophies. Books which were practical guides to a man's spiritual and temporal life.

Although David crossed the room to his sister, Enid did not move from where she was seated, glaring with a barely concealed hostility at her daughter. Granville turned from the window to watch with clinical interest the events about to unfold in the library.

'Angus is gone, Fi,' David murmured softly as he placed his hands gently on her shoulders. 'He was murdered by the blacks at Glen View. Father has buried him on the property.'

Fiona wanted to cry but Angus was almost a stranger to her. They had seen very little of each other over the years. Angus had lived with her father while she and David had gone to live in England. She felt a touch of guilt for the relief that it was Angus who had been killed – and not her beloved father. But she wished she could feel something more for her dead brother.

'It seems, Fiona,' Enid said coldly from behind the mahogany desk, 'that this Michael Duffy person whom you have been seeing behind our backs is the son of the man who helped the murderer of your brother escape retribution.'

Fiona stared disbelievingly at her mother. How could she know so much about Michael? And the answer came almost immediately.

'Penelope confirmed that this Michael Duffy you have been seeing is the son of a man called Patrick Duffy. David was told by your father that this Patrick Duffy stopped a police officer from performing his duty in apprehending the black

179

murderer of your brother. The irony of the whole situation is that the blacks repaid the misguided man's gesture by spearing him and his black companion to death. It was certainly God's will that the man died for the sin he had brought on himself.'

Fiona gave Penelope a withering and accusing look that said: How could you betray the confidence that I had placed in you? And why? It was the 'why' that puzzled her most.

Penelope looked away with the guilt of her betrayal etched in her face. Any sorrow Fiona might have been able to muster for Angus was soon replaced with bitterness towards all her family.

'I find it hard to believe that Michael's father would help a murderer, Mother,' Fiona spat defiantly. She could still feel Michael as if he were inside her. It did not seem possible such a man could be born of the man her mother spoke of. 'There must be more to the events than you have told me.'

'Lieutenant Mort of the Native Mounted Police confirmed to David the events I speak of, Fiona. It is not likely that a Queen's man such as Mister Mort would tell lies. No, the only person who has been involved in lies here has been you, sneaking away like some common whore to see your Papist Irishman.' She said this venomously with all the hatred she could muster for her daughter's unforgivable betrayal. A daughter who had knowingly stepped outside her assigned station in life. Her duty was to her family first – and last.

Granville watched with great interest. With Angus dead, David was the next in line to inherit the family wealth. He regretted the unexpected change in the line of succession, as dealing with Angus was far easier than dealing with the sanctimonious David Macintosh. Oxford learning had put in his head strange and dangerous ideas about social reform and equality for all.

Then a not so disturbing thought occurred to Granville as he brooded on the implications of the eldest heir's untimely demise. If something happened to David, Fiona would be the next apparent heir to the family business ventures. But David was young and healthy and it was unlikely he would die of natural causes for many years. Only an *unnatural* cause of death could change his luck. Granville tried to shake the troubling thought from his head. But, as an ambitious and ruthless man, he could not completely discount the murder of his cousin. Under the right circumstances . . . He turned his attention to Fiona's predicament.

Tears of rage and frustration had welled in Fiona's eyes as she was left speechless by her mother's invective.

'I think I should be taking Miss Macintosh out of here, Missus Macintosh.' The controlled anger in Molly O'Rourke's voice cut across the room. 'I think Fiona has had enough suffering for one day,' she said as she went to Fiona and placed her arms around the young woman's trembling shoulders. Molly O'Rourke, servant, and Enid Macintosh, mistress of the house, locked eyes.

'I did not call on your services, Miss O'Rourke,' Enid said imperiously. 'So I would ask that you leave the room immediately. This is family business and has nothing to do with you.'

Molly stood her ground and refused to budge. She had held Fiona as a baby in her arms and had travelled to England with her to care for her in the Whites' home there. No, she was not going to let anyone hurt Fiona. She was not leaving the library unless it was with her baby. 'We will, Missus Macintosh,' Molly said firmly as she gently guided Fiona to the door.

'Damned old Irish witch,' Granville swore when she was gone. 'You should throw her out on the streets where she deserves to be.'

'Over my dead body,' David said unexpectedly. 'No one dismisses Molly while I'm alive. That woman has given everything to Fiona and me over the years, cousin, and no one dismisses her.'

Granville glared at him then looked to Enid for support. 'I am sure the decision to dismiss the services of that Irish hag is in your mother's hands, David, not yours,' he said smugly.

Enid felt her son's eyes on her. It was not a bullying stare, but one of a request. 'As much as I detest the woman, David is right,' she replied quietly. 'With all her faults, her greatest virtue is that of loyalty to Fiona and David. No one will be dismissing her.'

Loyalty, David thought. More like love. But that was not a term used in the Macintosh house. Words like *position* and *duty* described their family relationships and David could not remember ever hearing his mother use the word 'love'.

Another example of Macintosh solidarity, Granville thought bitterly when he observed Enid bow to her son's request. Another example of David flexing his authority just as Penelope had predicted. He was becoming a dangerous man.

'If I am not required any longer, I think I will leave, Aunt Enid,' Penelope said, as there were matters to be discussed in an attempt at reconciliation between herself and her cousin.

'I would hope you would go to Fiona and convince her that seeing that Irish boy has no future,' Enid said to her niece. 'I would rather you do it that way, than have me take stronger measures to prevent her seeing him.'

'I will try,' Penelope replied. 'But I fear she thinks she is in love with the man.'

'She only thinks she is in love with him,' Enid snorted. 'Remind her of who she is and her duty to the family. Remind her that the Irish rendering of love is a house full of dirty squalling children and the eternal stink of cabbage, while the husband spends all his time drinking himself into a stupor. Just remind her of that.'

Penelope nodded. 'I am sure your description of life with the Duffy boy will change her mind,' she replied facetiously then turned her back and, with a rustle of her dress, swished from the library.

Granville tried to make light of his sister's parting sarcasm. 'One would think Penelope was in sympathy with Fiona. Possibly have some sort of liking for the Irish lout herself.'

Neither David nor his mother could see the humour in his attempt to excuse Penelope's retort. From what Enid had heard about Michael Duffy, she would not be surprised to find that her niece indeed had a 'liking' for the Irishman, as she was well aware of Penelope's scandalous sexual escapades and she blamed her daughter's

183

infatuation with the Irishman partly on her niece. But the matter of Penelope's morally degenerate influence on Fiona was something that could wait for the moment, as the events concerning the existence of Tom Duffy were of more pressing concern. She turned her attention to her son.

'You mentioned that this Patrick Duffy had a son with him at the time he was speared?' she queried.

'Yes . . . and no. It appears that the son was with the dray when the natives speared his father and their darkie. At the time Lieutenant Mort found the deserted bullock team, one of his native troopers told him of the existence of the second white man, who we now know was Tom Duffy. According to Mort, Duffy would not last long out in the bush without assistance.'

The Duffy name was like an Irish curse on them. First in Queensland where Patrick Duffy had knowingly taken sides with the murderer of her son, and now in Sydney, where one of his sons had . . . she shuddered . . . she could not even entertain the thought that her daughter might have slept with the man. And now she had learnt of another of the man's sons in Queensland. In all probability the son was dead and her husband had nothing to fear from him. But there was just that tiny irrational fear . . .

'Biddy, I am going to need your help with Michael,' Frank Duffy called to his wife from the kitchen.

She dropped the well-worn rosary beads on her bed and quickly threw a shawl over her long nightdress as she hurried down the staircase to the kitchen. She had recognised both anger and concern in her husband's urgent entreaty for her to join him and her own concern was heightened by the muffled sound of Constable Farrell's booming voice. She knew the voice well as the huge Irish policeman was a frequent visitor to the back door of the Erin Hotel for the occasional drink while he was on his beat.

'Dear God. Not Michael,' she muttered as she hurried to the kitchen where her husband met her with a scowl on his face fit to frighten the devil.

'What has happened to Michael?' she gasped, throwing her hands to her face. 'Is he hurt?' she asked anxiously with a maternal concern.

'Worse than that . . . he's drunk. And he didn't make it to work today when I most needed him to help Max in the cellar. Constable Farrell has been kind enough to bring him home when a night in the lock-up might have been a better idea.'

She glanced at Michael who was sitting slumped over the heavy slab kitchen table. 'Dear God! What has happened to you, Michael?' She gently lifted his bloodied head from the table. His clothes were torn, a sweet and sickly smell of alcoholic spirits wafted from him and it was apparent that he had been in a brawl.

'Sorry, Aunt Bridget,' he mumbled through split lips. 'Got into a bit of a fight.'

'Get a bowl of hot water . . . Not too hot, Francis, and a couple of clean cloths,' she ordered. This was not the first time she had cleaned Michael's wounds after a fight. But then the injuries were not as severe as now, and it was obvious that he had not fared well in whatever donnybrook he had been involved in.

'I wouldn't be feeling too sorry for him if I were you, Biddy,' Frank grumbled irritably as he filled an enamel basin with warm water. 'It's obvious that the man has decided to get drunk and get into a fight rather than do a day's work. Never thought he would be one for taking to strong liquor. Never has in the past.'

'Then he must have had a good reason to be this way, Francis,' she snapped as she carefully prised away a section of blood-matted hair from Michael's scalp to reveal a deep cut.

'I will be all right. It's nothing,' Michael said apologetically as he gave her thin and fragile hand a gentle squeeze.

'It is more than nothing to be sure, Michael,' she countered softly. 'You have a serious cut on your head and heaven knows where else you are hurt. We will clean you up first and see if we have need of fetching Doctor Hughes.'

'I will live, Aunt Bridget,' he protested. 'I just let my guard down.'

'What happened to get you into this state?' she asked.

He knew she meant more than his physical injuries, and he could not look at her when he whispered hoarsely, 'Da is dead. So is Old Billy. Tom is missing. Probably dead.'

'God almighty!' Frank swore and almost dropped the enamel dish of warm water he had filled. 'How do you know this?' he asked and Michael focused on his uncle's face through a haze of rum and pain.

'I know, Uncle Frank,' he replied. 'It would be hard for me to tell you how I know but, believe me, I believe what I know to be true. Da and Old Billy were speared by the blacks on the Tambo trip. I don't know all the details, except that it happened in November. I don't know much about Tom's fate. I suppose that is why we have heard nothing from them all these weeks.'

Frank collapsed into a chair and his face crumpled like wet paper as he stared past the battered face of his nephew. *Pat dead! And Tom missing!* The sudden and unexplainable lack of letters that had arrived regularly from the colony of Queensland now had a logical explanation. But not this terrible explanation. It was almost impossible to comprehend that a man like his brother, who had once defied the might of the British Empire both in Ireland and the colony of Victoria, could have fallen to the primitive spears of the wild black men of Queensland. Poor Katie! She was somewhere north and expecting to be reunited with a father and brother.

'Dear God, Katie will be on her own!' Bridget said, reflecting her husband's unspoken thoughts. She ignored the fact that her niece was now a married woman as she had little faith in Kevin O'Keefe's ability to be strong for his wife. O'Keefe was a city man, a womaniser, whom Katie had the misguided idea she could change with the words of the marriage vows. Bridget had never liked him but she had never told Kate of her doubts concerning the man she had married. She knew that any words against him would have only alienated her niece.

'You will have to go north and find your sister,

Michael,' Bridget said firmly as she brought her tears under control. 'She will need you now more than ever.'

'I have thought about that, Aunt Bridget,' he replied. 'And I think we have to let O'Keefe look after her now. Kevin is her husband and it is up to him to look after Katie . . . not us.'

'You would desert your sister at her moment of need?' she said with a flash of anger.

'Aunt Biddy, Kate is a lot stronger than all the men I know,' Michael protested. 'She might only be sixteen, but she has the iron of both the Duffys and the Fitzgeralds. If anything . . . and knowing my sister . . . she will cope.'

Bridget listened to her nephew's words. The strength was in the Duffy blood. There were those people who lived their lives frightened of change, or only dreamed about adventure. And there were those who did not know the former existed. To the latter, change and daring were the normal essence of life itself. There was a name for such people – pioneers! Kate was now a pioneer on a wild frontier. But she was also pregnant, and a long way from her family, with a man of doubtful qualities.

'Yes . . . yes. I suppose I am like a mother who does not want to admit my little girl is a woman,' she said softly as she reflected on her niece's inner strengths. She had always been a mother to both Patrick's children and although Kate had many of the characteristics of Elizabeth, her natural mother, she had also acquired many strong qualities from her aunt.

'Katie will no doubt learn about Da and Tom,'

Michael said. 'She will know what to do when she finds out.'

'Do you think she will come home when she finds out?' Frank asked.

Michael shook his head. 'No. Somehow I think she will stay in Queensland and build her hotel . . . with O'Keefe's help.'

Francis sighed. 'She has no reason to remain up there with Pat and Tom gone.'

But he had to admit there was a perceptiveness in Michael's observations. Patrick had been so different in his outlook on life. Not for his restless brother the city life, but the untrodden vastness of this new land and its far horizons. It was Kate who had also inherited the restless spirit of the Duffys to go beyond the paling fences and seek the places where only men normally went in search of adventure.

Only Michael was a little different to the rest of his family as he was very much like his poor dead mother, Elizabeth, with her creative spirit. For Elizabeth, it had been a sweet and beautiful voice that could create images sad and joyful in men's minds with her songs.

Bridget finished cleaning the wounds and washed away the blood from his face, and impulsively she wrapped her arms around him and held him to her ample bosom as if he were a little boy.

Michael was emotionally drained. It had not taken much for the three soldiers to provoke him at the Sovereign Hotel. Just a derogatory comment about the lack of intelligence of the Irish race. But the brawl with the soldiers had dissipated his anger

189

and grief, and all three soldiers had required treatment at the military infirmary as a result of their confrontation with the young Irishman. It was fortunate for him that an Irish police officer had been called to intervene in the brawl. And more fortunate still was the fact that the same policeman happened to be Constable Farrell who knew the Duffy family well.

When Bridget was satisfied that Michael did not require the services of Doctor Hughes, she prepared a cup of tea for him. He thanked her and she could see that her nephew wished to be alone. She indicated to her husband that they should leave him for the moment.

Michael stared with vacant eyes and confused thoughts at the corners of the kitchen. So much had happened in the past twenty-four hours. So much had changed his life forever.

The wooden keg rattled down the chute and slammed into the cellar floor with a thud. Michael strained and, with a grunt, hauled it sideways away from the chute. He was stripped to the waist and his muscled body bore the imprints of bruises from the brawl two days earlier. Sweat streaked his face, even though the cellar was the coolest place in the hotel.

'Ve vill haf a drink, my friend,' Max said, as he straightened to ease his aching back. He too was stripped to the waist. 'Ve vill try this ale.'

Michael wiped the sweat from his face with his shirt and sat down next to the German who produced two enamel mugs. He spiked a keg and tipped it carefully to pour the brown liquid.

Michael sniffed at his cup and wrinkled his nose at the unpleasant smell.

'Not really something to slake a thirst,' he said of the odious beverage. Max took a mouthful and spat it on the dusty cellar floor.

'You are right, mein friend. This country vill never haf a goot beer.' The local beer was brewed with dubious astringent substitutes to the hops normally used in beer-making. It was no wonder that the imported English beers remained popular despite their higher price. 'In Hamburg, vee haf the best beer, *ja*,' he added wistfully as he recollected the cold lagers with their creamy and frothy heads flowing over the lips of huge drinking steins. 'Vot you need in this country is such a beer. Vot you need is a goot Bavarian brewer to teach you how to make the beer.' Both men stared down at their mugs and simultaneously poured the contents on the floor.

'I've got a couple of bottles of English beer,' Michael said as he reached behind a wooden crate.

'Horse piss, your English beer,' Max said as Michael began to pass him the brown bottle. He shrugged, making a movement as if to replace the bottle. But Max grabbed it from him.

'But I vill force myself to drink it,' he said with feigned reluctance.

Michael grinned mischievously. 'I think you shouldn't drink it, Max. You are getting fatter every day. Soon even I will be able to beat you in a couple of rounds,' he said cheekily.

Max patted his ample belly. 'Missus Duffy is a fine cook. It is not my fault.'

Michael laughed at the twinge of embarrassment

shown by Max for the sad loss of his once fine body. Around Max, it was easy to laugh and hard work had been a good panacea for the emotional ills of the past few days.

'If you think Aunt Bridget's cooking is good, you should see what Uncle Frank has planned for the Erin starting next week,' he said as he took a swig from the bottle of English beer. It was not cold, or even cool, but it was still pleasant to the palate of a thirsty man.

'You mean like that other hotel vhere people pay for meals,' Max growled disapprovingly.

'Uncle Frank thinks he might give it a try,' Michael ventured. 'It will certainly be a change from what we usually serve up in the bar. Rabbit soup, saute of goose with olives, kidneys in champagne, mayonnaise of lobster, beans, peas, cauliflower, artichokes, spuds ... Sounds like something I ate only a couple of nights ago ...' Michael's voice trailed away as he remembered the night at the Macintosh cottage.

'Ach! Too rich for the people who come to the Erin, mein friend. Vey vill not pay three shillings for such a meal. Vey are mostly dumb Irishmen like you ... potato eaters,' the German said good-naturedly, but Michael did not hear his friend's good-humoured insult. His thoughts were across the harbour in another place with another person.

Max noticed the faraway look on the young man's face and gave him a nudge in the ribs with his elbow. 'Dumb Irishmen!'

Michael sighed and focused on the present. 'Sorry, Max. I was just thinking about something,' he apologised.

'Your papa and brudder, my friend?' Max prompted gently. 'Patrick vas the best of men. He saved my life when the British came to kill us all at Ballarat and I vill never forget him.'

'No. I wasn't thinking about Da or Tom or Billy.'

'Vot is troubling you, young Michael?' Max prompted. But before he could reply, they were surprised to see Daniel with his coat over his shoulder climb down the stairs into the cellar and pick his way carefully to them through the wooden crates and kegs.

'Have you any spare bottles down here, Mike?' Daniel asked by way of greeting. Michael rummaged behind the crate and found three more which he opened, passing one to Daniel who took a long swig. At this time of day, he was normally at the chambers of the law firm of Sullivan and Levi and leave from the chambers was unheard of – except to attend family births and deaths. When Daniel had finished half the bottle's contents, he made himself comfortable on a wooden crate.

'I gather from your look,' Michael said in a serious tone, 'and the fact you are home early, you have found out something?'

As an articled clerk to a firm of solicitors in the city, Daniel was in a good position to hear things. 'Yes,' Daniel replied as he stared down at a point on the cellar floor. 'The man who was killed by the blacks was Angus Macintosh.'

'*Angus!*' Michael exploded. 'I remember Fiona saying that was the name of her oldest brother. God almighty! Penelope said that Da had protected the murderer of a white man. She must have

193

meant that the white man was Fiona's brother and it's no bloody wonder she hasn't tried to get in contact with me in the past couple of days.'

'That's not all,' Daniel added. 'It appears, from a report by the police lieutenant in charge of a dispersal, that Tom's body was never actually found by him or his troopers. The trap only made a presumption that Tom was killed.'

'How did you find out all this, Dan?'

'Better you don't ask questions,' he replied with a mysterious smile. 'That way I don't have to tell you any lies.'

Michael nodded. His cousin had devious ways about him, and it was no wonder he had chosen to be a lawyer. In fact, Daniel had used money to bribe a clerk in the Macintosh firm of solicitors for all the information they had on the affair in Queensland. The clerk had met him at a city hotel for lunch and information had been exchanged for money and a few free drinks.

'What else did you find out?' Michael asked as the news about Tom held a sudden ray of hope.

'Apparently Uncle Patrick held the police at gun-point so that some wounded blackfellow could escape,' he answered as he took another swig from the bottle. 'It seems that the blackfella was responsible for the death of Angus Macintosh.The trap, who was in charge of the dispersal, reported that he left Uncle Pat and Old Billy alone and rode off. He said he then heard cries for help and when he rode back he found both Uncle Pat and Old Billy speared to death. Later he came across Uncle Pat's bullock team and he made a decision to destroy the dray and bullocks so that supplies would not fall into the hands of any of the hostile natives that might be around.'

Michael frowned. 'There is something about the trap's story I don't like, Dan,' he said slowly. 'Something that doesn't sound right.'

Daniel nodded, and it was Max who intervened. 'A trap would never let Patrick go for stopping him in his duties,' he reflected. 'A trap vould arrest him, not ride avay and leaf him.'

'You are right, Max!' Daniel said, recognising the fundamental flaw in the police story. 'The bastard could have killed Uncle Pat and Old Billy and somehow he missed Tom.'

'Jesus, Mary and Joseph!' Michael swore. 'Did you get the name of the trap by any chance?'

Daniel racked his memory. He had not considered the police officer as a suspect for murder before, but what Max had said made a lot of sense. It was not probable the inspector would allow Patrick to go free after harbouring a man wanted for murder.

'Mont . . . no! . . . Mort, Lieutenant Mort of the Native Mounted Police. Mort is the name of the murdering bastard!'

The three men sat in a short silence, and the taste of the English beer soured in Michael's mouth.

'What about Fiona's father? Was he anywhere near the scene?' Michael finally asked, breaking the silence.

'Yes. He was with Mort when Uncle Patrick bailed them up,' Daniel replied, as he repeated the details given to him by the talkative clerk.

'Then he is just as responsible for murder,'

Michael said quietly, and his eyes glowed feral in the gloom of the cellar.

Daniel shifted uncomfortably. 'I doubt if we could prove anything against anyone,' he said. 'Without any witnesses, it would be our word against that of the police and Donald Macintosh. And . . .'

'I know that,' Michael snarled. 'Murder gets done and we are without the law. But there is a thing called natural justice.'

'Forget what you are thinking,' Daniel said quickly to cut short the dangerous ideas he could see forming in his cousin's mind. 'You will only end up swinging on a rope with your neck stretched if you go after either Donald Macintosh or the trap.' But Michael ignored his cousin's warning as his mind was set and he knew what he must do.

'I have some more news for you,' Daniel added in an attempt to distract his cousin's murderous thoughts. 'Miss Fiona Macintosh has left Sydney with Miss Penelope White. It seems that their whereabouts is a mystery even to the family solicitors. There is a rumour that she was sent away on the orders of her mother because of some love affair she was having with an Irishman.' Michael gaped. 'Don't worry, your name did not come up,' he added, by way of reassurance.

Michael had planned to see Fiona that very evening. Now she was gone to God knows where! It was as if the devil were playing a sad and iniquitous game with him. He had not known exactly why he wanted to see her or what he would do and say when he met her again. All he knew was that he must see her – at least once more – before he travelled to Queensland to ascertain the truth concerning the death of his father and Old Billy. And possibly find Tom.

'Dan, thanks for all you have done,' Michael said as he stood and stared at the pile of kegs that he and Max had stacked. 'I think I need to talk to Uncle Frank about finishing up here.' Both men exchanged worried glances.

'You are needed here, mein friend,' Max said as he placed his brawny arm around Michael's shoulders. 'I vould haf no one to drink vif.'

Michael smiled at him. 'There are a lot of things I have to do, Max,' he replied quietly. 'And when they are all done, I promise I will come home.'

13

Penelope's home was not as luxurious as the Macintosh mansion. But it was still a house that reflected the considerable wealth of its owner, Granville White.

Originally built for a wealthy Sydney land developer, the house had been purchased by Jonathan White, father of Granville and Penelope, when he had come out from India to invest his modest fortune in the Antipodean colonies. It was ironic that he should survive the rigours of India only to die from a fall from his horse during a fox hunt in England's green and hedgerowed fields two years past.

Sarah White, his wife, had remained in England to live her life out as the mistress of the traditional White estates. She had never visited Australia. Life in the colonies had no appeal for a woman who had always yearned, through the blistering hot and sunbaked days of the Indian dry season, for snow at Christmas.

Her children had chosen to join their father in the far-off colony of New South Wales. Although she had not fully approved of her daughter returning to Australia, the scandal of her sexual escapades around London had helped Sarah decide that a short sojourn to the colonies might be in the best interests of the White family's reputation in polite London social circles.

Sarah accepted that her son, Granville, must be close to her sister-in-law's family if he were to realise his ambition of uniting the two fortunes. There had always been a presumption that he would eventually marry Fiona as a means of cementing the amalgamation of the two family fortunes.

The library, in which Granville sat brooding, held many mementoes of India. On the teak desk was a small but weighty brass statue of a Hindu deity. On the walls an array of traditional Indian weapons was displayed; exotically shaped swords, wickedly curved knives and small battle shields. Above the swords and knives was a long and deadly lance that had once been part of the arms of the Indian regiment in which his father had been an honorary member. Jonathan White loved India, but the terrible mutiny of the Bengal Army in '57, and the end of the rule by the East India Company for whom he'd worked, had decided him to seek more stable avenues in which to invest his wealth.

Australia had been a natural choice based on the advice of his sister, Enid, who had extolled the opportunities in the colony of New South Wales. Jonathan had left the management of his colonial business ventures to his only son when he sailed to England on the visit from which he never returned. Granville had inherited the family colonial enterprises under the conditions of his father's will, and his mother, the smaller estates in England. The large and comfortable mansion he now lived in with his sister was part of that inheritance.

A stately grandfather clock in the corner of the dark library ticked away the minutes as Granville sipped a port wine and puffed on a large cigar reflecting on the events that had transpired in the Macintosh library and their implications concerning his future ambitions. More than ever it was vitally important to secure Fiona as his wife if he was to move one step closer to the final amalgamation of the families. But this was a matter not easily obtained, as the stupid girl had become infatuated with the Irish oaf Duffy. So David Macintosh was not the only obstacle between himself and gaining almost total control of the vast fortunes of the Macintoshes. He also had the Irishman to contend with and, although any formal union between Fiona and the Papist was unthinkable, he was still an obstacle. While the Irishman lived, he knew Fiona would be under his influence. Duffy seemed to have a magnetic quality about him that attracted women and he would have to be removed from Fiona's life in a way that was absolute in its permanence.

The thick smoke from the cigar curled around Granville's head and the warm night brought a moth fluttering into the library through an open window. It circled the flames of the candles and sizzled as it flew too close to the flame, before spiralling to the floor with part of its wing seared away.

'A flame!' he said softly as he watched the

doomed moth fluttering helplessly on the library floor. 'All I need is a flame to burn you, Mister Duffy, and there will be nothing between Fiona and myself.' And he knew the very flame was at his fingertips.

Only days earlier he had been advised not to hire one of the men who had reported for a place in the crew of the *Osprey*. The first mate of the Macintosh barque knew well the man's unsavoury reputation for disruptive violence and had told Granville that he was extremely dangerous – a violent man with a reputation for killing. But a man who had enough animal cunning to avoid the traps of Sydney Town. What was his name? Damn! What was the man's name? Jack Horton! Yes, it was Jack Horton!

If anything went wrong, Granville knew he could be facing the gallows. But if everything went well, he would have eliminated the major obstacle between himself and Fiona. Unconsciously, he wrapped his sweaty hands around a small brass statue that he used as a paperweight. He glanced down at it and realised with a start that it was the statue of Kali, the Hindu goddess of destruction, whom the dreaded thuggees of India worshipped. Surely this was an omen, he thought. Yes, he would talk to the first mate and arrange to see the infamous Jack Horton.

It was time to deal with his sister and prepare the next stage of his plan because, as far as he was concerned, Duffy was already dead. The next step was to procure his cousin's hand in marriage. A less easy task than plotting the murder of a man, he brooded, as he climbed the stairs to his sister's room and opened the door without knocking.

Penelope stood in front of a full-length mirror naked to the waist, cupping her large but firm breasts in her hands and she did not notice her brother enter the room.

'You have certainly grown into a beautiful woman, Penny,' he said, admiring his sister's breasts.

Startled by his intrusion, she turned to face him, snatching a shawl from her bed. 'How dare you enter my room without an invitation,' she snapped as she held the shawl up to cover her breasts.

'I go where I like in my own home, dear sister,' he answered, nonplussed by her anger. 'Remember that well. Besides, it is not the first time I have seen you naked.'

She turned her back to her brother, slipping on a silk chemise which only accentuated her firm and desirable body. 'That was a long time ago, Granville,' she retorted in an icy tone. 'And I swear I will kill you if you ever try to do that to me again.'

He knew her threat was real. His sister was not a woman one crossed. She had the inherent vindictiveness of the Whites. 'You seemed to enjoy yourself at the time,' he smirked. 'If my memory stands me well. I know I enjoyed myself. You were always more than willing to comply with my . . . ahh . . . rather unusual requests for your services.'

She glared at her brother with a burning hatred for memories of a time and place that still haunted her. The unspeakable acts he had forced her to do could never be undone, and she had experienced at first hand the physical power of the male to degrade a female. But as time went by, she was able to use the very act of sex against men in subtle and devious ways that made them unwittingly comply with her ambitions. Lust was an unbridled need for men, she had learnt. But it was a need that she was able to use as one would tame a rampant lion.

And she knew with a burning certainty that one day she would revenge herself on her brother for the lost years of innocence. But for now, he stood smirking in her bedroom for the perceived power he still thought he held over her.

'And I suppose it was that time with me that gave you a taste for young girls,' she said with a mysterious and savage smile.

His smugness disappeared. 'What do you mean by what you just said?' he asked quietly with a touch of fear in his question.

'This house is not big enough to hide all its secrets,' she replied with a bitter smile. 'Not big enough to conceal the cries of that young girl. What's her name? Oh, yes, Jennifer. The gardener's daughter. I think she is only eight years old. About the same age you used me. Or could she be a year or two older, dear brother?'

Granville paled. So his sister knew of his meetings in the library with the young girl. The pact with Harris to provide his young daughter had been sealed with her visits to the library. Although the man knew what was happening he chose to let the stupefying effects of the gin that his boss freely supplied obliterate the reality of his daughter's pain. And he justified it, in his alcohol-riddled mind, by telling himself that although his daughter was a pretty girl she was most likely to become a prostitute – as her mother had. A large strawberry birthmark on one side of her face was God's punishment upon her for her mother's sins, and the harsh reality was that no man would want her when she came of age, or so her father thought. At least for the moment she had all that she could possibly want – good clothes and plenty of food on the table for both of them.

'Better you forget what you have just said, dear sister,' Granville replied menacingly. 'Better we both forget the past and think about the future. Your future as well as mine. I think I have something that you want very much.'

'My future. What can you do for *my* future?' she asked sarcastically. 'And what do you have that I might want?' But she knew her brother was capable of anything and was curious to hear what he would propose.

'This house,' he said with a wave of his arm. 'And all that goes with it.'

Her interest was aroused. She had always been bitter that her father had not left the house co-jointly to them. Jonathan White was a chauvinist. To him, females were mere property to be bartered in marriage to further family interests.

'And how do I get the estate, dear brother?' she asked with less sarcasm and he smiled.

'All you have to do is help me convince Fiona that she should marry me,' Granville replied. 'Nothing more. When you have done that I will sign over the house to you. And a sum of money to maintain you in the life that you are used to.'

Penelope sat on the edge of the bed with her long golden hair falling around her shoulders and framing her beautiful, almost angelic face. But the proposition disturbed her. There was something in her own feelings for her cousin that rebelled at the thought of her brother gaining access to Fiona's body.

Granville watched his sister's face and could see that she was troubled, but he waited patiently for her response to his proposal. Then she smiled enigmatically, as if she'd had a divine revelation, which made him feel a little uneasy.

'I will help you,' she replied. 'But I must warn you that convincing Fiona to marry you will not be easy. Not while she thinks she might be in love with the Irishman.'

He flashed his sister a victorious smile, which reminded her of the smile on a cat's whiskered face before it kills the helpless mouse.

'I don't think Fiona will be in love with Mister Duffy for much longer, dear sister,' he said, and his sister frowned as she had a tiny suspicion which she preferred not to dwell on. Was it possible that he was planning to have Michael Duffy disposed of in some way? But she dismissed the thought with another that satisfied her needs first and foremost. Very deliberately she lay back on the bed in a way that allowed the silky chemise to glide seemingly innocently up her thighs, exposing for a brief and erotic moment that which her brother had used for his carnal pleasure.

Her provocative act was not lost on Granville who stared with undisguised lust at her, and she was pleased to see that her power over him had not diminished with time. She smiled seductively and his face reddened with his desire. If only you knew my ultimate plan, dear brother, in helping you win the hand of Fiona, you might think very carefully on what you have asked me to do, she thought, as she watched her brother struggle with his lust. The divine revelation had told her how she could wreak her ultimate revenge on her brother as only she knew his true weakness, and it was this vulnerability she would use against him in the future.

'I think you should leave my room now,' she said, adjusting the chemise modestly to cover her exposed thighs. 'Or you might confuse me with Fiona . . . and that would not do. I think you should return to the library to seek your relief. I believe the gardener's daughter is due to visit you tonight.'

He glared at her with a rage for what she was deliberately doing to him, and the memories returned of their times together in the stables and the hidden places of the big house in England. How was it that she had been able to take his power from him when it had always been he who had controlled her, he thought. He stormed from the room, leaving his sister to gloat in her subtle victory.

14

The *Osprey* lay at her mooring and her timbers squeaked incessantly as she rubbed her hull against the wharf protesting like a lonely dog chained too long in the night.

Her sails were furled and her masts pointed like skinny fingers at the constellations of the Southern Hemisphere.

She was a barque, whose proud career had taken her into the rolling seas of Bass Strait and the calm of Moreton Bay as she plied the waters of Australia's east coast with a sound history as a supply ship for the Macintosh companies. But now the barque was undergoing a refit to carry human cargo rather than the trading goods she usually carried in her holds.

A lone man stood nervously under the bow of the *Osprey* and baulked at every unexpected and unidentifiable sound. His hand never left his coat pocket where it gripped a small pistol.

Granville cursed himself for choosing to meet Jack Horton at such an ungodly hour, but it was a time when he could be sure very few people would be witness to the meeting. Horton was late. He had stipulated 4 a.m. and it was now a quarter past the hour. Granville yawned and thought about lighting a cigar to pass the time.

'Bin later I'd might have seen you.' The voice, which came softly from nearby, startled Granville who almost fired the pistol in his pocket.

'Good God, man! You gave me quite a fright,' he exclaimed as Horton emerged cautiously from behind a news stand on which a half-torn poster declared a Confederate victory in the far-off American Civil War.

'Don't trust anyone . . . an' you don't get caught out,' Horton said matter of factly. 'I was waitin' to see if you was alone before I introduced meself.'

Granville eyed the bulk of the man who stood squarely in front of him. It was a mutual appraisal.

'Spect you has a gun in your jacket in case I turn nasty or somethin', Mister White.'

'How do you know who I am?' Granville replied, as he felt his spirits sink. 'I might not be this Mister White you called me.'

'I knows you, Mister White. Don't take a genius to know who you are round Sydney Town. I knows you are the man who wouldn't give me a job on this 'ere boat,' he said as he pointed to the *Osprey*. 'Now you give the *Osprey*'s mate a message for me to meet you down 'ere. But 'e don't say who I was to meet. So I'se jus' stan's over there and watch youse real careful like, in case it wus the traps tryin' to pinch me. But I recognises you and decides it wus all right.'

Horton spoke softly, which belied his hulking appearance. Although there was not enough light to make out his features, Granville could smell the rum on the man's breath and feel his menace as if it were something tangible. Yes, Jack Horton appeared to be the right choice. His caution proved he was also a thinking man, despite his crude grasp of the English language.

'I presume you are Jack Horton.'

'That's who I am when me mother named me, God rot her soul,' Horton spat.

'Well, Mister Horton, as I was about to say, who I am is best forgotten. To make this point, I will offer you a job within your ... er ... domain of skills, and pay you extremely well,' he said, relaxing his grip on the revolver in his pocket.

'What's this "domain of skills" mean?' Horton asked suspiciously. 'I never 'eard that word before.'

'I believe you are capable of doing away with a man for a price?'

'Ah, so that's what the word means,' he replied, pleased with his grasp of something new. 'Well, youse could be right ... and youse could be wrong. It depends on how much we is talkin'.'

'Hundred pounds.'

'Hundred guineas ... an' youse can purchase my domain o' skills, Mister White,' he countered.

Granville baulked at his asking price, but could not help admire the man's shrewdness as a hundred pounds was a small fortune to any man. 'A hundred guineas is a lot of money, Mister Horton,' he sighed, as if the figure might bankrupt him.

'For a hundred guineas you can call me Jack like youse would any of your other employees, Mister White,' Horton said with a sly smile that bared yellow and broken teeth.

'Well, er, Jack . . . I suppose a hundred guineas it is.'

'Good. Now that I am an employee of yours, you can tell me the person or persons youse want done away with.'

'Only one person. An Irishman by the name of Michael Duffy. He . . .'

''E comes from the Erin, don't 'e?' Horton said.

'Is this man a friend of yours?' Granville asked apprehensively, as he had not expected Horton to know the Irishman.

'No friend, Mister White, but 'e's no pushover, an' 'e's got a lot o' friends around the old Sydney Town. If I'd a knowed it was the pretty boy youse wanted done away with, I'd 'ave asked more than a hundred guineas. No, to do away with Michael Duffy will require a little 'elp.'

Granville weighed up what Horton was saying. Was it a ruse to extract more money from him? 'Why is Mister Duffy a problem to a man like you?'

Horton scrunched his shoulders and slipped his hands in the rope belt about his waist. 'The man 'as a reputation on the other side o' town for being handy with 'is 'ands. I can take 'im, but I'd feel better wif some backup . . . jus' in case, youse know.' For a man like Jack Horton to make such an admission impressed Granville.

'Another fifty guineas . . . to buy extra help. How you pay for the help is up to you . . . but at no time will you mention who I am to anyone. I need not impress on you that we are talking murder here,' he cautioned.

Horton grinned before replying. 'Not murder

. . . jus' me usin' me domain o' skills. But I need youse to do somethin' else before I'se can do the job.'

'What else?' Granville asked as he tried to keep his feelings of annoyance under control at the man's persistence in extracting further concessions from him.

'I'se'll need to get out of Sydney Town after I'se do away with the pretty boy. Youse can give me a berth on the *Osprey* here as a mate,' he indicated with a flip of his thumb.

Granville did not have to ponder very long on the suggestion. For Horton to disappear from Sydney after the task was completed made a lot of sense. 'A mate's job requires experience. Do you have the experience?' he ventured cautiously.

'I'm a quick learner. An', besides, if the work is like I think it's gunna be with the darkies, you are goin' to need men like me. Men who knows how to get the job done properly for the right kind of boss. Someone like you.'

'You could be right, Jack. I think you have a fine future with the company,' Granville replied with a short and mirthless laugh. 'Now I will tell you how and when you and Mister Duffy will meet.' He explained to the big man his carefully thought out plan and he could see that Horton was impressed. When he asked the man if he had any questions, he said no.

Business complete, Granville was eager to leave the wharf and return home in the carriage waiting for him at Circular Quay.

'Before youse leaves, Mister White, I have a habit of shakin' on any deals I'se makes,' Horton said.

Granville saw the big man offer his left hand and automatically moved to offer his left hand. A warning clicked in his mind. The left-handed shake was not right! He froze in absolute terror when the knife appeared in Horton's right hand.

'You see how easy death can come to a man. It can come as easily as a 'andshake between gentlemen.' He grinned at the sudden terror on Granville's face. He had made his point and knew Granville White had recognised the message in the simple but potentially deadly gesture. 'An' I knows youse is a gentleman, Mister White, who wouldn't go back on any deal.'

Granville did not move as Horton shuffled into the dark shadows of the wharf. His legs felt like jelly and he realised that his breath was coming in short desperate gulps. He could almost feel sorry for the last moments of Duffy up against such a man.

Granville hurried back to Circular Quay where his coach was waiting for him. Even the anticipation of having the young girl's body in his bed when he arrived home did not take his mind off the short distance the knife had been from his groin.

From his office window, David Macintosh could see across the rooftops of the warehouses to the waterfront. And as he stood with his hands behind his back he could view the *Osprey* being refitted for his cousin's Pacific venture. Worry lines creased his forehead as he turned away from the window and walked back to his desk.

There was very little paperwork to be seen as papers and files were located in the anteroom adjacent to his office. On the other side of the door, his private secretary, George Hobbs, sat engrossed in lists and correspondence that generated the Macintosh business interests for shipping in the colonies and the Pacific.

An unobtrusive kock at his door indicated that Hobbs wished to see him.

'Yes, Hobbs.'

Hobbs poked his bespectacled face around the door and, although he was twenty-eight years of age, premature baldness had put ten years on his appearance.

'Missus Macintosh to see you, sir,' he said with a welcoming smile reserved for the introduction of family to the offices of Macintosh & Sons. Except now it was the singular of sons that would appear on all the business signs. The problem was George's to wrestle with. Should he have the 'S' dropped from the signs by erasure? Or should new signs be painted? The former option had the less than tactful touch of obliterating the 'S' as if wiping out a life.

'Thank you, Hobbs,' Enid said with a warm smile. Hobbs gave a courteous nod of the head as acknowledgement to the mother of his boss, whom he genuinely admired for the professional manner in which she had run the business in the absence of her husband.

He closed the door behind Enid as she swept into the room. She wore a satin dress of black with matching hat which suited her as it contrasted with her smooth and milky white skin.

'Hell, Mother,' David said, and he guided her to a thickly padded divan set against the wall. 'Your visit comes as a pleasant surprise.' She sat and placed her hands in her lap, which was a rather demure gesture, her son reflected, if out of character for a woman who had grown used to using this very office in the past to make critical decisions that had at times brought others to their financial knees.

'I was talking to Hobbs,' she said without any idle chatter. 'He tells me you are having problems with the crew of the *Osprey*.'

David frowned. 'Not all the crew. Just the first mate, Bill Griffin. He approached me when I was making an inspection of the *Osprey* this morning. He was rather agitated about a decision Granville has made. It seems he has put a man on as assistant first mate to Bill Griffin. A man whom Granville had originally rejected on the advice of Mister Griffin.'

'That is Granville's prerogative as to whom he hires . . . or rejects,' Enid commented. 'We agreed Granville had full control of the operational side of the venture.'

David strolled over to the window and placed his hands behind his back. Enid could see that her son was worried. He gazed at the *Osprey* and all seemed to be normal. Supplies were going aboard and sailors went about their routines. He turned away from the window.

'Mister Griffin has threatened to resign if the man Granville hired goes aboard the ship,' he said. 'The man has a bad reputation as a trouble-maker and cannot be trusted.'

Enid raised her eyebrows as her nephew's decision to hire such a man against the advice of a proven employee flew in the face of logic and good sense. 'What do you think you should do about the situation?' she asked.

David was in a quandary. He could not interfere in the operations unless he thought the venture might, in some way, bring scandal upon the good name of the Macintosh companies.

'I suppose I should try to talk to Mister Griffin and placate him,' he sighed. 'The man Granville hired has done nothing to cause any problems at this stage and we can only give him a chance to prove his worth, one way or another.'

'In your shoes, I would have made the same decision,' his mother said. 'Just let the matter ride for now.'

David was pleased at his mother's support for his decision, except that he could not help but wonder why Granville had hired the man called Jack Horton.

'Now that is out of the way,' she said with a cheeriness in her voice that David had not heard since the tragic news concerning the death of Angus. 'I actually came to see if you would like to join me for lunch. There is a French chef at that new cafe in Pitt Street and I have heard he is very good.'

'I wish I could, Mother,' David apologised. 'But I have an appointment with the bankers in an hour. A matter concerning Father's proposed expansion in Queensland.' Lunch with his mother was definitely preferable to the stuffy boardrooms of the Bank of New South Wales, a place inhabited by pale and starched men.

'Well then,' his mother replied in a disappointed

voice, 'I suppose I should discuss with you the matter I was going to at lunch. Fiona's forthcoming marriage.'

David blinked. 'This is the first news I have heard about Fiona getting married. Who in Hades is she marrying?'

'I thought you would have made a logical conclusion on the matter. You rather surprise me. She is going to marry Granville, of course,' Enid answered.

'Granville! Does Fiona know she is going to marry Granville?' David uttered with a burst of surprise. 'Since when has all this come about?'

'Since he approached me on the matter this morning,' Enid replied calmly. 'Oh I know you are not overly fond of Granville but I have agreed for a very good reason. An important reason that concerns you,' his mother said to placate her son.

'Me?' he questioned. 'How does Granville's marriage to Fiona have anything to do with me? Oh, except for the fact I dislike the man as he has only one true love in life. And that is for the Macintosh companies and his chance of running them by himself.'

'That is why I think Granville is the right choice to join the family through marriage,' Enid said gently. 'You cannot hide from me that you are not happy at being thrust into the role of manager of the family's business. I have known for some time that you were offered a position at Oxford. And that the position means more to you than managing the companies.'

He did not know how to reply to his mother's very perceptive summation of his lost dream. Yes, a position at Oxford was his greatest hope. He had been an outstanding student – *even for a colonial* – and Oxford's cloistered halls were where he felt most at home. He had never considered being thrust into the position of managing the business because his brother Angus had always been the heir apparent. But an Aboriginal spear had changed all that.

'You are right in what you are saying, Mother,' David replied. 'But I also know my duty.'

'I know you do, David. But I do not think you will be a good manager. You will be an outstanding scholar, but not a very good manager. Granville can build on our interests even bigger and better in the tragic eventuality of your father finally passing on.'

'You are giving the family's interests to Granville?' David asked. He was astonished at the idea of his ambitious and ruthless cousin with so much power.

'No, your father will be giving the companies to his grandsons ... eventually,' she replied quietly. 'When Fiona and you produce them for us. You will always be a very wealthy man and share in the profits. And so will your children.'

David stared disbelievingly at his mother who appeared so deceptively fragile. Yet she had just schemed to cut him off from the management of the family business all for the sake of the Macintosh empire to expand. She was absolutely ruthless.

'You talk as if any sons of mine', he said, 'just *might* be the rightful heirs to the estates, Mother, and not as if this were a natural assumption.'

'What if they follow in your footsteps, David?' she reasoned. 'What if they decide they would rather be scholars like you. I hate to say it but, if nothing else, the blood on my side of the family is determined enough to make the Macintosh blood the strongest in this country. And it would only be through another union of White and Macintosh blood that I think this would occur.'

He shook his head disbelievingly. 'You make this sound like breeding horses or cattle. What if Fiona decides she does not want to marry Granville? Have you selected another stud with the right lines?'

'Don't be coarse! Fiona *will* marry Granville. There is no question on that matter,' his mother said firmly, as she did not doubt her daughter's ultimate loyalty to the family. Fiona had, after all, given her solemn word that she would never see the Irishman again.

So his sister was to be a brood mare for the Macintosh line.

His mother continued, 'I can see that you are upset. But I know you will eventually understand the rational reasoning in all of this and agree with the decisions I have made for Fiona's future.'

'Not Fiona's future, Mother – *your* future.'

'You are wrong, David,' Enid said quietly. 'I only care about the prospects for the future for all of us. And that includes your best interests above all. It is our duty to follow the path I have chosen for us and if you cannot see that, then I am sorry. I think I should leave you to think over all that I have spoken of,' she said as she rose and brushed down her dress.

There was nothing left to explain. She was upset by her son's lack of acceptance of her plans. She did not bid David goodbye as she left him to hurry down to her carriage waiting outside the Macintosh offices.

Enid had tears in her eyes as she stepped into the carriage. David, I have done this for you, she thought bitterly. You are too gentle and kind. Men like Granville White would eat you up, and you would grow old and miserable doing something that your heart was not in. No, David, I love you too much to let you get hurt. If only Angus had lived . . .

'Pitt Street, Missus Macintosh?' the driver asked.

'No. I think I would prefer to go home, thank you, Harold,' she answered, ducking her head so that the driver could not see the tears in her eyes.

15

Molly O'Rourke was not at the King George Hotel.

Michael sat in a corner patiently waiting but she had not appeared by closing time and the letter, embossed with the Macintosh family crest, delivered that afternoon to the Erin Hotel, had stipulated that it was most urgent that he meet her in the saloon bar. Molly had hinted that she would be able to tell him where Fiona was.

The message had come at a critical time as Michael had booked passage for the colony of Queensland and the ship was to sail the following week. But finding Fiona had also been a lover's priority and, bitterly disappointed, he left the hotel when the Macintosh nanny had not made an appearance.

His long walk back to the Erin took him past the tangle of streets best avoided at night along alleys where the heady scent of incense, opium and the spices of the Orient prevailed. The route from the King George to the Erin had brought him into the markets area where, by day, the horse traders and wheelwrights vied for space with the Fukien

220

Chinese traders, and where, by night, a woman might rob a man while his throat was being slit by her male partner.

Something was wrong! Jaundiced light from the gas lamps added to the ominous and hushed atmosphere of the lonely place as Michael stopped to get his bearings and remember something of vital importance. Then the terrible truth dawned: the message could not have come from Molly O'Rourke because she could neither read nor write! Michael sensed that he was in trouble – serious trouble!

'Ah, pretty boy. She's stood youse up . . .'

He spun around as Jack Horton emerged from the shadows of the lonely and deserted street.

An ambush!

With him was another man of equally repulsive appearance who grinned a broken-toothed smile. Michael noticed that both men were barefooted, which explained how they had followed him so silently. He felt a sick fear in his stomach.

'. . . But then she was never comin' anyway,' Horton continued. 'So me an' me brudder . . . well half-brudder, 'ere, says we's should make sure youse got home all right. Now didn't I say that, Benny Boy? Personally, I would never come this way at night. Very dangerous an' no one sees much down 'ere. Not like The Rocks where we is all mates,' he said as he continued his advance on Michael, who had no doubts that both men were armed. Nor did he have any illusions about Horton's offer for safe escort, and he dared not take his eyes off the man who approached with the stealth of a hunting feline.

Michael crouched and balanced himself for the attack he knew was coming. This was not going to be any rough and tumble bare-knuckle fight. It would require all the skills of a street fighter to stay alive. But he had been taught well by Max the dirty tricks he was going to need to survive. 'Keep your distance . . . both of you,' Michael growled.

They hesitated uncertainly as they had expected the Irishman to turn and run, exposing his back to them. A cunning and calculating look passed across Horton's face.

'Me an' me brudder don' mean you no harm, Mister Duffy,' he said in an oily voice. 'As a matter of fact, me brudder had heard 'bout your reputation roun' Redfern an' Benny 'e says to me, Jack, I'd like to shake the 'and of such a fine gentleman as Mister Michael Duffy.'

Benny Boy stepped forward with his right hand extended and grinned innocently. At first, Michael thought foolishly that the man was retarded. He could see the extended right hand was empty but remembered what Max had once warned him. He is left-handed, Michael thought with swelling fear. The knife is in his left hand!

'Sounds fair to me,' Michael said, trying to sound casual and unafraid although every instinct told him he had but a fleeting fraction between life and death in the next vital seconds.

'Good thing to all be friends,' Horton said with a hint of cunning in his voice. The two men were now at arm's length.

Michael's unexpected attack was sudden and violent. He reached out to shake Benny Boy's hand and simultaneously spat in Horton's face. Stepping inside Benny Boy's guard, Michael seized his left wrist and brought it through in a sweeping arc.

Momentarily distracted by the spittle, Horton clawed at his own face and heard his half-brother grunt as the long knife that Benny Boy was holding punctured his chest. Horton swung blindly at Michael with his knife. The blade missed its intended target and buried itself in the side of Benny Boy's throat.

Michael did not wait for Horton to realise his terrible error. He spun and delivered a well-aimed boot into Horton's groin. Horton and his dying brother collapsed together in a pool of Benny Boy's blood and Michael turned on his heel to run.

The bellow of rage that echoed down the narrow street spurred Michael as he sprinted for his life, and he did not stop running until he reached the Erin, where he hammered on the front door.

A lighted lantern appeared in an upper room. 'Who in hell is that?' his Uncle Frank called down irritably.

'Me, Michael ... Uncle ... Frank,' Michael gasped and in a matter of seconds the door swung open and Michael fell gratefully inside.

'Jesus, Mary and Joseph!' Frank said, as he dragged the young man to his feet. 'What's happened to you, Michael? You're covered in blood!' Michael could not reply immediately as he was winded from the fight and his flight from Jack Horton. 'Biddy! Wake up Daniel and Max and tell them to get down here straightaway,' Frank yelled up the stairs as he helped Michael into the kitchen. He lit an oil lamp which flared, illuminating the room with flickering shadows.

Both men responded to the urgent call and Max appeared standing in his long johns, bare-chested and bleary-eyed. Daniel wore a dressing gown over his nightwear and they all hovered anxiously in the kitchen until Michael was able to recover sufficiently to speak.

'I was ambushed on the way back to the Erin by Jack Horton and his brother,' he finally explained. 'I don't know why . . . but they were out to kill me. I got in first. Got Jack's brother with his own knife.'

'Did you kill him?' Daniel asked.

'Think so,' Michael replied as he reflected on the seconds of terror in the confrontation. 'The knife went in pretty deep. Then Horton missed me and stabbed his brother as well. In the throat, I think.'

'If they set on you, Michael,' Frank said, patting his nephew on the shoulder reassuringly, 'then what you did was self-defence. We get to the police and tell them what happened and they will round up this fellow Jack Horton.'

It was Daniel who expressed a reservation. 'What if Jack Horton tells the traps that Michael attacked his brother and killed him?' he said pessimistically. 'This will come down to Mike's word against Horton's.'

'What do you think Michael should do?' Bridget asked her son.

'I don't know. Possibly stay out of sight while Max and I go and see the police and explain the situation,' he replied.

'Won't the police want to know why Michael is not with you?' Frank asked.

'We will say he is hurt, a knock on the head, and is unable to come straightaway. That should gain us some time until we are sure of what is happening.'

Francis Duffy nodded his agreement because his son was the legal mind in the family and the best judge of how to handle this. 'We will do it your way, Daniel,' he said. 'I will hide Michael in the cellar until your return. In the meantime, I think you need a shot of good brandy, Michael. It will help clear your head.'

'I think Michael needs a good clean-up and a change of clothes,' Bridget said as she fussed around him. 'The boy has had a terrible time.'

'He can have both.' Francis shrugged as he stoked the smouldering fire of the stove with a fresh log. 'Max can fetch some water.'

Michael was spent and tired and the warmth of the kitchen lulled him into a sense of wellbeing. Had he killed a man? It was hard to believe. Everything had happened so fast!

While the water boiled in a big iron pot on the stove, Frank poured Michael a half glass of his best French brandy. Michael accepted it gratefully, took a long swig and the strong liquor fumed in his head.

Both Max and Daniel returned to the kitchen after they had hurriedly dressed and Daniel gave his cousin a reassuring pat on the shoulder.

'We will go now, Mike,' he said. 'Everything will turn out all right.'

Michael smiled at his words and they were on the verge of leaving when a persistent and ominous knock at the front door of the hotel froze them.

Bridget's eyes widened and she glanced fearfully at her husband.

'I will see who it is,' Frank said calmly, although he felt sick with apprehension. Max grabbed Michael by the arm. He yanked him unceremoniously out of the kitchen and down to the cellar as Frank left the kitchen to answer the front door.

'Constable Farrell. And what might I be doing for you on this night?' Frank asked the grim-faced policeman who filled the doorway. 'Would it be a cooling ale to pass the time?'

'And what a grand idea, Mister Duffy,' the big Irish policeman replied. 'I was passin' this way and I thought I might share a jar with you. But first I would prefer just you and I have a short chat about strange happenings on the beat tonight.'

Frank held the eyes of the big policeman. Both men knew they were playing a game and Frank knew by whose rules. 'I think you should be coming in, Constable Farrell,' he said, 'and having a drink with me in the kitchen.'

The policeman followed the Irish publican to the table where only the brandy bottle remained beside an empty glass, which Farrell eyed. Frank noticed the focus of the policeman's gaze. 'Would a good brandy be the thing for tonight, Constable Farrell?' he asked as he took down a second clean glass from the shelf above the stove.

'That it would, Mister Duffy. That it would.'

'And what strange happenings have occurred this night to interest the guardians of Sydney's streets and homes?' Frank had to fight to control the tremble in his hand as he poured the brandy.

'We found a fellow dead in Haymarket this

evening,' the policeman answered. 'An unsavoury character well known to us and, if I must say so, God preserve his soul, better for leaving this world of temptations.' He took a long sip from the half-filled glass of brandy and sighed with pleasure. The glass was refilled to its rim.

'Ah, but there is terrible crime nowadays in the streets,' Frank said with a sigh. 'The trouble is the people of Sydney do not appreciate the work you do. Now if I could be giving . . .'

'It's not for the giving I came, Mister Duffy,' the police constable said quietly. 'It's for the taking of one Michael Duffy who resides at the Erin . . .'

Frank attempted to protest but the big Irish policeman held up his hand. 'Before you say anything, Mister Duffy, I must be warning you that it is my duty to search the hotel for the said person. But I don't think I'd be searching your cellar because only a foolish man would go down there to hide.'

Frank Duffy kept eye contact with the police officer and understood clearly what he was saying.

'If I may be asking, why is it that you want young Michael?' he asked, with feigned innocence.

Farrell took another swig from the glass before answering. 'While I was on my beat tonight, I stopped Jack Horton. I stopped him because he rarely leaves The Rocks to come to this part of town. So I says to myself when I saw him, Jack Horton, why are you in this part of town on my beat? And the answer came to me that he was up to no good. As soon as I pinched him, he babbles on that his brother was murdered by Michael Duffy. He says Michael set upon the both of them for no reason. Now, I know the story is away with the fairies, but he produces a body and I take him down to the station to talk to the detectives. And they believed him. So I told them that I knew where I might find Michael and bring him in to be charged with murder.'

'You came alone?' Francis asked anxiously.

'Yes. The detectives know I always get my man,' he answered with a conspiratorial wink. 'Well, almost always. But you realise I still have my duty to search the hotel and report back.'

'I do, Constable Farrell. Duty,' Frank replied, 'even to the English Crown, duty must be done.'

The big Irish-born policeman finished the rest of the brandy in one gulp. He was a hard-drinking man but he could hold his grog and showed no signs of the effects of the strong and fiery liquor.

'I suppose if I were young Michael,' he said, as he heaved his massive bulk from the chair, 'I would be on a ship out of here tonight. Until the matter is cleared up in time.'

'You think the matter can be cleared, Constable Farrell?' Frank Duffy asked hopefully.

'I think so,' he replied and followed Francis into the dining room. 'There is no argument that would support Michael attacking two men like the Horton brothers for no apparent reason. But the law being what it is has swung men and women before in this town, then found them innocent later. Better young Daniel get good advice for Michael before we speak to him.'

They wandered from room to room in a pretence of a search and when they passed the door to the cellar, Farrell gave a wry smile and moved on. He thanked Francis for his cooperation as he walked with him to the front door.

'I'd be saying to the boys down at the station that I heard Michael had gone west to the colony of South Australia,' Farrell said in parting. 'Big place, this country. He might even have gone north to join his sister.'

The publican watched the departing policeman stroll at a measured pace casually down the road. It would take him time to get back to the police station at Darlinghurst . . . and time was precious!

Being a publican had its advantages. Especially when one of the patrons happened to be the skipper of a ship leaving on the early morning tide. It also happened that the skipper was an Irish Yankee out of Boston and a Republican with no love for English law.

It did not matter where the ship was going. But hopefully to the Americas where Michael could lose himself until he was cleared of the stupid allegations. Francis closed the door and hurried upstairs to dress. There were not many hours to dawn and the turning of the tide.

The young man, who had been smuggled aboard quietly with the captain's permission, stood at the starboard stern rail of the American schooner. The crew knew not to ask questions about passengers who arrived under such conditions.

It was almost dawn when the *Eagle* cleared Sydney harbour. She punched into the rising waters of the hissing sea and plunged bow first into the rolling troughs while the young man continued to stare back at the slowly disappearing headlands that blazed orange under the glare of the rising sun. It would be a hot and muggy day in Sydney when the sun rose, he thought sadly. The pub would do a good trade.

'Cap'n says you can join him for coffee.'

Michael turned to the sailor who had a toothless grin and a wizened face which mirrored his lifetime before the mast. 'Thanks,' he replied and he took another gaze at the disappearing land. 'We headed for America?'

'No, mister. We sailin' for New Zealand.'

'New Zealand,' Michael echoed with no expression.

'Yeah, New Zealand. But I wouldn't want to be stayin' there too long if I'se was you,' the old sailor said conversationally. 'Them big cannibals ... Maoris theys calls them ... is bustin' fer a fight with the Limeys an' I'd be puttin' my money on them Maoris. They is one hell of a fightin' man when they get goin'.' With a cackling laugh the old sailor, bow-legged from his life at sea, made his way back to the bow.

Drifting pillars of smoke from fires burning on South Head marked where Australia lay off the clipper's stern as Michael watched the mainland disappear before the horizon.

He waited until even the pillars of smoke were gone from sight, then picked his way along the rolling deck to the captain's cabin.

Ahead of him lay the islands of New Zealand and an uncertain future. Behind him lay Australia and the person he had once been. A person he could never be again.

* * *

Jack Horton came in the early morning and his hammering on the front door woke not only Granville, but also Penelope.

An angry maid, wrenched from her sleep by the din, answered the door with threats of summoning the police. But Horton simply pushed the frightened woman aside. As he forced his way into the house, she shrank from the blood-stained man with the foul breath who stood belligerently in the hallway glaring at her.

Granville appeared in a dressing gown at the top of the stairs holding a .32 calibre pistol levelled on the intruder and the cowering maid breathed a sigh of relief.

But instead of threatening to shoot the evil-looking man, he gestured Horton to follow him to the library. The servant shook her head as she pulled her dressing gown around her throat and toddled back to bed. It was nearly five o'clock and she could only expect another half-hour's sleep before she rose to start her day's work around Mister White's house.

Granville closed the door of the library. In her room, Penelope quickly threw a shawl around her shoulders. She padded cat-like down the hall to eavesdrop. Outside the library door, she could hear the muffled conversation of the two men. After a brief and heated argument, the door opened and both men came out of the library.

They did not see Penelope as she had returned to her room only moments earlier when she realised the conversation was over. But not before she had heard enough to learn of Horton's failure to kill Michael Duffy.

Horton left the house and returned to The Rocks. He was weary, as he had spent a long time being grilled by the traps before going to Granville's house to report on the events of the previous evening. Despite Horton's failure, Granville confirmed the deal they had concerning his job on the *Osprey*. He still had nightmares about a razor-sharp knife inches from his groin.

At the breakfast table, Granville was unusually quiet as he sat staring at the newspaper. Penelope sat across the table from her brother and smiled to herself. It did not surprise her that Michael had escaped her brother's trap. She felt a small amount of savage pleasure. After all, he was surely a dangerous man. She could hardly contain the delight that she felt for the visibly shaken demeanour of her despised brother.

'Pray that Michael Duffy never finds out that you tried to have him killed, dear brother,' she said casually as she nibbled delicately on a slice of toast. 'Or he might return the favour one day.'

Granville blanched with absolute fear. Not for the fact that his sister knew of what had transpired between himself and Horton, but for the fact that she had reminded him the Irishman was still alive and might learn of his role in the botched conspiracy to murder him. Duffy had now become his worst nightmare and he knew his life would never be safe while the young Irishman lived.

'I don't think it is likely he will ever know of any such thing, dear sister,' he snarled. 'Especially from you, if you wish to have this house to yourself.'

'Oh, I can promise you my silence,' she replied with a smile, 'if you abide by the pact we have made. And I will still help you obtain Fiona's hand in marriage, for that matter,' she added and noticed the expression of relief flood his face.

'You do that,' he said as he rose and placed the newspaper on the table, 'and I can promise you that you will have my undying gratitude.'

She watched him leave the dining room and glowed with contentment. Dear brother, she thought. If you only had the slightest inkling of what lay ahead of you.

WHISPERS ON
THE WIND

1863

16

Sir,
I beg to report . . .

Perspiration from Mort's hand smeared the paper
and obliterated the words which dissolved and
formed a watery inkblot. Sweat ran in rivulets
down his chest under his heavy police jacket and
he cursed the stifling heat.

With an explosive outburst of temper, he hurled
the nib pen at the wood slab wall opposite his
desk. A tiny lizard scuttled for safety as the pen hit
the wall, spraying a fine mist of dark ink across
the wooden floor. In his rage, he swept the blank
pages of the report from his desk.

Lieutenant Morrison Mort was not a happy
man. The infernal heat, the acrid smell of bushfires

and the existence of Tom Duffy plagued him in the silent hours of the night and he cursed his decision to leave the colony of Victoria for a position with the Native Mounted Police on the Queensland frontier.

Upon his return from the western patrol, he had learned who the third man was and that he was no less than the son of the Irishman he had murdered. The intelligence had come to him through the routine inquiries carried out by Sergeant James in Rockhampton. The inquiries had not been sanctioned by him, as some things were better unasked and therefore unpublicised. Solomon Cohen, the storekeeper who had provisioned the teamsters for the Tambo trip, had told the big sergeant about Tom Duffy. The picture drawn of Duffy by the Jewish storekeeper did little to allay Mort's fears. Cohen had described Tom as a tough bushman who could easily live off the land. He had been taught well by the old Aboriginal who had travelled with the Irish teamsters. Worse still, Duffy had a reputation as a man no one in their right mind would want to cross.

Mort eased himself from his chair, stretched and walked over to the only glass window in his office. He stared out into the hot night. Distant bushfires burned with a deceptively soft glow on the horizon and he found himself looking at his own reflection in the windowpane. He saw a man he knew women found irresistible and he laughed silently. For the person in the reflection was another man, a man who functioned as an efficient com-missioned officer of Her Majesty, Queen Victoria, and was well thought of by his superiors both in

Queensland and Victoria. A man the ladies vied to be in company with at social gatherings because of his brooding charm, dashing good looks and conversation.

'Fucking whores! All of them,' he snarled. The fever was on him this night and he knew he must have a woman to ease his pain. Oh, so little did they know of his pain! For the thirty years of his life he had carried the unforgivable betrayal of his mother's love. He counted thirty years because the betrayal had been with him from birth.

He turned his back on the reflection and stared at the sword hanging on a rack on the wall behind his desk. It was an infantry sword that he had won in a game of cards from a young subaltern of the Fortieth Regiment just days before the attack on the Eureka Stockade. Mort had carried the sword into action that hot summer's morning in the year of 1854 at the Ballarat diggings and on that day he had found the sword was the true extension of his manhood.

Long and straight, with a sharp point, it was designed to impale rather than hack like the cavalry sabre. The infantryman's sword was a weapon where the man who killed with it was for a moment joined to his victim as they died. A moment of awesome adrenaline-surged power where the executioner and victim looked into each other's eyes.

He slumped in the chair behind his desk and stared morosely at the paper he had scattered on the floor of his office in his rage. Maybe tomorrow he would write the report. The curse of his murky and violent past was with him, with its terrible grip in the present. He had grown up in the infamous Rocks of Sydney Town but he had broken with the area when he ran away to sea to eventually earn his mate's ticket as a first-class mariner. But his past was always with him as a curse that haunted him with the memory of a prostitute mother who had sold him as a six-year-old boy to a syphilitic drunken sailor for the price of a bottle of gin. Oh how she had laughed in her drunken stupor as he screamed in pain for her to stop the man hurting him.

In the filthy rat-infested room that backed onto a tannery, he had been ravished as his mother watched, and she had shouted raucous encouragement to the sailor grunting over the young boy. And there were many nights that followed when the men used him, while his mother took their money and laughed at his pain. They had used him in obscene ways that his mind had long tried to block out, ways that continued to haunt him regardless of his efforts to forget.

But a day came when he could take no more and he had hacked his drunken mother to death as she screamed for mercy in that putrid little room.

The investigating police attributed her grisly death to an unhappy customer and did not suspect the ten-year-old boy who stood stony-faced in the corner, watching on with cold blue eyes. A particularly sadistic assault, one of the policemen had said, as he squatted to examine the mutilated body. The bastard's cut her mouth up with something sharp. Young Morrison Mort knew she could never laugh again at his pain, and nor would any other woman in his life.

From a career as a mariner he had deserted his ship in Melbourne to join the goldfields police, where the graft provided a lucrative income for the smart and enterprising. His years of slogging self-education at sea had paid off with a rapid promotion to the rank of sergeant, and he was recognised by his superiors as a ruthless and intelligent man able to command others under difficult conditions.

After the massacre of the rebel miners at the Eureka Stockade, he remained in the Victorian police force before resigning to transfer to the Native Mounted Police of Queensland as a lieutenant. For Mort, the transfer was a necessity and not an opportunity, and the mutilated body of the little girl was never found in the bush where he had buried her outside Melbourne.

The hesitant knock at the door brought him out of his morose recollections. 'Enter,' he bawled and the door opened to reveal Trooper Mudgee standing with a young Aboriginal girl. He shoved her through the open door and she stumbled into the room to stand in front of Mort's desk. She wore a dirty cotton dress that clung to her skinny body and Mort guessed she was around ten years old.

'Me get gin for you, Mahmy,' the trooper said as he came dutifully to attention.

'Very good, Trooper Mudgee,' Mort acknowledged softly, as he gazed at the trembling girl staring with large frightened eyes at the floor. 'You tell no one about the darkie girl you got me tonight, and I promise you will get Corporal Gideon's stripes before the year is out. Tell anyone about this gin, and I promise you I will know and will flog you until there is no skin left on your back. You savvy well?'

Trooper Mudgee nodded. 'Yessa, Mahmy. My word, Trooper Mudgee tell no one 'bout this gin.' He knew well that the *debil debil* on the other side of the desk was more than capable of promoting him to Corporal Gideon's job – or flogging him to death.

'Very good, Trooper. You are dismissed,' Mort said. The trooper saluted, executed a regulation about-turn, and left the office.

When he had gone, Mort rose from behind his desk to go to the frightened girl and, with a strange faraway look in his eyes, he pulled the dress over the terrified girl's head. She knew not to resist, as Trooper Mudgee had told her of the white man's terrible wrath if she did so.

The dress fell to the floor and she stood trembling and naked as he came behind her and ran his hand slowly down her stomach. She winced and attempted to pull away. 'Don't move, slut,' he barked in her ear as tears of pain ran down her face. 'You are nothing,' he said as he used his free hand to unbutton his trousers, allowing them to drop around his ankles.

He stepped out of the trousers then rummaged in the drawer of his desk and found the two articles he required to complete his task. He smiled. The girl's trembling turned to an uncontrollable shaking as he stuffed a rag in her mouth and expertly lashed her wrists with a leather thong. He pushed her roughly face down across the desk and mercifully she did not see him reach for the sword hanging on the wall. Had she known what he was about to do to her she would have fought with every ounce of strength in her tiny body.

Sweat glistened on Mort's face reflecting the fever in his twisted mind as he stared with drooling pleasure at the opening between her legs. The fever was at a pitch and needed quenching!

Her long scream of agony was muffled by the rag thrust deep in her throat, and the sword entered deep inside her.

Sergeant Henry James had never had a trooper desert on him before.

He stood in the scrub staring down at the cause of the trooper's disappearance. Seeing the mutilated state of the young Aboriginal girl's body, sprawled in the red dust not far from the barracks, he could see why Trooper Mudgee had not wanted to face white man's justice.

Corporal Gideon stood behind him a short distance away, holding the reins of their mounts, and spat with disgust. 'Bad bastard, my word, Sar'nt Henry,' he said, reflecting on the horrific wounds to the young girl's gaping and bloodied mouth.

'Looks like he used a knife on her,' Henry said as he squatted and rolled the corpse over, causing a cloud of flies to buzz angrily in their protest at being disturbed. Henry gagged. 'Jesus! Look at that!'

Gideon shook his head at the sight of the mutilations to the girl's vagina. 'Blackfella got a *debil debil* in 'im,' he said sadly.

'Maybe Trooper Mudgee has been around

243

whitefellas too long,' Henry said softly as he spat in the dust. According to Mister Mort, Trooper Mudgee had been the last person to see the girl alive, which made a fairly straightforward case for a warrant to be issued for his arrest.

Henry rose and limped back to Corporal Gideon. 'Get some of the gins at the barracks to come out and do something with the body,' he said as he reached for the reins of his horse. 'You say she was one of the girls taken in the dispersal last year?'

Gideon nodded. 'Gin come from a Maranoa tribe,' he said. 'Got no 'lations here, Sar'nt Henry. Got no one to sing for her.' Henry swung himself into the saddle and cast a last look back at the dead girl who was once again covered in flies.

'No matter. Just give her a decent burial anyway,' he said as they rode away.

Lieutenant Mort was satisfied at the report that his sergeant had submitted on the murder of the Aboriginal girl. It was brief and it clearly identified the murderer as the Aboriginal trooper who had deserted the troop. And why wouldn't he desert, when he had been the one who had dumped the girl's body, on Mort's orders. The stupid man had been drunk when he took the body away, and had not left her in the river for the crocodiles as Mort had directed.

As slow as he was, Trooper Mudgee had been able to put two and two together very quickly when the young girl's body was found by the Aboriginal women from the police barracks. He knew his word against that of a white officer would count for very little in a white man's court of law.

Mort hummed a tuneless melody as he poised the nib of the pen over the half-completed sanitised report on the November dispersal at Glen View. Outside his office, Sergeant James drilled the police troopers on the dusty clearing that was the barracks parade ground. Curious and wide-eyed Aboriginal children mimicked the troopers' actions with sticks used to imitate the police carbines. A thin blue haze of smoke lay in the still hot air from the bushfires that had raged in the hills around Rockhampton. Eventually the clouds over the hills would billow into heavy rain-bearers which would break on the parched and burnt landscape to wash away the smoke and ash. But, for now, the heat was a tangible thing to the sweating troopers.

'*Preesent h'arms!*'

Henry glared along the rank to ensure that the men did not waver as they held the carbines thrust forward and vertical. They stood stone still, staring directly ahead as they had been trained to do, and they waited with muscles aching for the command to 'order arms'. But Sar'nt Henry seemed to be in a trance . . . as if his spirit had deserted him and flown away.

They watched him staring vacantly at the bark hut that was the office of the *debil debil* Mahmy on the far side of the parade ground. Something about the death of the Aboriginal girl nagged the sergeant and he now regretted submitting his report so quickly to Mort.

A strange and illogical suspicion had crept into his thoughts as he drilled the police troopers. It was a stupid suspicion, and he dismissed the foolish notion that his commanding officer might have murdered the girl. After all, Trooper Mudgee had deserted, and that seemed to confirm his guilt.

He shook his head and returned to the present reality of the parade ground. The Aboriginal troopers sighed with relief when he bellowed out the command to order arms.

17

The emu blinked its reptilian eyes and stretched its long neck like a periscope to peer above the sea of tussock grasses. Then the ostrich-like bird took short and hesitant steps towards the strange and curious things wiggling in the hot still air.

Tom Duffy watched the big flightless bird hesitate and bob its head at the black things waving like the thin stems of some decapitated tree.

'Closer,' he hissed softly as he lay concealed among the tussocks of desiccated grass. A short distance away the Aboriginal boy, Young Billy, lay on his back, waggling his legs slowly in the air. Behind Young Billy crouched Wallarie, gripping a spear ready for the kill.

'Closer,' Tom whispered again. As if acknowledging his plea, the inquisitive bird took two more slow steps towards the skinny legs, making small circles in the air. Wallarie rose from the earth and let fly with the long spear which flew true and struck squarely in the emu's broad and feathered body. The stricken bird took only a few tottering steps before crashing into the parched black soil of the plains. Immediately the Aboriginal hunter was on her with his wooden nulla, while carefully avoiding the thrashing legs that ended in bone-hard club-like feet capable of disembowelling a man. The emu died instantly from the blow inflicted by the nulla.

'Bloody beautiful!' Tom cried as he sprang to his feet. 'Wallarie, you old bastard. You did us proud.' The tall warrior grinned at what was obviously praise for his hunting prowess and was joined by Young Billy who strutted with pride at his part in the successful hunt as they conversed excitedly with each other in a language Tom Duffy was attempting to learn. Although his grasp of their dialect was only rudimentary, he did understand the phrase '*your meat*' used by Wallarie. So the boy was of the emu totem, Tom mused, and would have to remember that in the future.

Wallarie spoke to the spirit of the emu and thanked it for providing its body so that they could eat well that night, and he promised the emu spirit that he would carry out the proper rituals when he prepared it for the cooking fire.

He pulled the spear from the emu's body and hoisted the large bird over his shoulders. Its dangling neck flapped as he trudged west to the camp where the remaining survivors from the Nerambura clan were waiting for the hunters to return. Tom followed. The thought of fresh meat to supplement the diet of lizards, yams and nardoo flour cakes they had lived on since leaving Darambal country caused his stomach to growl. He could almost smell the aroma of emu fat sizzling in the hot coals and his mouth watered at the ·thought of the feast they would have that night. As fine a feast as the stuffed goose Aunt Bridget had always prepared for the Duffy family at Christmas.

The recollection of the European celebration seemed so far away now. He had long lost track of the days as he had wandered with the handful of Nerambura survivors on the vast and lonely inland plains of western Queensland.

Not many of the Nerambura clan were left. Only Wallarie, the boy, a young woman he knew as Mondo and an old Aboriginal woman Tom had named Black Biddy. And the two Daramabal elders, Toka and Kondola. In the weeks they had been together, Tom had grown fond of his adopted Nerambura family, who had accepted him without animosity, despite the fact that he was a member of the same race that had slaughtered their people.

As the leader of the tiny clan of survivors, Wallarie had explained to them how Tom might be of the same colour as the white men who had come in the morning with the black police and guns but he was, in fact, of a different tribe to those murdering white men.

Since his flight from the men who had slaughtered Wallarie's people, Tom had burned a dark brown under the relentless sun of the inland plains and, at a distance, he could have passed for one of the people he wandered with. His European clothes had long since gone to tatters, shredded on the prickly scrub that they had traversed as they trekked always in the direction of the setting sun, until the brigalow scrub had eventually given way to a flat, almost treeless blacksoil plain.

The only vestige of the white man's world left to

him were his shorts, fashioned from the tattered trousers, and the heavy leather boots he wore. He had retained his Colt revolver, a flask of powder, a pouch of lead ball and a tiny pouch of percussion caps, and had kept his water canteen and a Bowie knife tucked behind the broad leather belt that held up the remains of his trousers. His hair and beard were matted with animal grease and dirt and, although he had lost some weight on the spartan diet of traditional Aboriginal food, he was still an imposing figure with his broad shoulders and barrel chest.

As the three trudged across the plain of dust and dry grass, Young Billy chattered incessantly with Nerambura words the Irishman did not understand. But the lack of comprehension did not deter the boy in his prattle, as he had attached himself to Tom from the first day of their meeting.

Wallarie was a hunter and warrior without need for the boy's company, and Wallarie preferred to sit with the two old men who had once been respected elders in the Nerambura clan. The three men would chat and gossip around the fire at nights and ignore the boy who craved their company, whereas the big white man did not chase him away when he sought male companionship. Although Mondo would kindly tolerate Billy's company from time to time, there was a barrier between the boy and the young woman as she was no longer a girl.

As they trudged towards the camp in the sparse late afternoon shadows, the Irishman thought back over the events that had led him on the trek with the few survivors of Wallarie's people.

He remembered the day he had buried his father and Old Billy, when he had found their mutilated bodies under the tall tree. The mutilations, he could plainly see, had been inflicted by a sword or bayonet.

He had carefully read the ground as Old Billy had taught him, and he had plainly seen the signs of many horses. He had recognised the imprints of police-issue boots, and the indent marks of chains on the smooth white trunk of the tall tree under which he had found the bodies of the two men. He knew about police manacles and the indent marks on the tree trunk which, coupled with the bruises he found on both men's wrists, made him conclude that his father and Old Billy had been murdered by the police. For what insane reason he did not know. Nor could he speculate on it. But the certain knowledge they had been murdered made him acutely aware that they might attempt to kill him also.

He had scraped out the two shallow graves in the crumbly red soil with his Bowie knife, and buried his father and his old friend side by side, marking the graves with a few stones as a pitiful memorial to their final resting place.

After he had completed the burials, he had grieved for the souls of the two men and he had hoped that his father was with Old Billy in his version of the afterlife, because that meant that he would be able to see his father as one of the many stars of the wide and sparkling black velvet canopy of the heavens.

Tom had noticed a spiralling pillar of smoke rising above the scrub into the cloudless sky, and he'd known it was rising from where he had left the bullock team. A short time earlier, he had heard the faint popping of carbines drift to him on the still air. So the traps had slaughtered the bullocks and burnt the dray. He was now alone in territory where all men were his enemy. He had sat with his back against a tree, cradling a loaded Colt, waiting for the night.

When the night had come the dingo howled to its kind about the places of death and once, during the still hours, Tom thought he had seen the outline of a dark figure in the bush. But the figure was gone in the blink of an eye and did not return. Hallucinations? Maybe . . .

At sunrise, he had gone in search of water, avoiding the slaughter ground where the bodies of the dead Nerambura would be swelled to hideous, bloated, black balloons under the blistering hot sun. He had not lingered in the terrible area but struck out west towards the small range of hills which he could see looming above the brigalow scrub. He had dared not travel east as this might bring him into contact with the men who had murdered his father and Old Billy.

But, as he trekked to the hills, he'd had the uneasy feeling that he was being watched. Were his observers the spirits of the dead? He shuddered superstitiously. Old Billy's belief in the pagan world of the spirits had rubbed off on him more than he cared to admit.

He had been careful to keep the Colt ready just in case the spirits turned out to be of a temporal nature and he had trudged west without any real idea where he was going. All he'd known was that the path west would take him beyond the leases of the squatters and the patrols of the Native Mounted Police. He needed time to gather his thoughts, to plan a way back to the coast where he could seek help in tracking down the killers of his father and Old Billy.

His wandering had drawn him inexorably towards the small and craggy range of hills that was dominated by a single brooding summit of an ancient volcano. When he had reached the base of the hill, he'd found more grisly evidence of the troopers' work. He had presumed that the troopers were responsible until he'd found a spent bullet on the ground. His knowledge of firearms was extensive and he'd known at once it was not a police bullet, but one from a revolver most often used by squatters. He'd found two more that matched the first. So, it had not only been troopers involved in the slaughter. There had been other white men. Probably a squatter and his shepherds, he'd guessed. It had confirmed his suspicion that no white man – or black trooper – could be counted on as a friend in this country.

The hill had seemed to beckon him and the young Irishman had an eerie feeling that the rocks and scrub had a life of their own. Too long listening to Billy, he'd told himself. But, despite his attempts to shake off the strange attraction of the hill, he'd known it was a place where he'd be protected. By whom . . . by what?

Tom had found a well-worn trail. He'd struggled upwards to the peak and, as he'd climbed, he'd become uncomfortably aware that someone . . . or something . . . watched his progress with great interest.

When he'd finally reached the summit, he'd rested to behold a panoramic view over a seemingly endless plain of scrub. He was suddenly overwhelmed with a dark despair that caused him to consider ending his life with a single shot from the Colt.

He'd raised the pistol to his head. Did not the priests forever remind the faithful that suicide guaranteed eternal damnation to their Catholic souls? He'd eased the barrel away. No, suicide was not an option. He had a sacred duty to the soul of his father – and the spirit of Old Billy – to track down their killers. But he was alone and on foot in a land barely explored. And he was possibly being hunted for some insane reason by men he had never met. There was only one thing left that he could do. And laugh he did. A deep booming laugh that had rolled echoing off the hill and into the tough, stunted scrub-choked ravines that hid the wallaby and rock python.

Weary from the climb, he had sat with his back to an outcrop of ancient rock. The sun warmed him and he had fallen into a deep sleep until he was disturbed by a shadow falling across his face.

His eyes had snapped open as he instinctively reached for his gun. The gun was gone! And he'd stared into the smoky eyes of the big warrior who stood over him, examining the gun with an expression of curiosity. Behind the big warrior was a young woman who smiled shyly at him when his gaze settled on her. He could see that the warrior had been wounded recently. Other than the woven human hair belt about his waist he was naked, as was the girl behind him.

'Careful. That thing is loaded and you might just put another hole in yourself,' Tom had said without fear. He sensed that the Darambal warrior meant him no harm. The man could easily have crushed his skull with the nulla he carried while Tom slept, and the fact that he had taken the gun so easily spoke well for the warrior's stealth.

Wallarie had heard Tom's words without understanding them. But he knew the white man had a similar sound to that of the white sorcerer who had saved him from the murderers of the Nerambura people. He hoped Mondo was right in her perception of this white man.

She had watched Tom bury his father and Old Billy, and she had watched him through the night as he grieved by the graves and instinctively sensed that he was a victim like themselves. It was she who had become the spirit of the night that Tom had glimpsed in the dark shadows of the scrub. She had told Wallarie all that she had seen.

'We have the same enemy,' Wallarie said. Tom did not understand the words but he'd understood the gesture of trust when the Aboriginal warrior handed the pistol back to him.

'I don't know who you are, friend,' Tom said, holding out his hand to Wallarie who stared at the Irishman, puzzled by his gesture, 'but, thank you.' The young Irishman had reached out and taken Wallarie's right hand, pumping it twice.

It dawned on the Aboriginal warrior that the handshake was some kind of ritual of the white man, most probably a token of friendship, as he could see that there was no fear or animosity in the grey eyes. He had smiled as he let go Tom's hand

to walk away and Tom knew that he should follow
. . . and follow he did.

As he walked behind Wallarie and the girl, he
noticed her steal shy glances at him. When he had
caught her doing this, he'd flashed back a smile
and she'd giggled as she ducked her head. Her skin
had not been scarred by the totem signs and he
guessed, from what Old Billy had told him about
the rites of the Aboriginal people, that she had yet
to be initiated into the secret rites of womanhood.
Her nubile and naked body was that of a young
girl verging on puberty and he'd surmised that she
was the big warrior's woman. Ah the pity of it, he
thought wistfully. She was a handsome lass in any
man's language.

It had been close to sunset when Wallarie led
them into a small valley concealed by steep cliffs,
and the Irishman had first seen the few survivors of
the Nerambura clan. A young boy stood beside
two old men and an old woman sat cross-legged
beside a small fire.

When they saw him, they rose hesitantly, then
pointed at him chattering in excited voices with
consternation on their dark faces. Wallarie's commanding voice had cut their excited chatter short
and they fell into an apprehensive silence as they
joined them at their camp site.

Tom saw that they all bore the recent scars of
wounds inflicted by the men who had carried out
the dispersal. One of the old men had a scalp
wound and the other a bullet wound in the calf of
his leg.

The Nerambura elder who had been wounded in
the leg had limped when he walked to greet

Wallarie, while the old woman had launched into a tirade that was obviously directed at the presence of the tall white man. Wallarie had delivered a speech that seemed to mollify the old woman, who turned her back on the young warrior and sat down. Mondo joined her and the two women went into a huddle, whispering between themselves.

Suddenly the old woman had stood up and shuffled towards Tom. She then reached down, grabbing him between the legs before he could react. He had winced as she broke into a cackling laugh and said something to the others. The old men too had broken into loud guffaws that racked their thin bodies as they fell about laughing. Mondo smiled shyly and Wallarie had grinned. Tom guessed to his shame that the old woman had established his sex, hidden inside his trousers.

She gave a final yank on his manhood before hobbling away, cackling to herself, and in her wake she had left the young Irishman flushed with embarrassment. He was soon to learn that the Nerambura people had a rich and raunchy sense of humour.

From that day on his fate had been in the hands of the Nerambura survivors, led by the tall warrior. And in time he'd grown to know them for all their individual ways, as much as he had known his own family in Sydney.

Old Biddy was cantankerous and he dared not guess her age. But she must have been older than Old Billy. She would harangue the two elders, and often enough she would receive a blow from a gnarled fist from one of them. But she liked the young white man and would give Tom a choice fat wood grub to eat when the women dug them up around the roots of trees. The grubs were delicious and he'd regretted that he had nothing to give her in return for the choice morsels she brought him. Whenever he tried to thank her with his English words, she would cackle and hobble away shouting to Mondo, which caused the girl to giggle and drop her eyes shyly.

Kondola and Toka had tended to remain aloof from Tom. Kondola was the quieter of the two elders and was a man who wore the scars of many tribal duels on his body as badges of his prowess. He had once been a warrior and hunter of great repute among the Nerambura.

Toka had been known for the craftmanlike weapons he chiselled, and he was one with the spirits of the wood that he carved so expertly with the razor-sharp flints. Tom had noticed that it was Toka who did most of the talking when the two old men sat cross-legged together under the shade of a tree or by the camp fire at night.

Then there was Mondo, who Tom had gleaned from observation was not Wallarie's woman. It was hard to believe that a marriageable woman such as Mondo was not with Wallarie, but the Irishman had not yet learnt of the strict taboo of the Darambal people which banned marriage between persons of the same totem.

Finally there was the boy, Young Billy, who Tom had guessed was probably about nine years of age and desperate – as young boys of his age are – to be recognised as a man worthy of hunting with Wallarie.

Now, as they trudged towards the camp, Tom gazed at the dark clouds tantalisingly low over the dusty plains.

Sometimes the distant rumble of thunder rolled to them, but no rain came. The rains were late and the plains tinder hot and dry to the naked foot. Tom had not seen the signs of the white man for a long time; no telltale ruts left by the wheels of the drays, nor the print of the horse's hoof. He sensed that they were well beyond the established white man's frontier. They still walked in a land in harmony with all that lived upon it. But sadly it was only a matter of time before the plagues of sheep and cattle came to ravage the native grasses and spoil the pristine water holes.

He sighed. Was this the only life he would ever know? To walk forever in the desolate lands beyond the frontier with a people whose fabric of life was as torn as his own? The melancholy lifted from him when he heard the welcoming cackle of Old Biddy praising them for the feast they were bringing into the camp.

Wallarie dropped the big bird beside the fire pit which had been prepared by Biddy. She had an unshakable faith in the warrior's ability and she had, with the help of Mondo, dug a pit with digging sticks. The cooking area was lined with rocks and a few precious tree branches and the aromatic scent of eucalyptus steamed up from the hole.

The two elders sat cross-legged under the shade of a scrawny scrub tree chatting to each other. When they saw the three hunters approaching, they heaved themselves to their skinny legs to hobble over and examine the carcass with admiring prods and pokes. It was a fat bird which would fill hungry bellies this night and there would be meat left over for the next day.

Tom slumped wearily to the ground and stretched his legs while Mondo gave him one of her regular shy looks from where she knelt, pounding the tiny seeds of the native grasses into flour between two rocks. But this time her eyes lingered on him for longer than normal and he was aware of her frank appraisal. She was gaining respect for his ability to keep up with them on the trek towards the place where the sun slept each night.

He returned her smile, which made her think that she should not continue staring at the strange white man any longer or he would think she was being too forward in her interest of him, which was true. But she did not want him to know.

Wallarie prepared the emu for cooking in the pit as Billy hopped around, excitedly, boasting of his own part in the taking of the big bird. With great care, Wallarie placed the stones and earth on top of the emu and while it was cooking, he sat with the elders discussing the events of the day.

There was little for Tom to do so he busied himself with the task of cleaing the Colt revolver while Young Billy squatted beside him, watching with childish curiosity. Each night, Tom checked his supply of ball and percussion caps.

Kondola sat cross-legged under a scraggly bush with Wallarie and Toka. As a boy, Kondola had walked the same route years earlier with his mother and his old eyes were still strong enough to see the signs around them on the plain.

'The Kajana are watching us,' he said, raising the disturbing issue for discussion.

'I know,' Wallarie answered. 'I saw them on the hunt watching us.'

Toka gazed past him to the fire pit. 'We have not gone on their land to hunt. They will leave us alone.' The elder referred to the route that they had taken on their trek west, which was a corridor of neutral territory established between adjoining tribes over countless years. While they remained within the neutral corridor, they would be left unmolested.

'There is little sign of emu or kangaroo for us if we stay on the track into the country of my mother,' Wallarie answered. 'We might starve before we get there.' Both old men nodded. The alternative would be a confrontation with their traditional enemy, the Kajana, should they leave the trail that gave them safe passage. The options were grim. Death by starvation or at the hands of the Kajana.

'The Rainbow Serpent will rise from His lagoon soon,' Toka said optimistically. 'And then there will be plenty of emu and kangaroo for us.' The glum expressions of the other two did not echo his optimism.

'We have plenty of food for now,' Kondola stated as he picked at the earth with a sharp stick. 'The women fetch the nardoo seeds and even a bandicoot for us from time to time. We will not starve for now. But if the rains do not come . . .' his voice trailed away.

Wallarie listened to the opinions of the two old men. As leader of his diminished tribal clan, he

261

would have to make a decision before they became too weak from hunger to hunt. The Kajana were fierce warriors who had raided the Darambal people over many seasons, back to a time no one could remember. Rarely had the Darambal been able to better the Kajana in the inter-tribal skirmishes fought with spear, nulla and boomerang.

Wallarie rose and left the two old men to continue speculating on the future intentions of the Kajana, who dogged them each day, but remained hidden on the vast plain.

When the Rainbow Serpent finally rose from His lagoon, He did not come as a gentle and refreshing rain but as a series of torrential thunderstorms.

Small dry depressions that had snaked across the plains became raging rivers as Tom and the Nerambura huddled together at night for warmth. In the open plains, under the deluge, they disregarded the traditional protocol that separated the men from the women when they slept.

For two days the torrential rains kept them in camp huddling together miserably. More than once they were beset by plagues of deadly snakes that sought the higher ground Wallarie had found to keep them above the rising waters. The unlucky snakes were killed and eaten raw by the wet and hungry survivors. A spiny anteater that had waddled into the camp became food for them. At least they did not have to go far for fresh meat.

On the third day, when the rains eased to a heavy drizzle, Wallarie knew that they must leave. It was not only the law of the Kajana that influenced the warrior's decision. Toka had warned him that the passage to the channel country was by now almost impossible to traverse. The rivers between them and the channel country had mysteriously swelled even when the rains ceased over the black-soil plains. The Nerambura did not know of the tropical monsoon in the north, which filled the catchment areas of the rivers that flowed south, but every year it was the same as the Nerambura elders had come to learn.

The game would now be abundant around the water holes in the traditonal lands of the Nerambura: wild duck, turtle, fish and the flowering of the edible plants. Wallarie had little choice in choosing to return to the lands that had been those of his people back to the Dreamtime. Had not the spirits of the trees, rocks and animals there impregnated the women? Was it not the place where the ancestors lived in the Dreaming? If he were going to die, as was the fate of every living thing, then it was better to do so among the spirits of his own ancestors and not those of strangers.

The Irishman could see the deep contemplation in the face of the warrior as he stared in the direction of the rising sun. The decision to retrace their steps lifted Tom's spirits because he would be returning to the world he had left behind.

By now the Native Mounted Police and their auxiliaries would have given up any search for him and he could make his way back to Rockhampton. From there he would be free to go after the men responsible for his father's murder. But he would be leaving behind the Nerambura family and this thought left him with a guilt that he did not attempt to contemplate.

18

The little paddle-steamer swung into the main channel of the Fitzroy River and puffed up a full head of steam. She had to fight the heavy flow of floodwaters that rushed to the ocean, staining the opal-like sea a dirty brown. The river was awash with debris and the occasional carcass of an animal drifted past, and her captain kept a sharp lookout for the submerged logs that could ram and hole his boat as she slowly manoeuvred her way up the river passing river banks alive with water birds; clumsy looking pelicans, graceful long-legged waders and flocks of gregarious ducks.

The boat bucked the heavy run of water and the very pregnant young woman who gripped the boat's railing watched the normally cumbersome pelicans glide gracefully across the calmer waters near shore. With almost childish joy, she saw them settle and float with their oversized yellow bills tucked into white-feathered breasts.

The thoughts of Kate O'Keefe – née Duffy – were not so much on the wild beauty of the river bank as on the anticipated meeting with her father and brother Tom. What would they look like now?

Tom would be a young man courting the ladies! What would her father think about being a grandfather for the first time? She guessed that they would gape with surprise and express the usual male doubts about a woman as young as herself with such grandiose plans as building a hotel, even with the help of her husband.

The carcass of a wallaby drifted off the portside bow and Kate felt a surge of pity for the unfortunate animal as it bobbed like a balloon in the paddle-steamer's wake. Something thrashed the muddy water and snapped at the bloated body. She gasped and recoiled at the terrible sight of the primeval reptilian head with its gaping mouth and rows of yellowed teeth. It was like something from one of her worst childhood nightmares. The wallaby disappeared as the big estuarial crocodile dragged the dead animal below the muddy waters. Her reaction of horror was observed by the tall man who stood beside her at the rails.

''Gator, ma'am,' he drawled in a deep voice. 'Can't hurt us here.'

She turned to the man who had obviously been aware of her distress. Although she did not know the tall stranger, she had been aware of him when he had joined the paddle-wheeler in Brisbane for the journey north.

She remembered how he had been standing on the Brisbane wharf with a bed-roll slung over his shoulder. He had stood aloof from the other passengers milling around him as they fussed over luggage and bade farewell to friends and family with tears and hugs. There had been something about the man that had attracted her interest then.

Something in the way he stood alone and proud.

He was not handsome in the classical sense and she mused that he was quite old – possibly in his late twenties or early thirties. He had a thick bushy beard and blue eyes that seemed to gaze far beyond the people around him. From his manner of dress, she guessed that he was one of the legendary Kennedy men she had read about in the Sydney journals. The Kennedy men were so named after the sprawling region west of Rockhampton and further north. A wild and untamed territory.

They were the stuff of daydreams of pasty-faced young clerks in dingy Sydney offices who dreamed of an adventurous life riding the sun-drenched mountains and plains of the northern colony. They were the tough, devil-may-care men who lived life without a damn for the morrow, riding with a six-gun on their hip and a stockwhip over their saddle. Yes, the tall stranger who stood alone on the wharf was obviously a Kennedy man, she mused, as he stood with his thumbs tucked in his belt, and at one stage she was embarrassingly caught appraising him. His smouldering blue eyes came alive with a faint trace of a smile as he looked up at her, and she had looked away with a touch of guilt for having been caught staring at him.

Now she was standing only a few feet from the man and she could see a long scar stretching from the corner of his right eye to disappear in his bushy beard. She did not think that the scar detracted from his appearance, but it gave him an interesting and mysterious aura of someone who had seen much danger and adventure in his life. She knew that the tall stranger's accent was that of an

American. She had often heard the soft and melodious twang of that nation's sailors who had ventured to her uncle's hotel in Redfern.

''Gators! Are they the same as crocodiles?' she asked the stranger. His smile was warm and she experienced the sudden and uncomfortable feeling of being scrutinised by the man.

'It's unusual to hear someone call the 'gators by their correct name,' he said. 'I gather you know something about the creatures in this part of the world, Missus . . .?'

Kate could see that he was waiting for her to introduce herself and she felt annoyed at his conceit in assuming she would do so. But he was smiling and his voice had a deep resonance that was also attractive. Her annoyance dissolved under the spell of his natural charm.

'Missus O'Keefe,' she answered with a tilt of her chin and the stranger swept the cabbage-tree hat from his head.

'Luke Tracy, ma'am,' he said. 'I gather the big fella I had the misfortune to play cards with last night was your husband, Mister O'Keefe?' She nodded sadly and turned away to watch the mangrove shore slide past the *Princess Adelaide*.

Ever since their stay-over in Brisbane, Kevin O'Keefe had made a habit of leaving her at nights to gamble. He would return in the early hours of the morning reeking of cheap rum and cheaper perfume. When he had suffered a loss at the card table his mood would be morose and violent, and, although he had never struck her, even in his worst outbursts, she had begun to fear his seething temper.

If he had a good win for the night, he would return to her as a warm and loving man – the Kevin O'Keefe she had fallen in love with and married – not the other man who preferred the company of gamblers and the pretty women they attracted. Kate was relieved when they finally left Brisbane behind and she'd prayed, as they came closer to Rockhampton, that he would begin to realise his responsibilities as a husband and future father.

'Did my husband win much from you, Mister Tracy?' she asked when she returned her attention to the American.

'Not much you can win from a down-and-out prospector, Missus O'Keefe,' he replied with a rueful grin. 'No, I got out before the stakes went too high. 'Bout the only gambling I should stick to is looking for gold.'

She glanced down at his hands. They were strong, with the palms of a man who had known hard physical work all his life. He was a strange mixture, she mused. He was brash yet shy, and she wondered about the women in his life.

'Are you and Mister O'Keefe settling in Rockhampton?' Luke asked politely.

'We are hoping to build a hotel. If not there, somewhere on the coast,' she answered. 'Do you live in Rockhampton, Mister Tracy?'

'Not since the Canoona rush in '58,' he replied. 'It's been almost five years since I was last here. Like thousands of other fools, I came here in '58 only to find out that all the gold was gone long before I arrived. Been that way for me since I left Ballarat in '54. Always seem to be chasing someone else's luck.'

'I was at Ballarat for a little while in '54 with my father and his brother, Frank,' Kate said. 'But I am afraid I was too young to remember much about life there. Father and Uncle Frank were among the more fortunate miners and they were able to purchase a hotel. Except my da decided he was not cut out to be a publican and used some of their good luck to take a bullock dray out bush. My older brother, Tom, went with him.' She paused and backtracked. 'It's the Erin in Sydney. Do you know the Erin, Mister Tracy?'

'Sorry, ma'am, can't say that I had much call to visit Sydney,' he replied, shaking his head.

'Well, my father and brother are now some-where in the Kennedy district with their bullock team,' she added proudly. 'My father was one of the miners who stood at the Eureka Stockade.'

The American turned to stare across the river. 'I was also there when the redcoats came for us,' he said softly, as he remembered the terrible Sunday morning when the British Army and the goldfield police launched their attack on the rebel stockade. 'What name does your father go by, Missus O'Keefe?' he asked.

She did not hold much faith in him knowing her father. Many miners had stood against the British Army that terrible morning of the massacre.

'Patrick Duffy. He was . . .'

'He was with us!' Luke suddenly beamed. 'Big Irishman who had a German mate . . . I just can't think of the German's name . . .'

'Max Braun!' Kate squealed with delight. 'Max works for my Uncle Frank in Sydney.'

'Your father fought beside us . . . the California

Rangers Independent Revolver Brigade . . . I thought the redcoats got him,' Luke said, and his eyes twinkled with pleasure at the news that the big bearded Irishman and the German had escaped the bayonets and swords of the soldiers.

Suddenly Kate was as happy as a little girl as she talked to a man who had not only known her father, but had also stood shoulder to shoulder with him in the fight for the miners' rights at the stockade.

'No, Father and Max escaped,' she said, and immediately thought about the scar that ran in a jagged line below the American's eye. 'Is that where you got your scar?'

He grimaced and touched the edge of the welt and the smile was gone. 'Redcoat bayonet,' he replied bleakly.

For the American there was a haunting memory of a hot summer's dawn in the British colony of Victoria and a time of killing; miner against British redcoat. They had been rebels fighting under the blue and silver flag of the Southern Cross. Men from all nations protesting the injustice of paying taxes to the British Government without representation.

When their complaints fell on the deaf ears of Governor Hotham, the protest had ended in the frustration of armed rebellion. But the military defeat of the rebel miners at Eureka had eventuated in a political victory for them, and their mates had not died in vain that Sunday summer's morning.

As they chatted, Kevin O'Keefe groped his way along the rail looking as ill as he felt. The pungent odour of the mangrove swamps had drifted to where he lay below decks in a world of self-inflicted pain.

He had dragged on his clothes and made his way up to the deck where he knew his wife would be. O'Keefe was annoyed to see her talking to the tall man whom he remembered from the evening before. A Yankee, he thought, with a touch of jealousy for the way his wife was engrossed in her chatter with the tall man. O'Keefe did not like the look of the American. He was a man who was too charming for his own good, he thought irritably. He knew that if he asked Kate what she thought of him she would probably say, 'An interesting man', which he suspected was a woman's way of saying 'attractive'.

Kate saw her husband approaching and broke off the conversation with Luke. Both men greeted each other with a nod and she launched into a discourse on all that had happened prior to her husband's arrival on deck. She told him about the crocodile taking the body of the wallaby and of how this had led to meeting with the American. 'Mister Tracy has lived in Rockhampton before,' she said cheerfully to her surly husband. 'He might be able to tell us something about this part of Queensland.'

Luke eyed O'Keefe with a hint of contempt in his blue eyes and wondered how a man could leave such a pretty and pregnant wife alone at nights. He had noticed how O'Keefe flirted with the ladies when they were playing cards and he felt sorry for Kate. He figured O'Keefe as a ladies' man, one of those men who could never settle with one woman

271

no matter how pretty she was. And he had to admit to himself that the girl was more than just pretty – she was downright beautiful.

'Not much I can tell you about the place,' he drawled. 'When I last saw Rockhampton it was just a few bark huts on the southern side of the river. Friends tell me a few of the diggers from the Canoona settled there and that the town has got pretty much civilised.'

'You have work in Rockhampton, Mister Tracy?' O'Keefe asked as he scratched at a night's growth of dark bristles under his chin.

'No, I plan to push on as soon as I can,' he replied. 'Probably scratch around to set myself up for a grubstake, then head out west.'

'Doing what?' O'Keefe asked bluntly. He was in no mood to be friendly to the American.

'Looking for the big one,' Luke drawled.

'Big one?'

'Yeah. Find a gold strike the world will remember. Like Dunlop and Regan did back in '51 at Ballarat,' Luke replied, with a slightly wistful sigh for the recollection of great events in history.

'Oh, look!' Kate exclaimed. A huge flock of wild ducks rose with a rapid beat of wings from a lagoon adjoining the river and flew towards the flat grass-covered plains interspersed with tea-tree. 'Isn't it beautiful?' she said in an awed voice, as she gazed over the river at the scenery of the hills. Her husband grudgingly admitted that there was beauty in the country, although he would have preferred to be looking over the dirty rooftops of Sydney's mean streets.

'Certainly is handsome country,' Luke echoed for Kate's sake.

'Is the town far away?' she asked, her eyes wide with excitement.

'Not far,' he answered. 'Just a bit up the river.'

'I think then, Kate,' Kevin said as he steered his wife by the elbow away from the American, 'that you and I should go below and prepare ourselves to go ashore. We might see you in Rockhampton some time, Mister Tracy,' he added without conviction.

'Could do, Mister O'Keefe,' Luke replied, tipping his hat politely at Kate. He stared after her as she walked away with her husband. 'It was good making your acquaintance, Missus O'Keefe. I hope all goes well for you.' Luke had seen something in her eyes that had worried him. He had seen the same thing before in other places and other times in the north. He wondered if O'Keefe knew his wife was a very sick woman. She had the beginnings of the fever. Still, Missus O'Keefe was not his concern. She had a husband to look after her, he thought, as he shrugged and turned to stare at the ragged range of forest-covered hills.

A drifting log slammed into the bow of the little paddle-steamer but she took the knock and ploughed on. Soon the frontier township of Rockhampton came into view as Luke had promised Kate it would.

A colourful crowd of frontier people thronged the river bank for the arrival of the *Princess Adelaide*. Bearded Kennedy men flirted with the few single women who came ashore and prosperous

273

landowners vied for immigrants to work as shepherds on their leases.

Women seeking work were eagerly snapped up as domestic help for the families who could afford them, and busy customs men worked dutifully to ensure that taxes were extracted for goods shipped between the colonies, while the Royal Mail was dispatched to Rockhampton's post office to supply news-hungry citizens with precious letters from 'home'. A handful of Aboriginals, wearing ragged and discarded European clothing, watched through rheumy eyes the new wave of white invaders disembarking.

Kevin and Kate came ashore amid the bustle and the first impression Kate had of Rockhampton was the stifling heat which hit her like the opening of a furnace door. Heavy clothes, that were fashionable in the cooler climes of Sydney, were inappropriate for the town located just above the Tropic of Capricorn.

O'Keefe went back to ensure their luggage was safely unloaded, and when Kate moved away from the cooling breezes wafting off the water she suddenly felt very ill.

A man was frying a steak on a long-handled shovel over a makeshift fire on the river bank and the overpowering queasy smell of the meat frying in its own fat made her feel even more nauseous. She moved away from the frying steak, then experienced an unpleasant unbalanced feeling, as if she were walking on air. The shimmer of the early morning sun off the river seemed to melt red before her eyes then explode into a shower of black sparks. She felt disembodied and sensed herself falling down a long tunnel towards a voice. Stong hands caught her as she sank to the ground in a swooning faint.

Luke had decided to follow the O'Keefes off the jetty. It was apparent that her husband did not know the signs of fever or he would not have left his wife alone. The American prospector had kept close to Kate when her husband left her to supervise the unloading of their luggage, and he was close enough to catch her when he saw her sway.

'O'Keefe! Over here!' he bellowed and O'Keefe pushed his way through a small crowd of people who had congregated around Luke holding the pregnant young woman in his arms. The women in the gathered throng clucked sympathetically and the men voiced the need to get the young woman to a doctor. Luke lowered Kate gently to the ground and held her head in his lap.

'What happened?' Kevin frantically asked when he reached his wife's side.

'She's got the fever,' Luke answered. 'We have to get her somewhere out of the sun and fetch a doctor quick.'

Kate was just barely conscious and she mumbled incoherently that she would be well . . . if she could take her clothes off and sit under a waterfall. Luke could see as well as hear that she was already delirious.

'You get a dray,' he ordered brusquely, 'so we can find a doctor.' O'Keefe seemed lost to know what to do, but the tough American was decisive and he rightly felt that it was better that he remained with Kate. At least *he* had recognised she was sick.

O'Keefe moved away as a sympathetic group of bearded bushmen helped carry Kate along the river bank. They found the horse dray whose driver had been press-ganged into service with threats and bribes from O'Keefe.

Gently the men laid Kate in the rear of the dray. O'Keefe sat in the back to cradle his wife's head in his lap while Luke took a seat beside the driver. She tried to mumble reassurances to her anxious husband but a bilious attack suddenly came on and she turned her head to vomit.

'Does Solomon Cohen still have a store here?' Luke asked the grizzled dray driver, who scratched at his straggly beard and stared at the young woman being sick in his dray.

'Youse mean the Jew?' he asked.

'Yeah, that's him,' Luke answered.

'Yep. You want to go there?' the driver asked obtusely.

'That's why I asked,' Luke growled.

The driver gave the order to walk on and the big draughthorse lurched forward. The dray rumbled along a deeply rutted street bouncing the passengers uncomfortably around in the back. On either side of the primitive road were the stumps of trees and gangs of men sweating profusely as they rooted them out of the ground. Luke gave only a cursory glance at the new shops and houses that had sprung up since he was last in Rockhampton. His primary concern was to get the very ill young woman to a place where she could receive medical help.

When the dray reached Solomon's store, Luke was surprised at how his slab and bark hut had turned into a reasonably neat shop of sawn timber walls and shingle roof. The shop even had a verandah at the front from which various articles, such as pots and pans, dangled on display from hooks and it had also expanded to include living quarters with glass windows. It was obvious that Solomon Cohen had done well since the gold rush.

The Jewish storekeeper was sweeping the verandah with a straw broom when the dray came to a stop in front of his store. He paused in his work and immediately recognised Luke, who had leapt from the dray to the roadway. Solomon broke into a broad welcoming smile as he dropped the broom and threw open his arms to the tall American striding towards him.

'Mister Tracy, my friend,' he said joyfully, hugging the American. 'So you would be visiting me and Judith. Oi, what a wonderful surprise to see you again.' Solomon was clean-shaven and wore spectacles on the tip of his nose. He was dressed in an expensive pair of suit trousers and wore a waistcoat over a clean white shirt. He was short in stature and, at thirty-nine years of age, the little man bore the scars of the lash of the convict cat-o'-nine-tails.

In his youth, his crime had been forging bank notes in London and his sentence had been transportation to the colony of New South Wales. But forging was not the only skill he had and he soon proved a valuable asset to the penal authorities with his ability to keep meticulous records for less-learned men. Upon his release as a ticket-of-leave man, he was joined by Judith, who had defied her family to follow the one she loved across the ocean to the land so far away. With her natural astuteness in business dealings, they were soon able to build their future out of a loan long repaid and business was obviously booming as Luke could see.

With suitable sounds of sympathy, Solomon directed the two men to lift Kate down from the dray and carry her into the store to a stack of soft cloth bales. Solomon disappeared into the back and when Kate was comfortably settled, Luke took her husband aside to quietly suggest that he should go back with the dray and fetch a doctor. The dray driver would know where to find one in town and then he should go to the jetty to supervise the unloading of the luggage they had brought with them while the doctor saw to Kate.

Kevin hesitated, torn between being with his wife, and watching over all that they had brought with them from the south. Judith Cohen appeared from the rear of the store and with quiet competence assessed the situation. She ordered the men to take Kate through to a spare room and Kevin decided that his young wife was in good hands. He left with the dray to carry out the American's instructions.

Judith quietly issued orders to Luke and Solomon; cold water to be fetched, clean sheets and privacy for Kate. The woman, who moved carefully around her patient, had dark flashing eyes reflecting her ancestral Spanish blood. Her long raven hair was tied back from her olive-complexioned face, which always seemed to be in a state of perpetual calm. Although she was not pretty, she had a strange beauty in the tranquillity of her spirit that seemed to envelop those around her.

Judith was eight years younger than Solomon and the pair were an unlikely couple at first appearance – Judith tall and serious, Solomon short and jolly – but Luke knew the odd-matched couple loved each other with a passion present in their subtle glances and discreet touches.

When Judith had settled Kate behind the store, Solomon guided Luke from the room. In the store, they could wait for the doctor. Surrounded by every possible item required on the Australian frontier, Luke sat on a barrel of molasses while Solomon poured him a tumbler of thick raw rum. There was a lot of catching up to do between the two men as it had been four years since their last meeting.

'And how is it that you are not married, my friend,' Solomon inquired lightly, 'with a family around you?'

'I was,' Luke replied sadly as he sipped gingerly at the raw spirit and Solomon knew he should not pursue the question. He tactfully changed the subject.

'And such a pretty girl as you have brought to us, Luke,' he said. 'I gather she is the wife of the young man you sent to get the doctor.'

'Yeah. His name is O'Keefe,' Luke said, staring into his glass of rum. 'The young woman is the daughter of a man I once knew back at Ballarat. Good fellow. Big Irishman who fought with us at the stockade. I thought he was a dead man when I last saw him. He was holding off a parcel of redcoats with a pike then. Missus O'Keefe says he is working round these parts as a teamster.'

'What is his name?' Solomon asked. 'I know most of the teamsters in the Kennedy.'

'Patrick Duffy,' Luke answered, as he tried another sip of the raw spirit.

The little storekeeper looked sharply at his friend. 'There was a Patrick Duffy . . . a bullocky . . . who was speared by the blacks out at Glen View late last year. A big fellow who had a brother who owns a pub in Sydney,' he said as he frowned and leaned forward with his face almost in Luke's. 'The young lady obviously does not know of her father's death.'

'Jesus, no. I don't think she does,' Luke said, shaking his head sadly. This was sure not the time to tell her.

19

The wedge-tailed eagle spread its massive expanse of wings and was swept skywards on a thermal. Perched on a rocky outcrop, Tom Duffy watched the great bird seemingly hover in the high blue yonder.

Then suddenly the undisputed master of the Australian skies plummeted towards the scrub in a lethally precise dive and Tom was vaguely aware that he was holding his breath as the bird disappeared from his vision below the summit of the hill.

Tom loved the big eagles as they had always represented a majestic independence and freedom to the young teamster as he plodded the dusty plains of outback Australia. The eagles were not constrained by flooded rivers and creeks as were the bullockies. Nor by the steep slopes of hills and thick, sometimes impenetrable scrub. They could go where they wished with no natural enemies to fear.

Tom was once again inside the European frontier. But had Wallarie's decision to return to his traditional lands been wise? They were in mortal danger of discovery as the distant smoke of the white man's fires crept closer each day.

On their trek to their traditional lands, the Nerambura had come across the ever-increasing signs of the presence of the white man: tracks of horses and sheep, empty meat tins and the ashes of fireplaces made by the roving shepherds as they moved their flocks to fresher pastures to graze.

But even more disturbing than the signs that the white man left were the footprints of Aboriginals now working for the squatter. Wallarie knew that they were of a black people from another place who posed a deadly threat to the Nerambura survivors, as they had the perceptive eyes the white man lacked. Eyes to see the Nerambura moving through the lands that had once been their traditional home.

When they had finally reached Darambal country, the two elders had gone to the sacred cave to daub the paintings of the final act in the broken existence of the Nerambura clan. They had painted, with mixtures of coloured earths and resin as adhesive, the figure of a man on a horse and the stick figures of black people standing defiantly with spears poised. But it was more of a wistful representation of how the old men would have liked to remember the last moments of their people. Death had come so quickly that few warriors had been able to resist the terrible onslaught.

Tom had not been invited to attend the ceremony of the wall painting as he was not an initiated Nerambura warrior, although the old men had come to respect him. His standing had increased proportionally to the Nerambura language he had mastered and he was now included in their camp fire discussions.

Tom stretched and yawned as he scratched at his unkempt beard and thought fleetingly of being in a barber's chair back in Rockhampton. But the pleasant thought was rudely interrupted when he gazed out over the plains below. The smoke was closer this time, he mused. It was just a tiny grey wisp rising as a lazy thin column above the brigalow scrub. The fire of white men boiling a billy for a mug of tea.

The previous day the smoke had been further north and Tom had felt very uneasy. If the unknown white men continued on their present course, then there was a chance that they might stumble on the camp site.

The cooking fire made him think about a pannikin of salted beef stew, hot damper bread straight out of the ashes, washed down with a mug of sweet black tea. He felt his stomach growl at the memory of the European food he had once taken for granted. Or a leg of mutton roasting in a camp oven with . . .

Just the slightest rustle . . . not even a noise.

Hunting with Wallarie had honed Tom's instincts and he had quickly learnt to interpret nature as a living storyteller. There was definitely someone behind him. A tiny lizard basking on a rock suddenly skittered away. Something, or some-one, had frightened the lizard and Tom felt the tip of the spear prick his neck. 'Too slow,' came the teasing chuckle. 'You are too slow.'

Tom grinned. 'I knew it was you,' he replied in

his broken Nerambura. 'Otherwise I would have turned and shot you, Wallarie.'

The warrior squatted beside him and peered out at the smoke on the horizon. 'I would not have given you time to turn around. I would have put my spear through your neck before you moved,' he said as he continued the friendly banter. 'As I will all white men I meet,' he added bitterly. His visit to the sacred cave had brought home to him the enormous loss that he had suffered in his lifetime; the eligible young women who would be wives were gone, as were the elders to pass on the stories to the young people. Who would he tell the stories to when he was an elder? All gone.

He glanced sideways thoughtfully at his friend and remembered that the same white men who had slaughtered his people had also killed Tom's father. The recollection reminded the Darambal warrior that they were bound together by the death of those most important in their lives.

On the next sunset, they would join the others at the camp site and bring meat. The women would now be digging for the edible tubers and gathering the grass seeds to be pounded into flour for cakes. But for now he was content to squat and gaze out at the rich green patches of grass that sprouted in the red soil of the Darambal lands.

The smoke, rising from the camp fire that Tom had observed, eddied in a willy-willy and the little tornado-like column of air caused the two Glen View shepherds standing at the camp fire's edge to duck their heads. They wheezed and coughed from the smoke and ash thrown up in their faces, while a younger shepherd squatting on his haunches nearby quickly snatched at his newly acquired cabbage-tree hat to prevent the wind carrying it away.

When the willy-willy had whirled like a dervish dancer off into the scrub to wreak mischief elsewhere, the shepherd known as Monkey rubbed the grit and smoke from his eyes. He blinked and snarled at the older man beside him. 'Don't piss on the fire, you bastard.'

'Why not, Monkey?' Old Jimmy answered with a malicious grin. 'We got to put it out before we leave.' The men eyed each other like two dogs manoeuvring for dominance.

'Cos me mug o' tea is just there,' Monkey snarled. 'An' I know where your bum-fuckin' dick has been. I don' want you pissing in me tea with it.' His angry retort brought a howl of laughter from the younger shepherd who sat nearby watching the two older men locked head to head.

The laughing shepherd had joined the Glen View workers early in the New Year after stepping off an immigrant ship from England. And when Young Joe had arrived at Glen View, he was soon regaled with tales of Old Jimmy's preference for young Aboriginal boys. He had studiously avoided the old shepherd's company ever since.

The drunken bragging of the shepherds about their 'battle' with the Nerambura myalls had enthralled the impressionable young man. He had listened with rapt attention to the highly coloured tales of the courageous stand that they made against the massed ranks of painted warriors, who came in screaming and blood-curdling waves against them.

The rape of the helpless Aboriginal girls was described in explicit detail to a wide-eyed and gaping young lad from England. How exciting that day must have been, he had thought with wonder. If only he could have the chance to stand heroically beside his comrades and fend off the savages. What stories he could recount when he was an old man sitting by a warm fire with his grandchildren gathered about his feet.

When they had finished the midday meal of cold boiled mutton and damper bread, the shepherds were careful to ensure that they had extinguished the fire by scattering earth on the glowing coals. Flood and fire seemed to be the two perennials of life in the Outback. Floods, fires, snakes . . . and myalls. All could kill you if you got careless.

Monkey swung himself into the saddle of his horse and shaded his eyes as he squinted at the hill through the early afternoon haze.

'Never know, Young Joe, we might even find a nice set o' bones for you to fuck,' he said with a grin and a wink. 'Or Old Jimmy can look after you tonight when you go to sleep.'

Jimmy leered at the boy with drool at the corner of his mouth and Young Joe shuddered. Monkey's joke did not strike him as funny but the tough frontier shepherds were always ready to kid a 'new chum', as recently arrived immigrants from the Old Country were patronisingly called by the native-born.

Young Joe patted the butt of the carbine nestled in the saddle scabbard on his horse. ''E tries an' 'e gits this up 'is arse.' He was not smiling and his growled threat brought forth howls of laughter from the two older shepherds. Still laughing, they went in search of lost sheep.

They would not find the lost sheep but what they would find would forever change the life of Tom Duffy.

The crow flapped its shimmering black wings with insolent disregard for the two men approaching the mutilated body. It hopped a few paces before flapping into the sky with a lazy cawing protest at having been interrupted in its grisly work of tearing strips of bloody flesh from the body that lay huddled in a grotesque parody of final resistance to the killers. A clenched fist was still holding a digging stick. And eye sockets were plucked empty by a sharp and cruel beak.

The wallaby's plump body fell from Wallarie's shoulders.

Tom swore as he slipped the Colt from the holster and both men scanned the sea of scrub for warning signs of an ambush. But the killers were long gone and Tom stumbled towards the body in the grass. 'Dear God! How could you let this happen?' he wailed as he fell to his knees beside the bullet-riddled body of Old Biddy, who lay on her back staring at the cloudless blue sky through empty eye sockets. 'Ah Biddy, you old trouble-maker. Did you put up a fight before they slew you?' he choked back as he lifted and stroked the old woman's wrinkled and leathery hand in his. The same frail hand that had caused him the embarrassment of their first meeting, and the same hand that had touched his when

287

she gave him the choice witchetty grubs.

No longer would there be the sound of her cackling laugh around the camp fire nor her incessant nagging of the men for their supposed lack of manhood. He felt tears sting his eyes. How could a harmless old woman be a threat to the might of the white man's pastoral empires? Had not the dispersal been enough? There were no answers in the hush of the brigalow scrub and he shook his head for the senseless cruelty of the men who had brought obscene death to the harmless old woman. Her bullet-riddled body bore testimony to wanton and senseless murder by men who saw her as nothing more than a target for their marksmanship.

Wallarie touched him on the shoulder and Tom let her hand slip from his as he rose stiffly with tears of rage in his eyes. No words were said as he stumbled after Wallarie to the site that the Nerambura survivors had used as a camp.

Tom gagged and Wallarie shifted his eyes uncertainly from the grisly object spreadeagled over the now cold ashes of the camp fire. Such was Wallarie's confusion at the white man's need to inflict unnecessary pain that his mind told him what he was seeing could not be possible. He turned and walked to the edge of the scrub where he squatted and threw dust on his head, wailing a song for the spirits of the dead.

Tom broke into an involuntary sweat as he pieced together the last tortured moments of old Toka's life. His skinny and frail body had been held by hands and feet over the fire while he was roasted slowly across the red-hot coals. The pain must have been terrible as the fire seared firstly at the flesh, then burnt away what little body fat he had, before muscle and sinew were charred into black leathery strings.

When he was finally able to bring himself to stare into the old Aboriginal's eyes, Tom saw the last tortured moments of his life. Death had not come quickly. Only the pain had come instantly as he had screamed and struggled at the hands of his sadistic torturers in a futile attempt to escape the excruciating and lingering pain.

It was not the sickness of horror that came over Tom, but a rage of hate for the people who had committed this unspeakable act. He tore his gaze from the old Aboriginal and walked slowly over to Wallarie, who squatted in the dust chanting the death song. The Irishman's grey eyes blazed with a fire that only blood could put out.

'We have to find the others,' he snarled and trembled in his rage. 'And we have to find the . . .' He was lost for a description to give a name to the bestial creatures who had committed the crime and, although Tom had spoken in English, Wallarie sensed what his friend had said to him.

The boy and Kondola were missing but Tom held out little hope of finding them alive after what he had just seen. He could only hope their deaths had not been as obscene as that of Toka. But he held out some hope that Mondo might have been taken alive for the value she provided to the men's sexual needs, although he also knew that there was a good chance they would kill her when they were finished using her body.

There were at least three men responsible for the deaths of Biddy and Toka, from the three sets of different bootprints he had been able to distinguish around the fireplace.

Gripping his spears Wallarie rose from the ground and skirted the cold fireplace refusing by tradition to look upon the dead. Nor did he want to remain in this hideous place of death, as the ground was now taboo to him.

Tom did not need to ask where he was going. He knew. And it did not take long before they picked up the trail of the three horses and the two sets of footprints mixed with the horses' tracks. Even Tom could recognise the prints as those belonging to the young boy and Mondo. At least Mondo and Young Billy were alive.

But neither man could find any trace of Kondola's tracks outside the camp area. Inside, they were clearly displayed where he had gone about his daily routine, and it was eerie for Tom to see Wallarie puzzled. Had the wily old warrior covered his own tracks? Was his skill at evading his enemies better than Wallarie's skills at tracking?

'Kondola?' Tom asked and Wallarie shook his head with a frown. Had the old man turned into a spirit to escape his hunters?

Tom guessed the sun would set in five hours and he knew that the daylight was vital to keep visual contact with the trail of the three men on horses with their two prisoners. He had no doubts as to what he would do when he caught up with the murderers of his Nerambura family.

The two men dodged the prickly low branches of the scrub as they loped through the bush. Tom was careful not to trip on the ankle-high termite nests that littered the scrub as they alternately jogged and walked. He suspected that Wallarie only broke into a walk for his benefit and his stamina amazed him. The warrior was all muscle and no excess weight as he jogged, trailing his three long spears and a stone axe. Tom carried his battered water canteen, Bowie knife and big Colt pistol with its powder flask and pouch for lead ball.

As Wallarie jogged, he used his spears as a balance to his loping stride and Tom felt awkward in comparison with the pistol holster and water canteen flapping at his side.

Just on sundown Wallarie slowed to a walk and gave the hunter's signal to rest. Tom slumped to the ground, praying self-indulgently that they would remain there and sleep for the night. He took long gulps of water from his canteen which he passed to Wallarie, who only took short sips. He had barely time to stretch and ease his stiffening muscles when Wallarie hissed softly in the lengthening shadows, 'We go on. I know where the white men will be camped.'

Wallarie knew that all creatures in the bush sought a source of water at sundown and the only water ahead was a creek he knew they could reach before dawn.

Tom groaned as he struggled to his feet and gave Wallarie a grim smile to show that he was ready to follow him once again. At least they were walking and not running this time, he consoled himself, as he followed the broad-shouldered and naked black warrior ahead of him.

But even the walk was exhausting as they followed a star trail in the sky. To fight his tiredness, Tom forced himself to remember Biddy's and Toka's mutilated bodies. And there was also just the slightest chance that they might find Young Billy and Mondo alive if they kept up the killing pace.

It was just on dawn of the relentless trek that the two men were rewarded with the distant sound of snoring and the glow of a dying camp fire reflected off the trunks of coolabah trees by a muddy water hole. The last of the stars were leaving the night sky when the two men silently stalked the unsuspecting shepherds, sleeping soundly by the warm glow of the camp fire.

The attack was sudden and swift.

Wallarie's spear hissed across the short distance between hunter and hunted and the barbed point caught Young Joe in the throat as he rose groggily from under his blanket. He had been disturbed by the whinny of his horse hobbled nearby as it sniffed the presence of the two strangers approaching.

The spear exited from the back of the young shepherd's neck, cutting short any attempt to scream, and Young Joe had finally faced a myall warrior as he had dreamed he might one day, except that he never saw the warrior who had killed him.

In his death throes, he thrashed about wrapped in his blanket and crashed into Monkey beside him. Blood spattered the old shepherd's face and when Monkey opened his eyes to curse irritably, he looked directly into the terrified and bulging eyes of the young shepherd, clutching at the long hard-wood shaft projecting from his neck.

Monkey screamed in his terror. He grappled desperately for his revolver but froze when he stared up into the smoky grey eyes of the strange myall standing over him with a Colt levelled at his head. Turning, the Glen View shepherd saw the terrible spectre of a giant black man bring his stone axe down with a bone-crushing crunch on Young Joe's head.

'You have only two ways of dying,' the strange myall said to Monkey, and it was only when he spoke that Monkey realised the myall was a white man. 'Either I kill you in a relatively civilised manner, or I let my black friend over there kill you. And he's not civilised.'

Monkey felt a wet warmth spreading in his crotch and Tom wrinkled his nose at the foul stench when the terrified man's bowels also voided.

'Please, matey, please . . .' he pleaded as he grovelled towards Tom. 'Please don't kill me. I ain't done nothin' to no one in me life. I never done wrong by . . .'

Tom swung the barrel of his pistol at the side of the man's face and the stricken shepherd howled his distress, falling back with blood oozing from a long slash over his eyes. He lay curled in a foetal position, whining like a whipped dog. 'Please don't hurt me, matey.'

'Last time. Do you want a quick death? Or a slow death?' Tom snarled. 'Or maybe we might even give you the same death you gave the old man over the fire. Eye for an eye, the Bible says,' he added casually and Monkey snapped out of his fear-induced stupor to seriously consider his limited options. He knew there was something worse than death. It was how you died.

'You, matey. I want you to do it,' he croaked as his crazed eyes flicked from side to side, searching for any slim hope of escape. But the gun, inches from his head, and the hard grey eyes of the man staring at him with such malevolence, let him know that pleading for his life was an utter waste of time. He held no hope whatsoever that he would live to see the sun set that day and was gradually resigning himself to death at the hands of the white man.

'Well, now that you know that your death will be "civilised" I have some conditions,' Tom said in a flat voice as Monkey slowly came out of his foetal position and sat up, shaking uncontrollably. 'Then if you answer truthfully, I will honour the deal we have made between us.'

Tom squatted on his haunches and dropped the barrel of the pistol away from the trembling shepherd while Wallarie stood a couple of paces behind him, deceptively relaxed with the deadly stone axe swinging casually at his side.

'Firstly, I would like to know where the third man, who was with you before last night, is now?' he asked quietly as he fixed the shepherd's eyes with his own.

'Old Jimmy, the bastard!' Monkey flared with a touch of ironic anger. 'He took the gin and shot through just after we put our 'eads down las' night.'

'Where was he taking her?'

'Probably up to the Balaclava 'omestead,'
Monkey answered carefully as he was acutely
aware that Wallarie was standing behind him with
the axe he had used to crush Young Joe's skull.
'The boss there, Mister Bostock, was looking for a
nice bit of black velvet. An' the gin wasn't a bad
looker for a darkie,' he said tactlessly, but Tom
kept his temper at the shepherd's crude and
demeaning reference to Mondo.

'What do you know about a dispersal here-
abouts?' he asked. 'Maybe half a year ago?'

Monkey hesitated. He was going to die anyway.

'I was there,' he mumbled and looked down at
the ground. He dared not stare into the cold grey
eyes of the man opposite him.

'Do you remember if you saw a big white man
with an old Aboriginal offsider at any time?'

Monkey's narrow eyes widened with a sudden
recognition. 'You is Tom Duffy. I knows of you,'
he exclaimed as he lifted his eyes to stare at Tom,
who was startled by the man's knowledge of his
identity. How could he know who he was? 'Mister
Macintosh told us youse might be alive,' Monkey
continued to babble. 'He said there was a bonus in
the pay for anyone who found you, even . . .' he
hesitated as he realised what he was about to say.

'Even if what?' Tom prompted.

'. . . Even if youse was dead,' Monkey replied in
a hoarse whisper.

'Jesus!' Tom blasphemed. He had been right to
avoid all white men in the area after the dispersal.
'You mean I might have had an "accident". Why?'
he asked. 'Why was I to be killed?'

'Because youse was helping the darkies the day

295

we were tryin' to clear them off the land,' Monkey replied. 'The day when Mister Angus was killed by them.'

Tom was puzzled by the shepherd's explanation that he had been accused of aiding Wallarie's people. Especially since he had been judged and sentenced by a man he had never met.

Monkey volunteered an explanation. 'Your ol' man 'ad us bailed up after some darkie speared Mister Angus,' he said. 'An' your ol' man gave the darkie the chance to get away. When we left to go after 'im, the darkies speared yer old man, and the nigger 'e was with.'

'You are lying,' Tom snarled. 'My father was killed by a white man.'

Monkey appeared genuinely confused at his accusation, as the big Irish teamster had been in the custody of Lieutenant Mort when the shepherds had last seen him alive. Had not the trap reported that he had left the two prisoners chained to a tree and when he returned to pick them up he found them speared to death? There was furtive talk around the Glen View camp fires that Mort had actually done away with the Irishman. But few were stupid enough to voice their suspicions, not even when drunk, as it was not wise to bring the wrath of Mister Macintosh down on you.

'If 'e was killed by a white man then it was by the trap, Mort,' Monkey ventured.

'Mort who?'

'Lieutenant Morrison Mort of the Native Mounted Police,' Monkey replied. 'That's who probably killed yer old man.'

Tom noticed that something had attracted

Wallarie's attention, as he had suddenly tensed then walked warily towards a stand of coolabah trees not far from the water hole where he froze, staring into the trees. As Tom watched Wallarie, he knew he had found something and he had a sick feeling he knew what it was. Monkey followed Tom's gaze to where Wallarie stood among the coolabah trees and began to tremble violently.

Tom swung on him with a burning murderous rage and the shepherd instinctively cringed away. 'I don't want to go over there,' Tom said in a cold and flat voice. 'Because if I go over there, I will probably break my word and hand you over to my black friend who appears to be a bit upset at what he is looking at right now. So I am going to ask you. Is it what I think it is?'

Monkey had trouble finding enough moisture in his mouth to talk.

''E's found the darkie boy,' he croaked. 'Old Jimmy decided to cut off 'is cock and balls after he fucked 'im last night.'

'While he was alive?' Tom asked with a deadly and controlled fury.

The shepherd could only nod his head as he stared bleakly at the ground between his feet.

'I want you to look at me,' Tom said quietly. 'I want my eyes to be the last thing you see before I send you to burn in hell. Look at me, you murdering bastard.'

Slowly Monkey raised his head and tried to avert the grey eyes staring at him. But the voice was soft and lulling, almost hypnotic, and the last thing he remembered was that the young man's eyes were like the big Irishman's eyes that had

297

bailed them up the day of the dispersal. Monkey was hardly aware of the sound of the gun or the lead bullet that tore a hole through his forehead as he pitched backwards into the warm ashes of the camp fire. His death was merciful as Tom had promised.

When Tom Duffy pulled the trigger, he had crossed from his own world and irreversibly into Wallarie's. For now he was truly a white myall and one with the avenging spirit of the sacred hill of the Nerambura.

He no longer cared for the white race he had been born into. His people were now the people of the plain, of the brigalow scrub and the wild places beyond the frontier. The personal execution of the Macintosh shepherd had sealed forever any hope of a way back to the white man's world of towns and cities, and the company of his family in Sydney.

20

The Aboriginal shepherd respectfully skirted the two bodies, as he had a deeply superstitious fear of the dead. He squatted reluctantly beside the body of young Joseph Blake.

The body was bloated and decomposing and Young Joe's hands still grasped the shaft of the spear in his throat. A few feet away, partially in the ash remains of the long-dead fire, Monkey lay on his back in a similar condition. Plump white maggots crawled and writhed in the orifices of his body.

'Tell me, Goondallie, how many men?' Donald Macintosh stood behind the Aboriginal shepherd staring at the bodies of his two employees.

Goondallie rose and searched about the ground with his eyes.

'Two fella, boss. One whitefella, one blackfella. Funny business,' he frowned, scratching his head, and Donald turned to the two young shepherds who had stood well back from the bodies with sickly expressions on their pale faces. They were 'new chums' recently from the shores of England. For them, the lurid stories recounted in the bars of the frontier hotels and grog shanties about sudden death at the hands of treacherous ambushing myalls had taken on a terrible reality. They stared with morbid fascination at the bloated bodies of Monkey and Young Joe, who they had laughed and drunk with only days earlier.

'Ross, Graham. Get down and bury them,' Donald snapped angrily as he walked over to his horse to get a water canteen.

The putrefying smell of the bodies left an unpleasant copper-like taste in his mouth and he spat the first mouthful of water onto the ground. Monkey had been clearly shot in the head. At first he had made the presumption that one of the blacks had somehow got hold of Monkey's gun and used it to kill him. But from Goondallie's more learned observations, it appeared that a white man might have used the gun.

'Get the spear out of Young Joe before you bury him. I want to have a look at it,' he called to Goondallie, who acknowledged his boss with a wave before going about his primitive and grisly operation with a sharp knife.

While Goondallie cut carefully around the spear, the shepherds scraped two shallow graves in the crumbly soil with a shovel. They dug the graves immediately beside the corpses. That way they only had to roll the repulsive remains of the dead men into the holes and not lift them.

Donald had mounted the search for the shepherds when Old Jimmy had returned home alone to the Glen View homestead days earlier and was evasive about why Monkey and Young Joe were not with him. He was, however, clearly worried that the two men he had left at the water hole had not returned to the homestead and he was able to lead Donald and the three shepherds back to the last camp site he had shared with his companions.

Now Old Jimmy sat astride his horse well back from his two former and very dead companions, wavering between guilt for having left them to meet their violent deaths alone and extreme relief that he had not been with them.

Donald noticed the old shepherd hanging back and bellowed, 'Get over here, you sodomising bastard, and tell me what happened. Or I will shoot you off that horse, so help me, God.'

Old Jimmy reluctantly kicked his horse forward and eased himself down out of the saddle to stand contritely before his boss. He had trouble looking Donald in the face. He shifted from one foot to the other, displaying his extreme nervousness to the man towering over him.

'Why aren't you lying dead with them?' Donald roared angrily. 'Tell me the bloody truth or I swear I will shoot you right now.'

Old Jimmy picked at a sore on his lip and mumbled. 'We caught a young gin south of here and Monkey there says I should take her up to Balaclava to Mister Bostock,' he lied. 'Mister Bostock said he needed a darkie girl around the house.'

'Yes, Bill would,' Donald reflected sarcastically. 'How much did he pay you for the gin?' he demanded angrily.

'A fiver, Mister Macintosh. That's all,' Jimmy answered truthfully. He knew that there was no

301

sense in lying about the price. Bostock and Macintosh were neighbours who occasionally visited each other.

'How is it that Monkey let you take the girl when I know damn well that he would have done so himself had he thought of the idea,' the Scot demanded. He glanced back at the two shepherds sweating under the hot sun with bandannas around their faces to stifle the stench as they scraped out two graves.

'He was goin' to cut the gin's throat for a bit of fun before we left the water hole in the mornin',' Jimmy explained. 'But I figured I may as well make some money off 'er. It was a shame to waste 'er like that. An' besides, he and Young Joe had a good time with her, before I rode out. That's all, Mister Macintosh. On me mother's grave, that's all.'

Donald glared at him for an uncomfortably long time while the old shepherd shuffled his feet nervously like a dog expecting a beating from his master. His years under the lash of a penal system had taught him to cower in the face of angry authority. 'I don't understand,' Donald finally said as he pondered on the fates of his two dead shepherds. 'How could they have been taken so easily, by the looks of things, by just two men?'

Jimmy brightened because he had the answer and felt volunteering the information might ingratiate him with his boss.

'We were out 'ere a week and never saw a sign of any darkies until a few days back when we came across a couple of old darkie men. We caught one of 'em, but the other got away. Just seemed to disappear into thin air. Anyway, we had 'im, a crazy old gin attacks us with a digging stick. So we shot her. We had a look around after we . . .' he paused in his narrative of the events.

'Go on. I don't particularly care how your devious minds would have found ways to amuse yourselves with some old blackfella's death,' Donald said with a shrug of his shoulders.

'Well, we only found the young gin and a boy later on,' Jimmy continued. 'Figured they must have been the only Nerambura left after we dispersed 'em back in November. There was no sign of any young darkie men so we figured we were pretty safe. Didn't keep watch at nights.'

'And it got Monkey and Young Joe killed,' Donald said bitterly. He dismissed the shepherd with a growl of contempt. Jimmy scuttled back to his horse which had wandered a few yards away to graze. Donald wiped the sweat from his forehead with his hat and walked over to the shade of a tree to wait for Goondallie to finish his grisly task.

The shepherds paused to swig from their water canteens as Goondallie broke off the barbed end of the spear. He was careful not to scratch himself as he also had been taught the trick of plunging spears into the carcasses of animals that had died from snake bite. Death from such a scratch was a lingering and painful way to cross into the spirit world of the Dreaming.

He scrutinised the end of the spear and frowned.

He was shaking his head as he walked across to the squatter sitting on a log, puffing at his briar pipe.

'This fella spear all same spear kill Mister Angus, Boss,' Goondallie said as he gingerly turned over the barbed head in his hand. 'Same blackfella kill Mister Joe, kill Mister Angus.'

The Aboriginal's observation struck Donald with a cold chill as he had surmised that the death of the two Macintosh shepherds was down to some white renegade who had lived with the blacks. But this was a whisper of a spectre rising from the depths of the brigalow scrub to haunt him.

'*Duffy!*'

The name came to his lips as a strangled whisper. The Aboriginal shepherd looked questioningly at his boss. He knew fear when he saw it. And what he saw on his boss's face was pure fear.

Donald stared out to the brigalow scrub, baking under the hot sun, as if he expected to see a white man suddenly materialise, brandishing a gun and screaming ancient Celtic curses on him and his family. And standing beside the terrible apparition of the big Irishman, a tall warrior, with spear and boomerang, grinning at him.

Enid had mentioned in a letter the problems she was having in Sydney with another son of the dead Irish teamster. Of how his beloved daughter had become infatuated with the dead man's son. A terrible coincidence across time and space. Or was it some kind of myall curse on his family? He rose to his feet and banged the pipe savagely against the trunk of a tree.

'Hurry up and get those men in the ground,' he roared. 'Just throw some dirt on their faces. We will give them a proper Christian burial later. Then get on your horses and get back to Glen View.' The shepherds exchanged surprised looks. Something had agitated the boss in a big way.

Donald was already on his horse and galloping off before the two shepherds had covered the dead men in the shallow graves. They cast about with fearful looks. Maybe the darkies were watching them even now and were stalking them. They left the bodies unburied, as they did not want to be alone in the bush with their overactive imaginations.

Donald rode hard.

Although Duffy and the black killer had a few days' start, they were on foot. He knew this from finding the dead shepherds' horses still in their hobbles, grazing less than a mile away from the water hole. At the camp site, he had noticed that the dead men's guns and food were gone. But the horses had not been taken because they would be too easily tracked by his Aboriginal employees.

Duffy and the black killer were smart. Even Goondallie admitted to losing their trail not far from the camp. *But not smart enough.* Donald had a good idea where the two men would have gone, as Old Jimmy would have left a clear trail to track all the way to Balaclava station.

Now it was only a matter of rounding up an armed party from Glen View and going after them. If Duffy was with the black killer, then he would be shot down for the murderer he was. At least now he did not have to show 'accidental death' in an inquiry by the authorities. Duffy was now a murderer of white men. A common criminal.

* * *

It took a half day of hard riding to reach Balaclava station.

When Donald rode in with his party of armed shepherds, he was met by an angry Bill Bostock.

'Donald, I am going to horsewhip that damned man of yours for bringing that infernal gin here,' he raged as he stomped around the dusty yard in front of the tin and bark hut that was his homestead. 'The damned gin has brought nothing but trouble to Balaclava and all my blackfellas have gone walkabout on me. Seems the last couple of nights they were scared off by some wild myall out there in the scrub. They say he has powerful magic and those damned worthless blacks of mine even helped the girl escape last night. Appears the myall's name is Wallarie and he threatened to come in the night and cut their throats if they didn't help.'

Donald rubbed his forehead. He had a bad headache brought on by the hard ride and anxious thoughts that Duffy and the black killer he now knew was called Wallarie might evade him. He eased himself from his saddle stiffly. 'Fortunately for Jimmy's hide, I left him back at Glen View,' Donald said in a tired voice and reached for his water canteen. But he gave the water a second thought. 'Bill, you wouldn't have any real scotch, would ye?'

The English squatter nodded. 'Inside the hut. I have a feeling your ride here has something to do with the gin,' he said sympathetically.

'I don't hold out much hope of you ever finding her,' Donald replied pessimistically. But he knew Mort might have more luck. It was only a matter

306

of sending a rider to Rockhampton to tell the policeman the news of the confirmed existence of Tom Duffy. And that Duffy and the myall murderer of Angus were well and truly alive and travelling together with a darkie girl they had been able to spirit away from the Balaclava run. He trudged after Bostock towards the bark hut while his men dismounted to seek the scant shade under the verandah of the crudely built homestead.

Old Jimmy sat with his back against a gnarled gum tree under the midday sun. Flies buzzed their irritating song around his head and he swatted list-lessly at them. He dozed as he guarded his sheep with their heads bent, chomping at the luscious green shoots that would soon enough wither and die as the ground dried out.

His sheepdog, a border collie crossed with some breed from Rockhampton, dozed at his feet with her long nose on her paws keeping him company in his banishment to the furthermost part of the lease. His punishment was of little concern to him, as Donald Macintosh had let him keep the five pounds Bill Bostock had given him for the young Aboriginal girl, and he had already spent the money on a good supply of rum to help him pass the time.

Old Jimmy's throbbing head felt fuzzy from the bottle of raw spirits he had drunk the night before. Drinking was the only option available to kill the reality of his existence. The loneliness and bore-dom had driven more than one shepherd mad or to suicide. But at least he no longer had to fear the long spears of the Darambal tribesmen who had once roamed the territory. Their dispersal had finalised forever their existence as a threat to the Macintosh flocks and it was not likely that the murderers of Young Joe and Monkey would hang around the district with the Native Mounted Police assured to ride in search of them.

The dog pricked its ears and its nose came off its paws. Old Jimmy continued to doze until he heard the low warning growl from the dog, which stood tensely staring past the flock of sheep into the shimmering haze of the still bush. Old Jimmy snapped from his lethargy and blinked. She had detected something out in the bush that only her keen senses would notice and he pushed himself stiffly to his feet, reaching for the old Baker rifle that lay loaded at his side.

The dog exploded with barks as the black figure rose from the tussock grass on the furthest side of the sheep. The frightened shepherd raised the rifle to his shoulder but made the fatal mistake of snapping off his shot without aiming at the naked Aboriginal, who was taunting him with shouts and gesticulations. The heavy lead ball whined off into the bush, smacking into the leaves of a low shrub an arm's length from the warrior, who turned and displayed his naked buttocks to the terrified shepherd, who was now holding a useless rifle.

From the corner of his eye, Jimmy was shocked to see a big, bearded white man, almost as naked as the Aboriginal warrior, rise from the grass to point a brace of revolvers at him. But he recognised the Aboriginal girl who stood behind the big white man, as she was the one he had forced to walk to the Balaclava station behind his horse with a rope around her neck.

The dog snarled and made a valiant attack on the stranger, but a volley of shots brought her down and she lay quivering on the earth as her life bled away. Tom regretted killing the dog but the courageous animal would have died for her useless master anyway.

Jimmy knew he had no hope of reloading the cumbersome rifle. He had known fear many times in his life but this was a fear absolute in the futility he felt for his hopeless situation. He realised that he was at the total mercy of the man with the twin revolvers levelled on him. The rifle slipped from his nerveless fingers and he felt his bowels void.

'You ... you ...' Jimmy's toothless mouth opened and closed like that of a fish gasping out of water. For a second, he had a flashing recollection of a young Aboriginal boy screaming in agony, and he drooled like an imbecile because he knew God had sent an avenging angel to punish him for his wickedness. He watched with horror as the white man raised one of the pistols and the blast of the big Colt echoed in the hushed silence of the bush. Jimmy screamed and rolled on the earth, clutching at his bloody and mangled groin.

'An eye for an eye, the Bible tells us Christians,' the Irishman said softly as he watched the old shepherd writhe on the ground with a bloody stain spreading at the front of his baggy trousers.

'Oh, God, help me,' the shepherd screamed, oblivious to everything except his agonising pain. 'Kill me. For God's sake shoot me,' he begged, when he looked up at the man standing over him.

But all he saw were pitiless eyes staring down.

'God will kill you in His own good time,' Tom said as he slipped one of the revolvers behind the leather belt around his waist. 'Before He does, He will want you to pray for forgiveness for what you did to those poor bloody myalls a few days ago,' he said as he squatted beside the shepherd. 'You are fortunate that I have given you some time on earth to repent before you pass into the next world. Do not waste your time begging me for mercy because I do not have the power . . . or inclination . . . to give you the forgiveness which you crave.'

Then Tom stood and walked away from the shepherd, who alternately moaned and blubbered as he lay on the ground, clutching the mangled remains of his manhood. Tom walked over to Wallarie, who stood impassively watching the dying shepherd. 'I will teach you many things about the white man's ways, Wallarie,' he said as he held up the gun that he had used to shoot Old Jimmy. 'How to use one of these and how to ride the best and fastest horses we take from the bloody squatters. I will teach you a lot about the ways that have destroyed your people.'

The tall warrior listened to the words without understanding their meaning, but he understood what he saw in his white brother's face. He nodded and glanced at Mondo, who stood trembling. Was the white man an evil spirit? Mondo wondered. Or part of the powerful magic of the sacred hill? She cared not for the answer as she knew, with the certainty of a woman, that she would never leave this white man.

*   *   *

Two weeks later the shepherd taking supplies to Old Jimmy found the remains of his body. Donald Macintosh was informed of the discovery and Goondallie confirmed that the shepherd's death was the work of the same two men who had killed Monkey and Young Joe.

The employees at Glen View avoided their boss for two days as he drank himself into bouts of insane rage, ranting about evil myall spirits. They would hear his Gaelic curses shouted from the bark hut of his residence in the night, and wonder if he had gone mad. But none dared inquire, as their boss was in such a rage that he threatened to shoot anything that came within range of his drunken fury.

After a week, Donald Macintosh emerged pale and haggard to resume control of the Glen View run. His Garden of Eden had a serpent in it. A deadly serpent with a name . . . *Duffy!*

21

Sergeant Henry James followed the old bushman through the thick tangle of mangroves and swore profusely whenever he slipped on the exposed roots, causing tiny mud crabs to scuttle for safety as he lumbered towards them. Corporal Gideon followed as agile as a cat as he scrambled through the saltwater swamp after him.

As the three men emerged at the edge of the lagoon, the old bushman cast about with keen and wary eyes. He had a healthy respect for the big saltwater crocs that lurked in the lagoon waiting patiently for the careless to enter their domain.

'She'd be over there,' he said, pointing to a body half submerged under the overhang of the mangroves. 'Yep, never lose me bearings whether on water or on land. Me and Harry found her this morning. Surprised the 'gators haven't got her by now.'

Henry took the lead and sloshed through the warm shallows towards the body. When he came close he could see that it was that of a young Aboriginal girl. He bent over her as she drifted face down. He gingerly rolled her over and what he found did not surprise him. The numerous wounds showed that she had died a slow and painful death almost identical to the other two Aboriginal girls that he and Corporal Gideon had found murdered near Rockhampton.

When the second body of an Aboriginal girl had been reported to him by the frightened tribesmen living at the squalid Old Tree shanty settlement, he had discounted Trooper Mudgee as his prime suspect. The former Aboriginal trooper had been reported killed in a fight over a tribal woman outside Port Denison only a few weeks after the first murder. He could not have killed the second girl.

The water lapped warm around Henry's legs, washing away some of the glutinous mud that had caked his knee-length boots, and Gideon gave his boss a knowing look. It was their third body and in all cases the wounds were similar. Alone each wound was not fatal, but in combination the wounds would drain the life slowly from the victim.

The tough sergeant could feel no emotion at the sight of the mutilated body. He had seen so many on the frontier as a police sergeant in the Native Mounted Police. His only real emotion was that of puzzlement.

He understood what motivated men to kill under most circumstances, but he could not understand why this particular killer had a need to single out Aboriginal girls and torture them to death in an almost ritualistic way. Why Aboriginal girls? he asked himself and provided his own answer. Because they were easy victims! Who cared if a few darkie women got killed? Not the white police. But he also realised that the colour of the girl's skin might not be vital to the killer's twisted and perverted mind. Given the opportunity he might go after a white girl.

The significance of the gender of the victim, rather than just race, gave Henry the best ammunition to persuade Mort to treat the matter seriously.

'Thought I'd best report the matter to you blokes rather than the Rockhampton traps,' the grizzled old bushman said as he bent to get a better look at the wounds on the Aboriginal girl's body. 'Figure you blokes do all the blackfella stuff.' He was fascinated by the mutilation to the girl's mouth and vagina. 'Bloody myalls never done this,' he growled. 'Or if'n they did, there's a bad 'un roaming around out there. Myalls don't do this sort of thing. They might sneak up an' brain you with one of them clubs of theirs, but they don't do nothin' like this.'

Henry silently agreed with the old man. This was most probably the work of a deranged white man. A man capable of going beyond just killing Aboriginal girls. 'You know this gin?' he asked Gideon.

'No, Sar'nt Henry,' he replied, shaking his head. 'She not one of the gins from the barracks.'

Henry stood and stretched his leg as the old pain ached at the joint of his knee like fire.

'See'd her floating when we was out in the punt this morning,' the old man volunteered. 'Never would have worried about it until I see'd where she had them wounds when we rolled her over. I think you got a real bad 'un on your hands, Sergeant.

Might only be a matter of time before he goes after a white girl.'

Henry thanked the old bushman for his help and the man spat in the lagoon. The sight of the brutal wounds had left a sour taste in his mouth. He had learnt to respect the tribesmen whom he had encountered in his journeys and who, on more than one occasion, had saved his life with their unstinting generosity and kindness. But times had changed and he blamed the newcomers from down south for upsetting the trust that had existed between black and white. He picked his own way back through the mangroves leaving the two police with the corpse of the Aboriginal girl.

Henry bent and washed his hands in a mixture of sand and salt water.

'The other two gins were from the barracks,' he said as he wiped his hands dry on the side of his trouser legs. 'Is one of the troopers doing this, Gideon?'

The Aboriginal trooper shook his head. 'No, Sar'nt Henry. I would know if one of the boys was doin' this.' But there were frightening rumours among the women around the barracks. And none of the native police at the barracks were foolish enough to express what was being said. Not even to Sar'nt Henry.

Henry made a futile effort to wipe away the glue-like mud from his sleeve, but it stuck tenaciously. 'I want you to start asking questions around the barracks when the boys return from the patrol,' he said. 'I want you to find out more about the two girls we found like this. If you think you have found something, tell me immediately.'

He sighed and reflected angrily on his commanding officer's lack of concern. Admittedly there was little Mort could do for now. He had taken the Mounted Police on a patrol after some white man and an Aboriginal who had been reported by Donald Macintosh as suspects in the murder of two of his shepherds. Not that the finding of the two murdered Aboriginal girls earlier had caused Mort much interest anyway. Niggers killing niggers was of no real concern to white law. But Henry was not convinced it was a case of an Aboriginal killing the young girls.

And it was the odd thought that had occurred to him that day on the parade ground, after he had filed his report on the first murdered girl, that returned to him now. He shook his head and muttered, 'No. Not possible,' as he prepared once again to do battle with the maze of mangroves.

It was almost sunset and the air was cooling noticeably as the Mounted Police rode wearily into the Rockhampton police barracks. Horses' heads drooped and sweaty foam slathered their flanks. They had been pushed hard for the last sixty miles and the riders slouched in their saddles, covered in dust.

Excited women and children thronged to meet their men returning from the patrol and the barracks echoed with happy laughter as wide-eyed children scampered around the long legs of the horses.

The troopers filed to the saddling yard with Lieutenant Mort in the lead. Henry presented a salute at the gateway which Mort barely acknowledged. He was in a bad humour as he slid from his big roan.

'No good, sir?' Henry asked.

'No bloody good, Sergeant James,' Mort replied sourly as he brushed himself down and turned to yell at one of the Aboriginal troopers. 'Get those bloody gins away from the yards, Trooper. And make sure you take care of my horse or you will be in for a taste of the cat.' He was frustrated and this made him dangerously angry. The unlucky trooper obeyed immediately. He knew what the cat-o'-nine-tails felt like on his back.

Henry fell into step beside Mort as they strode towards his quarters.

'Did you get any tracks on them at all?' Henry asked with professional interest. Mort had not told him much about the patrol's purpose, other than it was on the request of Donald Macintosh of the Glen View run. All that Henry knew was that one of the suspects was a white man by the name of Tom Duffy. And the other, known as Wallarie, was the probable killer of Angus Macintosh. It appeared that both wanted men had teamed up in a dangerous combination of black cunning and white know-how, according to Mort's opinion.

'Not a damned trace,' he snarled. 'The bloody colony is just too big and we need more police up here. Those bloody politicians in Brisbane haven't a clue of our problems. Why don't they get off their fat arses and come up here to see for themselves?'

For once Henry sympathised with Mort about not having enough men to police the frontier. But the politicians were reluctant to increase the numbers of Aboriginal police as the city journalists hounded them with questions about the actual methods used in the dispersals. The politicians publicly condemned the tactics used to maintain the Queen's peace on the frontier, but at the same time they privately told the Native Mounted Police to continue their good work.

It was a no-win situation for the troopers and only the powerful influence of the squatters in Parliament kept the Mounted Police a viable force. But not all squatters supported the Mounted Police. Some flatly refused to allow the patrols to come onto their properties and they openly accused the police of stirring up trouble among the peaceful tribes.

When they reached the bark shack that served as an office for Mort, Henry chose to broach the subject he knew his commanding officer did not want to hear.

'Sir, while you were gone, Corporal Gideon and I found another darkie girl murdered.'

Mort sat with an audible sigh on the step of the verandah to his office. He was stiff, sore and tired from the hard ride. 'Help me get these boots off, Sergeant,' he said as if he had not heard Henry, who gripped the boot and gave a sharp tug, pulling it off.

'Sir, I think we have a serious problem around here. I think the man might go after a white girl,' Henry persisted stubbornly and Mort rubbed at his foot, ignoring his sergeant.

'Who won the sprint between Purcell and Jenkins?' he asked on a completely different tack.

'Little Boy Purcell. He gave Harry Jenkins a real

hiding this time,' Henry replied as he referred to the outcome of the long-awaited rematch between the local footrace hero, Harry Jenkins, and the out-of-town challenger, Willie Purcell. The race had attracted a lot of attention in the town and large amounts of money had changed hands on the outcome.

'Ah! Good. I had a fiver on Purcell,' Mort said, smiling for the first time since his arrival back at the barracks. 'Knew Jenkins was not up to it. About these killings, Sergeant James. If you ask me some deranged nigger is doing us all a favour and the more of those nigger women he kills, the less of their kind to breed in the future. So we don't trouble ourselves about him unless he steps out of line and goes after a white woman. Forget the matter and get on with running the barracks. That is all, Sergeant James,' Mort said bluntly, making it plain that he was dismissing him.

Henry stepped back smartly and saluted his commanding officer. Wait until he went after a white woman. How many more black women would have to die before something was done? He seethed as he limped away from the verandah. What occurred during a dispersal was unpalatable enough, but outside a dispersal the unlawful killing of any person – white or black – was a crime.

'*Corporal Gideon!*' he bellowed and his command was loud enough to cause a flock of white cockatoos to rise from a nearby tree and circle overhead, screeching their protests at having their rest disturbed.

'Sar'nt!'

'Over here . . . Now!'

Gideon doubled over and came stiffly to attention.

'You have anything for me about the deaths of those three gins?' Henry scowled.

'No, Sar'nt Henry,' Gideon replied as he remained at attention. 'The boys jus' got back.' Henry stared past his corporal to the troopers unsaddling their mounts and walking the weary sweating horses around the saddling yard to cool them down.

'Yes. You're right. Sorry, Corporal Gideon. You will need to talk to them tonight,' he said wearily, as he realised that his frustrating conversation with Mort had manifested itself in the way he had spoken to Gideon.

'Soon as they get some tucker, I will talk to the boys, Sar'nt Henry,' Gideon offered.

Henry dismissed him and rubbed his forehead as the white cockatoos swirled in a graceful arc to alight in a tree on the far side of the parade ground. It was not an Aboriginal killing the girls. It was a white man. He was sure of that now. Unless one of the myalls had learned the worst of the white man's nature. But where to start?

Mort had remained on the verandah and watched his sergeant talking to Corporal Gideon and he wondered what they were discussing. He was a troubled and paranoid man who had failed to find the killer of Angus Macintosh. But, worse still, he had failed to find Tom Duffy, who was a man who could cause him a lot of trouble if questions were raised concerning the death of Patrick Duffy and his nigger.

So far it appeared that Corporal Gideon had not said anything to Sergeant James about the incident in the scrub when Duffy had bailed them up. But it was only a matter of time.

He hurled a boot at a mangy dog that had skulked from the direction of the native troopers' quarters on the scent of a bitch. The boot found its target and the dog yelped with pain as it scurried away with its tail between its legs.

'Damned niggers and whores!' he screamed savagely. 'Worse than stray dogs!'

Someone had to die . . . And very soon!

'*Tom?*'

Judith felt an unexplainable chill and superstitiously glanced over her shoulder.

Kate was between two worlds: one of brilliant light and the living, the other a dark world of eternal shadows. Judith watched Kate toss feverishly as she sat beside the bed and mopped her forehead with a cool damp cloth. The young woman suddenly ceased her feverish restlessness and lay very still with an expression of awe and peace lighting her gaunt, fevered face. Two weeks of nursing Kate had not prepared Judith for the events that had suddenly changed in the fever.

Kate began to speak calmly to a presence in the room.

'*Father has gone, Katie. You will not see him in our world,*' the vision of Tom said to her.

'*Am I dead, Tom?*' she heard herself asking her brother.

'*No, darlin' Kate, you are alive but you must fight. Don't give in. I cannot tell you why it is you*' *who must live, except that you have been chosen by powers I do not understand. They have chosen you as a part in a great plan.'*

'Are you alive, Tom?'

'*Yes. I am asleep in a place of wilderness. And as I sleep, I think of you and Michael.*'

'*How was Da taken from us? Where does his body rest?*'

But Tom was gone before he could answer. He had left Kate as mysteriously as he had arrived to stand by her bed and speak to her. In his place, the vague and beautiful oval shape of a face hovered over Kate and a gentle hand stroked her hair. Kate felt the coolness of a damp cloth on her forehead. It was soothing and she drifted into another world of darkness with no memory of the past.

Judith felt her skin creep as a reaction to the unknown entity that had left the room. She rose and left Kate to sleep and closed the door quietly behind her as she joined her husband and Luke in the tiny dining room, just big enough to accommodate a table and four chairs. The Cohens did not have many guests and the room was adequate for their needs.

'How is she?' Solomon asked his wife.

'She sleeps,' she replied wearily as she sat down heavily in a chair. 'But it is still a fevered sleep.' The long hours of tending the sick girl had taken a toll on her strength. But Judith did not complain and it did not matter that the girl was a stranger. All that mattered was that she was her responsibility. 'She was talking to someone called Tom about her father's death.'

'Did you tell her about her father's death?'

Solomon asked with a frown, as they had agreed that she was not to be told until she was well and strong enough to cope with the tragic news.

'No, Solomon,' his wife replied irritably. 'But I think she knows in ways that we would not understand.'

'She must have overheard us talking about Mister Duffy,' Solomon commented, dismissing the matter.

Judith did not argue with her husband, as she did not expect him to understand things beyond the physical world men lived in. A man was too busy doing practical things to stop and listen to the disembodied voices that whispered in the dark. She excused herself to go to the adjacent kitchen and soon returned to the dining room with three plates of vegetable and chicken stew. The delicious aroma of herbs and chicken made Luke's mouth water.

'Ah, but she spoils you, Luke,' Solomon lamented. 'She never cooks me her chicken.'

Judith sat and placed a platter of oven-fresh bread at the centre of the table.

'I do make you this meal, at least twice a year,' she said gently, rebuking her husband. Solomon prepared to call blessings on the meal they were about to eat.

'So, Luke, how is your plan to go north faring?' Solomon asked as he poured a glass of red wine for him. 'Do you have the money for the horses?'

'Not enough for two horses,' Luke replied as he chewed a tender portion of chicken. 'I will need at least one packhorse for what I have in mind. Maybe another month of work and I will be able to head out west.'

'I can lend you the money,' Solomon offered. 'It's the least I can do for all your help you gave us when we first came here. I can afford it.'

'Thank you, Sol,' Luke replied gratefully. 'But in my business I can't promise results, so I will decline your generous offer.'

'I have faith in you, my friend. If you say this colony has much gold to be found, then I think it will be you who will find it. And then, when you are a very wealthy man, you can pay me back ... with interest, of course.' Both men laughed at his self-deprecating reference to the supposed usury tradition of his European relatives. Luke knew full well that Solomon had no intention of charging him interest.

'Well, your faith in me is good enough,' Luke said. 'I'll get by. I've got work and you know I don't need much to get by on in my life.'

As the two men carried on a banter over the table, Judith cast a glance at the clock ticking on the wall. It was late and, as usual, Kevin O'Keefe was away in town. She felt anger welling in her breast. O'Keefe went out every night to gamble and drink in the hotels and grog shops, while his pretty young wife hovered close to death. He would return in the early hours of the morning and sleep until late in the shed at the back of the store.

Once she had taken him to task about staying with his wife more often and he mumbled something about not being able to handle other people's sickness. In a cold rage, she had walked away from him. She knew the kind of man O'Keefe was and wondered why Kate had married him. Granted he was charming and handsome, but he was also a man who had no idea of responsibility to others. A selfish man who always put his own needs before those who loved him.

And she had heard the disturbing rumours that she had prayed were false, for the sake of the pregnant young woman who lay critically ill in bed.

'That cursed man,' she suddenly exploded and both men gawked at her in surprise.

'Who?' Solomon asked blankly.

'Mister O'Keefe,' Judith replied bitterly. 'He should be by the side of that poor girl and not out every night drinking and gambling,' she snapped.

'O'Keefe doesn't deserve her,' Luke growled. 'She's just a girl.'

'She is not a girl, Luke,' Judith said, savaging his patronising comment. 'She is expecting a child and that makes her a woman.'

'Well, what I meant is that she is very young to have all those big ideas,' he replied feebly.

'And how old were you in '49 when you were on the California goldfields?' Judith snorted derisively.

'Er, sixteen, I think. But I was all grown up by then,' he protested weakly. 'Kathleen O'Keefe is only a girl.'

'And you think having a baby is less hard than digging for gold?' Judith snorted. 'You men have a lot to learn about life.' Her face was flushed with anger.

'Not me, Judith,' Solomon said, gently attempting to steer his wife away from her emotional attack on their friend. 'I have you to tell me.' He could clearly see that his wife was venting her spleen on the wrong person and Judith softened as she realised that she was attacking a man who had suffered personal tragedy not unlike the drama being played out in the room behind the store. Although Luke did not speak of the loss of his own young wife and child, she had heard the tragic story from others.

The American prospector had met Jane in Brisbane. She had been a pretty young girl of eighteen and by nineteen she had become Luke's wife and mother to their daughter. But both mother and baby daughter had died of typhoid fever before she turned twenty.

Devastated by the loss, the American had gone bush and had only re-emerged in the last year to face civilisation. The frontier was not a place where much was secret. Stories travelled with the teamsters, mailmen, drifters and merchants and gossip was recounted to avid news-starved listeners in the grog shanties along the tracks and in the hotel bars of the frontier towns. It had been in the store that a travelling merchant out of Brisbane had told Judith the tragic story about Luke.

When the meal was over and Judith had cleared the table, Solomon pushed his chair out to fetch the box of cigars he kept for special occasions. He was standing with the cigar box in his hand when they heard the hammering on the front door of the store.

'Mister Cohen, are you in there?' the voice bellowed. 'Mister Cohen, I have to talk to you.'

Luke rose from the table as he cast Solomon a questioning look.

'That is Mister Wilson,' Solomon said,

answering the American's unspoken question. 'He has the Traveller's Rest Hotel in town.'

'You want me to come with you?' Luke offered. 'Sounds like a heap of trouble.'

Solomon shook his head. 'No. I know Mister Wilson,' he replied. 'He is no trouble.'

Luke resumed his seat at the table opposite Judith as Solomon left the dining room. They sat silently listening to the murmur of voices coming to them from the verandah. They could hear Wilson's voice raised in hysterical anger until the conversation ceased and they heard Solomon walking up the verandah back into the house. He was ashen-faced when he entered the dining room.

'Something has happened to Mister O'Keefe,' Judith said when she saw the troubled expression on her husband's face. He sat down heavily in his chair and poured himself a glass of wine which he swallowed in one long gulp.

'Something has happened to Mister O'Keefe all right,' he replied bitterly as he wiped his mouth with the back of his hand. 'He has run off with Mister Wilson's wife and she took the day's takings from the hotel when she left.'

'Goddamned son of a bitch,' Luke swore. 'God damn the man to hell!'

But it was Judith who responded to the news in a way that took both men by complete surprise.

'Good! I am glad he has gone away from her,' she said quietly. 'I hope she will never see the man again. Kate will do more with her life without him. I feel that she is destined for things beyond our understanding. Only God knows what He has in store for her.'

Solomon did not doubt that his wife was right, as he had long learned to trust her intuition. She was rarely wrong.

In the early hours of the following morning, Kate went into premature labour. Her cries of pain brought both Judith and Solomon to her bedside. In her agony, she had called for her absent husband.

Judith sat with her while Solomon went to fetch the midwife and the baby boy was born into the Cohen home two hours later. But the midwife shook her head sadly, and, before the first rays of the Queensland sun had crept over the town of Rockhampton, the infant died in Kate's arms.

Neither Solomon nor his wife could bring themselves to tell the distraught young woman that her husband had deserted her with another man's wife. That she would learn in time.

22

The earth had sprouted a scraggly cover of dry and brittle grass over the tiny grave and a spray of wildflowers lay against the headstone, etched with the simple words: Michael O'Keefe, born and died March, 1863.

Kate stood alone beside the small mound where her baby lay under the Queensland soil and prayed silently as she brushed away the pestering flies from her face.

It had been over twelve weeks since the baby's death and she had taken that long to fully recuperate from the debilitating fever. Little Michael O'Keefe. Oh how I miss you. You had such a fine life ahead of you. If only . . . The tears streamed down her pretty but gaunt face. At least his little soul would not be an anonymous entity in heaven. Michael was the name she had chosen for her son. A strong name, not unlike her brother's character. Now he was lost to the family as were Tom and her father. How could so much tragedy be visited on them like some awful Dark Angel? Why was God doing this terrible thing to the Duffy family?

The sun was losing its sting as the shadows of

the late afternoon crept over the cemetery. A low dust haze on the distant horizon took on the softness of a mauve filter. She dabbed at her tears with a handkerchief, knowing that there was nothing else she could do for her baby, and she walked slowly down the dusty and gently sloping hill to Luke Tracy who was standing patiently with his arms folded, smoking an evil-smelling cheroot by the buggy.

From a distance she was struck by his boyish appearance. It was not like the first impression of the tough and independent Kennedy man she first remembered standing on the wharf at Brisbane. For a fleeting moment she had an urge to throw her arms around him and hold him to her breast for being the gentle and wise person that he was. It had been he who had brought her the spray of wildflowers and suggested she take them to the grave of her baby. And he had been able to make her laugh when she thought it was not possible to do so. In so many ways, the American reminded her of her brother Michael. He was tough when he had to be, but he was also tender, funny and intelligent when she was in his company.

It had been his friends, the Cohens, who had nursed her through the deadly fever and always he seemed to be there for her in one way or another. Kate felt guilty for allowing herself to let her thoughts settle on him with such ease as she was, after all, still the wife of Kevin O'Keefe.

It was also just over two months since her husband had deserted her for Mister Wilson's young and pretty wife. Kate had heard that he had lost money on the big footrace between Jenkins and Purcell and that he had left town owing a lot of debts. His desertion of her at a time when she needed him most was bad enough. But he had also cleaned out their bank account, and left her practically destitute.

That the publican's wife had left O'Keefe in Brisbane for a wealthy landowner was small consolation. As much as she wanted to, or felt she should, she could not hate the man who had betrayed her in every possible way. She even harboured the burning hope that he might return to her. One day he would walk through the door a chastened man and humbly beg forgiveness for erring. But she was not sure how she would react to him if he did return to her.

A letter had arrived from Aunt Bridget which told Kate of the events surrounding Michael's flight from Australia. Bridget also wrote of how they had known of Patrick's and Old Billy's deaths and of Tom's misfortune.

With some bitterness she wrote that Tom's reputation as a bushranger had quickly spread, even to the mostly Irish patrons of the Erin, who sang rowdy songs about him as he was now in the pantheon of Irish folk heroes, alongside such legendary bushrangers as Bold Jack Donahue. He was the 'white myall of Queensland' and his daring raids on the squatters' properties were hailed as 'acts of war' by the small army of sympathisers who followed his exploits avidly in the newspapers.

To the landed gentry and their sympathisers, he was a renegade white man who merited no more consideration than the pesky blacks and there was a shoot-on-sight policy although this was not officially condoned by the law.

Bridget had hoped that the Australian colonies would provide a new start for the Duffys away from the never-ending troubles of Ireland. But now her nephew was repeating an old history in this new land with his supposed war against the Establishment. Would the Duffys be forever cursed with the hot blood of rebellion in their veins?

As Kate walked towards the American, she knew what she must do. She must find Tom and the final resting place of her father. A powerful and ancient force, linked to the future, had reached out to her in her fevered dreams, drawing her inexorably towards a place that was the centre of the universe for two families bound by a rip in the fabric of destiny.

Luke watched her walking towards him and wondered about the inner strength of the young woman. Although she had lost some of the gauntness the fever had left in its wake, she still had dark rings under her eyes which he guessed were from crying.

'Thank you for bringing me here, Mister Tracy,' she said with a sad smile as he helped her up onto the buggy and took up the reins in his callused hands.

They travelled in silence for a mile or so with Kate deep in her thoughts of past and present. The past was tragic and the future grim. She was almost penniless, had lost her baby and had been deserted by her husband. And for the future: her dreams and ambitions had not changed. Luck and hard work were the answers, as she well knew.

They clattered past flocks of white sulphur-crested cockatoos in the branches of the majestic gum trees and she gazed at the western horizon with a sense of peace. There was a special serenity about the dusk with its changing colours, crimson and mauve under a few scattered clouds like a beautiful but torn tapestry hanging delicately in the darkening sky.

'Are your parents still alive, Mister Tracy?' she asked unexpectedly, breaking the silence between them.

He did not answer immediately as he thought back over time to a place, far from Rockhampton, on another continent. 'No, Ma'am. Both folks are dead and buried in California,' he reflected.

'Then we have that in common, Mister Tracy,' she replied, staring out at the setting sun on the distant hazy horizon.

Luke glanced at her from the corner of his eye and saw her thick dark hair move softly with a slight breeze as the scent of lavender water wafted across to him. She appeared so vulnerable that he felt his own heart ache for her pain as he had the day he buried his own wife and baby daughter.

'Are you planning to return to your folks in Sydney, Missus O'Keefe?' he asked conversationally.

'No, I won't be going back. I have things to do here,' she answered as she continued to gaze at the sunset. 'No doubt some day I will visit my family in Sydney. But I don't think that will be for a long time yet. Have you ever thought about returning to America?'

He turned his head in surprise to look directly at

her, as it was a question he had often asked himself. 'I guess I am a bit like you, Ma'am,' he replied. 'I have things to do here before I ever go home. And right now with the war going on over there, and the fact of me being pretty broke, I guess that is a possibility but not a consideration for the moment.'

'Yes, I suppose the war forces terrible decisions for a man,' Kate said softly. 'Who to fight for, Mister Lincoln or Mister Davis. If you were back in America, who would you be fighting for, Mister Tracy?'

'Hard to say,' he replied with a frown. 'I was born in Virginia but spent most of my time in California. I stood at the Stockade as a Californian and got my wounds fighting for this country against the Limey army.' He shook his head, reflecting on the confusing nature of international politics. 'I guess you could say I'm kind of undecided. I grew up believing that God intended the darkies to work for the white man. But, at the Eureka, I fought beside a big nigra, a fellow called John Josephs, and he was as fine a man as you could ever meet. He kind of changed my ideas on things about the darkies. Since California, I've travelled a mite and I've met men from different places and got to feel that all men are equal . . . like it says in our American Constitution. I guess Mister Lincoln is fighting for that. Maybe knowing what I do now, I'd be fighting for the North.'

'And who do you think will win the war in your country?' she asked.

'That's hard to say,' he replied. 'The South won't surrender so long as a man can stand and hold a gun, but . . .' his voice trailed away. He had read the accounts of the bloody battles being fought across the sea between brothers and he did not have to be a general to know the Confederacy was bleeding to death. 'It don't look good for the South.'

'I am glad you are not in that horrible war,' Kate said gently as she touched him lightly on the arm. 'Do you know, if you had not been here when I was stricken with the fever, I might never have known the wonderful generosity of the Cohens. Nor would I have had you to drive me out to see my child.'

'Had nothing else to do, Kate,' he replied, shrugging off her gratitude with a touch of embarrassment for her gentle words. 'Can't go anywhere until I get a couple of horses. And that don't look like for a while yet,' he said, avoiding her eyes. His familiar use of her name was the first time he had done so. He had found it hard to use her married name – as protocol dictated – under the present circumstances. There was a sharing between them that was too intimate for formal distance.

Kate liked the way he used her name in the familiar way and it was only fitting that he do so. He had been more than just an acquaintance to her. The American was a friend she had come to lean on when she needed the strength to get her past the present and into the future. A very special friend, she thought, with the confusion of her feelings, as she sat beside him.

'Mister Cohen . . . Solomon . . . told me you were working to get enough money to buy your

335

horses. If you had them, would you leave Rockhampton?' she asked brightly in an attempt to shake off her thoughts.

'Yes, Ma'am! Head out and find gold,' Luke replied. 'I have a strong feeling in my bones that tells me there is gold somewhere out there to be found by someone looking for it. The colony is such a big place, there's got to be a really big strike waiting for me and as soon as I get a grubstake together, you won't see me for dust,' he responded optimistically.

Kate returned to gaze at the setting sun as she did not want him to see the frown on her face. She did not know exactly what it was in his statement that made her frown, but she did know she did not want him to leave her.

'What are your plans, Kate, since you have decided to stay?' he asked, pleased to see that she was not brooding on the past.

'First, I will go and find where my father is buried. And then find my brother Tom,' she answered without hesitation.

He looked surprised. A tall order for such a young woman. From what he had heard around Rockhampton, Patrick Duffy's last resting place was unknown. And Tom Duffy could be anywhere in the colony. Her ambitions were mere pipedreams, he thought sadly, and he decided to remain silent lest he express how foolish he thought her ideas were. Such a venture required supplies she could not afford and the services of a bushman, which she did not have. Kate O'Keefe was living in a dream world, but he was not about to waken her and force her to face reality.

But what he did not know was that Kate had

336

already formulated a way to find her father's grave, and then her brother Tom. She smiled enigmatically which made Luke feel a touch uneasy.

A week later, Luke Tracy answered a mysterious summons that he was required immediately at the Cohens' store. The message was delivered by a young boy at a stump-clearing gang where the American prospector worked grubbing tree roots. He handed his shovel to the gang boss then hurried to the store, where he was met by Solomon.

'I got your message,' Luke said anxiously as he removed his hat and wiped the sweat from his brow. 'The lad said you needed to see me as soon as possible. Has something happened to Kate?'

'Don't sound so concerned, my friend. All is well.' Solomon chuckled as he guided the puzzled man through the store to a paddock, where Kate and Judith were feeding handfuls of oats to three fine-looking horses. The two women chatted happily as the big horses bustled each other to get at the feed the women held in the palms of their hands.

'Luke! You came,' Judith cried delightedly as she turned to see the two men approaching across the paddock. 'What do you think of them?'

Luke gave the horses his expert appraisal as he stroked the nose of the biggest, a mare with an intelligent look in her eyes. The horses were at the peak of their health and strong. 'Not bad. Must have cost you a bit by the look of them,' he reflected as the mare nuzzled his bushy beard.

'Not us,' Judith replied with a mysterious smile. 'They cost Kate a small fortune.'

Luke frowned as it dawned on him why she had

purchased the horses.

'You can't be thinking of going west, Kate?' he said. 'It's utter foolishness for a girl as young and inexperienced as you to even think about travelling country as tough as it is out there. Believe me, I know.'

'Oh, yes I can,' she replied defiantly as she continued to feed oats to her horses. 'And nothing . . . or no one . . . is going to stop me.'

Exasperated by the young woman's defiance, he turned to Judith for support, but she ignored him and began to stroke the broad neck of the mare. This was a matter between Luke and Kate. She approved of what Kate had in mind, as they had discussed the matter before the purchase of the horses and she agreed it could be done with the right help.

The money had been a loan from the Cohens which Judith knew Kate would one day repay. She had already sensed with a woman's intuition that the young woman was destined for something important in life. Kate had survived death and desertion and was able to rally her life forces to plan an expedition of her own into wild country that was barely settled. Such a woman had a strength that could not be broken by adversity.

'There are a hundred ways you can die out there, Kate,' Luke protested. 'Believe me. I have seen at least fifty ways a healthy, well-armed and experienced bushman can die.'

Kate turned on him with a strange blaze in her eyes he had not seen before. 'You are a bushman, Luke,' she said, and he suspected that she was challenging him. 'So why do you go out there if what you say is true?'

'Because I am a man!' he replied simply.

'A man! Ah!' Judith snorted with amusement. 'Let me tell you, Luke Tracy. When I was Kate's age, I followed Solomon out to this land to be with him. My family were shocked that a young girl should dare travel to a place as far away as New South Wales to join a man convicted of forgery, and they tried their best to stop me. But I came, and when I got here I worked while Solomon was in chains. And when he was given his ticket of leave, we travelled to places against the advice of our friends in this country. And you say that being a man makes you special! Did not your own mother, alone in the world without a man, travel with you halfway across America to California? And did she not care for you until you were ready to take your place in the world as a man? And you say that only a man could go out west.'

Luke hung his head sheepishly at her tirade. She was right. But he could not admit he was beaten.

'My mother was older than Kate,' he said lamely, 'when we travelled to California.'

'That may have been so,' Judith retorted. 'But she was still a woman.'

Luke knew he was trapped and he stood with a pained expression on his face staring towards the west before finally turning and speaking softly.

'I will guide you, Kate, if you are foolish enough to go ahead with your plan.' He was also angry at himself for letting the young woman manipulate him so easily. A man had little chance against the devious schemes of a woman.

'You don't have to,' she snapped unexpectedly. 'I

339

am sure I could manage without a man.'

'I said I will guide you, Kate. And that is final,' he flared angrily. He was not prepared to have a girl of her tender years patronise him. 'We can leave as soon as I get supplies together. Maybe early next week.' Goddamn women, he thought. They know how to twist a man around their fingers.

The two women exchanged knowing looks when Luke turned to Solomon to discuss supplies for the journey west.

'Luke?' Kate called softly, before the two men were to return to the store. 'I am sorry that I will not be able to pay you now. But if you will put your trust in me, I will repay you some day.'

Luke scowled and shook his head. 'I'm not doing this for pay, Kate,' he said and stormed away with Solomon hurrying to catch up with him.

'He is a good man, Kate,' Judith said as Kate gazed at the departing back of the tall American. 'With him, you will always be safe.'

'Yes, he is a good man,' Kate echoed with a sigh. 'I wish my husband had been more like him.'

Judith could see that Kate was on the verge of tears and she guessed she was thinking about the past. 'I think Luke likes the mare, so the gelding is my present to you,' Judith said and Kate impulsively threw her arms around her.

'Thank you, Judith,' she whispered. 'Thank you for everything. I will never forget all that you have done for me.'

'I got the horses cheap from those robbing horse traders,' Judith said with a small laugh and Kate replied with tears of gratitude.

'You have asked nothing from me,' she said. 'I will always be grateful to you and Solomon.'

Judith was trying not to cry herself. 'The men must not see our tears or they will think we are just poor weak women. And we know different to that,' Judith said, pushing Kate gently an arm's length from the embrace. 'Your journey on the rest of your life will start somewhere out there, Kate. And I think God has given you a task as He gave to Deborah for my people. I don't know how I know this. I just do. There are people who need you, and I think it is out there in the wilderness you will find the answers.'

Kate listened to Judith's words with awe. How could the tall woman know of her own strange premonitions? Then Judith changed the subject.

'Come. I think we should choose for you suitable clothes to wear for your trip. And I think you should have a gun. Most of the women out here have guns.'

When they joined the men in the store, they found them haggling over the price of supplies. Solomon moaned as if he had been stripped of all that he owned and Kate smiled at the sight of the two good friends locked head to head in a loud dispute with each other.

But, even so, she felt a small fear creeping into her thoughts. Why was the journey to find her father so important? Was the answer somewhere in Tom's words that had come to her in her dream those many weeks past? And Judith's words . . . She knew the answer was somewhere out in the wilderness of central Queensland.

23

'Sar'nt Henry! Sar'nt Henry!'

Henry James rolled on his side and reached instinctively for the revolver in its holster by his bed. There was an urgency in the voice that called to him from outside his bark hut and he knew something was very wrong. Trooper Barney would never disturb his sleep unless it was literally a matter of life and death.

'What? Trooper Barney . . . what's happened?' Henry mumbled as he tried to shake off the sleep still upon him.

'You come quick, Sar'nt Henry. Corporal Gideon . . . he bin killed, Sar'nt Henry.'

'What in hell are you saying, Trooper?' Henry bellowed as he crashed open his door, waving his revolver wildly. 'What do you mean Corporal Gideon has been killed?'

The Aboriginal trooper stood at the foot of the verandah steps wearing a pair of old European cast-off trousers two sizes too big for him. His eyes rolled wildly in the garish glow from the lantern that cast his face in a mask of terror.

'Mister Mort. He bin killed Corporal Gideon

down at One Tree camp tonight,' he babbled. 'Mister Mort a *debil debil*, Sar'nt Henry. He bin crazy and stab Corporal Gideon until Corporal Gideon, he die. All finish.'

Henry snatched the lantern from the terrified trooper and bounded up the steps into his quarters where he slammed the light on the small table at the centre of the cramped room and hurriedly dressed in his uniform.

The news had spread rapidly through the troopers' quarters and an eerie keening wail of the women rose as an unearthly sound in the night. It reminded the sergeant of the crying of the curlews in the bush.

When Henry was dressed, Trooper Barney followed him to the saddling yard. The horses skittered as they were readied. The wailing of the women had unsettled them.

'Tell me what happened?' Henry snapped as he adjusted the girth of his saddle.

'I don't know, Sar'nt Henry,' Trooper Barney replied. 'I was with the old men when I heard Mister Mort had come into the camp. He looked funny . . .'

'What do you mean, funny?'

'He was jus' smilin' all the time an' said he was goin' to get Corporal Gideon for killin' those gins,' the Aboriginal trooper continued. 'Corporal Gideon was with one of the One Tree gins an' Mister Mort told him to go with him to the bush. Corporal Gideon, he looked scared . . . we all was . . .' Henry knew why they were scared. They had been caught infringing the no-alcohol rule for troopers and such an infringement was likely to bring a lashing with the cat-o'-nine-tails. '. . . Then we hear Corporal Gideon scream,' he added fearfully. 'We run away an' an old man tell us he see Mister Mort stab Corporal Gideon with his sword.'

'Jesus!' Henry blasphemed savagely. So Mort had gone mad and murdered a trooper. Killing of Aboriginals during a dispersal was one thing but the outright killing of a servant of Her Majesty – black or white – was another matter.

He felt sick at the decision he must make: to arrest a senior officer for murder was unprecedented in the Native Police and he was unsure of his lawful right to do so. Although he had never liked Mort, he had an inbred respect for authority. As the sergeant and the black trooper rode in the night to the One Tree camp, Henry was not sure what he would do when he confronted his superior officer . . . if he was stupid enough to stay around after murdering a man!

It did not take long to reach the Aboriginal settlement.

The camp's fires cast eerie flickering shadows on the bark gunyahs of the dispossessed people who lived on the fringes of Rockhampton. The place was deserted except for the half-wild dogs that were always present in Aboriginal camps and Henry knew that the inhabitants, to a man, had gone into hiding in the surrounding scrub. The dogs snarled and barked at the intrusion of the horsemen as the two police officers reined their horses to a halt. But the camp was not completely deserted.

By the largest fire sat Mort in his best dress uniform, warming his hands as if he had just stopped
to rest. He was smiling with a curious and fixed
expression on his face, with his infantry sword
across his lap. Even in the dim and flickering light
cast by the fire, Henry could see the long blade was
dark with blood and there was a terrible madness
in the officer's face. Mort did not appear disturbed
at the arrival of his sergeant. In fact, he appeared
pleased to see him.

Trooper Barney edged back into the protective
darkness outside the fire's glow. He did not want
to be in the presence of the white devil.

'Ah, Sergeant James,' Mort said casually. 'I see
Trooper Barney has fetched you. I was hoping one
of the charcoals might.'

Henry remained astride his horse and stared with
amazement at the man sitting so complacently
by the fire with a smile reminiscent of a hideous
grimacing death mask.

'What do you have to say about Corporal
Gideon . . . sir?' he growled. 'Trooper Barney tells
me you killed him.'

'Yes, that I did. His body is over there in the
bush,' Mort replied with a flourish of his sword
towards the darkness. 'Most regrettable that I was
forced to take action. All the man had to do was
come with me to the barracks for questioning
about the killing of those nigger women, but he
chose to try to kill me instead and I took the
necessary action to defend myself.'

'Defend yourself, sir?' Henry asked. It was
incredible that the man could offer such a weak
excuse. His smug composure was unnerving.

345

'Yes, Sergeant,' Mort replied as if explaining something difficult to a child. 'Corporal Gideon was the man killing all those nigger women around here. I came to that conclusion from my own investigations. And when I came out here to speak to him, he panicked and tried to strangle me. Fortunately, I came armed . . . or should I say . . . unfortunately, for Corporal Gideon.'

Henry dismounted, keeping his eyes on the officer by the fire. The bastard had covered himself. Or he might be telling the truth. Had Gideon acquired a taste for the killing? Had the dispersals unhinged his mind in some way? It was faintly possible that he could have been the killer, as he had been with the Native Police for a long time and exposed to the white man's brutal ways of senseless killing. The questions haunted him as Mort's apparent calmness and self-assuredness planted a seed of doubt in Henry's mind. No, not Gideon. Not the big Aboriginal corporal!

Henry lifted a burning stick from the fire and held it aloft to walk cautiously in the direction where Mort had said he had left the dead trooper. Mort remained by the fire staring at the flickering flames. 'More to the left, Sergeant,' he called helpfully and Henry stumbled on the body.

It lay on the dry earth staring with sightless eyes towards the star-filled sky. Henry squatted beside the dead corporal and lowered the firebrand to examine his friend's corpse. The glow of the firebrand revealed the extent of mutilations to the body.

But the sergeant's attention was centred on one wound Gideon had suffered before he died. All doubts about the Aboriginal corporal's possible guilt were affirmed when Henry saw the terrible wound to his mouth. It was the trademark of the killer who had tortured to death the three Aboriginal girls. A sword! Henry thought. It had been a sword that had been used to kill the Aboriginal girls. Not a knife, as he had concluded previously.

'Jesus! Gideon,' Henry groaned softly as he closed the big corporal's eyes in a final gesture of friendship. 'The bastard slew you for no reason other than his insanity.'

When Henry emerged from the darkness, he was holding a pistol pointed directly at Mort's head. There was a cold rage in the sergeant's eyes that made the officer flinch nervously, losing some of his smug composure. He had not expected the sergeant's reaction although he knew that his sergeant and the Aboriginal corporal were as close as a white man could be to a nigger. But levelling a pistol at him was beyond any measure that he had expected.

Mort did not rise to his feet but stared into the fire and said calmly, 'You should put away that gun, Sergeant. It might go off should you stumble . . . and then it might cause me some personal grief.'

'You murdering bastard,' Henry snarled as he pulled back the hammer on the pistol. 'You killed Corporal Gideon the same way you killed those poor bloody gins.'

'I don't know what brings you to that conclusion, Sergeant,' Mort replied just a little shakily.

'You have no proof of what you are saying. So I suggest that you put that gun away and I will forget what you have done here tonight. Pointing a gun at a superior officer is an extremely serious offence.'

'So is murdering three girls and a police corporal . . . sir,' Henry snarled. 'Right now, I don't know whether I should shoot you down . . . or arrest you. If I shoot you, then I will know justice has been done. But I would have to make up some story of how you had an accident and I'm not good at making up stories like you. But I think I could do it,' he continued, and Mort knew he was actually contemplating killing him. This was not supposed to happen! He had seriously underestimated the man, whom he had always considered a slow-witted, lumbering fool.

'If I arrest you I know how the courts work,' Henry continued with a cold menace. 'I doubt if the evidence will get a conviction . . . though both you and I know you are guilty. But then your arrest might lead to an investigation into the death of that Irish teamster. Oh! I forgot to tell you, Corporal Gideon told me everything that had occurred when you and Mister Macintosh were bailed up by the Irishman, so killing Gideon was a waste of time. The only trouble is that he told me just one day too late. I was troubled by how I might go about reporting the matter to Brisbane, but I am sure your arrest will cause quite a stir down there when the facts are put together.'

Mort's mouth was dry with fear, as he knew the balance of power had shifted to the sergeant. Either way he was in trouble. A bullet . . . or a scandal!

'You realise if you arrest me you will be finished in the Native Police,' Mort croaked. 'You and I both know that the authorities hate a scandal. Anyone who brings this sort of trouble down on their heads is finished. They will find a way to drum you out as soon as I hit the dock,' he said, as a desperate attempt to stave off the big sergeant's deadly fury. But the gun rose in Henry's hand and there was a distinct glint of murder in the sergeant's eyes.

'No witnesses, Mister Mort,' he said with a deadly softness that belied the hatred he felt for the officer at his feet. 'I see Trooper Barney has made a tactful retreat and so it's just you and me here now, and all I can see is the stab wound through Corporal Gideon's mouth, just like the ones I saw on those poor bloody gins. That makes me get so angry my hand starts to shake and this gun will probably go off. I suppose I will have to think up something to say about your death. But it won't matter to you because you will be dead anyway.'

Mort tried to rise to his feet, but he found all his physical strength had deserted him. Instead, he rose to a kneeling position with his hands extended in a begging gesture, and pleaded desperately, 'Arrest me, if you think you should. There is no need to kill me. I might be dead but you will be in trouble enough to swing. Do you really want that?'

The gun blast exploded in the night and Mort screamed as he fell to the ground.

'Dear God, man! This is murder,' he blubbered, grovelling in the dust. 'You can't just shoot me down like some rabid dog.'

Henry cocked the pistol again, bringing it to

bear on the officer at his feet. 'Must have missed the first time,' he said casually. 'Never was good at using one of these in the dark.'

Mort held his arms over his head as if they could ward off the heavy lead bullets and, in the initial blast of the pistol, his world had come apart at the seams. The English sergeant's words came to him as a eulogy for the dead. 'You know, I killed Russkies in the Crimea, and they were fine men. But it was never personal in war. Killing you *is* personal and I suppose you could say I'm not killing you, but carrying out an execution.'

'Those nigger gins don't warrant this,' Mort said hysterically as he knelt before him. 'They were just niggers like all the ones we killed out on the dispersals. I . . .'

'Corporal Gideon may have been a blackfella but he was as fine as any man I ever served with in the Crimea. I'm doing this for him. And maybe that dead Irishman,' Henry said in a flat and disembodied voice.

The gunshot echoed around the night like rolling thunder and dust sprouted beside Mort, who flinched as if he had been shot.

'Dear God . . . Please . . . arrest me, but don't kill me,' he wailed, although a faint hope existed that the sergeant was toying with him for something other than his death and he was ready to listen to anything he suggested. The first two shots had not been intended to kill. But maybe the third? 'What if I resign? What if we go back to the barracks and I write out my resignation . . . effective immediately?' he offered with pleading desperation. He did not want to die in some filthy nigger camp.

'You know as well as I do that you have to give notice before you resign,' Henry said, considering his desperate proposition. 'If you were to resign now, then you would have to get out of Queensland and never return.'

A cunning look returned to the police lieutenant's eyes. Yes. He could promise to resign and as soon as they were back at the barracks and he had the opportunity, he would arrest the sergeant for his actions this night.

'Yes, I know what you are saying. If I resigned and left . . . I would be in breach of the regulations and it would not sit well in Brisbane. But my resignation should suit your sense of justice,' Mort rationalised.

'It will do,' Henry said, letting the barrel of his pistol fall away from the trembling officer's head. 'But should you try and renege on the resignation, I can promise you that you will have to kill me to stop me talking about everything I know. And I doubt even you will be able to explain away the deaths of both myself and Corporal Gideon should you decide to shoot me in the back on the trip to the barracks.'

Mort blinked. The sergeant was still one step ahead of him. Even if he arrested the sergeant, many things would come out that were best left unsaid and although it was all circumstantial, he knew what his sergeant could say would bring questions from all sorts of people . . . politicians, journalists and his own superiors. Yes, resignation was the only real answer.

With a shrug, he rose to his feet and brushed himself down. He was once again in control and an officer of Her Majesty's Native Police. The sergeant had not wanted to kill him any more than he had wanted to die, although it did not sit well to test the patience of the big sergeant any further.

'Well then, Sergeant,' Mort said, casually regaining his composure, 'I believe you have a report to submit on the matters concerning the death of Corporal Gideon. A report of how he tried to strangle me and I was forced to defend myself.'

Henry did not answer, but turned his back on his commanding officer. He was sickened by the pact he had made with him and he fully knew that they were both playing a game that neither could win. Better the murdering bastard was gone from the force than allow Mort to use his position to eventually out-manoeuvre him, he thought bitterly. He knew that it would only be a matter of time before Mort found a devious way to win in the end.

Henry made sure he was riding behind Mort as they made their way back to the barracks. Mort was true to his word and submitted his resignation to the sergeant for dispatch to Brisbane that night. Before the sun rose the next day, Mort was gone.

Four weeks later the young replacement officer sat at Mort's old desk shuffling the reports before him. He made noises in his throat like that of an officious clerk.

Henry stood stiffly at attention. His leg ached and he silently cursed the pompous officer, who could plainly see that he was in some discomfort. Standing rigidly to attention before him, he waited as the officer stared at a vacant point beyond

Henry to where Mort had always hung his sword on the wall.

'Highly irregular, Sergeant James,' the young officer finally said as he glanced up. 'I find all these reports highly irregular. We have a police trooper dead and the man who killed him suddenly resigns. Mister Mort will have to attend an inquiry, you know.'

'Yes sir,' Henry replied formally. 'I believe that is the procedure. But I don't think we will be able to find Mister Mort, sir. From my inquiries, he has disappeared and no one seems to know where he is.'

'Hmm . . . Well, I suppose we have his statement here about the incident with the trooper at the darkies' camp,' the officer mused as he shuffled the handwritten statement to the top of the files. 'Under other circumstances, Mister Mort might have been commended for his work in attempting to bring to justice this man who was killing the darkie girls. But headquarters is not happy with his sudden desertion from his post and he would have to answer charges on the matter of not giving the regulation notice.'

'Yes sir,' Henry answered dutifully.

'From what I have seen of your work, Sergeant, I must say I am not very impressed,' the pompous young officer remonstrated, but Henry knew it was a lie. His work was of the highest standard. He had maintained the police barracks in good order and he felt his spirits slump as he guessed that the word was out to remove him from his post at Rockhampton. 'I have been asked to recommend your future in the Native Police,' the young

353

officer continued and he was uncomfortable in what he had to do, as he personally could not find fault with the sergeant. Damned if he was going to recommend dismissal, no matter who this squatter was who wanted the sergeant out. 'It will be my recommendation that you be transferred from here to a place decided by Brisbane.'

Transfer. It could have been worse, Henry thought, as he stared stonily at the wall behind the officer.

'The transfer will be effective as soon as I get word back from headquarters as to your new posting. Do you have any questions, Sergeant?'

'No, sir. No questons.'

'Very good. I think you are capable of continuing with your duties until your replacement arrives. You can go, Sergeant,' he said, dismissing him.

'Sah!' Henry saluted smartly, turned and was about to march out of the office when he heard the young officer call to him quietly.

'I wouldn't be packing my bags in a hurry if I were you. Reports tend to get lost and these matters blow over in time.'

Henry smiled. So there was some justice left in the world after all.

On the verandah Henry relaxed and gazed across the parade ground to the stables which the troopers were mucking out. The work came to a stop when they saw their respected sergeant. They all knew that the call to the office meant something important, as Sar'nt James had reported in his best uniform.

'I'm not gone yet, you lazy and idle men,' he bawled good-naturedly across the parade ground. 'So get about your duties or I'll put the cat across your backs.'

They hurried into their work with grins on their faces. Sar'nt Henry was tough . . . but fair.

With Mort gone, life was returning to normal around the barracks. Henry limped across the dusty parade ground. Why was it that he felt he had not seen the last of the murderous officer? The thought struck Henry as surely as one of the heavy lead balls of the police carbines. He slowed to stare back at the office where Mort had spent much of his day brooding and the answer came to the English sergeant. Because men like Mort were survivors, just as rats were when a ship was sinking. They just simply moved somewhere else and started all over again.

'I should have killed him when I had the chance,' he muttered softly to himself.

24

The Aboriginal troopers, stripped to the waist and wearing loincloths as they cleaned their carbines under the cool shade of a big gum tree, paused to stare curiously at the tall man. Not many visitors made the trip to the barracks unless it was on official business.

The stranger rode with the easy style of a man who spent most of his life observing life from astride a horse. He stopped at the rifle-cleaning detail to ask them the whereabouts of Sergeant James and they pointed to a bark hut across the parade ground. He thanked them and reined his mount to the sergeant's office, where he swung from the saddle with the ease of an experienced horseman. The troopers went back to pulling pieces of oily cloth through the barrels of their carbines. Whatever the stranger wanted was white-fella business and no concern of theirs.

Luke Tracy hitched his horse to a rail outside the bark hut and knocked on the door. A voice boomed to enter and Luke pushed open the door to step inside. He saw an impressive man, by his sheer size alone, wearing the blue uniform of the Native Mounted Police, sitting behind a desk spread with official papers and a map.

'You Sergeant James?' Luke asked as he removed his dusty hat and slapped it against his thigh. The big man behind the desk glanced up at him from the map.

'I'm Sergeant James,' he acknowledged, fixing his visitor with a modicum of interest in his American accent. 'And I presume you're a Yankee.'

Luke grinned. 'Luke Tracy. Prospector out of California . . . and mostly out of luck.'

Henry warmed to the American's easy manner. 'What can I do for you, Mister Tracy?' he asked, leaning forward. 'Not many whitefellas come out this way . . . unless they need our help.'

'That's why I'm here, Sergeant. I heard you were on a dispersal around November last year on a run called Glen View,' Luke said and noticed a cloud cross the police sergeant's face. 'I was hoping you might be able to give me some idea of where a couple of fellas are buried. Believe they were speared by the myalls. A teamster by the name of Patrick Duffy and his boy called Billy.'

'If I may ask, Mister Tracy, why do you want to find them?'

Luke sensed more curiosity in the question than suspicion. 'Pat Duffy was a friend of mine,' he answered reasonably. 'We were on the diggings at Ballarat back in '54. I'm heading out west and I kind of hoped to drop by and pay my respects at Big Pat's grave.'

Henry rose from behind his desk and limped to the only window in the office, where he stood with his hands behind his back to gaze in contemplative silence at the Aboriginal troopers cleaning their rifles on the far side of the parade ground. 'If I knew where Mister Duffy was buried,' he finally said, 'I would tell you, Mister Tracy. But my former commander, Mister Mort, was the last man to see them alive . . . and he is no longer with the troop. He left a week ago . . . whereabouts unknown.'

'You must have some idea where they are,' Luke offered. 'Someone would have buried them. One of them Glen View shepherds mebbe.'

'I hope Mister Duffy got a Christian burial,' Henry replied. 'Under the circumstances.'

'What do you mean by that, Sergeant?'

'Nothing that is of your concern, Mister Tracy,' Henry replied firmly but not with animosity. 'Just the previous commander didn't handle the situation very well at the time.'

Luke was very perceptive when it came to dealing with men and the English sergeant's manner was rather strange. He played a hunch.

'I heard your boss killed one of the troopers a short time back. Apparently he was killing young gins . . . so I heard around the pubs.'

Henry's expression clouded. 'I can't help you, Mister Tracy,' he said abruptly as he resumed his seat behind the desk. 'I don't know where Mister Duffy is buried . . . or if he has been buried at all. So if that is all you want with me, I would suggest that our conversation is at an end.'

Luke sensed that he had touched a raw nerve and he realised he would get nowhere continuing with his questions.

He departed and returned to the Cohens' store, where he told Kate what had transpired at the police barracks. She expressed her disappointment but she was not deterred, even though he pointed out the magnitude of the task ahead of them. Finding a grave, if one existed, in such a vast place as the brigalow of central Queensland . . . But Kate persisted stubbornly and he shook his head.

A day before Luke and Kate were to ride out of Rockhampton, they received an unexpected visitor.

A puzzled Solomon Cohen hurried to Kate, who was sorting supplies with Luke in a storage shed behind the store. The shed was little more than a corrugated iron roof supported by timber poles for storing baled hay. But it also doubled as a relatively comfortable accommodation for Luke while he was in Rockhampton.

'Sergeant James from the Native Police wants to speak with you,' Solomon said and Kate glanced up in surprise from wrapping a canvas sheet around blankets.

'Tell him to come through,' she said and instinctively brushed down her dress.

Henry stood in the shed curiously eyeing the supplies scattered around him: tinned meat, small sacks of flour, demijohns of lime juice, twists of tobacco, ammunition for the guns and packets of sugar and tea.

'I heard you were heading out west, Missus O'Keefe,' he said after he had introduced himself to her. 'And I also learnt that your brother is Tom Duffy.'

359

She stared hard at him with the defiance her family had long displayed for representatives of the British legal system. 'How did you learn that, Sergeant James?' she replied coldly and a faint smile formed at the corners of Henry's eyes.

'I'm a policeman . . . and this is a small town,' he answered. 'Do you mind if I sit down, Missus O'Keefe? My leg gives me a bit of trouble.' She gestured to a bale of hay and he sat down heavily. 'Mister Tracy here rode out to ask me if I knew anything about where your father might be buried. I told him the truth when I said I did not know. But I have this,' he said, passing Luke a piece of paper. 'It's a map I made, to the best of my memory, of the area around the site of the dispersal. You will see the best landmark is a range of hills there and a creek line. I think if you search in the area around the hills you might find something. As for getting out to Glen View itself, that I believe is in your hands, Mister Tracy.'

The American folded the paper and placed it in a battered chocolate tin that contained the smaller essential items for the trip: needles and cotton spools, a small phial of laudanum and a brass prismatic compass.

'Thank you, Sergeant James,' Kate said, softening her animosity toward the police sergeant. 'But I cannot help wonder why you should assist us when I can only assume you have a duty to search for and arrest my brother.'

'Your brother might not have obtained such notoriety had it not been for the actions of the former commander of the troop,' Henry replied. 'Something happened to your father that I will never be able to prove. Not that it matters now because Mort has disappeared and could be on his way out of the colony, even out of the country by now. Whatever happened the day of the dispersal at Glen View I think was murder. And I think that your brother was innocently caught up in the circumstances because of the actions of Mort that day.'

He turned to Luke. 'As for Corporal Gideon being the murderer of those darkie girls, Mister Tracy, I can assure you he was an innocent man who also fell victim to Mort's insanity. That is all I can say except that I hope you get to your brother before we do, Missus O'Keefe.' He paused and Kate could see a subtle change in the man, not obvious to less perceptive people. 'I mean that as a man . . . and not a policeman, Missus O'Keefe,' he added softly and she was able to read in his eyes a gentleness that belied his gruff exterior. She could also see deeper to a terrible torment of the soul for the violence of his life and she suddenly felt a surge of pity for the man. 'If you intend to journey to Glen View,' he added, 'I would advise that you stay out of Mister Macintosh's way. It seems he has a great dislike for the Duffy name. Your brother is under suspicion for the killing of three Glen View shepherds and I doubt that he will welcome any relative of Tom Duffy on his property. I would fear for your lives if you did so.'

'Thank you for the warning,' Kate said. 'I do not have any intentions of meeting Mister Macintosh if I can help it.'

Henry eased himself off the hay bale and brushed down his trousers. 'I'm glad of that,

Missus O'Keefe,' he said. 'You appear to be an honest young woman from all that I have heard about you. And I'm sorry for your recent loss. I don't think I can give you any more assistance, so I will bid you both a good day.'

Luke extended his hand and Henry seemed surprised. 'My thanks also, Sergeant James,' he said. 'Hope we meet again one day under better circumstances.'

Henry accepted the offered hand. 'So do I, Mister Tracy,' he said as he made his departure.

When he was gone, Kate sighed. 'I think Sergeant James is a good man, haunted by his past.' Luke did not understand. But then he did not have a woman's intuition either.

The following day Luke and Kate set out from Rockhampton and, in the two weeks they rode the track west, she constantly amazed the bushman with her extensive knowledge of the flora and fauna they encountered on the journey. She could identify many of the plants and animals by name as they traversed the range of low scrubby hills to the west of Rockhampton, and even when they rode into the seemingly never-ending sea of brigalow scrub.

As a young girl she had read as much as she could about the bush. The colourful and detailed letters her father had scribbled concerning his observations of the land on his long journeys across the vast and seemingly endless plains had provided her with much of her knowledge.

She was full of surprises from the very commencement of their trek. Luke had been stunned to see her wearing men's clothing the morning they met to ride out of Rockhampton. But he was even more surprised to see her ride astride her mount as a man would. Riding side-saddle along the rough bush tracks was not practicable. It was spine-twisting and uncomfortable, she had explained to him, and he was forced to agree.

Luke taught her to ride and how to lead the pack-horse and very soon he took it for granted that it was just as natural for a woman to ride like a man as it was for a woman to wear the practical clothes.

Kate adapted to life on the bush track as if she had been born to it, although at times the bush was like an ocean devoid of landmarks. Luke was a good teacher and patiently taught her how to live with nature and travel through the country of endless horizons. She soon gained her confidence as he pointed out how he followed the seemingly invisible route west along the lonely track.

Often at nights when they were camped, the American would gaze at her across the camp fire and ponder on how lucky a man would be to have such a woman for his wife. O'Keefe must have been raving mad to leave such a woman, he would muse to himself as he sipped at his coffee and watched her prepare for the next day.

He did not consider that the beautiful young woman saw him in any light other than as a good friend, a guide and protector on the trek west, and he would sigh and dismiss his feelings as nothing more than wishful thinking. He was careful to hide them from her, but the further west they rode the more he realised that he could never love any woman as much as Kate O'Keefe.

In the two weeks travelling west, they had encountered only the occasional shepherd riding or
trudging back to Rockhampton. But near Glen
View they encountered a solitary bullock dray
returning to pick up supplies in Rockhampton.

The dray was stacked with bales of wool for its
return journey, and the man who walked beside his
team trailing a bullock whip was almost as wide as
he was tall. He was accompanied by a tough little
cattle dog which snapped and yapped at the legs of
the plodding bullocks.

They met the bullocky and his dog just on sunset and pitched their camp with the teamster, who
introduced himself as Harry Hubner and was
pleased to have them share his camp fire.

After the horses and bullocks had been hobbled
for the night, the four sat around a camp fire
sharing the evening meal. The fourth member to
share the fire was the dog, which considered itself
an equal to the humans. After all, did he not work
as hard as his master? The dog took a liking to
Kate and leaned against her, staring with adoring
eyes at the human whose voice was as soft as her
stroking pats were gentle.

'Bloody dog!' the burly teamster growled with
deep affection for his tough little mongrel as he
reached over and poured Kate another mug of tea.
'I feed him and give him a job and he wants to run
off with the first woman he meets!' The dog gave
his master a mournful recriminating look for his
attack on his supposed lack of loyalty, then placed
his nose contentedly in Kate's lap as she sat on a
log by the camp fire.

Under the brilliant canopy of twinkling stars, they shared food and gossip of the lonely outback tracks while wispy smoke rose from the flames as if trying to reach the shimmering stars and smother their crystalline brightness.

Harry watched Kate over his mug of tea. The American was lucky, he thought, to have a pretty young lass like this girl for his woman. From her manners and talk he guessed that she was from somewhere down south but he could see that the American was a bushman. He could tell by the way he moved around the camp site – always watchful and cautious – and he had the natural ease of being one with the bush. Although Luke's American accent still predominated, it was inter-mingled with words of the Australian bushman. They were a strange pair, Harry thought. She young and pretty . . . and a city girl. He older and tougher. A man more at home in the bush than around cities. But they were good company and a change from just being with the mongrel on the lonely stretches of the western track. 'Another mug o' tea, Mister Tracy?' he asked as he stirred the billy with a stick.

'No. I think my grandaddy would turn in his grave if he saw how much tea I was drinking,' Luke replied politely with a grin. 'He never was partial to tea after the party we had in Boston.' His reference to the infamous Boston Tea Party that had helped fuel the rebellion against the British Crown of George III was lost on Harry, who knew little of history except that the Americans were once the enemy of Britain. But that was a long time ago and now the Yankees were all over the

Australian colonies. There was Mister Freeman Cobb who had set up that stagecoach line down in Victoria. He was pretty famous, and there were many other Yankees the teamster had come across in his travels. And men like this Mister Tracy, who said he was a prospector. Generally they were pretty good fellows but they had some funny ideas about something they called Republicanism.

'Seen anyone else on the track in your travels?' Harry asked conversationally as he poured the third cup of steaming tea into his chipped and battered enamel mug.

'Just one or two shepherds heading down to Rockhampton a couple of days ago,' Luke replied. 'Said they was from the Balaclava run . . . and had a big thirst.'

'Be old Billy Bostock's boys,' the teamster said with a chuckle. 'They would be wantin' to watch out for young Tom Duffy and that wild darkie if they was Mister Bostock's men.'

Kate glanced at Luke with a startled expression. 'Do you know Tom Duffy?' she asked casually to mask her excitement at the mention of her brother's name and the bullocky gazed suspiciously at her.

'Yair. Know Tom,' he replied slowly. 'And knew Patrick too. We would run into each other on the track back last year. Good men, both of them. Shame to hear what happened. Big Pat getting himself killed. And Tom out there taking the squatters and the traps on a merry chase in the bush. Don't think they will ever catch 'im though. Not while he has the myall with him. I even hear it rumoured that the myall was the one who killed young Angus Macintosh. Heard the boys at Glen View talk about it when I was there for supplies. Matter of fact, I'm taking a load of Glen View wool right now.'

'Do you know where this Tom Duffy might be?' Kate asked with an eagerness that was not missed by him as he raised his mug of tea.

'I don't. But if I did, I don't think I would tell you if'n I knew,' he said defensively. 'No offence intended, Missus.'

'Would you tell his sister?' Luke asked quietly and the teamster stared at him with speculative interest. Then he glanced at Kate with a growing awareness.

'Well, I'll be damned,' he said slapping his thigh and peering closely at the young woman. 'You Tom's sister, Missus?' She nodded. 'And yer looking for yer brother?' he asked with a chuckle and she nodded again. 'Knowing this I would tell you if I knew where yer brother was, but I don't know where they might be. Last I heard they bailed up a squatter the back of Port Denison. Seems the two of 'em are moving north. They stays mostly out in the country beyond, livin' like darkies, an' I don't think you will ever find him if you go looking. They has to find you.'

Kate had not wanted to reveal her identity as Tom's sister but, in an attempt to locate her brother, Luke had gambled on the teamster telling the bushranger's sister of his possible whereabouts. As her relationship to the Irish bushranger had now been revealed, Kate made a decision to ask the teamster all he knew about her father and brother. Harry told as much as he could, mostly things about the past and the respect that father and son had commanded from those who knew them. Eventually the conversation shifted to Macintosh and Harry mentioned that he had seen a former police officer by the name of Mort staying for a while with Donald Macintosh on his property. He also recounted how Mort had 'cleaned out' all the myalls in the district and he warned them to stay away from the tribes further west, as they were wild and fearless. More than one bushman who had gone their way had not returned.

Kate listened to the old bushman recount all that he knew about the country and its people. He was more than happy to talk, especially as one of his audience was such a pretty girl, and the sister of the infamous bushranger Tom Duffy. What a story he would have for the next traveller he met on the track!

The constellations whirled in a slow arc overhead and the soft crackle of the fire lulled Kate into a weariness. She found her eyes drawn to the dancing flames of the camp fire where vague and disturbing images pirouetted in the glowing embers to suddenly swirl around her like whispers in the night. The whispers seemed to be everywhere and she shivered. Who calls? Where are you? Was the fever returning? She rose unsteadily from the log and excused herself to retire for the night.

She unrolled the coarse blankets for her bed and wrapped them around herself to ward off the creeping chill of the still and cool night, while the comforting murmur of the men's voices and the familiar sounds of the possums scurrying in the branches of a tall gum tree nearby provided her with a gentle bush lullaby. The peaceful sounds of the bush at night had become as familiar to her as the clip-clop of the milkman's cart at her home in Redfern.

In a short time she fell into a deep and troubled sleep and the images that had flitted before her eyes as she had watched the flames now crept out of the shadows of the hushed night to enter into the sleeping world of her dreams.

Luke continued to swap yarns with the teamster as they sat by the fire. He asked him many questions about his observations on rock outcrops and creeks he had come across in his travels. But none of the answers sounded promising from a prospector's point of view. When the fire was almost out Harry stoked it with fresh logs which would burn through the night until piccaninny dawn and he bade Luke a good sleep.

Luke rose and walked over to where Kate slept. He quietly checked to see that she was well rugged against the chill that would increase during the crystal-clear night. He pulled the blankets up to her chin as she tossed restlessly in her sleep and he frowned. She was being troubled by nightmares, he thought, and he felt helpless in the face of the things that haunted her. Or was the fever returning?

He placed his hand on her forehead and felt that her brow was cool. He breathed a sigh of relief as he stared down at her, but remained concerned for her troubled dreams. He would have given his very life to take away her pain. 'Oh, Kate,' he whispered softly. 'If you only knew how much I love you.'

He took away his hand from her forehead and gazed at her for a long time before leaving her to prepare his bedroll a short distance away. According to what Harry had told him, they were presently camped on Glen View land and very close to the hills that Henry James had described where the dispersal had been carried out. That knowledge alone could bring on nightmares, he thought, as he fell into a deep but untroubled sleep of his own.

25

Kondola sat cross-legged before the fire crooning his song, while tiny stick figures danced a corroboree and surreal kangaroos hopped. The flickering flames of the fire brought them to life on the wall of the cave and not even the distant and mournful howling of the dingo in the depths of the night could interrupt the old warrior. Nor the inquisitive little possums watching wide-eyed from the branches of a gnarled gum tree would dare disturb the song as they listened in hushed silence. In time they would tell the story to their children of the last of the Nerambura elders who came to the cave on the wings of an eagle to sing the last song for his people in the Dreaming.

Soon the dingo would cease its howling and the calls of the curlews would rise as a sad symphony to the star-filled night sky as the old Aboriginal warrior tugged at his grey beard and remembered with deep and unremitting sadness how it had been before the white man came with his flocks of sheep to chase away the creatures of the bush.

And he mourned for himself, as no one was left to mark his passing with the rites accorded to a man who had proved himself a great warrior among his own people. No relatives to place his body on a dais of sticks and stones so that the young warriors could anoint themselves with the dripping secretions from his body as future aspirants to his title of great hunter and warrior. And no one to tie his legs and bury him in a shallow grave until the time came for his bones to be removed and placed respectfully in a hollow log to sleep with the possums and cockatoos that made their home with him. Now he was totally alone with the spirits of those he once knew as the people of his clan.

His gaunt ochre and feather-daubed body marked his hunger. But there were no young men to hunt the wallaby or women to make the nardoo cakes and his stomach growled. He had subsisted on the lizards and wild honey he had found in the crevices of the rocks on the hill.

They were coming. Not the white men on their horses who tended the sheep. No, the woman was coming. The Spirits had spoken to him in his sleep and had told him that he must guide her to the sacred place. They did not tell him why he was to help the woman, but he sensed that she had the power to see and remember all that had happened in the shadow of the sacred hill.

The chanting had wearied the old Aboriginal warrior and he lay on his side by the fire to drift into a deep sleep from which he would never return.

Just before dawn Luke came awake with a start.

The whimpering was not very loud, but to

Luke's experienced ear it was definitely out of place in the early morning sounds of the bush. He groped for the Colt, always within his reach, and rolled on his belly. 'Kate?' he called softly. 'Can you hear me?' The whimpering ceased and Luke crawled like a stalking leopard across to her, fully alert to any danger that might present itself.

'Luke!' Kate mumbled as she fought off the last remnants of the dream and saw his face inches from hers.

'Are you all right?' he asked anxiously.

'Yes . . .' she answered hesitantly. 'Yes, I am all right.' She sat up and rubbed her eyes. 'Where did the old black man go?'

Luke scanned the scrub of the early morning, but only the soft and gentle sound of the cowbells jangling and the distant cry of curlews came to him. The dog would have barked had an intruder entered the area around the dray. Nothing moved in the early morning chill. 'I didn't see any blackfellas. You sure you weren't dreaming?' he observed quietly.

Kate was now fully awake and she could see him clearly outlined against the last of the morning stars.

'I must have been dreaming,' she mumbled. But the old Aboriginal had spoken. And she had understood every word he said. No wild Aboriginal could have done that. He had been so real and she could vividly remember the strange scars on his back and skinny chest and the strange painted designs daubed over his body. There were feathers of wild birds stuck to him and she remembered that he was very old and seemed

373

to know who she was. The dream had not been a nightmare but it had still frightened her by its reality. It was like the time Tom had come to her in the fever. Who are you? Where are you? Now she understood.

'Luke, I know where my father and Billy are buried,' she said softly. 'And I know why I am here.' The meaning of the dream came back to her and she trembled for the terrible things he had shown her.

Luke instinctively put his arms round her shoulders and she did not resist his embrace. 'I saw it all,' she whispered in an awed voice. 'The little children being killed by the troopers. It was horrible. Those poor innocent children slaughtered.' Her voice quavered as the woman born in Ireland spilled tears for a people slaughtered under the red sun of the Australian plains. 'They came in the morning and the mothers watched helplessly as the troopers laughed and slaughtered their children.' Kate's tears of grief splashed down her cheeks and her voice was choked as she forced herself to continue. 'They tried to run but the white men were waiting for them at the hills and . . .' she hesitated. 'The old man told me why I am here but he could not show me the future. He told me there was too much pain for me to know. Oh, Luke, I'm frightened.' He held her tightly in his arms and rocked her gently as she sobbed with the terrible memory of the dispersal.

The little cattle dog sleeping beside his master lifted his head from his paws, rose and padded across to Kate, where he put his wet nose in her lap. The little dog understood the pain she was experiencing. Luke held Kate in his arms until the first warming rays of the sun kissed the brigalow scrub.

Kondola had taken her to a place where no woman had ever stepped before in the history of the Nerambura clan. It was a place taboo to women. But he had taken her into the sacred cave and shown her the painted wall as the Spirits of the rocks and stones of the hill had told him he must.

The place by the creek was eerie and frightening.

There were the sad echoes of children's happy laughter at play and the lazy melodious voices of old men and women at gossip around the cold ashes of fire.

Luke stood among the bleaching bones with his rifle over his shoulder. He bent and scooped up the tiny skull of what would once have been a child. There was a hole through the skull marking the entry of the lead ball from a trooper's carbine and he felt a twinge of guilt as if he were desecrating a graveyard. He replaced the skull carefully where he had found it. 'This must have been the site of the blackfellas' camp,' he said unnecessarily. 'Sure must have been some massacre.'

He was prompted to reflect on his own experiences at the Eureka Stockade almost a decade earlier. 'I think I know how the Nerambura felt,' he said softly, 'when they saw the troopers come down on them . . . poor bastards!'

Kate sat astride her horse watching him. A great sorrow swept her as she gazed down at the tiny scattered bones of a baby and thought of her own dead child. Unrestrained tears welled in her eyes.

'Those poor mothers seeing their babies killed. Seeing them trampled by the horses,' she whispered and felt her sorrow for the slaughtered children replaced with an avenging rage as she watched Luke pick his way through the scattered bones towards her. She even hated the big English sergeant because he had been part of all this. But her hatred was tempered by the memory of his guilt-haunted eyes. Henry James was already in hell.

Luke swung himself into the saddle. 'I don't think we should stay here any longer,' he said and she wholeheartedly agreed.

They rode in silence with Kate taking the lead away from the forlorn place of slaughter and they did not look back. In time, the bones would be obliterated by nature and become little more than a distant sad memory.

'Here! We are here, Luke,' Kate exclaimed as she stood in the stirrups to peer across a clearing in the scrub and Luke reined in beside her. The ground looked little different from what they had traversed since leaving the site of the massacre hours earlier, except that there was a big old gum tree at the edge of a natural clearing and two untidy piles of stones under the tree. 'This is where my father and Old Billy are! I just know it,' Kate said and her eyes shone with the revelation of discovery.

Luke slid from his saddle and Kate followed his lead. Neither knew who had buried the two men but, as she knelt beside the graves, Kate felt it must have been her brother.

'I have come all this way,' she sighed, 'and I do not know in which grave my father is buried.' Luke placed his hand on her shoulder.

'If your father and Billy were mates, like you told me, I don't think your father will be too concerned whatever grave you grieve over,' he offered gently. 'Mates out here share a special kind of friendship that I haven't seen anywhere else.'

She reached up and placed her hand over his. 'You are right,' she said quietly. 'Father loved Old Billy. Thank you.' Luke felt the warmth of her hand in his and her touch was gentle.

Kate scooped a handful of the red soil and sprinkled the earth on both graves as she prayed silently for her father and Old Billy. Graves were becoming a part of her life. First it had been the grave of her baby, and now these. Although Luke did not consider himself much of a churchgoing man, he found himself silently wishing the spirits of the two men eternal peace as he stood with his battered hat in his hands. Pat Duffy had been a friend who had stood with him against the guns and bayonets of the British at the stockade, and now he rode with the big Irishman's daughter as her guide and protector.

'It is time to go.' She sighed as she stood. 'We have a long ride ahead of us.'

He nodded and followed her back to the grazing horses.

The craggy hill rose above the scrub like a majestic cathedral and Kate gazed at the hill knowing she was seeing the spires of an ancient place of worship, except that this cathedral was of stone covered in dry scrub and many thousands of years older than anything in Western civilisation.

'Thank you,' she whispered as she gazed upon the summit where she sensed that the old Aboriginal was resting in an eternal sleep. She turned her attention to Luke, who rode ahead and looked so much a part of his horse . . . like a sunburnt centaur, she thought. But admiration for his skills as a bushman were not the only thoughts she was having for him. There had been times when she had felt guilty about her yearnings to surrender herself to him, but she dismissed the erotic thoughts as a natural part of her loneliness. If she were to give herself to him, then he would have to shave off his beard first. It would tickle, she mused, and she giggled self-consciously at the image of the American without his beard.

Luke twisted in the saddle, casting her a quizzical look as she stifled her giggling and she flashed a reassuring smile at him. He frowned and returned to scanning the bush.

He was always vigilant! Possibly she could shave the beard off while he was asleep, Kate thought, and the image of him waking to find his cherished beard gone caused her to break into uncontrollable laughter. This time Luke brought his horse to a halt and turned in the saddle to give the young woman a longer and more concerned look.

'Are you all right, Kate?' he asked with a worried look. Had the woman got too much sun?

'I am well, Luke,' she answered between bouts of laughter as she tried to bring her mirth under control. He shook his head, muttering opinions on the sanity of young women, before spurring his mount forward into the mottled shadows of the sparse scrub. He had only ridden a hundred yards when he suddenly reined his mare to a stop and signalled to Kate to halt. Luke stood in his stirrups to peer through the scrub.

Something was wrong, Kate thought with a frown as she watched him staring tensely ahead and slip his Snider from the rifle bucket beside his knee. With the butt of the rifle on his hip, he waited with the tension of a coiled spring. Then she heard the distant thunder of galloping horses and she shared his tension.

The four heavily armed horsemen galloped into view and reined to a dusty halt a few yards from them.

'Are you Kathleen Duffy?' Donald Macintosh asked belligerently. She was about to answer when Luke cut her short.

'Who are you, Mister?' He asked the question, while he held the rifle on Donald. 'You tell me that first.'

Donald eyed the American and was acutely aware of where the rifle pointed at him.

'I'm the owner of the land you are on,' the Scot growled. 'And that gives me the right to ask the questions.'

'I thought there was a custom around these parts', Luke said calmly, 'that a man could pass through land without being bushwhacked.'

'Anyone can,' Donald snarled, as his shepherds stared curiously at Kate, 'so long as they aren't a Duffy.' The shepherds had never seen a woman dressed like a man riding astride a horse before

379

and they could not help but notice how pretty the young woman was, despite the fact of her manly attire.

'I am a Duffy . . . Mister Macintosh,' Kate cut across him defiantly. 'And this land will not always be yours to decide who rides across it,' she added imperiously.

The Scottish squatter flared at her impertinence. He instinctively reached for his revolver but he froze when the American growled, 'You planning to be buried here, Mister?' Donald dropped his hand away from his pistol and the shepherds looked to their boss for orders. But none was issued, as Donald sensed that the man was prepared to die to protect the girl. The deadly determination was clearly reflected in the cold eyes of the tall man watching him like a hawk. A bloody American, from the sound of the man's accent, Donald thought angrily. A man just stupid enough to go down fighting for the Duffy woman. He was very aware of the terrible damage a Snider bullet could do to a man's body at close range.

'Get off my land now,' he snarled. 'And don't ever come back. If you ever come back, I will take steps to ensure that you leave in less than a civilised manner.'

'We will leave, Mister Macintosh,' Kate said, 'but one day this land will not belong to you. And I have sworn on my father's grave that I will do everything in my power to take this land from you, even if it takes me all my life to do so.'

Luke felt uneasy. He could see in the squatter's expression that Kate's calmly delivered threat had pushed him to a point where he was liable to forget the rifle levelled at him.

'So long as I am alive,' Donald replied as he leant in the saddle towards Kate, 'I can make you a promise that will never happen, lassie.'

'We can both agree on that point,' she said softly. 'Your years are numbered by the spirits of the people you slaughtered, for they will be avenged as certainly as the sun rises every day.'

Donald felt a superstitious chill in the hot still air of the midmorning and he shivered. It was not in the words that she uttered but in the cold grey of the eyes that locked with his. In their depth, he saw a fleeting glimpse of a spear with the distinctive long hardwood shaft that had taken the life of his son Angus.

Without replying, he wheeled away and his men followed reluctantly. They had been looking forward to killing the Yankee and taking his woman.

Donald Macintosh rode away knowing the Irish bushranger was not the only threat he faced from the Duffys. Like some ancient Celtic witch, the woman seemed to have a presence about her that was dangerous in ways that only a Gael could understand. 'I should have killed her,' he muttered as the distance between them increased and he knew with a certainty that they would meet again one day and in the meeting would be a final resolution.

Luke remained alert until he was satisfied that Macintosh and his shepherds were out of effective rifle range before he rode slowly over to Kate and reached out to take hold of her hand. 'Are you all right?' he asked gently.

She nodded and her words came as a whisper. 'I thought they were going to shoot you, Luke.'

He shook his head and gave her a reassuring smile. 'Better men have tried and failed. As a matter of fact, the whole bloody British army tried once.'

She felt reassured at his bravado and the colour slowly returned to her face.

'I think we should take Mister Macintosh's advice and leave,' she said as she gave his hand a squeeze. She added with a wan smile, 'I think somehow that you will always be there when I need you.'

He felt her hand close on his and he wished that what she had said could be true.

Two weary weeks later they rode into Rockhampton.

The confrontation with Donald Macintosh on Glen View had been a pivotal point in Kate's life. She had expressed in words the sacred duty that had been passed to her from the old Aboriginal. But she was at a loss to how she was to achieve the seemingly impossible task. Had the old Aboriginal asked too much from her?

In Rockhampton, she surprised Luke with her present of the three horses that she had bought with the help of Judith and Solomon Cohen. He tried lamely to tell her that he could not accept the horses, but she insisted. She brushed aside his gratitude with explanations that he had earned them for all that he had done for her. Judith was quick to see the dark expression of sadness cloud the American's face. It was obvious that the man was in love with the young woman, she mused, with some annoyance at the way Kate was apparently blind to his feelings. Kate O'Keefe, you are a stupid woman sometimes, she thought.

Kate was aware that Luke would leave one day. She could see his restlessness when he stopped off at the hotel where she worked as a barmaid. He would sit with the bushmen and talk of distant places in the northern colony and she understood his yearning to once again ride the vast open plains in search of gold. The same love of the harsh but beautiful plains had infected her.

For a while he worked at odd jobs for Solomon or worked at his old job of clearing timber, until he had enough money to outfit himself for a prospecting expedition. Whenever he could, he would spend time with Kate on her days off from the hotel and they would take a picnic hamper into the bush and sit under the shade of a tree, talking about everything and nothing, like courting lovers.

Although she accepted his leaving was inevitable, she had hoped that he might stay a little longer as she had grown used to him being in her life. But she was careful never to express any feeling for him other than friendship. It was not that she did not feel strongly for him, but she was still married, and wondered if her husband might return to her.

One day Judith told her that Luke was gone and that he had left at first light with the three horses. He'd left no details about where he was going or if he would ever return. Kate's disappointment was evident when she turned on Judith and asked angrily, 'Why did he not at least leave a message for me? I thought we were friends.'

'Because Luke is in love with you, Kate,' she remonstrated softly. 'And he carries the pain that you do not feel the same way about him.'

Kate stared wide-eyed at Judith. How did he know how she felt about him when he had never asked her? she thought, in her stunned surprise at Luke's sudden disappearance from her life. Deep down she was forced to admit to herself that she could not express her feelings for Luke. But she was not sure why. Was it that she had a need to protect her feelings? That love was the only emotion powerful enough to destroy her? She had once loved her husband and he had abandoned her. Whatever it was, she sensed that Luke Tracy held a power over her she could not afford to experience.

On a ridge overlooking Rockhampton, Luke reined in his horses.

He sat astride the mare Kate had given him and he gazed down on the town nestled on the banks of the Fitzroy River. Kate was somewhere down there, he thought. If only you knew how much I love you. But Kate had not seen his love for her and the pain of loving without that love returned had grown into an ache he knew he could no longer endure. There were too many reminders of her existence in his life around Rockhampton and he knew he must leave. Beyond the range was the seemingly endless horizon of the colony and somewhere beyond that horizon was the undiscovered gold strike that could give a man's name immortality.

He knew in the months to come he would ride with the image of Kate O'Keefe sitting across from every camp fire he made. She would be sipping tea from an old enamel mug and laughing at his wry stories of the bush. With a deep sigh of regret for all that he had lost in the past, and for all that was not to be his in the future, he gave his mount a gentle kick to spur her forward as he tugged on the lead rope of the packhorses. Love was not something that could be destroyed by a bullet. His love for Kate hurt worse than a bayonet wound.

26

A carriage drawn by matched greys rumbled down the finely crushed gravel driveway. It rattled along an avenue of trees standing naked against the drizzle of a wet Sydney afternoon and it came to a halt in front of the main entrance of the two-storeyed house.

Enid Macintosh alighted from the carriage unassisted. She was a woman who had grown accustomed to doing many things on her own and she preferred to dispense with trivial social niceties in favour of getting on with affairs. She issued crisp orders for the coachman to take the parcels piled in the carriage to her room.

She shivered as she moved from the cold wet day into the warm and dry interior of her house, while behind her struggled the coachman with an armful of parcels. A bountiful result of her shopping trip to the David Jones store in town.

There had been many things to buy for the arrival of spring. It was a time of social engagements as the city came out of the cold winter to celebrate the birth of life and the normally frugal woman indulged herself lavishly when it came to buying clothes to meet the round of dinner parties, picnics and balls.

The front door was opened by a pretty young dark-eyed maid wearing a spotless white pinafore.

'Mister White is in the living room, ma'am,' Betsy announced as she helped Enid remove her damp woollen cloak. 'He arrived a short while ago.'

'Thank you, Betsy,' Enid replied. 'Tell Mister White I will see him in a little while. Oh, and see if Mister White might like a sherry or port while he is waiting,' she added as she removed her kidskin gloves from her hands.

'Yes, ma'am,' Betsy answered dutifully as she took her mistress's cloak away to dry it by the kitchen fire.

Enid was puzzled by the unexpected arrival of her nephew, as she thought he was still in Melbourne discussing future loans with the bankers for the expansion of their pastoral interests in Queensland. He had been gone four months and the protocol of requesting a visit to the Macintosh residence had been flouted by him on his return. Enid was mildly annoyed at his rather rude assumption that he could visit her without a formal invitation. To her, social etiquette existed to maintain the dignity of established conventions and deviation from etiquette bordered on anarchy. She went straight to her room to change from her damp clothes.

Enid entered the drawing room as her nephew stood warming himself in front of the huge open fireplace. He was watching the tiny flames flick from the red coals of the burning logs as he toyed with a glass of sweet sherry. He turned from his brooding silence to acknowledge her entry.

'Hello, Aunt Enid,' he said as she swept into the room. 'I am sorry I did not have time to send around my card. But I have an idea you know why I am here.'

Enid guessed Penelope had told her brother the news. 'I think I have a good idea what you want to discuss, Granville,' she said imperiously. 'You were going to be told . . . All in good time.'

Granville glared at her and struggled to find the words to express his fury for the ultimate betrayal. 'She is ruined goods,' he finally exploded. 'She is carrying the child of that Irish bastard Duffy.'

'No, I believe Mister Duffy was born in wedlock,' Enid replied serenely as she sat on a sofa watching her nephew's anger with some amusement. He needed to be kept off balance from time to time, she mused, and said calmly, 'His child will be the bastard . . . And as for being "ruined goods" as you put it, no one will know except for the immediate family and Molly O'Rourke. I have told my friends that Fiona is visiting relatives at Goulburn.'

'What happens when she arrives back in Sydney with the child? Or have you already thought about that?' he asked unnecessarily as he knew his aunt would have considered all ramifications of an unwanted child to their interests.

'I have. Fiona will not be coming back to Sydney with the child, as I have made arrangements with Molly to dispose of the baby,' she replied as if she were talking about the disposal of an unwanted puppy.

388

Granville stared at his aunt with just a touch of respect and awe. She was most certainly a formidable woman! Ruthless and possibly even dangerous to anyone who might dare to attempt to thwart her ambitions.

'By dispose,' he said quietly, 'I assume you mean the baby will be born dead.'

Enid displayed the slightest smile of contempt when she replied. 'We do not all require the services of men like Mister Horton to achieve our ends,' she said sweetly and Granville baulked at the mention of Jack Horton's name. But he made no comment as he did not know how much his aunt knew. Or even how she knew at all! 'Oh, it was not hard to realise what you had done when I read in the newspapers about Mister Duffy being wanted for murder,' Enid continued serenely. 'I supposed it had to be more than just a coincidence that you employed Mister Horton, especially when he has a reputation as a very violent and dangerous man.'

Granville swallowed his glass of sherry which had lost its pleasant taste. 'What would you have done to rid us of Michael Duffy, dear Aunt?' he asked with a bitter edge of sarcasm. 'Request him not to see Fiona. Tell him he was not of a suitable pedigree, although that does not seem to have entered his mind when he put Fiona with child. What would you have done?'

'Probably what you did,' she replied frankly. 'I have no intention of allowing my daughter to marry outside her station in life. Let alone to some grubby Irishman. As for the child, it will be suitably disposed of by Molly.'

She was so devilishly confident as she sat with her hands in her lap, Granville reflected. It was so strange that Fiona had not inherited her mother's ruthless nature. Or had she?

'Now I see why you chose November for the wedding,' he said as he refilled his glass from the crystal decanter on a sideboard. 'Fiona should be sufficiently recovered by then.'

'That is part of the reason,' Enid answered. 'The other part is that November marks the death of Angus. And I think it is appropriate that his memory be celebrated with a new start in life for the family, with you and Fiona marrying. Mister Macintosh and I have decided that a passage to Europe is a fitting wedding present for you both and I am sure the tour will do Fiona good. An opportunity for you to have Christmas with your dear mother in England.'

He was pleasantly surprised at her generous wedding present and he responded graciously. 'Thank you, Aunt Enid. It will be an honour having you as my mother-in-law,' he said with just a faint touch of sarcasm, and he raised his glass as a toast to their future relationship.

'Oh, there is one other thing I should mention,' Enid said, ignoring her future son-in-law's sarcasm and toast. 'When your children are born they will be christened under the name Macintosh-White.'

Granville did not need to consider what his future mother-in-law had proposed, as he felt that the union of the two families in the next generation was a fitting gesture and, besides, *he* would be controlling both sides of the family through his marriage to Fiona.

'Oh, one more thing before you leave,' she added, as if she had just thought of it, and he felt uneasy about the facetious edge that had crept into his aunt's tone. 'I want you to get rid of the gardener's daughter from your house, as you will not need her services when you are married to my daughter. For that matter, get rid of the gardener. The stupid man does not know how to prune roses.'

Granville's bottom lip dropped. The damned woman knew everything!

When Granville arrived at his home he was not surprised to see a strange carriage outside. It was not pretentious but bespoke moderate wealth. He was greeted by his old cook, whose talent was just as much for discretion and loyalty as it was for her wonderful cooking.

'Yer sister is entertainin' a gen'leman friend,' she said sarcastically as he shook off the outside cold. 'I think she will be down from 'er room soon.'

Granville frowned and thanked her for the information then went directly to the library, where he poured himself a single malt scotch. He stood staring down at the footman and carriage waiting in the driveway below. He soon saw a well-dressed young gentleman come out of the house and climb into the carriage to be whisked away.

Granville swallowed the last remnants of the expensive scotch and left the library to go to his sister's room. This time he knocked before daring to make his entrance. Penelope opened the door to him with a smile which quickly turned to a frown.

'Your gentleman friend has left,' Granville said as he appraised her wearing little more than a silk chemise. 'As I suspect, your smile was for him and not me, dear sister.'

'I did not expect you to return so soon from Aunt Enid's,' Penelope said as she turned and walked back into the bedroom. He felt the old lust as he watched the inviting sensual movement of her buttocks rising and falling under the short garment. 'I expect that Enid has informed you of her plans for the wedding in November,' she added as she sat down in a chair in front of a large mirror to brush her long golden tresses.

'She has,' he said as he plonked himself on her large bed, where the sheets were as dishevelled as her hair. 'You have obviously satisfied your part of the bargain we agreed to.'

'It was not easy,' Penelope replied as the brush of sterling silver inlay swept the full length of her hair. 'Fiona has a childish and romantic idea that Michael Duffy will return to her. I suspect that it has something to do with the condition she suffers,' she added, as though pregnancy were a mind-altering disease.

Granville felt the ghost of an old fear return. While the damned Irishman lived, his hold on Fiona would never be certain. If only Horton had been successful. What if Duffy returned and was cleared of his supposed crime of murder? 'But she has agreed to marry me,' he said as part statement, part question.

'You have nothing to fear,' his sister replied, staring at his worried reflection in the mirror. 'Fiona has always done what I wanted her to do in the past. She will give up her baby, marry you and bear your heirs, dear brother. And in time I'm sure you will find ways to help her forget her Irishman. Wealth has that effect on women. All else is simply icing on a cake.'

'You are obviously not a romantic,' he said lightly.

'You should know,' she retorted bitterly as she turned to him. 'You made me what I am, Granville. I might have been like Fiona had you not taught me well in the ways of men. Or is it that I am truly like you in every way? That I have inherited the darkness that has always been in our side of the family, an unnatural desire that our wealth is able to buy ... as you do the girl, Jennifer, to satisfy your physical needs? I suppose I shall never know who I am because you took that opportunity from me a long time ago.'

She wanted to pour out the venom of her feelings to the man she most loved – and hated – in the world, but she checked herself, knowing that any further outpouring of feelings might disclose her burning desire to hurt him as much as he had hurt her.

Instead, she turned back to the mirror and continued brushing her hair with long strokes, even though her hands trembled.

'Don't expect an apology from me,' Granville said coldly, rising from the bed. 'I do not apologise for what I take for my needs.'

She paused from brushing her hair. 'No, we don't apologise for what we take,' she said with a bitter smile creasing her full lips. 'We are Whites and destined to rule all that we see. But remember well, dear brother, no one knows you as I do. And, in knowing you, I know the ghosts you live with. For that, I would feel great fear if I were you, because one day I might use them against you.'

'I doubt that you would do that,' he scoffed. 'You might think you can frighten me but when it is all said and done you are still a mere woman at the mercy of your emotions. Like all other women, your pleasures are simple and your desires predictable. You need a strong man to provide you with the wealth to satisfy your mercenary needs, children to give you an identity and the never-ending social engagements to show off the pretty clothes you wear. No, there is nothing you could do to me, dear sister, that I could ever perceive as a threat, despite all that you might know about me.' He shook his head and flashed her a smug smile as he left her alone in the bedroom to reflect on his self-assuredness.

Her first instinct was to hurl the hairbrush at his departing back. Instead she smiled grimly and returned to brushing her hair. She would not give him the satisfaction of an emotional display and she realised that her hands no longer trembled. Dear brother, if you only knew . . .

An icy flurry of sleet lashed the stone cottage at the end of the narrow gum tree lane. The cottage had a commanding view of the sweep of valleys below. Although it was small in comparison to the more grandiose Macintosh house overlooking the harbour in Sydney, it was large enough to accommodate four people plus three staff. For the moment, the isolated cottage high up in the Blue

Mountains west of Sydney was being lashed with a late winter cold snap.

Fiona Macintosh sat in the cosy kitchen with a blanket over her knees and stared wistfully at the neatly written copperplate invitation in her lap. She sighed regretfully, and placed the invitation beside her other correspondence on the kitchen table.

'Lady Manning is having a ball at Walleroy and I shan't be able to attend,' she said to Molly, who sat beside her knitting a woollen swaddling rug.

'There will be other balls, Fiona,' Molly replied maternally as she expertly manoeuvred the big needles. 'It won't be long before you will be the prettiest girl at all the spring balls.'

Fiona sighed again and put her hand to her swollen belly. The pregnancy had come as a shock. Oh, if only she had spoken to Penelope about ways to avoid such occurrences. But the baby was a fact of her life now and because of the pregnancy she had had a reason to initially decline Granville's proposal of marriage.

It had been Penelope who had finally convinced her that under no circumstances could the raising of the illegitimate child of a man wanted for murder be a practicable option. And Molly had promised her that her baby would go to a good Christian family. Although Fiona did not fully trust Penelope, she knew she could trust Molly completely. If she promised that her child would be given to good people then she was to be believed, and so she had relented to Granville's proposal.

Reconciled to her forthcoming marriage to her cousin, Fiona often thought about what life with him might be like. He was rather handsome and there was something deep and dark about him that fascinated her. It was as if he was Heathcliff from Miss Bronte's novel that she had read in the garden, rugged against the biting winds that swept up from the valleys.

She had chosen to read the novel with the mountains, valleys and mists as her companions because they gave greater pleasure to the atmosphere of the haunting and dark tale of love and passion.

Fiona had often cried alone in the garden when she placed the leather-bound book in her lap and she remembered Michael's strong arms around her. But she was also practical enough to know she would probably never see him again.

She had read in the Sydney papers of his being wanted for questioning in regard to the murder of a man only days after their wonderful time together at Manly. Despite the newspaper reports, she knew Michael could not be a killer as they described him. He was far too gentle and loving to cold-bloodedly kill another human.

Fiona had confided her feelings to Molly, who was a sympathetic listener.

''Tis a terrible thing, my darlin' girl. But life must go on,' she would always say, as she held the young woman to her breast, as she had when Fiona had been a child suffering nightmares after reading the terrifying novel *Frankenstein*. Fiona had found the book, which belonged to David, and she had avidly consumed the ideas of a creature made from the parts of dead men. She was only ten then, and reality and fantasy had been difficult to differentiate for an impressionable young girl.

Molly had provided her ample bosom then for Fiona to lie against as protection from the nightmares. Molly was always there for her.

Molly paused in her knitting as the wind reached a howling violence outside and a tree limb cracked in the night like a rifle shot. The foul weather brought back memories of her own childhood in Ireland before they had sent her as a young girl to the far-off convict colony of New South Wales.

Raped repeatedly by the soldiers and sailors of the convict transport ship, she had become pregnant at fourteen and her own child had died in the workhouse at Parramatta before Molly was Fiona's present age.

Enid and Donald Macintosh had secured her release from the terrible place to work for them as a domestic servant under a government scheme to use the services of convicts. She had proved a reliable servant and she had been appointed nanny to all three of the Macintosh children. But it was Fiona she felt closest to.

Fiona had been rejected by her natural mother from birth. Enid preferred to lavish her attention on Angus and David. It was as if she despised the fact that Fiona had been born a girl instead of a boy. And now Molly was going to hold the baby of the young woman whom she had once held squalling in her arms seventeen years earlier.

She glanced across at the pretty face of her little girl and felt a loving maternal ache for her. She was so young and the pregnancy had taken her childish innocence from her forever. The ache of nostalgia for things past turned to a terrible guilt and she looked away lest she see the pain in her face. God forgive me for what I am going to do, she prayed silently. Fiona, me darlin', if you only knew the pact I have made with your mother, you would kill me without hesitation.

But the pact was sealed with Enid Macintosh and Molly knew what she most wanted. So strong was her desire for her final dream to become a reality that she was prepared to betray the one person who most loved and trusted her in the world.

The wind rose even higher in its wailing cry and to Molly it was like the shriek of the banshee. She shuddered superstitiously. Had this been the answer from God to her prayer for forgiveness? Could there be forgiveness for what she was to do when Fiona's baby was born? She well knew the reputation of the infamous baby farms of Sydney. Baby farms was a strange way to describe places that committed systematic infanticide on unwanted babies. And the unwanted fruit of the Duffy and Macintosh bloodlines was destined for such a place.

The storm raged through the night but the morning came as a brilliant burst of sunshine in the mountains. Butterflies appeared as if conjured by the spirit of spring to fill the garden with their fluttering colour. Birds warbled their welcome to the blue sky and the tall and majestic gum trees stood as salutes to the sun.

Fiona harried Molly to assist her to dress for a day in the garden, where she could luxuriate in the warmth of the wonderful spring day under the shade of a spreading eucalypt. Being with nature this day had a strong call for the young woman expecting her first child. It was as if the beauty of the mountains could be absorbed by her body to give strength to the unborn child.

Molly fussed around her with blankets and slippers to keep her warm. She only agreed to leave Fiona alone so long as the blanket remained across her lap and she promised that she would call on her if she required anything.

Before midday, Fiona complied with the promise to call for her nanny. It was not so much a call as a cry of distress, as the pains came in crippling waves.

Molly came running and, with the help of the brawny coachman, she helped the pain-racked young woman inside the cottage. Urgent orders were snapped at the various members of the staff to fetch hot water, clean cloths and the doctor from the nearby settlement of Katoomba.

But before the doctor had time to arrive, Molly held the red and slippery baby boy in her arms. The coachman paced up and down the stone verandah outside the cottage like an expectant father while the cook made cooing sounds of wonder between cleaning mother and child.

Fiona lay exhausted against the sheets in a lather of sweat and she was hardly aware that her labour had lasted into the early evening while she had held Molly's hand and cried out in her agony. It had been a difficult birth but the Irish nanny's skills as a midwife had helped ease her pain.

The doctor had arrived by buggy, examined his patient, and declared that she required nothing more than rest and time to recover. He'd dispensed a draught of laudanum and left with a fat envelope swelled by pound notes to buy his silence. Enid's meticulous planning left nothing to chance and now it was up to Molly to dispose of the baby as they had agreed in their unholy pact.

In the early hours of the following morning, Fiona awoke from her deep opiate-induced sleep to call for Molly. Molly did not come to her. But the milk in Fiona's swollen breasts did come without having her baby to suckle.

All she could remember as she lay in the darkness of her bedroom, of the life that had lived in her body, was that it was a wet, slippery and squirming thing that had bawled when exposed to the world for the first time. A boy, Molly had told her, before he was taken from the room and from her life.

Fiona sobbed as she had never sobbed before. For now she knew what it meant to experience the greatest sorrow of a woman and somewhere in the depths of the night, in the dark corners of the room, she thought she heard echoes of a frightening whisper. A spirit whisper, swept off the harsh brigalow plains, and carried on the wind from a place where children lay dead in the arms of their mothers.

27

For two days and two nights Fiona called for Molly. But still she did not come.

The staff assigned to her confinement whispered outside the young woman's bedroom and shook their heads sadly.

On the third day her mother arrived and, after a short conference with the staff, Enid went to her daughter's bedroom where Fiona lay against the pillows gaunt and hollow-eyed. She turned her face slowly to her mother, who sat in a chair, watching her with maternal concern clearly etched on her face.

'I was informed by Missus Weekes that your labour was difficult,' Enid said formally as though addressing a stranger rather than her daughter. 'Although Doctor Champion informed me at Katoomba that you would recover fully with a few days' rest.'

Fiona stared at her mother. 'Where is Molly?' she asked in a hollow voice.

'No one seems to know.' Enid frowned. 'The damned woman was supposed to report to me in Sydney but she has not. I fear she has broken her service without notice and cannot expect any reference if she comes begging to me at a future time. Disloyalty is an unforgivable sin.'

'Where did she take my baby?' Enid was aware that her daughter was fixing her with feverish eyes as if a revelation had come upon her in her re- covery period. Without waiting for her mother to reply, she answered her own question. 'She took my baby to one of those terrible baby farms I have heard Molly speak of. She has taken my baby to be murdered. Hasn't she, Mother?'

The accusation caused Enid to glance away. 'I will not lie,' she replied defiantly. 'So I will not answer your question, Fiona. I expect you to understand your duty to the family. To appreciate how important your place beside Granville is to the future of the family. It will be you who will bear the children who will carry our blood heritage into the next century.'

'I carried a child in my body all these months,' Fiona said in a pleading voice. 'Did not that child carry our blood, Mother? Was not that child part Macintosh?'

'Tainted by Popish Irish blood,' her mother retorted angrily. 'A bastard not born to our class, and my decision was the only one that could be made under the circumstances. I would suggest that the sooner you forget this episode of your life the better it will be for your future happiness. Oh, I understand that you will naturally grieve for your loss for a little while, but time will heal your grief just as it has mine for the death of your brother. What has happened has been God's will and your sacrifice is His way of helping you repent for your sin . . .'

'Sin? My sin? Does the murder of my child constitute a sacrifice?' Fiona spat. 'Is our God the pagan god Baal of the Bible, who demands human sacrifice?'

'Do not blaspheme,' Enid shot back savagely. 'God will not be mocked by your blasphemy, Fiona. God has ordained that we must provide generations to give wise guidance to those people born of inferior blood . . . the black people . . . the Irish . . . and others like them.'

'I want you to leave, Mother,' Fiona said, turning her face away. 'I do not want to be in your presence unless absolutely necessary. Not because you have killed my baby, not because what I have done in allowing him to be taken from me makes me as guilty as you . . . but because you dare to justify murder in the name of God and duty. Go, Mother. Go now and leave me with my pain. A pain I doubt you could ever be capable of knowing.'

Enid stood and stared at the back of her daughter's head. She could hear Fiona's sobbing and she wanted to reach out and hold her, despite the bitter words that had come between them. Instead she consoled herself in the knowledge that her daughter would heal with the natural progression of time and Doctor Champion's doses of laudanum.

She swept from the room and called for the coachman who tended the horses at the cottage. He ambled from the stables, wiping axle grease on the sides of his leather apron. He was a big and brawny man whose powerful arms bespoke his time bending red-hot iron in the blacksmith's forge.

'Tell me what transpired after the baby was born, Hill,' she commanded as she stood like a diminutive doll before the huge man. 'And get that surly look off your face.'

'Sorry, Missus Macintosh,' he mumbled as he bowed his head. 'I done what you asked. I took Miss Molly down to Sydney an' she left with the kid.'

'Left her where?' she snapped. The big man shuffled his feet and could not look her in the eye. 'Speak, man. Where did you leave her?'

'At the place you said to go.'

'Why didn't she return with you then?'

'I doan know,' he mumbled. 'She never come back to the carriage. I looked for her but she weren't anywhere to be seen. She jus' disappeared into thin air.'

Enid stared at him for a short while, but he did not elaborate any further on the Irish nanny's disappearance. 'Thank you, Mister Hill,' she said formally. 'I am sure you are telling the truth and I'm sure Miss O'Rourke will make contact with me in the near future.'

'That all, Missus Macintosh?' the coachman asked and was relieved to be dismissed.

He had never liked the thought of taking the baby to one of the infamous baby farms as he had too often been involved in the delivery of life himself, albeit horses and sheep. The idea of destroying a perfectly healthy creature was against all he held precious. But the whims of the gentry had to be pandered to if he was to keep his employment. He had actually been relieved when Molly had not returned to the coach, although he had wondered what had happened to her. He hoped the baby would be safe somewhere. The little mite had grasped his thick finger with his tiny hand during a stop at an inn on the way down to Sydney. In doing so he had infused the brawny coachman with a part of his little life. No, it was not easy to be a part of destroying a helpless little life – man or animal.

David Macintosh sat at his desk in his office and stared at the newspaper article. If what it said was true then the ramifications would certainly ripple around his family circle. So engrossed was he in the article that he had forgotten the cup of tea George Hobbs had placed on his desk and the tea was cold by the time he neatly folded the paper and placed it beside the cup and saucer.

He leaned back in his swivel chair with his hands behind his head, staring at the door to the office. He wondered what Granville would say when he was told the news. News that would certainly affect his soon-to-be brother-in-law.

David glanced up at the loudly ticking clock on the wall and he noted that it was almost ten o'clock in the morning. Granville would be on time for their appointment. Whatever else he found irritating about his cousin, punctuality was his one saving grace.

The appointment had been made to discuss the implications of Robert Towns landing his first cargo of South Sea Islanders in Brisbane, where they were to be assigned to work on his cotton plantation on the Logan River, south of the growing colonial town.

In turn, Granville would introduce the newly appointed captain of the *Osprey* to him and discuss the islands he had identified as the most likely places to recruit black labour for the Macintosh sugar and cotton plantations.

But David did not have to be introduced to the new captain. He already knew the man. They had met earlier that year on his trip north to Queensland.

The clock chimed ten and, on cue, Hobbs poked his head around the corner and formally announced Mister Granville White's arrival.

David rose from his chair when Granville entered the room with the new captain of the *Osprey*.

'Ah, Granville,' David said as he put out his hand to Mort. 'I see you have Mister Mort with you.' Mort accepted the extended hand and David was surprised to feel how limp his grip was. It was not what he expected from the reputedly hardened former Native Mounted Police officer.

'Pleased to make your acquaintance again, Mister Macintosh,' Mort said with polite deference to one of his new bosses and released his hand. 'Your father forwards his good wishes to you,' he added solicitously.

Granville sat in a leather chair in a corner of the office. He crossed his legs as he brushed back his thinning hair with a swipe of his hand. It was an unconscious gesture as his receding hair was a blemish on his vanity. 'Our Mister Mort is a man of many talents, David,' he said, wiping down his trousers of the imagined grime from David's office. He was fastidiously clean to the point of obsession.

David tended towards being untidy at times, which irked Granville's sense of all things having a place – and a place for all things. 'Appears our Mister Mort holds master's papers from his days prior to joining the Victorian constabulary back in '54,' he added. 'One could say the right man in the right place for our South Sea venture.'

'That is correct.' Mort was quick to confirm Granville's disclosure of his previous experience at sea. 'My original career was on the Hobart-Melbourne route. I was the first mate of the *Vandemonian*.'

'If I remember rightly, the *Vandemonian* was a brig,' David said as he returned to his chair. 'So the *Osprey* should suit you. Have you inspected the *Osprey* yet, Mister Mort?'

'I've taken Mister . . . should I now say, Captain Mort . . . aboard before we came here,' Granville said, answering David's question. 'I think, considering Captain Mort's considerable experience with dealing with our black brethren, he will be admirably suited to the task ahead of him. And I think your father was rather astute in recommending him to us.'

But David was not so sure about his father's wisdom. His own discreet inquiries about the enigmatic man's background had tended to paint a picture of someone with a dubious past. And there was the matter of his rather sudden resignation from the Queensland Native Mounted Police where it was rumoured, albeit unsubstantiated, that he had unnecessarily killed a trooper and he had been forced to tender his papers by his second-in-command.

And it was also rumoured that Mort was the illegitimate son of a serving girl from Sydney who had been dismissed when her unfortunate indiscretion with her employer could no longer be concealed from the man's wife. The young girl had been thrown on the street and turned to prostitution in Sydney's infamous Rocks, where Mort was born. But despite the man's lowly origins he had to give Mort his due. He had been able to rise above his past to get where he was now.

Seeing Mort and Granville together in his office, David felt they were two men cut from the same cloth, except from vastly different sides of society, and it was a comparison that did not sit well with him. One Granville to deal with was bad enough, David thought, but another! However, his father had recommended the man for the position as captain of the *Osprey*, and his father was the ultimate decision maker in the family. His wishes were to be respected regardless of the doubts David harboured concerning Mort's suitability.

David suddenly remembered the article he had been so engrossed in before his cousin's arrival. 'To digress for the moment, Granville,' he said. 'Have you read the report in the *Bulletin* covering the campaign in New Zealand?'

'No. I haven't had the chance as yet.' Granville frowned. 'Why, is there something I should know?'

'Well, if it is of any interest,' David replied, 'I have just read that a Michael Maloney was reported killed in a skirmish with the Maoris last week in the Waikato campaign.'

'Do I know the man?' Granville queried and was slightly annoyed at his cousin's theatricals.

'Apparently you did,' David answered, raising his eyebrows. 'According to the report, the man known as Michael Maloney was discovered to be an alias for one Michael Duffy. The report also says that he is reported to be the same Michael Duffy wanted for questioning by Sydney police on a matter of the death of a man here last January.'

Granville tensed. He quickly uncrossed his legs, stood up and snatched the folded paper from his cousin's desk. He flicked impatiently through the pages until he found the article reporting the Waikato campaign. As he scanned the report, his expression reflected his pleasure. So the Maoris had done what he had not been able to achieve – the death of Michael Duffy. The article also outlined how, after he had been killed, the soldier's real identity had been exposed by a comrade with von Tempsky's Forest Rangers. It was also reported that the man known as Michael Maloney – alias Duffy – had died in a courageous lone stand saving his comrades from a Maori ambush.

'I think Fiona should be told the tragic news as soon as possible,' Granville said smugly as he closed the paper. 'I am sure she will need a couple of days to grieve for the loss of a dear friend.'

With the Irishman well and truly dead, he knew she would lose any last flame of secret hope that she might harbour for his return. Now Duffy was nothing more than a ghost and he had never known of a ghost being able to physically hurt the living.

Jack Horton stood at the top of the *Osprey*'s gangplank as the ship lay tied to the wharf. He stared down at the labourers manhandling the last of the supplies aboard for the sea voyage into the South Pacific. He watched curiously as two men on the wharf, carrying a strange stool-like bench between them, struggled up the gangway.

At first he did not recognise the wooden bench for what it was. Then, as its purpose dawned on him, he flinched. 'A bloody whippin' stool,' he muttered uneasily. 'The bastard's got a whippin' stool.'

Close behind the two sweating men came the new captain, dressed in the fine dark blue uniform of the merchant seaman. He carried a sword on his belt and glanced around the deck with an expression of possessive pride as he came aboard.

'Good to have yer aboard, Cap'n,' Horton said solicitously as he eyed the bench being taken below deck to the captain's cabin. ''Aven'nt seen one of 'em in a long time.'

'You must be Horton, the first mate,' Mort said without extending his hand. 'I want to see you in my cabin now.'

Horton followed Mort below and watched nervously as the two labourers placed the bench in the little space the cabin provided. It sat like some heathen altar with its timber smoothed to a dark polish from much brutal use in its bloody past.

Mort ran his hand over the surface with a strange faraway look in his pale eyes. The first mate noticed this with a strange quiver of illogical fear. Was there a madness in the new captain? 'I was fortunate to find this,' Mort said, without looking up at him. 'Mister White knew just what to give me as a welcoming gift to the company.'

'If you don' mind me sayin', Cap'n Mort . . . It's a peculiar gift.'

Mort raised his eyes to lock with those of his first mate. 'He also told me about the circumstances of your employment aboard my ship,' Mort said, without commenting on the peculiarity of the gift. Horton sensed the deadly menace in the tone and he squirmed. 'Under the circumstances, he explained to me I could expect to have your total and unquestioning loyalty. Would I not, Mister Horton?'

'You would, Cap'n.'

Mort nodded and slid the sword from its scabbard. He placed it on the bench, where the blade caught a ray of sunlight through a porthole to gleam a fiery silver.

'He said I would be able to call on your "domain of skills" at any time. And in the difficult time ahead of us, possibly fraught with great perils, I expect your loyalty to be total,' he continued, fingering the sword as it lay on the bench. It was no idle gesture, as Horton could very well understand. 'So that will be all for now, Mister Horton. You can resume your duties overseeing the resupply.'

'Yes, Cap'n,' Horton said as he edged his way out of the cabin. He had met a lot of dangerous men in his violent life but none as dangerously mad as the new skipper of the *Osprey*, whose almost effeminate looks and diffident manner belied a savagery that he sensed and did not want to cause to be unleashed.

The predominantly Irish patrons of the Erin were unusually subdued as they gathered in the hotel's bar to discuss the latest happenings in the popular publican's family. The news had spread rapidly of young Michael Duffy's death at the hands of the Maori heathens in New Zealand.

Many a sympathetic comment was passed on the God-cursed tragedy that had befallen the Duffy family since Patrick's tragic death at the hands of the wild blackfellas in Queensland, although it was rumoured that there was more to the death than met the eye. Tom was a wanted man in Queensland for robbery under arms and he was suspected of murder. And now Michael had been slain in the war across the Tasman Sea.

Frank Duffy was not in the bar as he usually was in the evenings bellowing good-naturedly at unruly customers and shouting occasional drinks for a select few. The pretty, buxom barmaid, Elsie, was in tears as she fumbled with the glasses of ale for the customers, spilling much of the precious liquid. It had been well known that she had been in love with Michael and it was also wickedly rumoured that she had introduced him to the pleasures of the flesh when he was eighteen. Ah, but the Duffy men were wild lads, the customers mused. They had got it from their father, God rest his saintly soul.

Glasses were raised as toasts to Michael Duffy's innocence and bravery and then glasses were raised to Tom for giving the traps a merry chase in the far-off colony of Queensland. And glasses were refilled to toast Patrick, the rebel father of the Duffy boys, who had himself assisted one or two English soldiers to their graves in Ireland, and Victoria at the Eureka Stockade.

Then glasses were raised to Francis Duffy as the

finest publican outside of Ireland. Saint Patrick was next. The downfall of British rule at home was not forgotten and finally glasses were raised to dear old Ireland itself.

To be sure the copious quantities of rum and gin flowed down the thirsty throats of men toasting all that was important in life. And that led in turn to push and shove from the non-Irish drinkers who objected to the outpouring of Irish sentiment.

Before long, Max Braun was up to his muscled armpits in brawls with the *verdammen* drunken Irishmen. He had long learnt that it took little in the way of an excuse for an Irishman to get into a fight and it was no wonder they were found in the ranks of most of the mercenary armies of the world.

Above the din of breaking glass and thumps of men hitting the floor, amid drunken oaths in English and curses in Gaelic, Bridget sat by her bed in her old rocking chair with a well-worn set of rosary beads slipping between her fingers as she muttered her prayers, seemingly oblivious to the riot just below her bedroom.

The salvation of Michael's immortal soul held her attention, as she had no illusions about her nephew and his wild ways. To be sure, Michael was a terrible sinner when it came to matters of the flesh. But he was also a gentle man who dreamed of beautiful paintings, and he had loved her as if he were her trueborn son.

The tears flowed but she was hardly aware that she was crying and it was not for Michael alone that she wept. Her tears were also for little Katie, who had suffered the unspeakable pain of the loss of her child, and Bridget Duffy prayed that she might return to the family that loved her dearly. So much death and suffering had been visited upon her dead brother-in-law's family in the past year and only God knew why.

The tentative knock at her door interrupted her Hail Mary. She brushed the crucifix with a kiss and placed the well-used rosary beads in her lap. 'Come in,' she called with a feeble attempt to brush away the tears.

She did not recognise the woman who stood beside her ashen-faced husband in the doorway, but she could see that the woman held a bundle in her arms wrapped in a fine swaddling blanket.

'Biddy, Miss Molly O'Rourke has brought someone to us,' Frank said as he ushered the woman into the bedroom.

Bridget rose from her chair by the bed and crossed the room.

'Missus Duffy,' Molly said as she reluctantly passed the bundle to Bridget, 'I have brought you the son of Michael Duffy. I have given him his name but he is yet to be baptised in the True Church.'

Bridget took the bundle and gazed down into the blanket where a baby with dark curly hair was asleep. She fought to stay on her feet. Michael now lived through his son. The shock of recognising the resemblance of the baby to his father was uncanny. 'Dear Mother of God!' She gazed down at the baby snuggled asleep in the warm rug and the little creature's eyelids twitched at the annoying sound of brawling patrons in the bar below their feet.

'What name have you given him, Miss O'Rourke?' Bridget finally asked as tears of grief turned to tears of joy.

'I have called him Patrick after the big man himself,' she answered softly with tears welling in her own eyes. 'I'm sure Michael would have wanted that name for his son. I knew Patrick Duffy in the old country a long time ago. Oh, I was but a mere slip of a girl then and I fell in love with Patrick himself like all the other colleens in the county. But he only had eyes for Elizabeth Fitzgerald, and not for the likes of a simple girl such as meself. Ah! but that was a long time ago,' she sighed.

Patrick Duffy was woken by a window shattering downstairs as the brawl spread. He opened his eyes to stare myopically at his new world. He balled his tiny fists and opened his little lungs to vent his anger for all to hear that he did not like being disturbed from his comfortable sleep. Patrick Duffy announced to the world that he had come to live with his father's family.

28

Although the two men appeared to be relaxed astride their horses, they were particularly alert. Tom Duffy and Wallarie had good reason to be vigilant. They were approaching territory that was home to tribesmen prepared to spear intruders on their traditional lands.

Wallarie's dark eyes also scanned the country around them for signs indicating the intrusion of white men beyond their established frontiers. The advance of white settlers usually meant the presence of the dreaded Native Mounted Police.

The two men rode in the style of the cavalryman, one hand swinging free while the other gripped the reins and led a packhorse burdened down with bags of flour and sugar, tins of tea and syrup, small boxes of ammunition for their weapons and a few precious tins of tobacco.

As they rode side by side through the low scrub of the Gulf, Tom Duffy's thoughts were on a place somewhere ahead of them on the banks of the river that flowed into the placid waters of the Gulf of Carpentaria. Wallarie assured him all the signs indicated that the Gulf tribe they had befriended months earlier were camped there. If all was well Mondo would be with them and by now she would have given birth to their first child.

It was six months since he had last seen her and the signs of her pregnancy were obvious then. Six months away from their sanctuary to raid the homesteads south of the Gulf Country, relieving the wealthy squatters of their cash and valuables to redistribute among the storekeepers of Burketown. The money was used for replenishing badly needed supplies to sit out the coming wet season of the tropical monsoon of the north.

'Blackfella by and by,' Wallarie said softly as he strained to listen to the whispers in the still and oppressively hot air that wrapped around them like a stifling cloak.

'How close?'

'By and by close,' he replied, shifting in his saddle to ease his discomfort. The hard ride from Burketown had been necessary to put a safe distance between themselves and the outpost of the white man's civilisation where a Native Mounted Police contingent was camped. 'Mebbe before billy time,' he added. His estimations of time were always measured in meal breaks. Billy time meant a half hour from locating the wandering tribe, as it was already around midmorning.

His estimation proved to be correct as they rode warily into the deserted Aboriginal camp. But the telltale signs of fires left smouldering and middens of unopened shellfish indicated that they were being watched from the surrounding silent scrub by wary eyes.

Tom slid from his mount and gazed cautiously

around him. 'Mondo,' he called loudly. 'It's us, Wallarie and me.' But his call was answered with a continuing silence as the warriors crouched tensely in the shadows of the bush, fitting spears to slings.

Wallarie remained astride his mount with his hand not far from the butt of the Colt tucked behind a broad leather belt. He did not trust the northern tribesmen.

Tom frowned. He could feel the eyes watching them and sensed his friend's tension as he sat astride his horse studying the silent scrub. Had their tentative truce with the Gulf tribe been forgotten already?

Their acceptance by the Gulf tribesmen had been founded on Wallarie's knowledge of the trade route language. He had established that he and the white man would bring precious supplies of tobacco and sweet thick cane syrup to them. In return they would allow Mondo to live with them. The tribesmen had agreed and the deal was sealed with gifts of tobacco and syrup.

But six months was a long time and Tom felt a growing fear well inside him. Not a fear for himself, but for the woman he had left behind. Had they killed her?

'Baal!' Wallarie hissed, fingering the revolver tucked in his belt. 'Blackfella watch us, Tom.'

'So long as they keep watching,' he said grimly as he strode across to the packhorse and loosened a wooden box containing the tins of syrup. The box crashed to the ground where it split open, spilling the tins in the fine red dust. Tom scooped up a tin to wave over his head.

'Tucker,' he called to the ominously silent scrub.

'We have good tucker.' Although the watching tribesmen did not understand the words, they did understand his gesture and recognition dawned in suspicious dark eyes. One by one, they emerged from the scrub trailing their spears and families behind them.

With a wide grin, Tom quickly passed the tins to the squabbling women, frantic to get hold of the sweet gooey gifts, as precious to them as gold was to the Europeans. Eager hands pried lids off and fingers of all shapes and sizes were thrust into the gold sticky liquid. All signs of wariness had gone from the tribesmen as they accepted Tom and Wallarie back into their lands with laughter and delighted squeals for the gifts.

Even so, Wallarie remained on his mount and kept the packhorse close by him, as he was aware that, given the opportunity, the tribesmen would have happily rifled all that was left of their precious supplies. But they respected his ownership of the stores he jealously guarded. The Darambal man was also a man greatly feared. He had come to them with an aura of powerful magic that only they understood. It was an aura that protected him in the lands of tribesmen who would normally kill such an intruder from another tribe.

Tom searched the faces of the people who now milled around in the camp, fighting over the last of the tins of syrup he had distributed. Then he saw the face he most wanted to see and with long strides he closed the gap between himself and the woman standing at the edge of the squabbling crowd. She was holding a baby on her hip and smiling shyly at him.

He stopped before Mondo to stare at the child at her hip, sucking his little thumb. The tough and feared Irishman was at a loss for words. She held his son!

The months of being hunted, the weeks of lying under the stars of Burke's Land, wondering and worrying about the shy and pretty Darambal girl, were all washed away in a moment.

'We will call him Peter. That's a good name. It means rock,' he said as he reached out to touch his son's face with a big callused hand. 'And our son will need to be as strong as the rocks of your land if he is to survive.' The little boy grabbed for his hand and held the big Irishman's thumb in a firm grip with his chubby little fingers.

Tom reached out to touch the face of his woman and he felt tears sting his eyes. 'Mondo . . . my little black princess . . . that I could promise you and Peter a good life, I would give my own gladly,' he choked in the white man's language she did not understand. 'Ahh, but that I could be free to raise our son without fear of the traps coming for us, and give him the future all free men are born to with a God-given right.'

His words trailed away and he shook his head as he gazed into the dark eyes watching him with a love that needed no spoken words. She smiled sadly for his pain, which she did not understand. They were, after all, alive and free, albeit in the territories of a foreign people. And she held at her breast the child that was of her man's spirit totem.

Wallarie watched the reunion and was glad that his kinswoman was well, as she was the only other survivor from his clan and a link to his Dreaming.

It was strange, he mused, as he watched the son of his friend and his kinswoman united, that the child carried the spirit of both the Irishman and the Darambal people.

Wallarie's attention was drawn to the nearby shallows of the river estuary where a brown and white feathered sea-eagle swooped to scoop up an unlucky fish that had swum too close to the surface of the tropical waters. For a brief moment, a terrible image flashed in his mind and it was not the sea-eagle itself but the image of the sea-eagle's shadow. An evil entity of absolute and boundless cruelty. He did not understand and he shuddered. How was it that the dead could return to destroy the living?

But it would be so. The spirit of the sacred hill had spoken to him across the vastness of the timeless land.

TO TOUCH THE
FACE OF THE
DREAMING

1867

29

The *Osprey* tacked between the great jagged walls of coral whose stone-hard fingers promised to rip and shred any ship foolish enough to come within its reach.

On either side of the Macintosh barque, the massive rolling waves of the Pacific Ocean crashed onto the jutting coral heads with loud booming smacks that carried to the tense black-skinned sailors. The ship's timbers creaked ominously as she wallowed for a short gut-wrenching moment in an eddy in the fast-running waters of the channel leading from the deepwater seas surrounding the flat and tiny jungle-covered island.

With an almost human sigh, the tough little ship was swept safely forward into the calmer waters of the island's lagoon where, with a rattle of her anchors dropping over the bow and stern, she floated serenely in crystal-clear waters gently lapping at her teak hull, and drifted off a white sandy beach of finely ground coral particles. Her presence in the lagoon was as ominous as that of a predator sea-eagle.

Captain Morrison Mort stood beside his first

mate, Jack Horton, and watched with morose interest the born-to-the-ocean islanders scuttle nimbly in the rigging of his ship and scramble with the self-assuredness of their immortality to furl the sails. Mort fiddled with the hilt of the sword at his side, as was his habit whenever he contemplated a forthcoming action.

Four years had passed since he had been given command of the converted barque and the four years had been good to the former officer of the Queensland Native Mounted Police. His long blond hair was swept back from his face and tied in a ponytail which reached down to the stiff collar of his serge blue frockcoat. Years of exposure to the tropical sun had tanned his face to an almost golden hue like his hair. Age did not seem to be a factor in his life as he had the youthful look of a man ten years younger than his mid-thirties. It was a handsome face, almost aristocratic, and it was a face set off by the pale blue eyes that burned with an intensity of their own . . . or that of the devil. A man of spartan diet, his slim body under the unsuitable frockcoat was whiplash taut with an abundance of nervous energy and his demeanour unmistakably that of a man used to command.

The Macintosh shipping company had paid him generously for the cargoes he had delivered consistently to the markets in Brisbane Town and the former policeman had been able to accumulate a modest amount stashed in a bank account in Sydney. In another five years, he calculated that he would be able to shift his accumulated savings into an investment in a small property at the outer-Sydney village of Penrith. Maybe an innkeeper's licence to sustain him into retirement when that day came. Maybe even more for a prosperous farm to provide him with a certain degree of respectability, in the snobbish social circles of colonial Sydney. Perhaps he could find a wealthy widow who would be smitten by his charm and maintain him in the genteel style that he aspired to. Women were such foolish creatures, easily swayed with a few choice words of flattery . . .

'Launch the boats,' he ordered quietly to Horton, who passed on his captain's command in the pidgin English of the South Pacific. The nine dark-skinned crew from the Loyalty Islands, picked for the raiding party, responded with eagerness for what they knew was to come.

The two longboats splashed into the placid waters, scattering tiny silver-scaled fish that had gathered in shoals around the *Osprey*'s stern, as the red ball of the sun was disappearing behind the watery horizon to the west. And, as the sun was swallowed by the ocean, the beach now marked a line between the ominous dark jungle and the lagoon. The rapidly approaching tropical night promised to be balmy. The ocean breezes would then waft onshore, through the lush verdant jungles, bringing relief from the shimmering glare of the day.

'You can distribute the arms now, Mister Horton,' Mort said, leaving to join the Loyalty Islanders who were gathering on the deck in their prearranged teams ready to board the boats. He could see that Horton had anticipated his routine by organising to have the sea chest hauled on deck. The excited Islanders were like children laughing and chattering among themselves as they bustled around the big wood plank chest bound with iron hoops and secured with a huge padlock.

Horton took a key from the broad leather belt around his waist and with a flourish opened the lid of the big chest. Eager hands snatched an assigned weapon: a single-shot rifle that chambered a combustible cartridge or a short-handled steel axe.

Under normal circumstances the weapons were kept secured in Mort's cabin, as he did not trust his crew. Close to their home islands, the natives tended to grow restless and the idea of a sudden and violent mutiny was never far from their minds. The blackbirder carried items more valuable than gold to the Islanders: tobacco, cloth and, of course, the new Westley Richards carbines. The breech-loading rifles, with their capacity for rapid fire, were a vast improvement over the slower rate of the ancient muzzle-loaders previously carried by earlier island traders. The possession of such rapid-firing weapons could easily make their owner a master of the perennial inter-island warfare that had plagued the South Pacific for centuries.

But the *Osprey* was not a trading ship in the strict sense. She was now one of the infamous blackbirders that scoured the South Pacific in search of strong black bodies to toil in the sugar and cotton plantations of Queensland.

Since Captain Robert Towns had landed the first cargo of South Pacific labourers at Brisbane the trade for indentured labour had brought out the ruthless and tough South Sea adventurers – Americans from the Marianas and Australians from all ports on the east coast of the continent.

Tough men of dubious reputation, with varied and colourful backgrounds, they shared the common bond of ruthlessness in pursuit of their trade in human bodies.

Recruiting labour from the South Pacific islands varied from wooing aboard recruits with promises of riches in exchange for labour in far-off Queensland to actual kidnapping and, often enough, killing those refusing to leave their island homes. It was a means of terrorising others who might be reluctant to accept the blackbirders' contracts.

The night's forthcoming action was in the latter category, as the cursed missionaries had warned the Islanders to stay away from the blackbirders.

Mort had clashed with the resident Presbyterian missionary of the island chain on a previous occasion and the missionary, the Reverend John Macalister, had become a thorn in his side.

Fearless and fiery, Macalister had influential contacts in Sydney who viewed blackbirding as a polite euphemism for slavery. Did not the overseers of the Queensland plantations ride on horses, and carry guns and whips, to ensure that the last drop of sweat was exacted from the black men labouring under the hot sun in the fields? Did not this seem reminiscent of the Southern cotton plantations of America before their bloody Civil War?

Tonight Captain Mort and his raiding party would be in and off the island before the missionary knew they had been there. Mort knew that the missionary was two islands away and news of the raid would reach him well after the *Osprey* was over the horizon.

Tonight's choice of tactics appealed to Mort, as they were little different from the tactics he had employed when dispersing the Aboriginal tribes of central Queensland years earlier. There would be killing to take native heads as a valuable commodity to use as barter with native tribes on other islands. But they would also take prisoners for sale in Brisbane's kanaka markets. Raiding the village on the other side of the tiny island would be like throwing a net in the sea for fish. After the raid they would sort out their catch – those who lived and those who died.

When the weapons had been distributed among the crew, Mort issued his final instructions to his hulking first mate, who was the only person the paranoid captain trusted. But it could not be said that either man liked the other as theirs was a mutual respect born out of a knowledge of each other's inherent violence.

Horton had personally witnessed Mort's swift and violent temper with any infractions of his rules, which were enforced violently and brutally with the flat of his sword or, on occasions, with its point. Horton preferred to use his fists or a knotted rope knout to enforce discipline. And besides the disciplinary nature of their mutual respect, both men were bound in an unholy pact of torture and murder.

The unholy pact had been made when the first native girl was taken aboard the barque in '65. Horton had heard her screams coming from Mort's cabin when they were out to sea. The crew had turned deaf to the young girl's cries and had cowered on the deck under the fierce gaze of the first mate as none dared interfere in the 'captain's pleasure'.

The first mate had been instructed to ensure their silence for a share in the 'entertainment' in the cabin. Horton had waited with lustful anticipation for his chance to join Mort. The captain was probably just 'teasing' the girl with a hot candle, Horton thought uneasily. Or squeezing her nipples just a little roughly. Nothing really serious.

The agonised screams tapered to a whimpering and Mort had called softly to his first mate to enter the cabin. When he did so, it was not as he had expected.

The young native girl was stripped naked and strapped face down over the old-style whipping bench. Although he was used to inflicting pain on women, he had never expected to see the extent a man could go in extracting pleasure from pain as Mort had perfected.

The captain stood naked behind the helpless girl with his body slick with the dying girl's blood. His eyes glittered with a feverish light, like the lanterns of hell shining out of a grinning skull. When Horton stepped inside the cabin, he sealed forever a perverted and demonic pact with the devil incarnate.

The young girl was beyond even terror. Her eyes rolled back into her head as Mort slowly passed the sharp tip of the blade through the fleshy parts of her thighs. The tightly restrained girl had tensed in a futile effort to resist the blade. Her agonised scream penetrated the gag in her mouth as he withdrew the blade and blood flowed down her leg forming a pool around the base of the bench.

Horton could see the girl's body had been punctured in many places. Mort stepped back with a maniacal smile to admire his work and gestured to Horton to take his pleasure.

The first mate overcame his initial shock to take his turn. He stepped behind the girl and dropped his trousers and gripped the girl by her slim hips. Grunting like a pig, he raped her with brutal thrusts until his back arched and he shuddered violently. He was vaguely aware that he had heard Mort crooning strange words to the victim as he had taken his pleasure. Words about never being able to laugh at little boys when they were hurting and only wanted love. Words of a madman . . .

He pulled his trousers up as Mort took his place with arrogant casualness. The sharp point of his sword slid between the girl's legs and even the hardened criminal from The Rocks could not restrain the involuntary gasp of sympathy for the girl's imminent excruciating agony.

With a sudden and powerful thrust, Mort forced the sword into the girl until it was buried to the hilt. She screamed with a final despairing voice for the hell that had come to her on earth. Mercifully the sword ruptured her heart so that she died relatively quickly.

It would not be the last time Horton would witness the hideous ritual. The second time came easier for the first mate and thenceforward he was a devotee of Mort's twisted and brutal rituals with the young island girls.

The longboats grounded on the coral beach as a huge yellow moon rose into the night sky obliterating the stars with its brilliant glow. The tropical moon was welcomed by the blackbirders who assembled silently on the beach. They were no longer like excited and chattering children. They were now what they had once been in their own lands – warriors stalking an enemy village. Mort had calculated they would be in position well before first light.

He gazed over the calm lagoon at the *Osprey* and could see that she was perfectly silhouetted by the rising moon. Under other circumstances, the silhouette of his ship against the big round yellow moon would have been a beautiful picture worthy of a romantic painting. But the kanaka ship had long lost her soul so that the silhouette took on a black and sinister shape and there was little that was romantic about the intentions of the black-birding captain and his raiding party.

He then glanced back at the longboats, resting with their bows on the beach, and decided that they did not need concealing in the jungle, which pleased his crew as the longboats were heavy to haul up from the water.

Mort left two of his men with rifles on the beach to guard the boats before leading the remainder of his raiding party into the inky blackness of the tropical rainforest. They would march in single file along a native track through the jungle until they came to the village, where they would halt and fan out into a U-shaped formation for the attack. Then they would sweep through the sleeping village and the U-formation would close to a circle trapping everyone inside.

If all went well, his men would take young men

and women as prisoners. Later they would be 'convinced', after they were well out to sea, that being indentured was a preferable choice to attempting to swim a hundred miles home through shark-infested waters. Those who resisted at the village were to be slain. Mort's men carried with their weapons ropes for securing prisoners and axes for taking heads.

From the deck of the barque, Horton had watched the longboats run ashore on the beach. The rising moon had cast a silver path to the shore. He could see the distant landing party form up on the coral sand, then plunge into the jungle. There was little for him to do until their return in the early morning except ensure the watch did not go to sleep and that the small brass cannon at the *Osprey*'s stern was manned at all times.

Precautions were necessary in the waters hostile to blackbirders. The first mate was aware that sandalwood ships, previously visiting the islands, had fallen victim to the swift war canoes of the fierce island warriors. He suspected that the captains of the unfortunate ships had been lax in keeping sentry duty. He had no intention of repeating the mistake, as headhunting and cannibalism were still practised in the islands despite the missionaries' zealous attempts to stamp out their ancient and traditional ways.

The moon shrank as it rose into the night sky while Horton perched himself on a hatch cover and idled with a short length of rope, twisting the Indian hemp fibres into a new knout.

As he worked on the latest addition to his already sizeable collection of knouts, he thought about the immediate future. Tomorrow, all going well, there would be a new victim to provide entertainment for himself and Mort. He did not know where and when the captain had first started his bestial practice. Nor did he care, for he had soon acquired a perverse understanding of the feeling of absolute power the torture of the young girls gave Mort.

A big fish splashed on the silvery and smooth surface of the lagoon and a bigger fish snapped it in two. Horton heard the noise and it made him aware that he should check the Islanders manning the stern gun.

He rose from the hatch cover and padded silently to the stern, where he found the two men chewing betel nut. In the grip of the mildly narcotic drug, they were dozing with their backs against the gun and the first thing they knew of Horton's presence was when his newly plaited knout came down with painful stinging blows on their shoulders. They yelped and scrambled to their feet as they covered their heads.

Horton grinned as he walked away from the two Islanders, now wide awake. The new knout worked just fine.

Sweat trickled uncomfortably under Mort's cotton shirt as he crouched waiting in the night shadows of the jungle. All had gone according to plan and he had led his raiders into a position where they could settle down and wait for the first rays of the rising sun to touch the eastern horizon with a gentle kiss of pink.

He scratched irritably at his chest and cursed the

oppressively humid tangle of rainforest under-growth. Huddled around him, his raiding party also crouched and stared at the tiny cluster of thatch huts by the sea. Maybe no more than fifty people lived in the little fishing village, he had calculated, from the small number of palm leaf and thatch huts built on stilts to catch the ocean breezes.

According to his previous experience, he knew that he had sufficient numbers to carry out his mission and it was obvious that the sleeping villagers were not expecting trouble. The advent of the damned missionaries had brought a kind of peace to the once warring peoples of the South Pacific, he mused to himself with ironic satisfaction. And in bringing an uneasy peace to these people, the missionaries had unwittingly made the blackbirding captain's task easier.

He slid the infantry sword from the scabbard and, with a few muttered orders, his raiding party slipped away into the night to take up their positions around the unsuspecting village. For Mort, it was just like the old days of carrying out the bloody dispersals on the tribespeople of Queensland.

The village dogs barked and the scrawny village pigs squealed. But they were too late to warn the sleeping inhabitants that the raiders were descending on them with rifle and axe. A volley of shots and blood-chilling war cries tore the villagers from their sleep. Panic stricken, they clung together with only a handful of quick-thinking natives fleeing into the jungle, successfully breaking through the cordon of *Osprey* crewmen in the predawn darkness.

As it was not a large village, little resistance was offered. For those few who bravely tried to stand and fight, death was inevitable. Lead bullets cut them down and the razor-sharp axes wielded with deadly efficiency swiftly severed valuable heads from the bodies of the slain.

The horrific attack was over in minutes and the terrified screaming of the villagers became a despairing wail as they realised that they were now helpless prisoners of the black raiders, who herded them roughly at gunpoint to a clearing at the edge of the village. The wailing of the women who had lost sons, fathers and husbands became one strident sound, callously ignored by the raiders as they secured their prisoners with ropes.

Mort stood trailing his sword in the sand, watching his men go about their grisly work. He smiled. Give niggers a worthwhile occupation and they were easily led, he thought with a touch of pride for their absolute ruthlessness. He was never happier than when he stood as the master amid death and destruction.

Two of the *Osprey* crewmen squatting beside a grisly pile of freshly severed heads grinned happily up at their leader. 'Damned good work,' Mort muttered and stood impassively by as those not guarding prisoners fanned out, searching the huts for anything of value to loot. When the booty was removed, the looters torched the huts and a few pigs were dispatched with axes to provide fresh pork for the crew.

The dry thatch roofs and coconut log frames

crackled sluggishly, then blazed furiously as the flames spread, twisting and spiralling. The early morning sky was lit with an evil glow that marked the death of the village.

When the village was totally engulfed in flames, Mort had the bound prisoners file past him. As he inspected each one, he searched the cowed villagers for a victim for his pleasure. His feverish eyes came to settle on one young girl who stood beside an old woman. Her bare and budding breasts bespoke her blooming womanhood as did the hint of a swelling of her hips and buttocks. The influence of Christian modesty had not yet reached her tiny atoll island and she was naked except for a small woven grass loincloth.

She attempted to avoid the white devil's scrutiny but even with her eyes downcast she could feel the burning intensity of the man's stare upon her. It was an irresistible impulse that caused her to glance up. Quickly she turned her head away. The pale blue eyes were not of a human, she thought, with a chilling shiver of terror. There was a bestial madness in his eyes that she recognised from the stories that the missionaries had preached about the devil.

'A good haul. Sixteen men, all in their prime. Nine women. Only three young 'uns, and a few old 'uns,' Mort said as he appraised the huddle of prisoners on the deck of the *Osprey*, surrounded by their captors, who taunted the cowering natives still stunned into submissiveness by the swift ruthlessness of the unexpected attack. The village was gone now and the column of smoke rising in the distance above the jungle clearly marked its destruction.

'You keepin' the old 'uns?' Horton growled to Mort, as they were of no use in the Queensland fields as labourers. But the young girls would fetch at least twenty pounds each from the plantation owners. At least the male plantation owners.

The *Osprey* still had other islands to visit but Mort did not expect any further trouble. His method of recruiting would be less violent. The pile of heads, which his raiding party had forced the prisoners to carry back to the longboats, would ensure recruits would be volunteered by island chiefs eager to take possession of the grisly trophies as a means of impressing their women. He expected to have a full hold of recruits when he returned to Brisbane. But he knew one of the young girls would never reach the Brisbane River.

'You know what to do, Mister Horton,' he said as he studied the youngest of the girls he had chosen on the island. 'I'm sure the Kuri will enjoy his work,' he added and the first mate bawled to the leader of the Islander crew to report to him.

The leader was a powerfully built young man who had been a feared warrior on his own island. A long and livid scar across his chest bore testimony to his fighting prowess.

'Kuri . . . you kisim head belong lapun manmeri. You savvy?' Horton said to the Islander, who grinned with child-like understanding for the murderous task he was about to carry out. Still grinning, Kuri slipped the iron tomahawk from his waist belt, and grabbed the nearest old man from the huddle of prisoners on the deck. The old man struggled feebly as he was dragged to the stern of the *Osprey* by the Islander who forced the old

439

man's head down over the stern with one hand.

Kuri was careful in his aim. A miscalculation could easily slice off his own arm and the tomahawk's blade flashed in the early morning as it severed the skinny neck with one swift and lethal strike. Kuri held up the head triumphantly and the blackbirders shouted their praise for his deft stroke.

Blood spurted into the clear waters of the lagoon from the decapitated torso and Kuri was careful not to get the blood on the wooden deck that Mister Mort insisted be kept spotless. The prisoners wailed in their terror as they clung to each other while the headless body of the old man toppled over the stern and splashed into the lagoon, staining the crystal waters red.

Kuri turned away from the stern and strolled back to the huddled villagers. He flashed his captain a smile seeking his approval, and Mort nodded to acknowledge the young Islander's deftness with the deadly tomahawk.

By sunset the word had reached the Presbyterian missionary John Macalister, who raged with impotent anger when he was told of the raid and the slaughter of the villagers. He uncharacteristically cursed the blackbirders to hell without recourse to God's mercy. It was not the strict Presbyterian that spoke, but the tough Scot who loved his flock with the love of a shepherd for his precious highland sheep.

There was nothing the missionary could do but write another report to Sydney about the activities of the blackbirders in his waters. And another report that would end in some bureaucrat's top drawer to be forgotten in the interests of keeping the peace among the high-placed owners of the infamous blackbirding ships. What was needed was direct action by the Royal Navy in hunting down the blackbirders and curtailing their god-forsaken activities.

If it had been good enough for the steam frigate HMS *Curacao* under the command of Sir William Wise to shell the Tannese villagers in '65, whose only real crime had been to resist the Europeans imposing their civilisation on them, then it was good enough to go after the ungodly blackbirders, the missionary reflected. Why could not the navy hunt down the murdering blackbirders? But he already knew the answer. Britain did not see the Pacific as a major part of its global strategy. The islands in the Pacific were as far from Westminster as Westminster was from the moon.

The tough little Scottish missionary sat down in his hut to draft his report on the activities of the kanaka ship. He believed it to be the *Osprey* from descriptions given by the survivors who had eluded the raiders on the island. Even if the British Government was not sympathetic to his complaints, then at least the Sydney papers and the anti-slavery movements might be. They would listen.

And listen they did! Among the allies the Scot would muster to his cause was one who had a strongly vested interest in seeing the captain of the infamous blackbirding ship swing at the end of a rope. He was a young lawyer by the name of Daniel Duffy.

30

'You are to all intents and purposes, Missus O'Keefe, very well off from Mister Hubner's estate,' Hugh Darlington of the Rockhampton firm of solicitors Darlington & Darlington said as he leaned back in his chair.

Kate stared in a daze at the sheets of important-looking papers on the solicitor's desk. She had heard the rumours around the hotel bar where she had worked for almost five years that Harry had accumulated quite a deal of money from his hard work as a teamster. But the sum the solicitor mentioned was beyond her wildest dreams. Fourteen thousand pounds . . . after probate!

'And Mister Hubner has also left to you all other properties he owned,' the solicitor continued. 'Which, I believe, is a house in Townsville, plus four blocks of land. And his wagon and bullock team. I assume you will be selling the latter part of the estate for its monetary value, Missus O'Keefe?'

Kate was still in a daze. Fourteen thousand pounds! After meeting Harry on the track when she and Luke had travelled west to find her father's grave, Harry had met up with her at the Emperor's

Arms, where she had worked as a barmaid. Kate had always treated Harry a little more specially than the other teamsters who vied for the attention of the beautiful young daughter of the legendary bullocky Patrick Duffy. She had listened to the lonely man talk about his life whenever there were quiet times in the bar, and the news of his death had been a personal loss to Kate.

'Mister Hubner was very fond of you, Missus O'Keefe,' the solicitor continued, leaning forward in his chair. 'He said you were the closest thing he had to a daughter. And from what I can gather, Harry had no other relatives living. So I doubt that anyone will contest the will. All Harry owned is now yours.'

Hugh Darlington could not help but steal more than a glance at the young woman on the other side of his desk. The stories he had heard of the barmaid at the Emperor's Arms were true. She was indeed very beautiful. He also knew that she was married and had been deserted by her husband years earlier. Despite the rough clientele of the hotel, the young woman had a reputation as a true lady: charming, intelligent and she did not take up the countless offers to share the bed of even the most eligible of the young squatters' sons who drank alongside the burly teamsters.

Kate sat with her hands in her lap and was acutely aware of the handsome young man appraising her. It was a mutual admiration, unknown to the lawyer. Kate could not deny to herself that Hugh Darlington was an attractive man, with his dark brown eyes and thick wavy brown hair curling above his collar.

Unlike the bearded frontiersmen, he was clean-shaven and he had an aura of arrogance in his demeanour that was appealing to women. His hands were clean and his fingers rather delicate for such a big man. The slender fingers looked as if they would be very much at home on a piano keyboard and were not the hands of a man used to callus-hardening physical work. Not like the hands of the men at the Emperor's Arms – the teamsters, prospectors, stockmen and labourers.

'You asked me what I intended to do with the rest of the estate, Mister Darlington?' Kate finally said, gazing directly at the solicitor.

'Yes. I can arrange to have the properties sold for you – should you so wish to continue with the services of Darlington & Darlington,' he replied, assuming she would liquidate old Harry's property.

'I won't be selling any of Harry's property. I have a feeling Harry would have liked to see his bullocks continue working,' she said quietly, causing the solicitor to raise his eyebrows at her decision. He had naturally assumed that she would take the money and go south to Sydney. The frontier town of Rockhampton was not a place of genteel persuasion. It was a tough outpost to a wilderness where even tougher men went and from which some never returned.

'You cannot be considering taking over his team, Missus O'Keefe,' he said condescendingly. 'That sort of work is for a man. Not a young woman of, what I must say, such delicate beauty.'

Kate smiled and was aware that he had paid her a compliment. But he was also patronising in his attitude towards her ability to do a man's job.

'I don't intend to work the team myself. But I am sure I will be able to plan and organise a business. And hire someone who can look after the hauling side of the work,' she said sweetly in a way that left him in no doubt that she knew he was being patronising.

He attempted to extricate himself from his situation and could see now that she was not a wilting flower. She was more an Irish rose, beautiful, but prickly. 'Ah, yes . . . of course, you can. No doubt Rockhampton has one or two experienced men who would gladly work for you,' he said with a short and embarrassed cough behind his hand.

'Yes, it has,' Kate continued, realising she had made her point with the smug but extremely attractive lawyer. 'One of the advantages of working in a hotel is that you get to know people. You soon learn who can be trusted. And who has the right credentials. It so happens that I know of a reliable man who is looking for work with a team. Tonight he will be able to shout the bar when I tell him he is employed with the Eureka Company.'

Having uttered the words 'Eureka Company', she paused and reflected on the name she had chosen. What would it mean to the future of herself and her burning mission in life? Finally her dream was within her reach. She had come north to build a hotel but instead she had found herself following in the footsteps of her father, rather than those of her Uncle Francis. The bullock team would spearhead the beginnings of a financial empire of her making. Just exactly how, she was not entirely sure. But she was sure, before her life was spent, it would bring down Donald

Macintosh. As the only way to fight fire was with fire, the only way to fight wealth was with wealth.

'Mister Darlington, I would like you to prepare papers to set up the Eureka Company,' she continued with the self-assurance of someone who had been in business all her life. 'I gather you will accept the position as the company solicitor?'

He accepted the offer. 'The title Eureka is a rather interesting name, Missus O'Keefe. May I inquire why you chose that name for your company?' he asked.

She flashed him a sweet and enigmatic smile. 'It is the name given to a stockade where my father and other men whom I know fought for justice against the British. My company will also have to fight. It will some day take on the biggest and best British companies in Queensland. But *this* Eureka is going to win.'

The lawyer was taken aback by her grandiose ambitions but wisely made no comment. He switched to discussing a few matters concerning what would be required to set up the business and the company.

When their discussions were at an end, he rose from behind his desk and politely escorted Kate to the door of his office.

'Missus O'Keefe, I hope you don't think me forward . . . as we have only just met,' he said as he held the door open for her to leave. 'But I am extending an invitation to accompany me to a picnic on Boxing Day. I will understand if you decline the invitation.'

Kate turned and smiled and her hand brushed his arm in a way that made his pulse race. 'I would be delighted to accept your invitation, Mister Darlington.'

Hugh stood stunned by the reply as she brushed past him. Her acceptance was so readily given that he was left standing for some time by the door in a happy daze.

On the street, Kate flipped open her parasol. Not all the inherited money would go towards capital for the company. It had been a long time since she had spoiled herself and a visit to a draper was well overdue. 'Thank you, Harry,' she whispered. 'I promise that you will never be forgotten so long as I live.' With a spring in her step, she cut across the dusty street in a direct line for the draper's.

Hugh watched her from the window of his office and saw her dodge lightly between two massive bullock teams plodding down the street. He heard the teamsters bellow a hearty roar of greeting to Kate, whom they recognised from the Emperor's Arms. She flashed them a broad smile acknowledging their rough but good wishes.

It was a pity the young woman had aspirations beyond her, Hugh mused as he watched her friendly banter with the rough teamsters. Otherwise she might think about settling down with a man and raising a family. She had all the qualities and looks to be the wife of a man as socially accepted as himself in Rockhampton society. But she also had a foolish side to her. The idea that a young woman was capable of competing against the rich and powerful squatters and merchants . . . *absurd*!

From the moment he had set eyes on the

legendary beauty of Rockhampton, he knew he had to have her. Hugh Darlington was a man of considerable wealth himself. And Kate O'Keefe was a young lady with a considerable inheritance.

Little Deborah Cohen sat on her father's knee. She listened as Aunt Katie outlined her ideas to her parents and knew that they were impressed by what she was saying to them.

Deborah liked Aunt Katie. She was always full of fun. But now Aunt Katie sounded serious and the little girl watched the meeting wide-eyed. It was something very important the grown-ups discussed. The two-year-old precocious girl with the big lustrous eyes knew that much.

'It is such a big enterprise you propose, Kate,' Solomon said as he unconsciously stroked his daughter's silky raven hair. 'But I think we can do it. We have the capital to go in with you and I think Judith agrees already.'

Judith nodded. 'Kate is a young woman with an old and wise head; I agree,' she said. 'We open another store in Townsville and Kate's company will haul for us.' She hesitated, as the second part of the proposal worried her a little. Kate was talking of something beyond even the dreams of the Cohens – and they were ambitious dreams.

'The idea of buying a property and supplying our stores with our own beef requires either our own meatworks or relying on someone else. I think we would have to own our own meatworks. But that will cost a lot of money,' she added.

'We will make that the second part of the plan,' Kate said with measured thought. 'First we buy the property. We need somewhere close to Rockhampton. At least within a few weeks' drive for the beef.'

Solomon scribbled figures on a sheet of paper as Kate spoke. 'To buy a property . . . or lease?' he mused as he poked at the paper with a pencil.

'Buy!' Kate replied firmly. 'And I know just which property we should make an offer on.'

Solomon glanced up at her. 'Which property?'

'Glen View,' she answered without hesitation.

Solomon and Judith stared at the ambitious young woman. She was serious and they knew why.

'You are letting your heart rule your head, Kate,' Solomon remonstrated gently. 'Or is it your feelings for revenge?'

Kate knew that Solomon might baulk at her suggestion to buy the Glen View lease and she was ready to counter his doubts. She drew a breath.

'Glen View is struggling to stay in Macintosh hands. The present financial crisis in the colony has caused the price of beef to drop and I know the Macintoshes have put a lot of money into the shipping side of their businesses. Especially the kanaka trade. And cotton sales have suffered some setbacks since the Americans concluded hostilities between their states. The Macintoshes are shifting capital to their sugar-growing properties along the coast and I have learnt that Donald Macintosh is going to Sydney to try to raise a loan for Glen View. Now is a good time to make an offer.'

They listened respectfully. But Solomon still felt the young woman's prime motivation in wanting the property was because her father lay buried there. It was her way of revenge – one step at a time. First she wanted to show the Macintoshes that as a Duffy she could buy and sell them. Solomon knew of the Irishmen's love of fighting and he now realised that it spread to their women as well.

'Twenty thousand pounds will not buy Glen View and its stock,' he said, shaking his head slowly. 'You would need at least thirty-five thousand pounds. If we had that much I think your idea has merit. But thirty-five thousand pounds . . .'

Sadly Kate knew he was right. To purchase Glen View would soak up all their cash reserves and leave nothing for improvements. 'If we had that much, would you make an offer?' Kate asked. 'If somehow the money was there?'

'Yes, Kate,' Solomon replied. 'I know what you have said tonight makes a lot of business sense. Buy on a buyers' market. Glen View is just that bit far away and I think the financial slump will not stay with us forever. By that time, Glen View will be out of our grasp, so why don't you consider something a little less costly. There are other leases.'

She shook her head and looked away. 'It's Glen View or nothing,' she said stubbornly. 'Some day I am going to take Glen View off the Macintoshes.'

Deborah slid from her father's lap and went over to her Aunt Katie and put her arms around her, saying solemnly, 'I love you, Aunt Katie.' Kate held the little girl and gave her a squeeze.

When the talk had shifted from business, Judith brought out a plate of cold meats and bread. Kate shared their meal and it was during the light banter that Judith unexpectedly said, 'Kate, you should find a good man and have many children of your own.'

Kate almost choked on a piece of chicken leg as she burst into a strangled laugh and replied, 'What brought that on, Judith?'

'I see how you are with Deborah,' she answered simply. 'You were meant to be a mother.'

'I was a mother for a short while,' Kate reminded her in a sad whisper.

Judith reached out to touch her friend on the hand. 'You will be again . . . some day,' she said and Kate gave her friend a sad smile.

'I cannot be with a man while I am married, you know that, Judith.'

Judith gave Kate's hand a squeeze. 'That is not true,' she replied. 'I spoke to one of your priests about that very matter last week.'

Kate was surprised at the revelation. She knew of Judith's dislike for the Christian priests, who still held the Jewish people as the killers of the Saviour. For her to approach a priest was something very extraordinary.

'I spoke to a priest, Father Murlay. He was a very nice man,' Judith continued. Kate knew Father Murlay. He was a French priest whose attitudes varied somewhat from his Irish colleagues and he was less judgemental about matters dealing with the heart and marriage. Possibly it was his Gallic upbringing that made him more tolerant.

'And what did Father Murlay say?' she asked.

'He told me that in your religion there were ways to get an annulment. I think that is what he

451

called it. He said you should talk to him when he next visits Rockhampton.'

'I will speak to him on the subject,' Kate said as she placed a chicken bone on her plate.

She had not thought about seeking grounds for an annulment and she was vaguely aware that the canon laws were as complex as any laws on earth. She knew that in the Vatican there were priests who were employed to examine cases just as a lawyer would. Divorce was one part of the canon law.

'Good. And when you get your annulment you will find a good man and have children,' Judith said, as if the matter was finalised before it had commenced.

Solomon had listened to the conversation in surprised silence. He was also stunned to hear that his wife had gone to see a priest. But he knew how much his wife cared for Kate. They were bound to each other in that most sacred time for a woman – the birth of a child. It had been Judith who had brought Kate's child into the world for its very short life. And Kate was one of the first to hold the wet and slippery Deborah, squalling in her arms. After the midwife had done her work, it was Kate who had passed the baby to Judith's breast. That sort of thing could make a Jewish woman go and see a priest, he thought ruefully.

'Luke was in the district last week,' he said for something to say and he noticed the sudden expression of interest in Kate's eyes. But he did not know whether it was just curiosity . . . or something else. For that he would have to ask Judith when they were in bed that night.

'Oh! I didn't know that. I pray he is well,' said Kate. Judith thought that she detected just the slightest note of interest in her over-casual reply. 'I did hear talk at the hotel that he was planning to go north into the mountains,' Kate said in an off-handed manner. 'Some of the bushmen said he was foolish to try. They said the myalls further north are reputedly hostile. I suppose he would see the sense of turning back.'

'No, he didn't turn back,' Judith said quietly. 'Luke Tracy is Luke Tracy and God only created a few men like him. But the devil has made him pay. Luke has gone north a very sick man. He has the fever.'

Kate registered visible concern in her expression. She had often heard the bushmen yarn about the legendary but crazy Yankee prospector who, alone, crisscrossed the vast colony in search of his El Dorado. But they spoke with respect.

Although she had not seen the gentle and courageous prospector in over four years, she often found herself thinking about him. Was he alive and well? Why did he not return to Rockhampton to visit his friends?

It was on those occasions that she had wondered at her own deep concern but she had dismissed her thoughts as nothing more than what one would feel for a dear friend. Only once, many years earlier, had she cried alone in her bed as she remembered the man who had been beside her when they embarked on the dangerous journey in search of her father's grave. Although they had hoped to make contact with her infamous bushranger brother, the closest she had come was to hear the stories told around the bar at the hotel of his legendary exploits. Like the American prospector, her brother was a ghost in her life.

She instinctively felt that the lack of any communication from Tom was prompted by his deeply ingrained sense of honour, that he did not wish to bring shame on his sister by allowing any contact whatsoever. It was stupid male pride. But the American's total lack of contact had no explanation.

'How bad is his fever?' she asked calmly, carefully hiding her feelings.

'He would be a lot better if he had someone to care for him,' Judith answered and Kate did not miss the note of slight anger in her snapped reply.

'I would have thought Luke might have at least contacted me . . . us,' she retorted.

'And what reason would he have for that, Kate?' Judith asked with an edge of sarcasm. 'You are, after all, just friends.' Kate's face clouded with hurt at her friend's obvious recrimination and Judith regretted that she had been so hard on her. But it was hard to bite one's tongue under such circumstances.

'Do you know where he is now?' Kate asked, addressing Solomon.

'I'm sorry, Kate, but I do not know,' he replied.

Kate stared at him and asked icily, 'Why hasn't he written – at the very least – to us?'

'He is a man,' Solomon replied lamely, suspecting correctly that she would not understand because she was not a man. 'And some things a man has to do *because* he is a man.' Oi, but there were terrible and irreconcilable differences between men and women, he thought bleakly. And hoped that he would not have to try to explain himself as he did not know how to do so. All he knew was that Luke had told him he must do very important things before he could ever return and face the beautiful young woman as a man she could be proud of.

Solomon Cohen could not betray the promise he had made to his friend that he was in receipt of a letter that had arrived two weeks earlier from up north. Luke had written optimistically that he had a feeling in his bones where his El Dorado lay and it was only a matter of getting there and back alive that counted for the present.

But Solomon did not share the American's optimism, as he had heard disturbing stories of the northern districts of the colony. It was said the land belonged to extremely fierce and warlike tribesmen who practised headhunting and cannibalism in the little-explored country of the high jungle-clad mountains and searing arid plains.

Kate did not pursue the philosophy of the irreconcilable differences between men and women. Solomon breathed a sigh of relief. And the subject of Luke Tracy was quickly dropped from the conversation.

Dropped or not, it did not stop Kate from feeling anger towards the man who had chosen to ignore her. She was not used to being ignored by any man. But with the anger there was also a yearning to once again hear the slow drawl and see the bronzed face above the beard of the man who had come to find a place in her heart. It could not be love, she convinced herself. Merely a very deep affection for him.

31

The malaria had taken its toll on Luke Tracy and the fever was still on him as he shivered uncontrollably, slumped in the saddle astride his mount.

He knew from the bearings he had taken with his small brass compass that he was somewhere south of Cape York Peninsula in the shallow dry valleys of low and spindly trees left brittle by the long dry season. He also knew that his big and faithful mare was close to collapse as she plodded on without questioning the foolishness of man's quest for the yellow metal.

Together horse and rider had faced jungle, desert, scrub and hostile tribesmen. And together they had forged a bond based on mutual need. The big mare was tough and carried an old scar on her flank from a spear wound and she had many more scars from the terrible cuts of the rainforest vines as badges of her courage.

Time had lost all meaning for Luke as he swayed in the saddle, fighting to stay conscious, his existence now measured in the fact that he was alive to see the sun rise and set each day. The fever came to him in alternating waves of burning hot and icy cold deliriums, with each malarial attack threatening to be the fatal last.

His precious supply of quinine, his two pack-horses and most of his prospecting equipment were long gone to the terrible tangle of gullies and jungle that now lay behind him in the craggy mist-covered mountain range he had traversed weeks earlier. At least now he was beyond the terrible rainforest hell and back down on the plains. He also knew it could get worse if he persisted in pushing himself north. He might have survived the dark and green hell of the tropical rainforests but he still had the endless miles of scrubland and craggy hills that spread west, north and south ahead.

According to his last estimation, he was still eighty to ninety miles south-west of the river and if there was gold in payable amounts it had to be between his present location and the river.

Unconsciously he touched his damaged shoulder where the long hardwood spear had ripped through his body a year earlier in Burke's Land, when he had been camped by a water hole at night. His first inkling of danger had drifted on the balmy night breezes to his camp fire. He had immediately recognised the sweet and not unpleasant scent of burning followed by the crackling hissing sound of grass blazing with its deep orange glow that could be seen through the stark scrub trees of the red earth plain. A grassfire front sweeping down on his camp site in a place where he was alone, or at least he'd thought he was!

He had snatched for his pistol and rifle as the

wall of flames silhouetted the lines of naked Aboriginals advancing on him with spears fitted to woomeras. A volley of shots from his pistol had caused the advancing warriors to waver. Then a deadly shower of fire-hardened spears had plunged down around him and one of the spears had found its target.

Luke had been flung sideways as the barbed spear tore through his shoulder. The pain was beyond anything that he had ever experienced and he accepted death as inevitable. His revolver was empty and the ball and powder weapon too cumbersome to load under the circumstances. Badly wounded, he was helpless in the face of the overwhelming number of tribesmen advancing on him. It was only really a matter of how he would die: by a spear or a bone-crushing blow from a hardwood club. What occurred next gave the normally agnostic American a greater respect for the Divine Being whom he had taken for granted during his thirty-five years on earth.

Out of the night sky came the shattering explosive crack of lightning to hit between himself and the advancing warriors. Stunned, he stood and watched without comprehending that the tribesmen were scattering into the night to escape the spirit world's irrational bad temper. He had slumped with a groan and fallen heavily into the rich red earth of the Gulf Country as a gentle breeze played across the plains to force the grass-fire away from him.

Throughout the night he lay in a throbbing haze of pain, and when the morning dawned he was dimly aware that two bearded faces hovered over him, muttering how lucky he was to be alive.

The fellow prospectors had seen the grassfire from their camp site miles away and, acting on a hunch, they had ridden across the plain to the water hole. As they had suspected, the fire denoted an attack on one of their fellow trekkers on the vast plains of the Gulf. At the worst, they might find a body and they would provide a Christian burial for it, as such was the unwritten law of the frontier. Instead they had found Luke unconscious with the spear protruding from his shoulder.

The operation to remove the spear had almost killed Luke. One of the bearded prospectors had served in Britain's colonial army and his service had taken him through the campaigns in Africa, where such wounds were not infrequent.

With a thin knife blade honed to razor sharpness and sterilised in the fire, he'd cut and probed the wound from front and back while Luke was tied to a log and given the traditional gag of the wounded soldier – a lead musket ball which he succeeded in biting through in his searing agony. But the former soldier was a talented amateur surgeon and the operation was successful. Infection did not set in and, after two weeks of recuperating with his newly acquired friends, Luke was well enough to strike out alone again.

The parting carried no sentimentality. What had been done to save him was simply an expectation of bushmen for each other on the frontier. A few grunted words of thanks and good wishes and then the shimmering plains of the Gulf Country swallowed men who were most likely never to see each other again.

Alone, astride his mount on the lonely plains, Luke had often thought about the miraculous lightning strike that had certainly saved his life. The lightning had come from the northern sky. Providence dictated that his salvation meant that he should ride as far north as possible in search of El Dorado.

But first he had returned to civilisation to replenish his supplies. From Townsville, he had posted his letter to his old friend Solomon Cohen in Rockhampton, informing him of his plan to trek north into the Palmer River region.

But perseverance had a limit and now, finally, he had reached his. To go on was certain death from starvation or fever. To turn back now gave him a chance. To the south lay the white man's outposts and maybe a lonely homestead or even one of the tiny towns sprouting in the wake of the bullock teams where he could rest up and recover from his gruelling ordeal.

He now knew that it had been a terrible mistake to think he could take on the tropical rainforests that covered the coastal mountains of north Queensland. The tangles of liana vines that strangled the giant trees had been like binding ropes to hold him back and, in the dank and gloomy forests, he had found himself in a world of primeval cycads, ferns and fungi that lived off the wealth of rotting death under a canopy of tall trees whose majestic crowns paid homage to the sun.

On the ground were the phosphorescence of decay and the bone-chilling mists that swirled slowly, wraith-like between the trunks of the trees. And as he had climbed higher on the range, the colder the eternally swirling mists had become. Day after day of being beaten back by the parasitic vines that strangled the forest giants had sapped his strength and that of his brave and sturdy horses.

In the haunted forests of ghostly twilight, the carcasses of his two packhorses now became fodder for the buttress roots of the giant trees. The American had spent long and lonely nights ranting in a nightmare of fevered dreams at a world devoid of light. And there were days of sweat and exhaustion crawling ever upwards onto the ridges with the pygmy-like inhabitants of the forests watching curiously his every move from the silent shadows.

He had stubbornly pushed on until he was at the top of the majestic range where the rainforest gave way to the lightly timbered and undulating plains of the west. Then came the time of stumbling and crashing down into the narrow valleys in a cycle of pain, sweat and exhaustion that would have killed lesser men than the determined American.

The warming sun of the plains could not take away the cold mists that had seeped into his body to remind him of the silent terror that had been the tropical rainforests high in the ranges.

He now found himself in a land equally as hostile. It was a lonely place to die.

His mare picked her own way along a valley floor. She did not need his hand on the rein to guide her as she was an intelligent animal and she sensed that it was up to her to keep them going.

'We aren't going back that way, old girl,' he

461

promised her wearily as he rode slumped in the saddle, too sick and spent to care any more. He had pushed himself beyond the established white man's frontier. To continue was certain death and it was time to turn back. He pulled down on the reins but the mare propped of her own accord.

At first he thought in his fevered mind that she was able to read his despairing thoughts as she stopped with her ears pricked forward and pawed at the ground with her hoof. Something had caught her attention.

Luke dropped the reins and eased his Sharps rifle from its scabbard by his knee. He thumbed back the hammer and raised the rifle to his shoulder. The mare snorted as he scanned the silent scrub, searching for the shadows that moved. The fever was still on him and he knew that he had little hope of defending himself against a concerted attack by hostile tribesmen and he was in territory where a man needed all his senses to stay alive. The fever had effectively dulled his mind as surely as if he were in a drunken stupor. Luke felt very vulnerable in the sparse scrub.

He scanned the surrounding area searching for movement and saw nothing except the straggly rough-barked trees eking out a tenuous living from the termite-infested soil. A nerve at the corner of his eye twitched. What would it be? he thought in his despair. A stone axe or a throwing stick that might suddenly whirl through the still air? Or maybe the swift and silent hardwood spear to pluck him from the saddle?

His scrutiny came to rest on the bundle of rags to his front in a place where there should not be European rags. The bundle moved!

He kicked his horse forward until he reached the rags and slid from the saddle to kneel beside a white man, blackened by long exposure to the sun.

The man reacted by flinging up his arm as if to ward off a blow when Luke bent to help him. A fetid smell of decaying flesh rose and Luke could see that the stranger's leg was swollen with putrefaction under the remains of his tattered trousers. A broken shaft of a spear could clearly be seen embedded in the flesh. The man was dying.

'You a white man?' The man croaked the question feebly as he brought his arm down and turned his head slowly to blink at the framed silhouette kneeling over him.

'I'm a white man,' Luke replied to reassure him. 'Luke Tracy out of California.'

'A Yankee.' The man groaned painfully as he struggled to sit up. 'Help me up, Yank.'

Luke rolled him gently onto his back. It was obvious that the man was beyond any hope of surviving his exhausting ordeal. He skin was hot to touch and the rotting leg stank of advanced decay. He let out a loud groan when Luke moved him.

'Tried to get the spear out,' he said through gritted teeth. 'But the bloody shaft broke off in me leg. Don and Charlie gone. Myalls got 'em. Almost got me. Don't think they have seen many white men before. Not many guns anyway,' he gasped in short and pain-racked bursts. 'What are you?' he asked when he was able to focus on Luke.

'Prospector,' Luke answered and the dying man gave a choking and bitter laugh as if mocking the American. The laugh took much of the man's reserves of strength. 'Another bloody fool like meself,' he whispered.

Luke left the man to fetch a water canteen from his horse and he returned to press it to the man's lips. The prospector had trouble swallowing the brackish water and he sighed when he had finished drinking. An expression of serenity came over his bearded face.

'Thanks, matey,' he said gratefully, grasping Luke by the wrist. 'Almost as good as a cold beer on a hot day.'

Luke helped the man into a sitting position and placed him with his back to a stunted tree. The prospector gazed down at his putrefying leg where flies crawled on the wound seeking a place to lay their eggs. From death comes life.

'Too late to take the leg off,' he said more as a statement than a question. Luke nodded.

'Then I'm goin' to die soon,' he added bitterly. 'Die just when we found the River of Gold. Don, Charlie an' me. Found the bloody river. An' the myalls found us. Hit us on the river. Don an' Charlie never had a hope. The myalls was big bastards. An' their spears went straight through Don an' Charlie. But I got a few of 'em before they got me. Been a running fight . . . don't know how long. Two days . . . maybe three.'

Luke listened patiently to the dying man. 'You think I'm ravin' mad, don't you?' he said fiercely and he thrust his hand in his pocket. When he brought his hand out Luke's registration of utter surprise pleased the prospector, who held up a nugget of gold as big as a hen's egg. 'Just picked this one up as easy as you please. An' I got more.'

He struggled feebly to retrieve the other nuggets in his pockets but Luke stopped him. The dying prospector's exertions were overpowering his weakened condition. Each word brought him a step closer to death.

'I believe you. Just take it easy and I'll get you something to eat,' Luke said gently.

'Keep the tucker, matey,' the prospector countered. 'No sense in wasting good food on a dyin' man.'

Luke ignored his protests and rummaged in his saddle-bags for some strips of leathery beef jerky. Although the prospector had protested, he finally relented and took the food gratefully. Luke watched the prospector pop a piece of meat into his mouth and chew slowly, savouring the strong taste.

Luke guessed the prospector was his age . . . or thereabouts . . . and he had what Luke had come to recognise as an Australian accent, as opposed to the rich variety of predominantly British accents from all Britain's regions. He must have been one very tough man in his time, Luke thought. To have survived as long as he had. The prospector was near starvation and it was obvious that he had engaged the Aboriginal tribesmen of the north for more than two or three days. Luke could see that the leg had been rotting for some time.

'Terrible thing to die alone without a mate,' the prospector said dreamily after swallowing the jerky. 'All the gold in the world won't buy a good mate. That's something that just happens, Yank.' His shrunken stomach refused to take any more food and even the small piece he had swallowed made him feel nauseous. He was slipping in and out of a blissful world where there was no pain. Just a long and deep sleep. His spirit was ready to leave and tears streamed down his sun-blackened face as he cried silently.

Luke turned away. Better a man cry in private. For the prospector, his tears were those of regret. Regret for finding a fortune – but losing the woman he loved. Somewhere there was a woman waiting and she would wait no more. None of it had been worth the years on the plains and in the hills, forever searching for a dream that could not bring happiness. When his tears were spent, the prospector lay back and fell into a fevered sleep.

Luke set up camp after he made the prospector as comfortable as possible. Finding the dying man had given him a mirror to his own life. The dying prospector was himself, in another time and another place. A spear, starvation, snakebite or a fall from his horse. One way or the other, death would come.

But he did not want to die alone in a place so far from the giant sequoias of his beloved California. Never before had Luke realised how much he missed the country of his birth.

He gazed out at the endless grey scrub and the ancient eroded red hills that hedged the dry valley. Fleeting memories came to him of another place and another time. Memories of stately forests of dark green fir trees whose tops swayed and sighed to the cool mountain breezes of northern California. Homesick memories of the splendid beauty of the majestic Rocky Mountains under a white blanket of winter snows and the pristine clear mountain streams gurgling sweetly across the green grass-covered valley floors.

Memories of his childhood, growing up among the summer fields of golden maize basking in the warmth of a gentle sun, crept to him with a soft kiss of the woman who had been his mother.

How old was he now? Thirty-three ... thirty-four ... Luke could not remember. The years of roaming were a blur that stretched back to the singular pivotal points in his life. Of mining camps and the rebellion. Of his dead wife and child. He was hardly aware that he was weeping. He was homesick for the land of his birth and yet he had grown to accept the harshness of the land that he had spent half his life roaming around in search of the elusive big strike. Maybe it was time to go home.

But there was Kate ...

He could see her face in front of him, her beautiful warm smile, and for just a fleeting instant he thought he could smell the hint of lavender on the hot breeze. It was as if she were with him – as she had been with him when they had ridden together in search of her father's grave.

Instinctively he cast about to see if she was preparing the camp fire or hobbling the horses. But when he gazed around, he saw only the harsh and ancient land of the shallow sunbaked valley. Kate was gone from him and had become a part of the shimmering haze of the late afternoon.

Nearby, the dying prospector twitched in his sleep and his fevered words were a rambling non-sensical monologue. Luke settled in for the evening to wait for the prospector's death and hoped that it would be soon. The longer he had to stay by the dying man's side, the less chance he had of returning south alive.

During the night when the fire had burnt to a soft glow Luke heard the prospector call to him. He sat beside the man, who lay very still, staring with wide eyes up at the constellation of the Southern Cross.

'Half the gold is yours,' the prospector whispered hoarsely with a great effort and Luke knew that death was close by, waiting just beyond the glow of the camp fire. 'The other half give to Miss Rose Jones. She's a schoolteacher at Toowoomba. Promise me you will look for her. She's been waitin' for me for a long time. Always been true. A finer woman I have never known,' he said with tears in his eyes.

Luke gave his word.

'I trust you, Yank. That's all I can say. Nothing much else 'cept there's been good times . . . and there's been bad times. Expect you know that. Being a prospector yerself,' he said with a long sigh and he smiled enigmatically as if remembering something pleasant or funny. He continued to gaze upwards at the heavens at a sky brilliant with a myriad of stars where the Southern Cross was ablaze, lighting the way for the dying prospector.

'Never did get 'round to introducing meself,' the prospector whispered as he listened to the voices of his old partners calling to him from the shadows in the night. 'But names doan mean much when you're dyin'.'

Luke did not hear the voices. All he could hear

were the mournful cries of curlews and the soft crackle of the camp fire as the prospector's whisper trailed away and was followed by a rattling sound in his throat. He tensed, then with a final sigh, relaxed. Luke knew it was over.

The curlews called in sad and lonely songs to each other as the American sat beside the dead man. Names don't mean much when you're dying . . .

When the sun rose in the morning, Luke scratched out a shallow grave for the prospector. He sat with his back to a tree and carefully scratched out on a flat piece of rock with the tip of his knife: Prospector – Mate of Don and Charlie – 1867. The malarial fever was gone and Luke felt better, although weak from the debilitating effects of the illness.

He recovered the gold the prospector had carried with him. It was a small fortune. And he could see from the flattened shape of the nuggets that the gold had probably come from a water-course. If the size and quantity of the gold nuggets were indicative of what the dying prospector had found in the river of gold . . . And it was some-where to the north! The years of roaming Australia's desolate places barely making a living were about to pay off for Luke, who held the largest egg-sized nugget in his hand, testing its weight. But somewhere north might as well have been on the moon, he thought bitterly. He knew he was at the limit of his trek north.

To push on meant precious days he did not have. His food supply was down to a few strips of jerky and the tropical wet season was not far away. He could be trapped between the dry sandy creek and river courses he knew would turn into raging waters. He closed his hand on the nugget and walked over to his horse.

'Next time, old girl,' he said with an affectionate pat on her forehead. 'Next time we come north we'll find that river, and I'll make you a set of gold shoes to wear.'

Luke swung himself into the saddle and turned her head south, leaving behind the lonely grave that would be obliterated by the seasons that came and went.

32

The men who ran the shanty grog shops of Australia's frontiers were as tough as the men who frequented their bark and timber establishments, scattered along the bullock tracks that meandered through the endless miles of flat plains covered in scrub and eucalypt forests. The grog shanties provided more than grog. They were also an oasis of news and gossip for the stockmen and travellers at the end of a weary day. Burke's Land had its share of the shanties.

The Gulf Country is an ancient land of flat savanna plains where the monsoonal wet season of northern Australia arrives in the southern tropics. A place where the parched plains of withered native grasses drown for weeks – even months – under the inland seas of muddy waters until the monsoons leave for another year.

But in the wake of the destructive rains comes creation. The withered grasses are reborn as life thrives on the abundance of flora and fauna rejuvenated by the life-giving water. And for a brief and bountiful period between the wet and the dry, the Gulf is a land of plenty. The end of the dry was imminent upon the land but the Gulf Country was still scorched and arid under a pitiless sun.

John Hogan stood under the shade of the hessian bags that served as a verandah roof to his one-roomed grog shanty. With his massive arms folded across his chest, he surveyed the two men who had taken up residence near his shop. A stockman, the Australian equivalent of the American cowboy, slept in the thick red dust of the country under a coolabah tree beside the shanty while his hobbled horse grazed on one of the few remaining patches of dry grasses.

The stockman had been riding to Burketown but had stopped off at Hogan's grog shop for a preliminary drink. That had been two days earlier and Hogan had taken all the stockman's money over the wood slab counter in exchange for two days of blissful retreat from the harsh and lonely world that was the stockman's life.

The second man was a mystery.

Hogan could see the big man sitting by a fire he had built from white ant-riddled timbers. He was bearded and when he walked he did so with a noticeable limp. The big stranger drank very little when he came to the shanty and Hogan knew it was best not to ask too many questions. To all intents and purposes the man was probably a horse thief or one of the bushrangers wanted by the recently arrived Native Mounted Police force posted to Burketown.

Hogan scratched irritably at his crotch. Termites and crutch rot – one ate the timber away and the other ate away a man's crotch. The bearded stranger looked up from his fire and saw the burly

472

shanty owner watching him. He gave a friendly wave which Hogan acknowledged and then returned to the oven-like heat of his store. Another bloody hot day!

Sergeant Henry James poured tea into a battered enamel mug and sat with his back to a log. He sighed with contentment as the tea washed away the dryness in his mouth. One more day he would wait and then return to Burketown if the information proved to be false.

Henry stared idly at the sleeping stockman who had rolled over and made feeble efforts to brush away the cloud of flies around his head. He was not the one! He had watched the stockman carefully when he rode in to stop off at the grog shanty but the description did not fit.

Lieutenant Uhr had listened to Henry outline his plan and the young officer had given his hearty approval. If only Uhr had commanded the Rockhampton troop back in '63 things might have turned out differently, Henry mused as he watched the stockman feebly scratch at his face. He would not now be sitting under a searing sun waiting for the man. Yes, Mort had changed a lot of people's lives by his murderous actions so long ago.

As Henry sipped from the mug of hot tea, his thoughts were not on his tedious vigil but on his wife, Emma, and their young son, Gordon.

He had met Emma in '64 while on leave from the Rockhampton troop, visiting Brisbane to see the bright lights. While there, he'd met the pretty young woman, who had recently arrived on a migrant ship from Liverpool with her brother.

She had immediately fallen in love with the big

bear of a man twelve years her senior on a picnic outing on the banks of the Brisbane River. For all his size and strength she recognised in Henry the soul of a very gentle man. And she found in him the romance she had come in search of on the frontiers of Australia.

Henry courted her in his tender and passionate letters from Rockhampton and in the same year they were married by the Church of England minister when he returned to Brisbane on his next leave. Ten months later, Gordon James was born in Rockhampton.

It was only after they were married that he revealed to his wife the terrible things he had seen and done on the dispersals. The young woman had held him to her breast when he opened his soul to her and he'd talked haltingly of the horrors. She had held him to her with soothing words as if he were a little child and not a tough war-scarred veteran.

He had also told her of the injustice that had been brought upon the Duffy family by Mort and Donald Macintosh and he spoke of Kate O'Keefe's unconditional forgiveness for his role in the dispersal that had taken the life of her father.

Emma had been impressed by the way Henry held Kate in such high regard and she took it on herself to visit her at the hotel where she worked behind the bar. Kate met Emma James one evening when she had finished at the hotel. What Kate saw was a petite young woman with red hair, blue eyes and freckles. Emma looked no older than fifteen or sixteen and Kate was surprised to find that they were both the same age.

Emma was pretty in her own way, but she felt awkward in the presence of the young woman with the long, raven hair and flashing eyes. No wonder the men all talked about Kate O'Keefe's beauty in such glowing terms, she thought.

The two women warmed to each other almost immediately and from the evening of their first meeting they became firm friends.

Judith Cohen also warmed to the wife of the police sergeant and Solomon would often roll his eyes and complain that Judith spent all her time with Kate and Emma gossiping. He wondered at the strange bond that formed between women that brought them so close. Maybe it was because they felt no need to compete with each other as men did. Or maybe it was because they shared some female secret wrapped in a mystique of their primeval drive to bring children into the world. Whatever the bond, Solomon wisely decided no man could truly understand.

And it was with an empathetic joy that Kate and Judith welcomed the birth of Gordon James into the world. Then it was Judith's turn to become a mother and a time for Kate and Emma to welcome the birth of Deborah Cohen. The regular morning tea meetings were filled with the cooing of contented mothers and 'aunts'. And the bemused tots burbled with all the attention they received.

The horseman came from the edge of the sparse scrub.

He was a powerfully built man with a full beard and rode with a rifle across his saddle and a Colt in a leather holster at his hip. A smaller Colt pistol

475

was tucked in the broad belt of his trousers and the bandolier of cartridges across his chest was full with rounds for his rifle, as the cartridge belt around his waist carried ammunition for the pistol. He also had a knife tucked in the side of his knee-length boot.

Henry remained sitting beside his fire. Adrenaline coursed through his body and his heart pounded. What was most noticeable to Henry was that the horseman was particularly alert as he approached the shanty.

He turned his grey eyes in Henry's direction with a cautious and inquisitive appraisal and, with a courteous nod, each man acknowledged the other's presence. Henry was aware that the man's eyes were carefully scanning him for signs of any weapons. He found none. Then the grey eyes shifted to the sleeping stockman in the dust.

Yes, Henry thought. This has to be him.

His every movement was that of a man surveying the field like a military skirmisher picking targets on the battlefield. Henry was acutely aware that the rider's hand was on his rifle and that the rifle over the man's lap was pointed at him even though he seemed satisfied that Henry was not a threat.

Tom Duffy was not going to be easy to arrest. The very horse that Duffy rode was the final evidence Henry needed to identify the man. It was the well-known thoroughbred stolen from Pike Downs, south of Burketown, where Tom Duffy and the Aboriginal had been identified as the men who had bailed up the manager on the track a month earlier.

Tom rode slowly past him and the sleeping stockman, and Henry knew he could not make his move while Duffy was astride his horse. To do so gave the bushranger the advantage of flight.

Hogan heard the horseman approaching his shanty and strolled out to meet the man in the dusty yard. Henry noticed that the infamous bushranger dismounted with the horse between himself and the sleeping stockman.

'Mister Hogan. Good to see your grog hasn't killed you yet,' Tom said in greeting to the proprietor.

'Mister Docherty. Presume you'd be wantin' a drink this day?' Hogan answered casually as he turned his back and walked into the shanty. Tom hitched his horse to a makeshift rail.

'I'd be having a drink outside, Mister Hogan,' Tom called to the brawny shanty owner. ''Tis one of those days it is good to be alive and in the presence of God's wondrous generosity of bush and sun.'

Duffy was extremely wary. Not even going inside where he would lose his ability to see what, or who, might approach from the bush. It was no wonder he had stayed always one step ahead of the law.

And Duffy also had the help of the Darambal blackfella. The tracking skills of the Native Mounted Police were thwarted by the two bushrangers' intimate knowledge of the country. It was only the occasional visit to an isolated grog shanty that brought Duffy into contact with civilisation besides his occasional forays against the landowners for their money, horses and supplies.

So far he had not killed any man or molested any woman. His forays in Burke's Land and the death of three Macintosh shepherds in '63 were yet to be proved against him.

Tom took a mug of whisky from Hogan, who knew the man was good for as much as he drank. He always paid more than the grog was worth and the big man's generosity helped Hogan keep quiet about the occasional visits to his grog shop. Maybe Docherty was one of the cattle-duffers wanted by the traps. But he was also a reliable customer.

The two men threw down the whisky as if it was cold water. Tom liked to drink with Hogan, who became more talkative the more grog he consumed. Hogan would provide all the news of happenings around Burke's Land – and even further afield.

The police revolver was hidden under Henry's shirt and although Tom Duffy's rifle was leaning against the hitching rail, he still carried two deadly revolvers. Henry noted that the bushranger drank with his left hand, which left his right hand free to draw the Colt from its holster slung on his hip.

The police sergeant fought to keep his breathing steady. He knew he had good reason to feel the fear. Although it was not proved, the wanted man was capable of killing. And where was the black-fella? Was he watching even now?

With some effort, Henry eased himself to his feet and tried to appear nonchalant as he walked towards the shanty owner and Tom standing in front of the bark hut. But he felt that his heartbeat might hammer him to the ground and his legs were weak as if they might suddenly fold under him at any moment.

'Thought I might join you for a taste,' Henry called as he closed the distance. 'Bloody tea doesn't get rid of the thirst.'

Thirty paces between them.

'You got the money, I've got the grog,' Hogan said with a laugh.

Twenty paces . . .

'I've got 'bout enough for at least one long taste,' Henry replied, trying to laugh.

Ten paces . . .

For a split second Tom's eyes shifted across to the stockman, who had pushed himself onto his elbows. The mention of grog had reached the ears of the sleeping man across the dusty yard and had drawn him out of his befuddled alcohol-induced sleep.

'You got a drink goin', mate?' the stockman called to the trio. 'Count me in.'

It all happened in that shift of the eyes.

Henry clawed desperately at the pistol tucked under his shirt, but the hammer caught in the tough material and refused to let go. Tom swung his attention back to Henry and his right hand dropped over his holstered revolver. His gun was out and levelled at Henry's head. Tom's grey eyes blazed with cold fury. Henry froze with his hand still wrapped around the butt of his now useless pistol. All feelings were gone!

He braced himself for the fatal shot and was vaguely aware that Hogan had snatched up the rifle leaning against the hitching rail to point it uncertainly at him. It was obvious that Hogan was confused, as his eyes darted from the police sergeant and then to the bushranger.

'I suppose it's no good me telling you to stand in the Queen's name,' Henry said with a weak smile. It was all he could think of to say.

'You're a trap?' Tom snarled with his arm outstretched and the pistol levelled at Henry's head.

'Sergeant James of the Burketown Native Mounted Police,' he answered wearily and he saw the blaze in the bushranger's eyes grow cold and deadly. He knew Tom Duffy had no love for the men who had been responsible for his father's death.

'A bloody trap,' Tom growled. 'I ought to blow your bloody brains out as we stand here now.'

Henry could see that despite the bushranger's understandable hatred for the Native Mounted Police, he was wrestling with himself over his fate and a tiny flame of hope flickered. Henry made his desperate move.

'I was hoping to take you alive, Tom Duffy,' he said, as if confidently stating a fact. 'But I'm afraid Mister Hogan standing just behind you knows about the thousand-pound reward for your arrest and will probably have to shoot you.'

Hogan's eyes widened at the mention of the reward. The police sergeant's gamble was a desperate one but he noticed the barrel shift towards Tom.

'You Tom Duffy?' Hogan asked with a noticeable tone of awe. He had suspected that his regular visitor might have been wanted by the law for maybe horse-stealing or cattle-duffing. But not the infamous bushranger Tom Duffy, who was wanted for robbery under arms.

'Yair, I'm Tom Duffy,' Tom replied as he continued to level his pistol at Henry.

'And yer worth a thousand quid?' Hogan said ominously. The Irish bushranger was aware of the strange note in Hogan's voice and his survival instincts told him the Snider was pointed squarely at his back. Now it was his turn to attempt to get on top of the situation that had shifted in favour of the police sergeant.

'The Snider's not loaded, Mister Hogan,' Tom said without bothering to turn. But Hogan had made up his mind where his loyalties lay. A thousand pounds!

'Then if'n I pull the trigger nothin' will happen,' he countered casually.

Tom shook his head and lowered his pistol. As he lowered the gun, Henry unravelled the hammer of his revolver from under his shirt and levelled it at Tom, who dropped his gun to the ground.

'And all the others, Mister Duffy,' Henry ordered.

Tom removed the smaller pistol from his belt and placed it in the dust of the shanty yard. 'It was worth a try,' he said with a cheeky grin and a shrug of his massive shoulders. 'I tell you, Hogan, this will be the last time I drink at your establishment if you let traps drink here. You've got no class.'

For the first time in his life, Tom Duffy was manacled.

33

Wallarie had a bad feeling. He had watched his white brother ride towards the grog shanty with that easy indifference he had so often contemptuously displayed for danger. Mebbe he would be all right, he thought. There had been no sign of the Mounted Police in the area for a long time. His horse snorted and shifted under him as if sensing his unease. It was a baal feeling.

Wallarie reined his horse away and melted into the sparse shadows of the bush to keep the track from Burketown under surveillance. The afternoon passed and the shadows lengthened and still Tom had not come back to their appointed place of meeting. Something was very wrong.

Within minutes, the former Darambal warrior picked up the tracks of two horses and immediately recognised one set as that of a Mounted Policeman and the other as the familiar tracks of Tom's horse. Whoever was leading Tom's horse had skirted the track to ride across unbroken ground and he knew what he was doing. He was deliberately attempting to throw a tracker off the trail. That could only mean that the trap knew that Wallarie would be following them.

Wallarie smiled savagely. No white man could ever use the bush to cover his trail. It was not whether he would find them but merely a matter of whether he would use his rifle or revolver to kill the trap when he caught up with him. And he knew with the certainty of his considerable skills that he would be ready to make his move just after sunset. He would come like a spirit in the night to take the trap's life and free his white brother.

With a jerk on the reins he forced his mount into a canter. The tracks were easy to follow.

Tom had a grudging respect for the sergeant's bush skills. The policeman's attention was never distracted from his constant scanning of the mottled shadows of the country they rode through, and he noticed that Henry avoided any rocky outcrops as they traversed the land between Hogan's grog shop and Burketown, avoiding the better-marked track to the Gulf town.

He could see that the big Englishman was well at home navigating across the monotonous terrain of grass and woodland. With the tactical astuteness of a military scout, the big bearded sergeant always ensured he had a panoramic view in all directions as they rode north. Wallarie would have some problems keeping the sergeant close to him in the present country during daylight. But Tom knew that with the coming of the night, Wallarie was bound to make his move to rescue him.

Henry rode, never speaking a word, except to give his manacled prisoner orders. The manacles chafed Tom's wrists but he was at least grateful that he was riding and not walking as the sergeant could have made him do all the way back to Burketown.

What puzzled Tom was why the sergeant had not sprung the trap on him with more police. Either the sergeant was the best in the north or he was downright stupid. Sergeant James must have known he would not be alone and that Wallarie was bound to be with him or at least close by. But it was obvious from the way the sergeant traversed the country his first proposition could have some basis – Henry James was bloody good at his job. Tom was beginning to regret that he had not killed the policeman when he had the chance.

He pondered on what had stopped him from pulling the trigger of his Colt. Was it the lack of fear he saw in the sergeant's demeanour when he had levelled the gun on him? Tom respected courage. Was it that he was not naturally a killer? The shooting of the Glen View shepherds had not been acts of murder. They were acts of summary justice for the shepherds' torture and murder of his friends. Execution was the technical name, he thought. Yes, he was an executioner. But not a murderer. So it had been that he had hesitated in killing a man just doing his job.

At sundown, Henry selected a clearing with a gentle rising section of grassland to camp for the night and Tom noticed that the ground had an uninterrupted view in all directions of the surrounding plain, dotted with low and spindly trees. He was left manacled near the camp fire while Henry limped out from the camp site.

Tom watched with interest as the sergeant paced out distances and then stopped to mark the trunks of nearby trees with scraps of white rag he carried.

'I see you've been a military man in your time, Sergeant,' Tom called to him as he recognised that the policeman was setting rifle ranges for the Snider carbine.

'Crimea in '54,' Henry grunted when he returned and he cleared a space around the sticks he had gathered for a small fire.

'Then at least you weren't one of those murdering redcoats at the Eureka if you were fighting the Rooskies in '54,' Tom said as he gazed out at the shimmering haze of the plain and rubbed his wrists, chafed by the police manacles. He did not complain, as he knew with certainty that he would not for long be a prisoner of Her Majesty and the English sergeant who escorted him to Burketown. Wallarie was out there.

Although Tom had left Wallarie in the scrub to keep a sharp lookout for anyone approaching the shanty, he had not expected to be taken at the shanty itself in a cleverly set ambush. He had made the fatal error of underestimating the cunning of the traps, or at least the deviousness of Sergeant James. He vowed to himself that it would not happen again as he watched the sergeant go about, cautiously preparing the camp for the night. It was obvious that he also expected Wallarie to attempt a rescue when the sun set over the plains.

Henry knew it was no use concealing the camp site if the Aboriginal bushranger was tracking them. Better that he prepare his defences for an attack. Now he wished that he had brought the

troop with him from Burketown, as he had foolishly overestimated his ability to take both
bushrangers single-handedly. But he had his
reasons for choosing to attempt the arrest of Tom
and Wallarie alone.

Neither policeman nor bushranger mentioned
Wallarie. Some things did not have to be said, as
they both knew he was out there and what his
intentions were.

The sun sank as a cooling red ball over the tops
of the parched and stunted scrub. The hot air
cooled noticeably and the flames of the fire took
on the beauty of dancing wraiths.

The night was promising to be clear and crisp
and the full moon would soon rise to cover the
plains with its soft glow. A time when every
shadow would take on a sinister shape for Henry.

Very few words had passed between the two
men as they rode across the land to the gentle rise
but Henry had treated his prisoner with a strange
courteousness Tom could not fathom. He had
even offered Tom a plug of his precious tobacco.
Precious because it was a luxury that was not
always available on the frontier.

Tom gratefully accepted the plug of tobacco
Henry passed him and tamped it down in his
battered pipe with his thumb. He bent and took a
thin burning stick from the fire to light his pipe,
sucked until the tobacco glowed and then he
relaxed and puffed contentedly on the pipe.

Grey smoke curled lazily from the pipe's bowl in
the still air of the sunset. Under other circumstances, Tom thought, the evening might have been
pleasant.

'I'm just a bit puzzled why you didn't come better prepared than you are, Sergeant James,' Tom said as he puffed at the clay pipe. 'Thought Wallarie and me warranted at least a troop from Burketown.'

Henry poked at the fire, which sparked in a shower of red cinders. 'I didn't want you to get killed,' he replied quietly. 'Any more of us might have got you shot up.'

'Nice that you should say that, Sergeant,' Tom said with just a touch of gratitude for Henry's considerate view of the situation. 'But it doesn't make a lot of sense. Me and Wallarie being the scourge of Queensland and all that. It's not that you know me exactly.'

'I know more about you than you think,' Henry said with an enigmatic smile. 'Your sister Kate has told me a lot about you.'

The bushranger ceased puffing on his pipe.

'Kate! How do you know Kate?' he asked quietly as Henry began to prepare himself for the night. He slipped the loaded revolvers inside his belt and was now armed with three pistols as well as the Snider.

'I met Kate a time ago,' he said and stared into the flickering flames. 'Your sister is a fine woman you can be very proud of.'

Tom stared curiously at the police sergeant. It was a strange world where Kate might be friends with a trap, let alone an Englishman.

'I was on the dispersal when your father was murdered,' Henry continued softly as he scanned the plain, now under a soft light as the sun sank below the flat horizon.

'*Murdered!* You knew he was murdered?' Tom hissed across the space between them. 'You know about that murdering bastard Mort then?'

Henry nodded. 'I couldn't prove anything but I got him to resign from the Mounted Police at Rockhampton. I came very close to killing Mort myself. He not only murdered your father but he also murdered a good friend of mine.'

'Then why didn't you kill him if you had the chance?' Tom asked with an edge of bitterness, as Henry stared reflectively at the fire.

'Because I'm still here and free. And you are the one in chains,' he replied philosophically. 'You made your decision. I made mine.' Henry fell into a silence as he kept a careful eye on the horizon where he expected the moon to rise.

Tom understood what Henry was saying. If only the Macintosh shepherds had not killed the last of the survivors of the Nerambura clan and raped Mondo, things might have turned out differently for him and Wallarie. They might not have taken to bushranging. But that was past and the reality was the present. He was the one in chains and only one day's ride from a police lockup.

'How is Kate?' Tom asked, breaking the silence that followed Henry's revelation as to why he had not killed Mort.

'Kate is fine and well,' he answered. 'She lives in Rockhampton and happens to be good friends with my wife, Emma. Kate is like an aunt to my son, Gordon.'

'I heard she was working in a pub in Rockhampton,' Tom said, puffing on his pipe. 'You get the news out here along the track.' He leant back to look up at the first stars appearing in the sky. 'They say she is the most beautiful woman north of the border. Ah, but it would be good to see her again some day . . . little Katie.'

Henry listened to the bushranger talk about his sister as if he was talking to a friend. But as he listened to the bushranger's banter, he was fully alert to all the noises around them.

A quoll, the marsupial native cat of Australia, gave off a sharp screech as it encountered another male quoll. The ferocious animals, only a little larger than the common rat, fought over a female and the screeching of combat between them caused Henry to start nervously. But he soon settled down when he recognised the sound for what it was.

Tom noticed that the sergeant was tense and he knew he had good reason to be. If Wallarie came it would be with his natural stealth and a sharp knife. The quolls settled their dispute and moved away. One a winner, the other a loser.

'You much of a cook?' Henry asked Tom.

'Fair enough.'

'Then we get to find out. You get to make the tucker. I've got some rice, couple of tins of sardines, and a bit of curry powder. Also got flour and jam. See what you can do with that,' Henry said as he dropped the saddlebags at Tom's feet.

Tom grinned up at Henry. 'I might just poison you, Sergeant James.'

Henry wanted to eat before it got too dark as he did not want to be preoccupied with anything other than watching for the Aboriginal bushranger when night fell.

After an imaginative if not appetising supper of

489

curried sardines and rice, Henry strolled across to
the horses. He had not only marked out rifle
ranges with the cloth spotters but he had also carefully made a survey on lines of sight across the
tussock and scrub plain. He had left the horses in
dead ground, an area of hollowed earth, which
obscured an observer's view of their location.

He saddled the horses and was careful to keep
Tom in view at all times even though the ankle
chains were guaranteed to keep him from running
very far should he attempt to flee.

Tom watched with interest as Henry went about
his tasks in the hollow. Whatever he was doing was
a waste of time. Tom fully expected to gain his
freedom in the next few hours.

The moon was a big yellow ball on the horizon
and its soft glow brought to life the stark shadows
of the bush and tussock. If Wallarie was working
to the plan that Henry thought he would have
formulated for Tom Duffy's release, then the
warrior would even now be stalking them. When
the horses were saddled, Henry led them up the
rise to Tom, manacled by the fire.

'I want you to listen very carefully, Duffy, to
what I am going to tell you,' he said. 'But first, be
assured I will kill you if you should so much as
vary one inch from what I tell you to do. Are we
clear on that?' Tom could see in the sergeant's eyes
he meant exactly what he said and he nodded his
head. 'I do not want to have to kill you,' Henry
continued as he stared into Tom's eyes to keep his
meaning clear. 'But if it comes down to you or me
I promise you that it will be me who comes out of
this alive. I know that blackfella companion

of yours is probably out there watching us right now and I have no doubts he would kill me as fast as you can say Jack Robinson. So do as I say and we will both live.' Tom nodded again. He had underestimated the English sergeant twice now.

Henry released Tom's ankle chains which fell away and he rubbed his ankles where they had chafed him.

'Get on your horse. You ride in front of me and we ride north,' Henry said as he made a final scan of the surrounding moonlit plain. 'I figure your myall mate isn't going to be very happy when he sees us ride out of here,' he said with a quick and savage smile. And Henry was right.

Wallarie watched helplessly as the two men rode at a gallop away from what he had presumed incorrectly was to be an overnight camp for the sergeant and his prisoner. Had not the policeman marked the trees with the white rag as Tom had told him some men did to mark ranges for rifle fire accuracy? Wallarie used one of Tom's favourite curses. The bloody whitefella had tricked him.

Wallarie rose up out of the grass tussocks and flung his rifle to the shoulder. The bang of the rifle shot rolled across the plain and Henry instinctively ducked his head at the sound. It was a futile gesture, as he knew the sound followed the bullet and if the Aboriginal bushranger's aim had been true, then he would have felt the impact of the bullet first.

Tom and Henry were swallowed by the bush before Wallarie could reload. He strung together a string of invective words that Tom used when he was particularly angry at the world. Wallarie's grasp of the English language was improving.

Without wasting precious time, he turned on his heel and sprinted back to where his horse was tethered a half mile further into the scrub. The bloody white man had fooled him with the appearance of settling in for the night. But it was not over, as the moon was on his side and he knew where the policeman was taking Tom.

Henry did not believe for a moment that he had shaken off Wallarie. But he was able to console himself that the night made it harder for the Aboriginal bushranger to track them. When they had galloped for what Henry considered a safe distance out of Wallarie's reach, he ordered Tom to walk his horse.

'You're not going to throw him, Sergeant James,' Tom said as he let his mount find her own way in the dark. 'He'll be on you before dawn.'

Henry ignored the Irishman's confidently delivered warning, although he had a bad feeling he was probably right. For now they would ride until just after midnight, when Henry hoped that the setting moon would leave the vast plains under a cloak of darkness and he would snatch some sleep, shielded from the Aboriginal's searching eyes.

Henry knew with the coming of the sun it would be a long day of exhaustive vigilance for him as they drew closer to Burketown. Wallarie would become more desperate in his attempts to free his friend. Henry realised that he would always have to be looking over his shoulder right up to the front steps of Lieutenant Uhr's office.

* * *

Piccaninny dawn came with its soft light across the stunted tree plain as Tom felt his shoulder being shaken.

'Wake up ... time to start moving,' Henry whispered in his ear as he bent to unlock the manacles from behind Tom's back. The first of the diurnal creatures, the little bush birds, began to make sweet chirping calls as they stirred with the false dawn.

'Sleep well, Sergeant James?' Tom asked with an edge of facetiousness as he yawned and tried to stretch his cramped muscles. 'Hope you did because I . . .' The bushranger did not have a chance to finish his statement.

The strike was swift and deadly!

Henry yelped with shock and tumbled backwards. 'Jesus help me! I'm a dead man,' Henry screamed as he scrambled in the dim light to get away from the tree. Confused, Tom searched frantically for sight of Wallarie. But there was no sign of the tall warrior.

He suddenly froze and dared not move a muscle. The dark and sinister shape of the snake slithered away from near his foot and, with rising horror, Tom realised that the snake had nested in a rotting log behind him as had lain chained to the tree. In the half light of the dawn, Henry had not noticed the log which gave way under his foot, and the usually sluggish snake struck with blinding speed. The needle-sharp fangs had hit just above the top of his riding boot.

'Let me free, I can help you,' Tom yelled at Henry, who ripped at the trouser leg that was tucked into his boot. 'I've seen things the blacks do for snakebite.' Tom found himself suddenly and unexpectedly on the English sergeant's side. No one warranted the agonising death that came with the spread of the poison. Not even a trap. Death from the much-feared snakes of the Gulf Country was hideous and cruel. And death was certain if the bite was not treated.

Henry slumped to the ground feeling for the bite and located the puncture wounds in the calf of his leg. Blood flowed from the jagged short gash the snake's fangs had inflicted and the flesh around the wound was sensitive to touch. The pain had not yet come from the venom. He heard Tom's plea to help him but held little hope of his surviving the reptile's bite.

'I'll free you, Tom, but I doubt if you can help me. I'm a dead man,' he said bitterly. He was resigned to his inevitable fate. It was ironic, he thought, that he should survive a war and the events of policing on the frontier only to die from a snakebite. 'I can't leave you manacled to the tree in case your black-fella doesn't find you. I'll let you go.'

He fumbled for the keys and passed them to Tom, who quickly unshackled himself. Henry felt dizzy and slumped to the ground. It did not matter that Tom could take his guns from him now. For him to kill the bushranger served no purpose.

'Lie still and don't move around,' Tom ordered. 'Do what I say and you just might live.' He searched frantically about the area for a fresh piece of bark from one of the trees and was careful when he stripped a fragment from a fallen tree trunk. Where there was one snake there could be a nest of them, he cautioned himself.

Tom placed the fragment flat over the puncture marks on Henry's leg and strapped the bark down firmly with strips of cloth torn from his own shirt. Then he propped the sergeant against a tree and made him sit up.

That was all he could do for the moment and he did not know if he had the right bark or if he had done as Wallarie had once shown him. All he could do now was wait. Either the sergeant died or he lived. Tom hoped he would live. The police sergeant had risked his life to capture Tom alone and that counted for something.

Henry felt the nausea well up and he vomited. Tom sighed. It did not look good for the sergeant.

'I will kill him,' Wallarie's voice came from behind Tom's shoulder. He turned to see the rifle raised and pointed at Henry. 'He is a dead man anyway,' Wallarie said in the Nerambura dialect and Tom understood every word.

Henry did not have to know the Nerambura language to realise he was looking death in the face. And the face of death was black! The Nerambura warrior sighted down the rifle for the fatal shot. After all, had he not done the same to Wallarie's people when they were facing a slow death from the white man's bullets all those years earlier.

Henry closed his eyes and forced himself to picture the faces of his wife and son. He knew he was going to die and he wanted his last thoughts to be for the two people he most loved in the world.

34

Penelope could hardly refuse to attend her own farewell dinner, as Aunt Enid had already selected the guests for the occasion at the Macintosh residence. Penelope's pending visit to Europe early in the new year had given Enid the opportunity to bid farewell to her niece in a gracious manner.

As Penelope had very rarely visited the Macintosh house over the past four years, she accepted her aunt's gracious offer with thinly veiled cynicism. Fiona was settled into married life with her brother, Granville, and there was little reason for her to visit her Aunt Enid's home. Nor had she been able to visit Fiona very often in the years she had been married to her brother. Granville's presence in Fiona's life had been an awkward distraction to their friendship and had temporarily thwarted Penelope's plans for the ultimate revenge. When she had visited her cousin there had always been an ever-present sense that something had been lost between them. Fiona had adopted the role of a dutifully married woman. And yet Penelope had always sensed a tension at their brief afternoon teas in the garden or drawing room. How much she had longed to take her beautiful cousin in her arms and lull her with words and stroke her naked flesh. But she seemed lost to her. Only the unrequited yearning was left and a hope that something might happen to let Fiona see who could truly love her.

Penelope well knew that her aunt still blamed her as a contributing factor in Fiona's fall from grace when she became embarrassingly pregnant to the Irishman. The dinner was a hypocritical gesture by her as a supposed outward sign of her ability to forget and forgive the past.

Penelope's mother, Sarah White, had died the previous year in London and left her daughter a substantial legacy, which Penelope had decided to use in a long and luxurious tour of Europe. She had booked a passage via India and had intended to make her way to Prussia to visit the von Fellmanns, who were closely related to her deceased mother's side of the family. As a young girl in England, Penelope had once met her intriguing German cousin, Manfred von Fellmann. The meeting had had a great impact on her at the time, she remembered, and although he had been much older she remembered how as a young girl she had instantly fallen in love with him. He had married but was now a widower. So the visit to Prussia held a special interest for Penelope.

Penelope arrived late as a subtle display of contempt for her aunt. Her carriage rumbled up the driveway and she was helped down by a footman to be greeted warmly by David Macintosh. Penelope genuinely liked her quiet and scholarly cousin, who had recently returned to the colonies from his sojourn of teaching at Oxford. He no longer troubled himself with the management of the family companies as the day-to-day administration was in Granville's hands after he wed Fiona and the arrangement had proved to be a wise one by Enid. The family's coffers continued to swell with financial returns under Granville's competent and shrewd supervision.

David had acquired two new interests in his life since Penelope had last seen him: Miss Charlotte Frost and photography. His interest in photography had been aroused by his contact with Professor Smith at the newly established Sydney University. The daguerreotype process had come a long way since Mister Goodman had opened his gallery in Sydney back in 1842, when he had displayed the remarkable chemical portraits of well-known people around Sydney Town.

And the second interest in David's life, Miss Charlotte Frost, was pretty and demure. She was of the London Frosts with a well-established bloodline of wealthy merchant entrepreneurs who had growing financial interests in the colonies.

Granville accompanied Fiona to the dinner and they were a handsome couple as they stepped down from their carriage. But when they made their entrance, Penelope thought Fiona looked rather pale and ill. She knew that the birth of Fiona's second daughter had almost killed her cousin and although it had been three months since the delivery she still had not fully recovered.

Fiona's eyes sparkled briefly when she greeted Penelope but the dullness returned when she saw her mother approaching. It had been many years since mother and daughter had conducted a civil conversation between them.

Enid was her usual regal self as she moved among the carefully selected guests she had invited to the dinner. Whatever devious reasons Enid may have had for arranging the dinner, Penelope was rather pleased to see that one of the guests invited was the dashing and rather mysterious Captain Morrison Mort.

She had heard much of the captain's colourful exploits in the South Pacific islands recruiting the natives for the Macintosh plantations and her brother had often expressed his admiration for the *Osprey*'s captain. But she had not previously had the opportunity to meet the man.

Others who had met him thought the rather infamous sea captain cut a rather dashing figure even though it was rumoured that Captain Mort had a dark and violent past shrouded in controversy. Penelope found the man's history fascinating.

He was possibly in his mid-thirties, she mused, as she watched him discreetly from across the anteroom to the spacious dining salon. He stood stiffly chatting with one of Sydney's better known matrons and Penelope could see how the woman unashamedly vied for the captain's attention although her husband, a respectable banker, was standing beside her. He has a most dangerous and attractive aura, she thought, with a stirring of strong physical desire.

Penelope could not keep her eyes off him and she was annoyed that she was continually being intercepted by acquaintances desiring to wish her well on her European tour. She would have preferred to engage the handsome captain in conversation.

During the course of the dinner, Mort was seated at the furthermost end of the table away from Penelope. She was next to Fiona and was engaged in listening politely to her cousin prattle on about her young daughters, Helen and Dorothy. The topic of the conversation had little appeal to Penelope and she thought that Fiona was growing rather dull in married life as she talked incessantly about the girls. Gone were the secret discussions about men and the forbidden subject of sex. And gone was the tender talk of romance. Now Fiona could only talk about children's sicknesses and problems of teething and of Granville's desire to see her bear a son.

But Penelope was also aware of a haunted and frightened look in her cousin's eyes as she spoke of Granville's need for a male heir. It was the kind of look one would see in the eyes of a cowed dog, Penelope thought, as she listened and made the appropriate polite noises to her cousin. Although she feigned interest Penelope was watching Mort engaged in a deep discussion with her brother at the other end of the table. Captain Mort was certainly a handsome man. And she wondered how it was that he was not married.

She assumed that his roving way of life precluded marriage. He was no doubt one of those exciting men who seized love where and whenever they could. The thought of his rampant approach to love appealed to Penelope. He was not unlike herself in that regard.

With the tedious dinner finally over, the men prepared to retire to the library to smoke cigars and drink port while the ladies retired to sip tea and coffee served in the drawing room.

Penelope excused herself from Fiona's company and attempted to intercept Mort but she was unsuccessful, as he disappeared with her brother and the other men. Caught in the drawing room, Penelope continued to politely accept the best wishes from the ladies for her journey to Europe. She sighed. Would she ever be able to get the handsome and mysterious captain alone?

Enid had engaged a well-known soprano to entertain the guests and the recital would commence when the men had returned to the drawing room to rejoin the ladies. Penelope was bored with the occasion supposedly for her benefit. Frivolous chatter from dull matrons was not her notion of a good evening and she would glance occasionally across at Fiona, who she could see was also trapped by the mores of polite society into the same dull chatter.

She was finally able to catch Fiona's eye across the room. Fiona returned the look with one indicating I-want-to-speak-to-you-alone. They stepped discreetly out onto the verandah to take in the cool harbour breezes. Penelope had sensed during the evening that Fiona was eager to get her alone and that the frivolous prattle was really a cover for what she wanted to confide.

The lost years between them fell away as they shared the serenity of the darkened harbour from the verandah where they could hear the men returning to the drawing room with their laughter raucous from the amount of wine and port consumed. Enid introduced the soprano and her accompanist on the piano.

The two women on the verandah stood side by side watching and listening to the inconsequential sights and sounds around them.

'What is it, Fi?' Penelope finally asked gently as she could sense Fiona was on the verge of tears.

'I don't want to have any more babies, Penny,' Fiona blurted as she fought back the tears. 'Granville wants to keep trying until we have a son. But I'm afraid I might die in the next childbirth.'

Penelope placed her arm around Fiona's shoulders and led her further away from the sounds of the guests in the drawing room. 'You do what you want, Fi,' she said in a firm voice. 'My brother's ambitions are not worth your life.'

Fiona reached up to hold her cousin's hand resting lightly on her shoulder. 'I knew there was at least one person in this world who would understand,' she said gratefully as she smiled weakly and dabbed at her eyes. 'I knew I could confide in you.'

When they were at the furthermost end of the long verandah, Penelope guided Fiona to one of the cane chairs and took a seat on an adjoining chair. Penelope felt a surge of pity for her cousin, who had started life with so many romantic and foolish ideas about marriage and love. She even thought that it might have been better for her if Michael Duffy had not been killed in the Maori Wars. Michael Duffy might have been socially unacceptable, but at least he was a real man, she thought unselfishly.

'I wish you weren't going to Europe, Penny,' Fiona said with a sad sigh. 'I have only the visit of Father this Christmas to look forward to. And that will probably mean I will be forced to talk to Mother while he is here.'

'Well, your father will be very happy to see you,' Penelope replied cheerfully in an attempt to bolster her spirits. 'I know he is very fond of his only daughter.'

Fiona had ceased crying and stared blankly at the garden veiled by the night.

'I don't think he is much more fond of me than he is of one of his horses,' she said bitterly and Penelope moved to divert her from recriminations.

'Your father loves you, Fi. I know that in my heart,' she said gently. Fiona responded by providing the ghost of a smile for her cousin's benefit. Yes, she would miss Penelope very much.

The intimacy they had shared on the verandah was broken by Granville, as he had seen Fiona leave the drawing room with his sister and had come to fetch her away. He did not trust his sister any more than he trusted Enid and, over the four years he had been married to Fiona, he had noticed his sister's rare visits to his wife had an unsettling effect on her. There was something there that he could not quite put his finger on. What he did not understand, he did not trust. But it was something very deep.

Fiona excused herself and went obediently with her husband to join her mother's guests in the drawing room. It was important for Granville that he be seen with his beautiful young wife in public. He owned her and he wanted the world to see that she was his.

Penelope lingered on the verandah alone to enjoy the cool and refreshing night air and pondered on her cousin's soft hand against hers. The proximity of her beautiful body had rekindled old feelings of desire in her. Feelings that had long lain dormant but never forgotten and nor was the driving need to revenge herself on her brother for the pain he had caused in her life.

She was also aware that the time was not far off when she would take that revenge. Fiona was growing more vulnerable as each day passed and time was on her side.

She was on the verge of joining the guests in the drawing room when she noticed Captain Mort step outside. The soprano's rendition of the classics had little appeal to a man who had grown up in The Rocks.

'Why don't you join me, Captain Mort?' she suggested softly from the shadows. 'The breezes are much sweeter here.' With a nod of his head, he strolled down the verandah and sat beside her in the chair that Fiona had recently vacated.

'Miss White, I believe. I have not had the privilege in all these years of making your acquaintance,' he said as he lit a corona. 'A rather unusual situation when I have worked all those years for your brother. I had that opportunity earlier and I must apologise for being remiss in doing so. But I'm afraid business with your brother has taken up most of my time.'

Penelope was aware the captain's eyes had travelled over her with an undisguised appraisal of her voluptuous body and she liked the feeling of his attention on her which was frank with the lust he obviously felt. But there was something else rather disturbing about the pale eyes that she preferred to ignore. Or was the strangely disturbing aspect of the captain's stare also sexually exciting to her? They were the eyes of a male animal. She had a fleeting recollection of another man who had the same animal appeal. Michael Duffy!

'I have heard many stories of your rather colourful exploits in the islands, Captain Mort,' she said and was surprised to see a guarded expression cloud his handsome face.

His body seemed to tense when he replied suspiciously, 'What kind of colourful stories, Miss White?'

'Oh, just that you have had encounters with headhunters and cannibals. Is that true, Captain?' she asked with genuine innocence and Mort visibly relaxed.

'Yes. It is true. The *Osprey* has encountered cannibals and headhunters in her travels,' he replied with some pride for a distorted view of reality. 'At times we have been forced to defend ourselves against their unwelcome attentions and the rascals have rued the day they ever dared take on the might of the *Osprey*.'

He was quick to notice the beautiful woman's deliberately exposed ankle beneath the long skirt. The damned woman was trying to seduce him with her coquettish ways, he brooded. At the same time he found her strangely attractive, unlike many of the other women he had met ashore in the past. She had the brazen look of a woman who would not flinch at anything of a carnal nature and he felt an attraction to her that he had not known with

505

other women. Yes, he would play her game. But it was up to the sister of his employer to make the proposal, as he did not want to cross Granville. He could possibly lose the *Osprey* if the sister bleated that he, Mort, had made indecent approaches to her. But somehow he suspected that the woman was not the kind to run to her brother about such matters.

'I would assume, Captain Mort, that in your travels in the South Seas you must encounter strange and, how should I put it, ah, *exotic* native customs,' Penelope said huskily with the emphasis on 'exotic', which she clearly inferred to mean *erotic*. He was aware of what she meant and he smiled knowingly.

'I have, Miss White. But I am afraid I would not dare repeat to a lady the things that I have witnessed the heathen natives practising,' he replied with a slightly teasing tone at her aroused interest. 'I am afraid the pagan practices are not fit for the sensibilities of polite and beautiful company such as yours.'

Penelope leant forward and touched Mort on the knee lightly. He tensed, as it was not the act of a lady to do such a thing to a man she barely knew.

. . . *Make them stop hurting me . . .*

'Please tell me, Captain Mort,' she said softly. 'I am a student of human behaviour and I feel you could teach me much from your worldly experiences.'

Mort stared at her with a smouldering interest. There was little need to go any further with the game, as it had already been won. When he smiled and brushed her hand with his fingers, she experienced a delicious shiver of anticipation ripple through her body.

'Do you have a carriage, Miss White?' he asked quietly, fixing her gaze with his.

'Yes, I do have a carriage, Captain,' she replied, holding his gaze with brazen acceptance of his meaning, and she slowly withdrew her hand from Mort's thigh. 'Could I possibly take you somewhere tonight after you have completed your business with my brother?'

He nodded and with an enigmatic smile replied, 'I would be very grateful if you could take me back to my ship tonight. I think I have something in my cabin that will be of great interest to a student of human behaviour.'

Penelope had a strange feeling she was only hours from exploring a whole new world of pleasure.

Mort's cabin aboard the *Osprey* was cramped.

It was cramped because of the chunky wooden bench that took up much of the confined space in the cabin. The bench was a perversion of the beautiful timber that had been used in its construction and the once-living trees had lost their souls to hell in the crafting of the device.

Penelope recognised the whipping bench for what it was. She had an irresistible urge to run her hand along the smooth surface and she felt it grow into impulsive desire to feel the smooth and silky wood, which was mottled with dark blotches.

So the bench had been used for its intended purpose, Penelope mused idly, and she thought, for an erotic but perverse moment, of an altar used for human sacrifice. The kind of altar that might have been used by the Druids in the dark forests of northern Europe in a time before Christianity spread its repressive teachings.

Mort stood watching the beautiful woman stroking the bench under the sickly glow of the oil lantern that cast its feeble light in the tiny cabin and he could clearly see that she was reluctant to take her hand away from the smooth and oily surface of the timber.

'It is a whipping bench, Miss White,' he said unnecessarily.

Penelope answered in a distant and dreamy voice, 'I know.'

'Would you like a rum?' he asked as he ratted through a sea chest that was jammed against the single bunk fixed into the bulkhead.

'No,' Penelope answered as she gazed around the cabin, which had a lack of personal adornments, except for the sword hanging in its scabbard over the bunk. Mort was a very neat man who kept everything in its place. Just like Granville, she mused. Her social and sometimes sexual contact with the regimental officers of Sydney's garrisons had taught her the difference between a cavalry sabre and an infantry sword and she thought it was rather unusual for a man who had served with the Native Mounted Police to own an infantry sword rather than a sabre.

She turned to Mort, who stood awkwardly in the cabin holding the bottle of rum, and she slowly began to undress in front of him.

He stood expressionless as he watched the layers of her clothes fall away until Penelope stood wearing only the long pantaloons that were divided discreetly at the centre, designed for calls of nature.

She raised her arms above her head to undo the pins that secured her long silky tresses and her hair fell as a golden shower around her shoulders. Then she turned and lay forward across the whipping bench – gripping the stout legs with her hands. Her own legs spread enticingly to Mort's view as her lustrous long blonde hair cascaded to the cabin floor.

'I will have to secure your wrists,' Mort said in a hoarse voice thick with lust. 'For you to experience the full effect, Miss White,' he added as he placed the rum bottle carefully back in the sea chest and produced thin strips of leather.

Penelope smiled dreamily as he tied her hands securely to the legs of the bench. She was now completely vulnerable to whatever his fertile mind should conjure for their mutual pleasure. Bound and helpless, she imagined that she was a native girl being punished for resisting the captain's pleasure. She smiled with delicious anticipation of what he would do to her as punishment. She was unable to see Mort reach for the sword above his bunk because of the manner of her bondage, but she did hear the soft and metallic hiss of the blade slide from the scabbard. The lovingly oiled silver blade was out of its sheath and in the hands of its cruel master.

How could she know . . . ?

He stood behind the helpless woman and contemplated the erotic sight of her firmly rounded buttocks straining against the shiny and creamy silk of the pantaloons. A sweaty feverish sheen gave his face a garish and hellish look as the demons of his twisted mind took control of his actions and the murderous captain could see that she was utterly unafraid of him.

How could she know . . . ?

The sharp tip of the sword slowly caressed the exposed milky white flesh that was revealed where the pantaloons divided and its cold and unexpected kiss was an electric shock to her body. Penelope flinched when she felt the flat of the blade slide down slowly and precisely between her legs and over the most intimate parts of her body. She shuddered with the thrill of terror and sensual ecstasy and her moan of pleasure filled the small cabin.

How could she know . . . ?

The *Osprey* was once again at sea. And the helpless girl was begging to be impaled with the symbol of his manhood!

'I should stick the sword up you, you black bitch,' he hissed as the point of the sword lingered lightly at the entrance to Penelope's body.

'Yes,' she sighed softly with her fear heightened and an overwhelming desire to be entered. 'Do it!'

She could feel the tip caressing the entrance to her body and experienced the most extreme fear and anticipation of death she had ever known. Pain and pleasure came together as one. The creature born out of the depths of humanity's most evil and perverted desires was as old as the demons that had lived with the powerful who preyed on the weak.

The sharp tip of the infantry sword lingered

menacingly at the yielding flesh between her thighs and then, slowly and gently, the tip of the blade entered her just the shortest distance. Mort shuddered violently as the uncontrollable spasms swept him with waves of violent relief. The sword clattered from his nerveless grip onto the cabin floor and he buckled and fell to his knees behind Penelope. How could she know his terrible desire to hurt those with the power to bear life . . . to inflict an unspeakable perversity on little boys.

'Kiss me there,' she said in a commanding voice distant with her rapture. 'Kiss me there, Captain Mort, and drink of my body.'

He crawled forward to obey her order and his lips pressed against her. His mouth opened to receive her offering, which flowed warm into his mouth and he drank greedily. They were now bound as one in their mutual pleasure.

As Penelope felt the tip of the sword caressing her body, her brother stepped with his wife from their carriage at the house Donald Macintosh had purchased for his daughter as a wedding gift.

The house was much smaller than the Macintosh mansion overlooking the harbour but it was new and luxurious and Granville had gratefully accepted the wedding gift from his father-in-law, despite the fact that the house belonged to his wife. It did not matter, as one day all the Macintosh property would be his anyway.

Fiona bade the carriage driver a good evening, whereas Granville did not bother to thank him. It was not in his nature to give praise or compliments to people employed by him.

Husband and wife stood alone in cold silence on the driveway in front of their grand house as the carriage rattled away. Their conversation on the journey home had been limited to how well Penelope appeared. Or what a nice dinner Enid had provided for the guests. It had been trite talk between two people with little interest in each other and now Fiona was weary and looked forward to a good night's sleep.

She was about to walk towards the front door when they were startled by the figure standing in the shadows of the garden and Fiona gasped with fright. Granville gripped his wife's elbow and summoned as much courage as he could to demand the man step forward. The man obeyed and Granville felt a profound sense of relief to see that it was only Harris, his former gardener.

'Harris! What in Hades are you doing standing around here frightening my wife?' he demanded arrogantly as the gardener shuffled from the shadows. In the dim light, Granville could see that his former gardener was a very ill man who had all the signs of advanced consumption.

'Come to see you, Mister White,' he said quietly as he glanced at Fiona standing beside her husband. 'Rather you and I talk privately if you don't mind.' Granville felt uneasy about the request, as there was only one thing the two men had in common. And he was not about to let his wife know what that was.

'You go inside and see to our daughters, Fiona,' Granville said quietly to his wife, who stared at the former gardener. She remembered that he had once worked for her husband and she felt a touch of pity for the sickly man. She could not help but wonder why the gardener had suddenly decided to visit her husband. Years had passed since Granville had dismissed him from service. But she did not question Granville and did as he directed.

Fiona was met by the girls' formidable nanny at the front door. She cast the gardener a contemptuous look. It was not fitting that such a disreputable-looking person hang around the gardens of good Christian people.

''E came early this evenin' lookin' for Mister White,' the nanny said as she ushered her mistress inside the house. 'Told 'im youse was out but he refused to go until 'e saw Mister White. 'E's been no bother though.'

When the nanny closed the door, Granville turned angrily on Harris.

'I've told you, Harris, that you were never to come to my house and bother me,' he snarled.

The gardener looked Granville directly in the eye. 'Jenny had a baby today,' he said. 'She's had a baby boy. Your boy, Mister White.'

Granville felt a cold vice grip his chest. The stupid girl had got herself pregnant! 'I deny what you say to be true, Harris,' Granville snarled as he took a threatening step towards the gardener. 'And I suggest very strongly that you leave now or I will have the police fetched to throw you in gaol.'

Although Harris was not a robust man, as the insidious disease of tuberculosis had long drained his strength, he refused to be cowed by his former employer's threatening attitude. What more could be done to him that God had not already punished him for?

Harris coughed, a deep hacking cough that caused Granville to step back lest he catch the dreaded sickness.

'It's your kid right enough, Mister White,' he finally said, after he was able to bring the coughing fit under control. Dark mucus covered the gardener's shirt sleeve where he had wiped his mouth. Sweat covered the man's face from the exertion. The coughing had drained his reserves of strength. 'And I'll tell Missus Macintosh so if you don't listen to what I say,' he added in a voice wheezy from coughing.

Granville realised the gardener meant what he said, as there was a defiance in the man he had never seen before. Jennifer was twelve now and although he had seen the obvious signs of her body turning from a prepubescent girl into that of a young woman, he had been careless concerning the risk of pregnancy.

He had dismissed the gardener but had paid for a small tenement to house the man and his young daughter where he could visit the girl on a regular basis until six months earlier, when Jennifer had simply disappeared. Granville had the gardener evicted and sold the house, as the man was of no use to him without access to his daughter. Now it was clear why she had run away.

'You can tell Missus Macintosh anything you like,' Granville said contemptuously in an attempt to bluff the gardener. 'I doubt if she will believe your slut of a daughter is the mother of my child.'

Harris shrugged his shoulders and turned to shuffle away, but Granville sensed that the man was not leaving. He believed his threat that he was actually going to tell Enid Macintosh. He felt real fear verging on panic, as relations with his mother-in-law were tentative at the best of times.

'Wait!' he cried out to the gardener, who had taken a few steps. 'Wait, Harris. I think we can come to an agreement in the best interests of you and me.'

The gardener stopped and turned around. 'Not in my interests, Mister White,' Harris replied. 'In the interests of Jenny and her boy. You see I don't think I'm long for this world and when you're looking at the next life you get to thinking there are things you should do before you go.'

'If that's what you want . . . the interests of your daughter,' Granville said calmly as he resigned himself to dealing with Harris. 'I'm sure money can be arranged to see she is looked after for a while.' One of the great advantages of wealth was that money could buy peace of mind. 'How much?' he asked.

Harris stared at Granville with just a hint of victory in his rheumy eyes. He had always hated himself for the deal that he had made with his employer all those years earlier. He had always tried to absolve his guilt by justifying it as based on altruistic motives for his daughter's future. Or so he thought. But the deadly and insidious consumption, and the realisation he would have to answer to his Maker very soon, had changed the gardener's attitudes. He had come to realise that the life he had been partially responsible for creating was his only earthly immortality and he'd thought it was rather ironic that he was now tied by blood to the man he had always hated.

'Five hundred quid,' he replied and he watched with vicious satisfaction as Granville's mouth gaped.

'I can arrange for the death of a man for less,' Granville unwittingly replied.

'That may be so, Mister White,' Harris said quietly. 'But if I don't get five hundred quid for Jenny then I think you might have signed your own death warrant with Missus Macintosh ... In a manner of speakin'.' The analogy was not lost on Granville. The ensuing scandal that could emerge was the equivalent of a death warrant to his aspirations.

'You will get the money,' Granville replied. 'On the condition that you take your daughter out of the colony of New South Wales ... and never return.'

Harris smiled. 'Fair enough,' he agreed. 'I was told by the doctor I should go somewhere warm and dry. He says Queensland is as good a place as any. You get the money to me by next week and I can promise you that Jenny, me and the kid will be gone by the week after, Mister White.'

Five hundred pounds was not a lot to get rid of the girl and her father, Granville thought, and he would certainly miss the little slut's prepubescent young body. However there were others who could take her place. It was only a matter of careful searching in the right places.

As the gardener and Granville made arrangements for the money to be paid, Fiona watched them from the bedroom window. Although she was relieved to see that her husband was not in any danger from the man he spoke to, she was also curious as to why Harris had come so late to see him.

When Granville finally came to their bedroom, she did not ask her husband about the conversation he had had with Harris. But he volunteered that the gardener had spoken to him about a grievance of back wages not being paid to him. Fiona knew her husband was lying but she did not comment, as she preferred not to know whatever it was the gardener had come to the house for.

That night Granville forced himself on Fiona. His lovemaking was rough and quick, as if he were using her to relieve his sexual tension. And when he was finished, he rolled over to sleep.

She prayed that she would not fall pregnant as she stared into the silent places of the night, listening to a whisper of an unthinkable and forbidden yearning. Penelope was with her in spirit and she wished she was with her in body, holding and comforting her – as they had when they were girls so long ago.

In a row of squalid tenements adjoining the back-yards of the tanneries and gasworks, a young girl sobbed as she rocked her baby in her arms. He would not stop crying and she despaired that he ever would. She tried to get him to take one of her nipples in his mouth but he only screwed up his face and bawled at her attempts. Frightened, confused and facing utter despair, she tried to calm him by rocking him gently in her arms. And still he cried. Jennifer Harris buried her head in his thin wispy hair and whispered tearfully, 'Your grandpapa will be home soon and he will help us, Willy.'

The wax candle flickered and was snuffed out as the wick reached its limit of life. The tiny room, with only a dirty straw-filled palliasse as the major item of furniture, was cast into stifling darkness. But she did not mind. Here she was safe and he would not be coming for her body to do the unspeakable things that he had in the past to hurt her.

'When you grow up, Willy, you will be my little man and look after Papa and me,' she crooned as she rocked the baby in the dark. He continued to bawl irritably at the flea bites that were inflicted on his tender skin. 'And when you grow up you will hurt Mister White,' she said with mounting anger.

She stopped rocking him and hugged him to her so that he stopped bawling as he fought for breath to fill his tiny lungs. 'You will grow up and hurt Mister White. Hurt Mister White so that he can never hurt no one again.' Her words echoed as whispers in the night.

35

The law firm of Sullivan & Levi was well known. Its fearless reputation to take on cases not popular with the establishment brought many to its doors. Mostly the guilty who could expect fire in the belly of their defence.

Daniel Duffy was learning the rough and tumble of court work in a manner not too dissimilar to how his cousin, Michael Duffy, had learnt to fight with his fists. Except that he was learning to fight with his rhetoric and he was already being recognised as a rising star in the legal world. Daniel Duffy was humble enough to give credit for his skills to the two men for whom he worked.

Gerald Sullivan was an Irishman and Isaac Levi was Jewish Australian. Although the two men were opposites in every way – Gerald Sullivan was short, fat and fiery; Isaac Levi was tall, slim and urbane – they complemented each other. Daniel had found, in working with the law firm, the art and science of court work. The art he learnt from Gerald, the science from Isaac. Both men were ten years older than Daniel but a hundred years more experienced in the devious ways of law. Neither solicitor was popular with the predominantly English judges they fronted at the bench or the police magistrates in the petty sessions. So it was strange that a Presbyterian missionary should seek help from the law firm of Sullivan & Levi.

The fiery little missionary sat in Isaac's office bristling with both discomfort for being in the presence of one of those who was responsible for the death of the Saviour and being in the presence of one of the damned Papists who slavishly followed the rule of the Antichrist in Rome. But the Presbyterian missionary had realised reluctantly that his mission required the legal services of a firm well and truly out of the grasp of the English establishment. Even his own Scottish legal firm was suspect when it came to prosecuting the powerful Donald Macintosh company that owned the *Osprey* – that black ship of Satan. Their zeal in establishing a case against the captain of the *Osprey*, Morrison Mort, might lack for real punch.

And so it was that John Macalister sat bristling in the presence of those with whom he never dreamt he would be associating in his lifetime. It was bad enough to have to put up with the French Marist missionaries poaching his island congregations for converts. It was an unholy pact he was entering into.

Daniel sat unobtrusively in the corner of Isaac's office as an observer. Isaac was a handsome man who had presence whenever he entered a room. His thick dark hair was shot with grey although he was only thirty-five years old and the greyness gave him an appearance of wise maturity in the eyes of his clients. Gerald had no hair at all. He was the same age as Isaac.

The two lawyers had found common ground many years earlier in that they had both been spurned by the conservative English system. Jews and Irish were on a socially unacceptable par as far as the powerful Protestant ruling classes were concerned and it was not unheard of for the Catholic Church in the Australian colonies to rally behind the Jewish faith in secular matters, although the same tolerance might not extend to religious doctrine. In matters of professional partnership and religious tolerance, the Irishman and the Jewish lawyer were very close friends.

Daniel had been given the task of making notes for the meeting and he sat with a pencil poised over his notepad.

Neither partner had briefed Daniel about the case and he was amused to see that Gerald was getting a secretly perverse pleasure from watching Macalister squirm in the presence of so much heathenism.

Isaac ignored his partner's smirk, which he guessed was aimed at the obvious fidgeting discomfiture of their client, and he tried to put the missionary at ease. He felt that if Macalister was able to explain why he had chosen them for his Synod's case against Captain Mort he might feel better. A bit like how Catholics felt when they went to confess their sins to one of their priests, as Gerald had once explained to him over a bottle of good port.

Isaac Levi leant forward in his chair with his hands on his desk. 'Tell me, Mister Macalister,' he said, 'why did you choose *us* to represent your Synod's recommendation to prosecute the captain of the *Osprey*?'

Daniel froze and almost snapped the pencil in half. *So that was it.* Both partners knew of his unrelenting crusade for justice against the Macintosh family and Mort. He had long used his knowledge and contacts in law to try to find ways of bringing to justice the people who had done so much damage to his family, but to date he had nothing. Suddenly here was Mort being named for a prosecution of some kind. Maybe there was a god of justice after all!

Macalister shifted uneasily. 'It's not that I have anything against Jews and Papists personally, Mister Levi,' he said self-consciously in his thick Scots brogue. 'I would have preferred to have consulted my own kind but the Synod feels we should employ the services of a firm of solicitors with no vested interests in seeing Captain Mort is allowed to escape the wrath of God for what he has done in the islands to my people.'

'I cannot speak for God's wrath, Mister Macalister,' Isaac said with just a hint of mirth. 'But I hope I can speak for the wrath of British law against those who commit murder.'

Murder! So it was murder they were going after Mort for! Daniel almost forgot to take notes as the missionary explained the events of September and the raid on the helpless village. He told how neighbouring Islanders had identified the *Osprey* working in the waters around the New Hebrides at the time of the killings and how a handful of survivors who had escaped the cordon of raiders could identify the devil with the pale blue eyes. The villagers who had escaped had watched helplessly from the surrounding jungle as the white man took away their friends and relatives. None of those taken away had been seen since except for the headless bodies floating in the lagoon.

Daniel listened to the gruesome and terrible story unfold. He knew his chances of proving Mort guilty of murdering his uncle and Old Billy were pretty slim. But it did not matter if they could get a conviction against him that eventually led to the gallows. The *Osprey* was currently moored in Sydney harbour and, as far as the Scots missionary knew, the captain of the blackbirding barque did not suspect action was being taken against him.

Time was of the essence! They had to get the case together before the ship sailed again. God had sent Macalister to them, Daniel was sure.

After Macalister had finished his briefing, he gruffly bade his farewells. When the missionary had left the office, Isaac turned to Daniel, whose face was aglow with the savage joy of anticipated victory. Isaac smiled.

'Well, Mister Duffy. What are your thoughts?' he asked.

Daniel glanced at his notes before looking up.

'The case will cause a storm around Sydney,' the young lawyer replied. 'We prepare a case against one of the blackbirding captains and we will have a lot of influential people against us. But we will also have a lot of people on our side who want to see the trade stopped. The trouble is they are generally not the people with the money and influence.'

Daniel knew very well the political implications of a prosecution of murder against a captain of a kanaka ship. The ramifications could undermine the foundation of the cotton and sugar plantations of Queensland at a time when the colony needed every penny it could get. Queensland was suffering badly from the crash of the English banks. But this was not merely a murder case. It was the indictment of powerful vested money and political interests in the kanaka trade.

Gerald scratched at the tip of his nose, which was an affectation Daniel would unconsciously learn from the Irish lawyer and use in years to come when he was in court considering a vital point of defence. He then removed the pince-nez spectacles he wore and said quietly, 'To be sure it will give the British gentry in the colonies a bloody nose. They don't like us God-fearing Irish – or you godless Jews – anyway. Ah, but it will be grand to see them quake with terror when we use their own law against them.'

Isaac grinned at his partner's slur on his faith. He knew full well that the rotund and jolly Irishman did not have a biased bone in his body – except against the British establishment.

'We have a lot of work to do before we brief a suitable barrister,' Isaac said, standing and stretching his tall frame. 'We have an interesting case of murder committed outside the colony. It will not be easy in any way to prove jurisdiction. But I think we can.' Gerald and Daniel nodded.

No, it would not be easy, Daniel thought, and he knew he would not sleep until he had prepared a brief as tight as a noose around a hanging man's neck.

'I think we have a need', Gerald said, 'to move very quickly on this one. Christmas is not that far away and everything seems to come to an infernal stop around Sydney at this time of year. Damned clerks get careless about filing court papers and magistrates are hard to find outside public houses. I think we should employ a man to keep an eye on the movements of Captain Mort while he is in Sydney. Make sure he is not about to sail away and out of the grips of the courts.'

Isaac smiled. 'No doubt I can leave that matter in your hands,' he said with a sigh. 'I suspect that you have someone in mind, knowing your rather colourful contacts in the world of vice and crime.'

The rotund little Irish solicitor turned to Daniel. 'I was thinking that Mister Duffy could look after that side of things,' he said with a twinkle in his eye. 'His father owns one of the finest and most salubrious social establishments in town where just the right man can be employed for such a mission.'

Daniel blinked, as he tore his thoughts away from an image of Mort dangling at the end of a rope in Darlinghurst Gaol.

'I am sure my father will know the right man to employ,' he replied. 'He even has contacts in the police force.'

'Not a big Irish trap by the name of Constable Francis Farrell perchance?' Gerald said with a wink and Daniel appeared startled by his knowledge.

'Er . . . yes. How . . . ?' But he did not continue his question as Sydney was a small town and the Irish community close-knit. He rose and followed the two senior partners from the office. There was much to arrange to ensure that justice was done.

36

'Sir Donald and Lady Macintosh.'

The herald's announcement turned only a few heads to witness the grand entry of the newly knighted Scottish land and ship owner and his attractive wife into the glittering and packed ballroom. Knights of the realm were not an uncommon item at the 1867 New Year's Eve ball and their appearance hardly warranted the interruption of polite conversation. The guests of Sir John and Lady Susanna Merle continued to chat among themselves with hardly a glance towards the entrance while the regimental band played a medley of martial airs.

Candles, colours and elegance marked the evening. Colourful mess dress of the dashing regimental officers, both colonial and British; shiny dark dinner suits of the wealthy merchants and leading squatters. Their ladies with sweeping dresses of silk, satin and chiffon. Tiaras and precious stones caught and magnified the soft light of the many candles in the ballroom. The New Year's Eve ball also attracted guests other than the colonial gentry; ambassadors and a sprinkling of foreign naval officers on attache duty to their respective embassies. Politicians and their wives. Or, in one or two cases, their mistresses.

The grand entry of Sir Donald and Lady Enid was noticed by Granville White, who bent to whisper in his wife's ear, bringing a rare smile to Fiona's face. Granville took his wife's arm to escort her over to greet her mother and father, who were making their way slowly through a gauntlet of old friends and acquaintances congratulating them both on Donald's recent knighthood. The knighthood had been recommended by the New South Wales Government for Donald's outstanding services to the colony and was couched in the words of praise reserved for men of influence.

Fiona appeared radiant, like a young girl rather than a woman with two daughters, and the pomp and ceremony suited her because it gave her an opportunity to lose herself in the merriment and glitter of the occasion. Although she had barely spoken a word to her mother in recent years, she was still proud to see her appear so outstandingly elegant beside her gruff and burly father. She was even prepared to allow a short truce with her mother for her father's sake.

Granville shook Sir Donald's hand. 'Good show, Sir Donald,' he congratulated and Fiona gave her father a rather bold peck on the cheek, whispering, 'Well done, Father. You look magnificent tonight!' But she did not reserve the same warmth for her mother and they exchanged polite, but formal head nods, as recognition of each other's presence.

Granville was distracted by an acquaintance in the shipping industry and Fiona was glad to have an excuse not to remain in the company of her mother. She was escorted by her husband to meet the boring shipping man and discuss new opportunities along the trade routes of the rapidly opening north of Australia.

Sir Donald might have been a Knight of the Most Noble and Most Ancient Order of the Thistle but he was now feeling more and more out of place in the present company of urban merchants and bankers. He had been so long on the frontier that he felt more at home with the stockmen who had replaced his shepherds than in the company of the glittering colonial elite at the ball. He was more at ease sitting on the verandah of the newly built homestead at Glen View than standing under the imported crystal chandeliers of Sir John's ballroom. The dust of Glen View was in his blood as much as the memory of the purple thistle of his native land. He now found all the protocol and glitter of Sydney foreign, but he owed his wife his attendance at the ball, as her discreet lobbying and lunches had assisted in getting the knighthood for him.

Sir Donald cast desperate glances around the packed ballroom for any other Queensland squatters who might have been in town for the ball but he could see none and he resigned himself to a boring night being seen in the company of the colony's rich and famous.

'Jolly good show your knighthood, Donald,' Sir Ian Smythe said as he intercepted the knighted squatter searching for a waiter with the champagne. 'Well deserved, old chap.'

Sir Ian was not a squatter but he had interests in

leases in Queensland and he was pleased to be able to discuss pastoral matters with a man of such considerable reputation as the Scot. Sir Donald's capable management of Glen View was legendary in the south. 'Heard you cleared Glen View of the darkies a few years back,' Sir Ian said, striking up a conversation. 'One of my managers informs me he is having a spot of trouble on Cristabel Downs with them. Says the damned government won't deploy enough of those native troopers up his way.'

Sir Donald nodded his head sympathetically. At least here was someone he could talk to about the problems on the frontier. 'It's the damned liberals in the south who would like to see us humiliated,' he answered as he procured a crystal flute of the imported champagne. 'Always out to bring us down.'

The conversation was interrupted by the appearance of Granville, as there was a matter of urgency to discuss and it could not wait. Fiona was left in the company of Charlotte Frost, David's fiancée, to chat about the forthcoming wedding between her and David.

'Sir Ian, I pray you are well,' Granville inquired politely of the robust knight's health. 'Rather a warm night for the affair.'

'Damned warm! But the champagne is cold,' Sir Ian snorted. He could see from the expression on Granville's face that he was impatient to talk to Sir Donald. Sir Ian blustered his excuses to collar an influential member of the legislature on matters of political significance affecting his business interests. When they were alone, Granville steered

Sir Donald to a relatively quiet corner of the ballroom.

'Well, Granville, what bad news do you have for me?' Sir Donald asked gruffly. 'I know it is bad news because I can tell from the look on your face.' He would have preferred to stay with Sir Ian rather than talk to his son-in-law.

'Some damned Presbyterian missionary by the name of Macalister arrived in Sydney about four weeks ago,' Granville replied. 'He's lodged a complaint of murder against the captain of the *Osprey*. He . . .'

'Mort!' Sir Donald growled, cutting across his son-in-law. 'Damned fool. 'Bout the kanaka business, is it?'

'Well, yes,' Granville continued. 'But it could get worse. Mort has a suspicion that he is being followed and watched whenever he leaves his ship. He even fears that, if he sails, the navy will seize the *Osprey*.'

Sir Donald felt the beginnings of acid burn his stomach. The Royal Navy seizing the *Osprey* would bring an unwanted scandal to the Macintosh name and it would not look good in the newspapers that the newly knighted pastoralist was the owner of a ship whose captain was wanted for murder. He cursed himself silently for recommending the man to the job as skipper of the *Osprey* in the first place. But he knew with some guilt that he and the murderous captain were bound by the events of the dispersal years earlier. Mort knew enough to cause more than a scandal.

'How far has this damned missionary got with his complaint?' Sir Donald asked his son-in-law.

'I'm afraid Macalister is drumming up support from the old anti-slavery movements and the news-papers. He's launched a holy crusade against Mort and the *Osprey*,' he answered.

'This . . . on top of the troubles I am having in Queensland,' Sir Donald growled. 'I need this right now like I need a speargrass-infested flock of sheep.'

'I hate to tell you things could be worse . . . but they are,' Granville said with a pained expression on his face. 'Macalister is getting legal advice from the firm of solicitors Sullivan and Levi.'

'Sullivan and Levi,' Sir Donald growled irritably. 'Never heard of them.'

'They have one Mister Daniel Duffy working for them,' Granville continued, 'who has not tried to hide the fact that he is out to bring us all down.'

Sir Donald reacted to the Duffy name as Granville knew he would. Duffy! The damned name was still haunting him. The bloody Irish bred like rabbits and they were everywhere. But these were dangerous rabbits.

'What relationship is this Daniel Duffy to that blasted Irishman who was killed at Glen View in '62?' he asked, hoping that Granville would say 'no relationship'.

'Nephew,' Granville replied. 'I've heard that Daniel Duffy is a man with a reputation for not losing cases.'

The band struck up a Scottish reel and Sir Donald turned away. He toyed with the champagne flute without drinking a drop and brooded on the cursed name of Duffy. Finally he placed the still-full glass on a silver tray carried by a passing waiter, as he knew that the sparkling wine would sour his stomach.

'I think it is time we got back to the ladies,' Sir Donald growled and walked away to join his wife, whom he could see across the ballroom chatting with their son David.

She was still a handsome woman, he mused proudly, as he made his way to her. Straight-backed with little sign of the years and their responsibilities marring her beautiful and serene face. Fiona was fortunate to have inherited her mother's looks. But had she inherited Enid's ruthlessness? The notion disturbed him. Ruthlessness was a weapon of destructive qualities when turned against family.

Sir Donald was fully aware of the schism between mother and daughter, which was not unexpected as he had observed the tension verging on animosity between the two women over the years. Tension which had always been concealed by a polite and dutiful veneer.

But the animosity had risen to the surface at the time Fiona had given up the bastard son of Michael Duffy and he suspected that his daughter had allied herself with Granville in a way that might do Enid harm. But how? He did not know. But he knew Fiona was very different to the little girl he once knew. She was still outwardly affectionate to him but there was also a coldness he had not experienced from her before.

'Hello, Father. You look very distinguished tonight,' David said when he joined them.

'Thank you, David,' Sir Donald growled. 'But I feel less than distinguished among all these poodle fakers. Damned bankers and merchants living off those trying to turn this country into a place fit for good Christian men and women . . .'

'Donald! Do not let them upset you,' Enid gently chided. 'You promised no talk of business tonight.' She could see her husband growing belligerent as he glowered at the cavalcade of the colony's money manipulators, whom he saw as responsible for the July '66 crash of the prestigious Agra and Masterton Banks in England.

Queensland had suffered badly when the financial tidal wave had crossed the ocean to swamp the heavily indebted squatters of the new colony. The Crimean War, the Indian Mutiny, and finally the American Civil War had come together to cause the commercial crisis now in Britain and adversely affect the colony of Queensland.

Sir Donald acceded to his wife's wish. He had a Scot's tenacity to overcome tough times and for now it was his duty to forget falling cotton prices and the need for a loan to keep the Glen View lease. In the structure of the family companies, it had been agreed to keep the pastoral enterprises separate from the shipping and other ventures. As such, Sir Donald realised that his tenure of his beloved Glen View might face extinction and he would be forced back to Sydney. The thought did not rest well with him.

'I'm sorry, m'dear,' he replied contritely. 'You are right.'

Enid sat on a chair with a fan in her lap and asked David to fetch her a glass of ice water but the request was really an excuse to confer with her husband. When David was safely out of hearing she said, 'David has told me that he plans to go on the *Osprey* and voyage to the islands with Captain Mort.'

Sir Donald frowned. 'That is if we still have the *Osprey*,' he replied with a growl, and Enid gave him a questioning look.

'Damned missionaries are moving to have the Royal Navy seize her as a slaver,' he explained quietly. 'It appears that Captain Mort has done something to upset them.'

'But that's preposterous,' his wife protested and was indignant that anyone would dare link the Macintosh name with the abominable practice of slavery, although she was aware that the newspapers were attempting to liken the kanaka trade to slavery. Lurid stories had been reported in the newspapers of wretched souls crying out for freedom from the devilish blackbirders. Stories which inflamed public outrage. 'The *Osprey* is a legitimate ship of trade,' she continued, 'not some African slaver of old.'

'I know that,' Sir Donald reassured her. 'But it appears some missionary by the name of Macalister is saying Mort has done something rather nasty. I will ask Granville to give us a full report on Mort's activities and then put it in the hands of our solicitors. I'm sure there is nothing to worry about. As it is, the damned missionaries are always bleating about atrocities. Keeps them in the public eye when it comes to asking for money for their missions.'

Sir Donald could see that his wife had reacted to the news about the *Osprey* with mixed feelings. On the one hand she would have liked to see the

Osprey taken out of the kanaka trade. But on the other hand she also feared the scandal such a move would bring on the family name. Should the Royal Navy seize the blackbirding ship, then David would have to cancel his trip on the *Osprey*. He had plans of photographing native life in the Pacific islands, but Enid did not like or trust Captain Mort. She had met the notorious captain when he first commenced employment with them in '63 and she had taken an immediate dislike to him. It was in the eyes. A madness one would see in a rabid animal, she recalled later.

Nor did she like the first mate, who she knew for a fact was an extremely dangerous man. Mort and Horton were a bad pair in her opinion and worse still was the total loyalty they had to Granville as their employer. She strongly opposed the idea of her son travelling in the company of such cut-throats. Call it a mother's intuition but the feeling persisted that her son could be in mortal danger aboard the *Osprey*.

She had tried to talk David into taking passage on another ship if he was so determined to sail the South Seas but he had pointed out that the *Osprey* was the only Macintosh ship working there, and that he was, after all, a part owner. It was bad enough that David had resigned from his position at Oxford to pursue his foolish dream of recording history in his photographs, Enid thought. But to venture with the blackbirders into situations of dire peril was beyond foolish.

Although she would never admit publicly what she had learnt of the darker side of blackbirding, her intelligence network informed her that atrocities were being committed in the trade. She was fully aware of how dangerous the trip could be for her son.

'Do you think you could persuade David not to join the *Osprey*, Donald?' she said.

'I doubt if anything I said would do any good,' her husband replied. 'After all, he is your son and if he won't listen to you then he is not going to listen to me.'

Enid knew he was right. The family had always been divided in its loyalties. Angus to his father, David to her and Fiona . . . Well, Fiona's loyalties lay with her husband's interests now.

'I almost pray that Captain Mort and the *Osprey* are detained by the authorities,' she replied quietly.

David returned with both the glass of water and Miss Charlotte Frost, and the conversation turned to matters of the wedding four months hence. It was scheduled to take place upon his return from the South Seas.

On the other side of the ballroom, Fiona had met up with Penelope who was, for the evening, being escorted by an English cavalry captain posted to the colony from his regiment in England. She had made an excuse to leave him with fellow officers while she sought the company of Fiona. The captain was boring and his conversation limited to talk about the hunters he had brought with him to the colony. He complained incessantly about the lack of respect shown to him from the colonials as they did not seem to hold the captain in the same awe as he was shown in England. Even the street urchins followed him when he wore his uniform in Sydney, and mocked him with clever impersonations of his deliberately affected manner of an English fop.

Fiona giggled when Penelope made a mocking impersonation of her escort.

'Oh, Penny, you are awful to the man,' she said as she stifled her giggles behind a delicately splayed fan ribbed with mother-of-pearl. 'You are awful . . . and shocking.'

Penelope gave her sister-in-law a mysterious smile. 'Shocking, yes. But not awful. The man is a prude!'

'Prude, Penny? You mean he is a gentleman and does not share your attitudes to . . . well, you know what I mean,' Fiona said, alluding to those things better not mentioned in genteel company.

'Gentlemen are boring,' Penelope retorted. 'They think that we are passive receptacles for their relief. Why, Captain Hayes got off me last night after having mounted me like one of his brood mares and said, "There, there, old girl, do you feel better?" Feel better? Damn him! I was screaming out for relief.'

Fiona glanced around and fervently hoped that no one could overhear her cousin's explicit narrative of her interlude with the captain. Although she was embarrassed, an erotic and disturbing image flashed in her mind and she imagined her sister-in-law's naked body under the British officer.

'Penny, I think it might be wise if we change the topic of conversation,' she whispered nervously behind her fan. 'People may hear us.' But two glasses of excellent champagne and Penelope cared

538

little for the hypocritical mores of Victorian morality.

'Not *us* Fi, . . . *me*,' she replied in a more subdued tone. 'At least I know you have a married man who knows how to touch the dark places in a woman's mind. My brother might be a lot of things but one thing is that he knows how to go beyond that place between our legs. Yes, Granville is good at that. And so am I.'

It was then Fiona felt her face flush with shock at the realisation of just what her cousin was saying. Before she could reply, Penelope touched her arm above her wrist and whispered in her ear, 'If you think Granville is exciting, you should try me, my love.'

With the words hanging in the air, Penelope turned and in a loud voice greeted the English captain wending his way over to her. He was flushed from drinking and his expression was a repulsive leer that made him unappealing to both Penelope and Fiona. To the other young women at the ball, Captain Hayes was an attractive catch; handsome and dashing in his colourful uniform and he was also the second son of an English earl. That implied in its own right wealth and a position in society. Penelope would have been more than happy to let them have him. At least when the candles were blown out.

When the bandmaster struck up the traditional 'Auld Lang Syne' to mark the passing of the year, Sir Donald and Lady Enid linked arms, as did David and Charlotte with Granville and Fiona. Penelope had lost her beau to the drink, so she linked arms with her sister-in-law.

As the guests sang the refrains of the Scottish song of joy and lament, when voices were raised in a mixture of hope and cheer for the promises of the New Year, Enid felt David's arm in hers and she was content. Her fears for her son were almost forgotten as the voices swelled to the traditional hurrahs marking the midnight hour.

In another place another family also celebrated the coming of 1868.

It was not a splendid ballroom on a wealthy man's estate, but a simple kitchen in an Irish-patronised hotel in Sydney's Redfern district. The kitchen always seemed the most appropriate place for important occasions. For it was in this single room that so many events had transpired over the years and it was as if, by gathering in the kitchen, the spirits of the absent were one with those present.

The battered table was like an altar where the family met to exchange gossip, tears, fears and news. A place where Michael had been patched up so many times by his Aunt Bridget. An altar to Kevin O'Keefe's proposal to Kate Duffy.

Frank Duffy was more than jovial as he swayed on unsteady legs, roaring out an old Irish song. Beyond drunk, he almost splashed his whisky over Daniel and his pretty young wife, Colleen, who good-naturedly pushed her father-in-law away when he stumbled into the table where she sat watching the celebration.

Colleen wisely scooped Charmaine, her daughter, out of Frank's way as he bounced off the stove and almost pitched into Daniel, who stood swaying behind his wife's chair. Little Charmaine sucked at her thumb with wide eyes drooping for want of sleep. She was an intelligent two-year-old who had inherited her father's dark and curly hair. Her brother Martin, a year older, had inherited his mother's copper hair. Both children laughed at the drunken antics of their grandfather. It was a fine old time for the Duffy clan!

Bridget Duffy's face glowed. The usual one sherry a night before bed had been extended to five and she smiled at her daughter-in-law, who had proved to be a good wife for Daniel. The young woman had fitted easily into the Duffy clan traditions.

As the daughter of an Irish country publican from Bathurst, Colleen was all too familiar with the antics of an Irish New Year. At least an Irish New Year transported to the far-off land in the Southern Hemisphere. And she was pleased to see that her normally teetotaller husband had allowed himself to get merry from the effects of the rum that flowed.

Daniel was drunk and raised his glass in a toast: 'To the downfall of the bloody Macintoshes,' he roared above the din. 'And the hanging of Captain Mort.'

Colleen had never met a Macintosh, but from the things Daniel had told her she felt as if she knew them. She realised that the Macintoshes were, in fact, relations of a kind when she glanced at young Patrick asleep in the brawny arms of Max. He held the boy gently, rocking him as he crooned a German lullaby. The powerfully built man looked so out of place with his massive arms

541

wrapped around 'his Patrick'. Only minutes earlier the boy had been sparring with Max, who had pretended that the blows from his little fists were hurting him. And when Max would fall to the floor on his back, Patrick would leap on his ample stomach gleefully crying out for 'Uncle Max' to get up and fight more.

Yes, Patrick Duffy was half Macintosh, Colleen thought with a start, as she gazed at the sleeping boy in Max's powerful arms. She had been told of the events that had brought Patrick to the Erin Hotel and she had accepted the boy as if he were her own by birth. Young Patrick lacked for nothing when it came to love.

Patrick was definitely more Duffy than Macintosh, her husband would often say proudly, although the boy was not aware that Daniel and Colleen were not his natural parents. But the day would inevitably arrive when he would learn the confusing truth.

For now the family were together and it was a time to forget the pain of the past and think optimistically of what might be in the future.

Outside the Erin, the Duffys could hear drunken and happy voices call out New Year greetings. Francis Duffy was too drunk to remember his native Gaelic so instead he raised his empty glass and wished all a happy New Year in the cursed language of his old enemies, the English. Patrick stirred in the big German's arms and opened his eyes to gaze at all the fuss, but just as quickly he fell back to sleep.

37

Granville stood at the bow of the *Osprey* with the ship's captain beside him. To the inconspicuous dockhand sitting with his back against the sandstone wall of a warehouse in the shadows of the midmorning summer sun, the meeting was of no real significance.

He had been asked by Constable Farrell to follow the *Osprey* captain and report on where he was at all times . . . nothing more . . . nothing less. It was a mission he had reluctantly accepted from the big burly Irish policeman, but he'd had little choice. It was that or be arrested for being in possession of certain items from housebreaking. Farrell was a man who would have made an excellent criminal himself and only the uniform gave him respectability.

The observer did not recognise Granville White. He was merely a well-dressed man of gentlemanly appearance who was visiting the barque. To all intents and purposes probably a shipping merchant discussing business, the observer reflected, as he idled with the piece of driftwood he was carving into the shape of a whale.

* * *

Mort stood stiffly with his hands clasped behind his back staring up the harbour and Granville could sense the fear in the man, who had said little upon his arrival. Mort instinctively knew that his employer had come to discuss a way out of the storm that was gathering around him. His aspirations to eventually retire to the village of Penrith seemed to be disappearing as fast as a tot of rum in the hands of a thirsty sailor.

Granville placed his hands on the railing of the bow and did not look at Mort when he spoke.

'Your suspicions about being followed have been confirmed,' he said quietly between his teeth and Mort glanced at him with a touch of fear. 'They are not going to let you leave Sydney.'

'How . . . ?'

But Granville waved away his question. 'It doesn't matter how I know,' Granville replied. 'What matters is how *much* I know. And I know that papers are presently being compiled by a firm of Sydney solicitors to have you arrested for murder. You can thank the idleness that afflicts Sydney over this time of year for not already being thrown into Darlinghurst Gaol, Captain Mort.'

'They can't prove murder or any other crime, Mister White,' Mort mumbled weakly.

'I don't particularly care if they do,' Granville snapped as he turned to stare into the captain's face. 'What may occur to your personal welfare is of no interest to me. My only responsibility is to the good name of the Macintosh companies.' Both men's eyes locked and they recognised in each other their absolute ruthlessness.

544

Theirs was a mutual acceptance forged in the very nature of that ruthlessness and, in recognising this fact, Mort felt the compounded fear start to melt away. He knew that his employer would do anything to save the Macintosh reputation. And in doing so, he would have to save him.

'What do we do then to save the Macintosh name, Mister White?' Mort asked with an almost audible sigh of relief.

'I have set matters in motion that will buy us time,' Granville replied. 'All you have to do is play your part without question and I promise that you will not end up in Darlinghurst.' Mort nodded. Not that he accepted his employer's promise as anything more than words. White was too much like himself to honour his word. 'Saving your neck comes at a price,' Granville added. 'And I know I can count on your total cooperation in what I am about to tell you.'

Mort listened as Granville White explained what was expected of him and although he was not a man easily unsettled Granville's proposal shocked even him. Not that the taking of life unsettled him. It was whose life he was expected to take.

Granville leant away from the ship's railing and patted down his jacket casually as if they had been merely involved in a conversation about shipping prices.

'You have a good man in your first mate to assist you,' Granville said as he let his eyes rove over the docks below the bow of the ship to settle on a seemingly insignificant man, sitting cross-legged and whittling away at a piece of driftwood. The man assigned to follow Mort did not seem to show much interest in this meeting, he thought with some satisfaction.

The Duffys were not the only people with contacts in the ranks of Sydney's police force. Money and social position just happened to ensure even higher contacts than could be acquired by working-class Irishmen. 'Mister Horton will give you assistance when the time comes I believe,' Granville said as he prepared to depart from the barque. 'He also has the right domain of skills,' he added as his own private joke.

Mort stared at his foppish-looking employer as he walked away and he suddenly had a greater respect for his boss whom, until now, he had considered rather ineffectual. What the man proposed displayed absolute ruthlessness.

The observer glanced idly up at the well-dressed man who passed him by on his way to a carriage drawn by a fine set of matched greys. There was nothing of interest happening around the *Osprey* worth reporting.

Two days after Mort and White met on the deck of the *Osprey*, Daniel sat stunned in Gerald Sullivan's office as he listened to the Irish lawyer tell him the bad news. Gerald Sullivan placed an expensive bottle of imported Irish whiskey on his desk and he invited the young solicitor to pour himself a stiff drink.

Gerald had just been informed from his network of spies on the Sydney waterfront that the *Osprey* had sailed for the islands and its murderous captain had slipped their grasp. The devil protected his own, he thought.

'How?' Daniel asked in stunned disbelief, as all their intelligence corroborated the sailing date of the blackbirder to be at the end of January. Not early January! The shipping clerks had confirmed the intelligence.

'It seems the *Osprey* sailed last night under another name,' Gerald answered as he put away a generous shot of whiskey. 'All the papers for her departure had been prepared in advance. We seem to have underestimated the cunning of Mister Granville White. From what I have been told by Constable Farrell, Sir Donald's son-in-law was instrumental in arranging the deceit.'

'There must be something we can do to execute the warrant,' Daniel pleaded. 'Something within the law to aid us.'

The older lawyer shook his head. 'There is nothing we can do about it,' he replied glumly. 'We would insist on the police investigating the inadequacies of the port authorities but that would achieve very little other than possibly a prosecution against some corrupt government clerk. Little else, I'm afraid. We may have failed in this attempt but there will be others. And I propose a toast to the next time. That means you have to respond, Mister Duffy,' he added with a mischievous twinkle in his eye. 'I might even keep proposing toasts until we get falling-down drunk and Isaac orders us out of the office. We could go down to your father's salubrious establishment for the day.'

Daniel poured himself a stiff drink and joined Gerald Sullivan in morosely toasting future opportunities to bring down Mort and the Macintosh family. But the whiskey tasted sour in his stomach.

547

38

The boat trip to Curtis Island brought back bitter-sweet memories for Kate as she gazed across at the lagoons of the river. She remembered years earlier on the same water when Luke Tracy had first spoken to her with his soft and melodious American drawl. But that seemed a lifetime ago and she knew his memory should be forever relegated to those other ghosts of her past. Now she stood at the railing of the chartered paddle-steamer with Hugh Darlington beside her.

Kate wore a fashionable light cotton dress as white as the coral sands of the tropics, with a wide-brimmed straw hat. Her chic appearance had brought one or two jealous remarks from the matrons of Rockhampton, whose idle tongues wagged that the barmaid at the Emperor's Arms was nothing more than a brazen opportunist. Kate knew of the talk but did not care. She was stronger than the gossip and she knew that she had many friends who were quick to support her. They ranged from tough old teamsters to the dashing young Hugh Darlington. But most important were the friendships of the Cohens and the Jameses.

The weather had cleared, although rain clouds still boiled over the range of hills behind Rockhampton. It was muggy on shore, but out in the mouth of the Fitzroy River the sea breezes cooled the passengers who stood on the deck of the paddle-steamer with their picnic baskets.

The sea breeze toyed with wisps of Kate's raven hair that had dislodged from under her hat and Hugh could not help but admire the smooth curve of her slender neck. Her pale skin was like that of an alabaster statue and he had a strong urge to kiss the back of her neck . . . maybe soon, he mused. When Kate turned to speak to Hugh, she was acutely aware that he was standing very close and that his eyes held his deepest and most intimate thoughts. Kate felt a warmth she had not known for a long time.

When the paddle-steamer drew close to the shore of the island, rowing boats were lowered and the passengers were taken ashore in relays. When the boat taking Kate and Hugh beached on the coral sand, he stepped into the warm clear water, soaking his trouser legs to the knees, and grasped Kate by her slim waist. He lifted her easily from the boat and carried her to the beach where he was reluctant to release his grasp. She gently prised his hands away with a knowing smile.

They shared the picnic with Hugh's friends, who were mostly eligible bachelors escorting young ladies from some of the best of Rockhampton's families. There was also a smattering of young married couples and Kate noticed that Hugh mixed mostly with the clerks, government employees and their families. Kate found them rather stuffy with their affected formality and she missed the boisterous company of the tough and colourful sun-blackened men of the frontier; the teamsters, stockmen and prospectors who frequented the bar where she had once worked. That was gone now as she had given her notice at the Emperor's Arms to pursue her newly established business interests.

The publican had expressed his bitter disappointment in losing his most popular barmaid. The tough and weather-beaten teamsters had presented Kate with a beautifully plaited stockwhip, swearing her in as an honorary teamster to their ranks. Her rowdy farewell cost the generous publican four kegs of beer but he felt that she was worth the expense as her presence at the hotel had attracted a lot of patronage over the years.

Hugh had helped set up the office and depot which she'd rented for her transport business and the Cohens regularly met with her at their store to coordinate the purchase and dispatch of goods using Kate's bullock team for local hauls. The teamster she employed to handle Harry's team of bullocks proved an excellent choice and the Eureka Company was off to a promising start under her capable management.

When the picnic lunch was over, the men rolled up shirtsleeves and a cricket ball and bat were produced as two teams were organised. The alcohol flowed freely between runs; champagne and gin, English beer in bottles and dark rum. Kate was bored with sitting and cheering the men at their game and she decided to take in the beauty of the island.

She excused herself and walked down to the beach alone. Hugh had been buttonholed by a client who wanted to talk conveyancing. As he was an important client, Hugh was forced to apologise for not being able to join her.

Kate flipped open her parasol and kicked off her shoes as she strolled along the sand bordered by rainforest trees. The sand felt gritty but pleasant underfoot and she had not strolled very far when she noticed a familiar figure at the furthermost end of the pleasant beach.

'Emma!' she cried out happily.

'Kate! Oh, it is good to see you,' Emma squealed with delight when she saw Kate hurrying towards her. They met and embraced.

'Are Henry and little Gordon with you?' Kate asked, disengaging herself from the embrace.

'Yes. We have just arrived,' Emma replied. 'I left Henry and Gordon playing cricket with the others. I didn't know you were coming over for the picnic and I love your dress.'

Kate beamed with pleasure at her friend's compliment. 'You know, it is the first nice dress I have bought since I left Sydney,' Kate replied modestly and she gave her friend another hug to thank her for noticing.

'I heard about your good fortune,' Emma said as the two women walked over to the shade of the trees. 'Henry and I want to visit you as soon as he gets a little better.' An awkward silence fell between them at the mention of Henry's recovery from the snakebite. The story of the encounter with the infamous bushranger Tom Duffy had been told and retold in the bush shanty grog shops along the bullock tracks. And even as far south as Rockhampton's hotels.

'Your brother saved Henry's life,' Emma said in a more serious tone, breaking the awkward silence between them. 'Henry said that if he had not done what he did, then he was surely a dead man. Tom must be a good man and it's so tragic that Henry had to go after him the way he did. But he has his duty . . .' Emma's short and halting statement was as much an explanation as it was a plea for understanding. She had avoided Kate and Judith, as she had felt they would not understand what had occurred in Burke's Land.

'I should have realised how much you must have worried,' Kate said gently. 'How you must have thought that I would hate you for what occurred. I suppose that is why Judith and I have not seen you for a while.'

Emma nodded and there was the hint of a tear at the corner of her eye. 'I thought you might hate Henry for doing what he did,' she said, forcing herself not to cry. 'In arresting Tom.'

Kate took Emma's hands in her own. 'Any other policeman would have shot Tom out of hand,' she said with a gentle smile. 'But Henry cares. I know that. And he risked his life to make sure Tom would get a chance for a fair trial. I could think of no other man on earth who could have cared as much as your Henry. He is the finest of men, Emma, and a man I consider among my truest friends.'

Kate's gentle and reassuring words brought tears of gratitude and reconciliation to Emma, who still tried to restrain her feelings.

552

'Do you know?' Emma said, both sobbing and laughing, 'Henry told me that Tom actually went back and bailed up the publican of some grog shanty and paid him to help get Henry to Burketown. Henry said it was the first time he knew of a bushranger bailing a man up to *give* him money.' Both women laughed at Tom's exploit. 'Henry says it was not a robbery under arms but a giving under arms,' Emma added with more merriment. 'Mister Uhr was very good in sending Henry back to Rockhampton to recover.'

'You and Henry must visit me as soon as you are able,' Kate said wistfully. 'I have a thousand . . . no, a hundred thousand questions to ask Henry about Tom. He is the only brother I have left and I miss him every day of my life. Oh, I know what people say about Tom but I only remember how much like Da he was . . .'

Kate's sentence trailed away and Emma could see her friend was close to tears. 'We will,' she said, and hugged Kate. 'And Henry will tell you just what a fine man your brother truly is. I know, he has told me.'

Hugh found the two women sitting under the trees engaged in an animated conversation. He thought it was rather ironic that the sister of the bushranger Tom Duffy should be a close friend of the policeman who could claim the dubious honour of being the only man to get close to capturing the legendary criminal. But such ironies were part of the frontier in a colony with so few people to populate it.

'Missus James, how good to see you,' Hugh said as he joined the two women. His roving eyes

553

travelled over the slim figure of Emma James and he thought idly that the big policeman had done well for himself. She was pretty, in a wholesome way, although not as beautiful as Kate sitting beside her.

Emma politely returned the greeting even though she was aware of the man's eyes appraising her and felt annoyed. He had the reputation around town of being somewhat of a ladies' man, smooth and charming with his fine looks and delicate hands. But Emma was annoyed more for Kate, who might get hurt by the man at some future point. Then she glanced at Kate and smiled. On the other hand, Hugh Darlington might get his comeuppance should he ever cross Kate. She was a rare and special person. Equal to any man – if not better!

'I ran into the sergeant just a few minutes ago playing cricket,' Hugh said by way of polite conversation. 'He tells me that he has no sense of taste and smell as a result of the bite from the snake. Terribly peculiar!'

Emma returned a wry smile. 'At least Henry cannot tell whether I have made a mess of any meals I cook,' she said, causing Kate to laugh lightly, as she knew full well that Emma was an excellent cook and that Henry would be cursing the fact that he could not taste her meals.

'The good sergeant has told me you will be returning to Burketown,' Hugh said as he sat to one side of the women, 'when he is deemed fit to resume police duties.'

'You didn't mention you were going to Burketown, Emma,' Kate stated with a questioning glance at her friend.

'I told Henry', Emma replied, 'that if he didn't take Gordon and myself back with him I would leave him. He has this silly idea that I should be wrapped in cotton wool and left on the mantelpiece for safekeeping. I had to remind him that it was I who chose to marry him, and not the other way round.'

'Ah, yes. A man pursues a woman until she catches him,' Hugh said, meaning to sound witty on the subject. But he received only scornful looks from both women for his ineptness at humour on such a delicate subject as matrimony and he was wise enough to retreat from their company. He was learning something that Solomon Cohen already knew – that he was excluded from the subtle intercourse of the sisterhood.

By late afternoon the picnickers had packed and strolled down to the rowboats that would return them to the chartered steamers at anchor in the bay for the trip back to Rockhampton.

Hugh and Kate were among the last to take the trip out to their steamer. Hugh slipped Kate's arm through his as they strolled down to the waiting boats and she did not try to stop him from doing so. As they made their way back, they were alone for a moment under the canopy of rainforest trees. It was then that Hugh stole a kiss and was stunned by her reaction to his presumptive move. Kate returned the kiss with a passion that was totally unexpected.

That evening Kate went to Hugh's bed. And, even as she did, she was not sure why she had, except that her body was hungry for the touch of a man.

She did not fool herself that it was love as his delicate hands quickly and expertly undressed her. Hugh Darlington was no Luke Tracy, although she quickly dismissed any thoughts of Luke.

She was flattered by Hugh's audible gasp of admiration as she stood naked before him in his room. The flickering set of candles accentuated the curves and dips of her body as he sat on the bed to take in the beauty of the young woman. So many men would have killed to be in his place at this time. Kate wondered why she felt no shame in giving herself to the handsome and dashing lawyer. Was it that the need to be held and possessed was stronger than any of man's laws on morality and behaviour, she thought for a fleeting moment, as she went to him and sat on his lap with her arms around his neck.

'I could never have imagined in my wildest dreams', Hugh said in an almost hoarse voice as he held Kate, 'that this moment might occur so quickly for us.'

Kate placed her fingers on his lips to silence him. 'Don't say anything,' she said. 'Just love me.'

He drew her down onto the bed and kissed her as his hands slid along her body, searching for her thighs. She gasped and arched her back as the pent-up passion so carefully controlled for so long was unleashed. Hugh quickly shed his clothes, flinging them on the floor as he scrambled to capitalise on her need to be ravished. Neither needed the gentleness of arousal for they both recognised it had been present during the day's outing to the island and Hugh's thrusts were quick and hard. Within seconds he had spent himself with a long moaning shudder and he fell back against the pillows to sigh contentedly for the relief. Beside him, Kate lay on her back staring at the ceiling that reflected the flickering shadows of the candles as Hugh rolled over to find one of his cigars and light it. Kate could feel his wetness inside her and she wondered why she felt as if she wanted more. But it was not something a lady admitted to and she was grateful that he had found her so desirable. He was, after all, an extremely attractive and successful man. And she knew there were many other young ladies in Rockhampton who would have clawed her eyes out to be in her place at this moment.

Hugh Darlington could not believe his good fortune as he lay back against the sheets admiring the curves of the woman who lay asleep beside him. It had not taken a fortune to get the beautiful woman to his bed and now all he had to do was keep her there. But that would not be hard, as he knew he had the looks and charm to do so.

39

Curious glances were cast in the direction of the tall bearded man who stood self-consciously in the schoolyard as the children poured out of their tiny, one-roomed timber schoolhouse. Screeching like cockatoos they passed Luke who smiled at some of the frank stares directed at him by scab-kneed, snotty-nosed kids who ducked their heads and giggled. Like an army of marauding ants, they headed for a paddock, where they spread out in search of mischief.

A young and pretty woman was the last to leave the schoolhouse. She also cast a curious glance at the tall stranger, who strode towards her with his broad-brimmed and battered hat in his hand. He vaguely reminded her of someone else she had once known. It was in his face, the faraway look of a man who was used to seeing the distant horizons from astride a horse, she thought. And it was his sparse and lean frame ravished by privation and fever, and the gun tucked behind his broad leather belt, which marked him as a man of the frontier. The display of guns was rare in Toowoomba, which enjoyed a conservative reputation for staid respectability.

The tall man fixed her with his striking blue eyes and smiled shyly.

'Miss Jones?' he asked when he came to a stop in front of her, and Rose returned the smile.

'Missus Carr. I am married to Mister Robert Carr,' she replied diffidently.

'But you were once Miss Jones, I believe, ma'am?' he asked and she nodded. 'If I could just have a moment of your time, ma'am, I have something to tell you.'

'It's about Jack, isn't it?' she replied sadly, staring past the American at the departing backs of her brood of sometimes unruly pupils.

'If the man you mentioned is the same one I met up north, then this is the first time I've know'd his name.' He paused and continued politely. 'My name is Luke Tracy, ma'am. Should have said so when I first spoke to you.'

'Mister Tracy, I notice that you are an American from your speech,' Rose commented. 'Were you teamed up with Jack?'

'No, ma'am. I met Jack . . .' He hesitated and fidgeted with the battered bush hat in his hands . . . How could he break the news to the young woman who stared up into his face with such a stricken look of dreaded anticipation? 'Jack is dead, Missus Carr. I was with him when he died and I gave him a Christian burial . . . if it's any good to know,' Luke said gently.

Her expression crumpled like the shattered façade of a beautiful marble wall, but she quickly recovered.

'It was inevitable,' she said sadly. 'Poor Jack! How did he die, Mister Tracy?' she asked in a controlled and almost calm voice.

'Speared by the myalls south of Cape York Peninsula.'

Rose swayed and Luke took her by the elbow to guide her to a log seat erected in the schoolyard under a big old gum tree. He sat beside her while she recovered her composure. She had hoped that she would be in control when the news was eventually relayed to her of the prospector's inevitable death. But the actual realisation was no less painful.

She sat staring straight ahead in silence as if Luke was not even in her presence and, in the awkward silence that followed, Luke wondered if he should not leave her and return later.

'I must seem very cold to you, Mister Tracy,' she finally said. 'But you must also realise that I truly loved Jack for many years. And for those many years, I was young and believed in his dreams that one day he would find the gold he was always searching for. That he would return to me like some crusading knight of old to build me a castle. Jack used to have such foolish dreams of giving me the riches of the world, when all I ever wanted was to have him with me. But he could never see that I loved him for the wonderful, generous and gentle man that he was. Then one day he finally rode out and I told him I could wait no longer for him to return with his pockets empty . . . and the promise, that, just one more time . . .' She choked as the tears welled at bitter and beautiful memories of the man she had once loved.

Luke remained silent and he thought of Kate in Rockhampton . . . Was love such an important part of life, when a man's duty was to provide for his woman the best way he could?

Rose wiped away the tears that had streamed down her pretty face and she continued to speak. 'When Jack left a year ago I promised myself that I would never take him back. He would only laugh and he'd make another promise he would return with a fortune for me. But he had said that one time too many. And when Mister Carr came into my life, I realised that there were men who were prepared to remain by a woman's side. Men who would be there when they were most needed. A man so different to Jack. A man who did not have the need to face danger every day of his life with nothing more than a dream to keep him going. A good and predictable man who . . .' She hesitated and turned to Luke with pleading eyes and said, 'Do you know what I mean, Mister Tracy?'

He nodded and turned to stare straight ahead, as he did not want her to see the guilt in his own eyes. The good men stayed safe in their homes behind the frontier. And only the bad men went out beyond the frontier in search of dreams, he reflected bitterly. Maybe he should throw in his search for the elusive dream and settle down to a life in town as Solomon and Judith had always begged him to do. The little Jewish storekeeper had even promised him the management of a store he was planning to open in Townsville. But he had declined, explaining how he knew nothing of pots and pans.

'Some men are born with a different kind of blood, ma'am,' he said sadly as he stared at a trail of ants at his feet, labouring with the carcass of a dead grasshopper. 'Maybe it's a curse. But the blood makes those men restless and foolishly ambitious and they lose sight of what's really important in life,' he said wistfully and once again thought about Kate. Maybe too many years had passed between them for him to ever dream of finding her love.

'I can assume that you are a prospector like Jack, Mister Tracy,' Rose said gently to the man she sensed was also suffering from a deep loss, and Luke nodded. 'Then I pray you find your dream before it kills you,' she said as she touched him sympathetically on the back of his hand. Luke was reminded of a similar touch many years earlier from a woman who would be about the same age as the one sitting beside him. He smiled sadly, stood and reached into his trouser pocket to retrieve the package he had carried up from Brisbane.

'I made a promise to Jack before he died,' he said as he held out the cloth-wrapped bundle. 'And no matter what, he wanted you to have this.' She took the small bundle in her hands and stared at it curiously as he continued, 'I didn't know Jack long. But I figured him for a fine man who would have been happy to know that you found someone you could love. Someone who would look after you.'

Rose held the cloth-wrapped bundle without opening it, as whatever it was she felt that it should be opened in privacy. Hopefully it would be the journal he had always kept, recording his life on the lonely trails and his love for her. She was hardly aware of the parting words of the tall

American. 'Jack found his river of gold. But it done him no good in the end,' he said as he turned and walked back to his horse tethered at the front gate.

Rose remained seated with the package in her hands, remembering the bittersweet times she had spent with the man she had once loved to distraction. But a man she had finally given up for a stable home and life with a gentle and considerate man who would always be there. At least the journal would be a part of her life to remember those days.

She slowly unwrapped the cloth, which fell open to reveal a pile of banknotes. Stunned, she sat gaping at the money in her lap and she didn't have to be a teacher of arithmetic to know she was staring at a considerable fortune. The parting words of the American echoed in her bewildered mind.

'Jack found his river of gold. But it done him no good in the end.'

A fiddle screeched and a young and world-weary woman sang a sad and haunting song about Moreton Bay's brutal convict system on the banks of the Brisbane River many years earlier. Two weeks out of Toowoomba, Luke Tracy sat alone at a rough bush-crafted table just big enough to seat two men and two shots of rum. Pipe and cigar smoke clouded the room in a mist so thick that the American had no reason to light up a cheroot and smoke and he hardly heard the young woman singing her sad song, as he was engrossed in his own thoughts.

The patrons of the tiny hotel bar took little

notice of the prospector. They were preoccupied vying for the attention of two other ladies who made it known they were available to share their charms with the man – or men – who paid the most.

Ironically Luke Tracy could have been just that man as he carried in a money belt enough cash to not only buy all three ladies for the night, but also the hotel and a year's supply of its stock.

The Palmer River gold had been converted to pound notes through Solomon's contacts in a world of transactions where questions were not asked. The gold would eventually find its way into respectability as items of jewellery and the fancy ladies wearing golden chains would never know of the blood that had been spilled to enhance their vanity.

Selling gold without government approval could incur a hefty prison term under the laws of the colony, but to disclose the gold meant revealing its source and that invited a gold rush that might leave him behind. Luke had no intention of losing the El Dorado he had searched for over the long and lonely years of his life.

He picked up the tumbler of rum in front of him. The alcohol fumed in his head and made him feel good. At least a little less morose. But it did not take away his soul-destroying loneliness. He had a small fortune and yet it meant nothing compared to the love he had for years carried with him for Kate O'Keefe. If only she knew how much he loved her. If only she knew.

'Mister Tracy, isn't it?'

Surprised, Luke glanced up at the mention of his

name and focused on a tall and broad-shouldered man standing over him with something between a smile and a sneer on his handsome face.

'I know you?' Luke queried with a slight slur.

'We met at Rockhampton back in '63,' the stranger said. 'You don't remember?'

Luke remembered and the rum in his stomach suddenly felt like bile. 'Mister O'Keefe,' Luke answered somewhere between a hiss and a snarl. 'I remember. I thought you might not want to be recognised in the colony of Queensland.'

Kevin O'Keefe dragged a rickety chair to the table and sat down without invitation. 'That might be, Mister Tracy,' he said and he reached into the pocket of the fancy waistcoat he wore. 'But the colony is badly in need of enterprising men with a certain kind of business acumen to make this place fit to live in. I suppose I am one of those men.'

He produced a florin coin which he placed on the table and turned to call across to the girl singing her sad song. 'Get me and Mister Tracy another drink, Sally,' he commanded. The girl ceased her song and obeyed with a small display of reluctance. 'Bloody woman,' O'Keefe scowled as he watched her walk unsteadily to the bar. 'Should have left her in The Rocks to rot. She'll be too drunk by the end of the night to work.'

Luke momentarily turned his attention to the girl, who was not beautiful but had a sexual appeal which was for sale as he'd guessed correctly. He turned back to O'Keefe.

'All the women here work for you,' he stated bluntly and O'Keefe nodded.

'I hear you've been paying for your drinks with

pound notes,' he said leaning slightly forward into Luke's face. 'If I remember rightly from the last time we met, you said you were a prospector. So I can only surmise that you've made a good strike somewhere.'

'If I had . . . what concern would that be to you, Mister O'Keefe?' Luke answered without trying to conceal his hostility. 'You don't strike me as a man who would get his hands dirty doin' an honest day's work for an honest day's pay.'

O'Keefe's eyes glazed at the intended slur on his character. He did not fear the American, even if he did carry a big Colt revolver tucked in the belt of his trousers. Other men had threatened him in the past, and other men had been paid with a beating that had maimed them for life. Behind his fancy clothes was still the hard bare-knuckle fighter of the tough Irish part of Sydney Town.

'If I did what you call an honest day's work, I wouldn't be wearing these clothes, would I?' O'Keefe challenged. 'No, I provide a service no man can live without, Mister Tracy, and I am not concerned who knows. In your case, I was hoping you and I might talk about maybe a future location where men hungry for the gentle touch of a woman might go to dig for gold, nothing more than that. And I suspect you know such a place.'

Luke stared hard at the big man sitting opposite him and an image of a helpless young girl's face gaunt with fever filled his memories. It was the image he remembered for the absolute sense of helplessness he had felt at the time. The image of Kate in her dire time of need boiled up like a rage in his belly. The speed and fury of Luke's blow took even the experienced bare-knuckle fighter by surprise and O'Keefe felt himself propelled backwards where he hit the wooden floor with a heavy thump.

The crash of the table and chairs scattering in the small bar caught the immediate attention of everyone in the crowded, smoke-filled room. But O'Keefe was experienced in the ways of the street fighter and the blow had little more than a stinging effect on his reactions. The razor-sharp knife was in his hand in the blink of an eye.

A woman screamed and the girl who had been ordered to fetch the drinks let them fall to the floor with a crash of splintering glass. Luke was on his feet and the Colt in his hand was pointed directly at the head of O'Keefe, who lay on his back supported by his elbows.

'You're a lowdown son of a bitch, O'Keefe,' Luke snarled with murder in his eyes. 'And I should put a bullet in you right now for what you did to Kate.'

O'Keefe did not attempt to rise but he stared back at the man standing over him. He knew the American's threat was very real and he was looking at certain death. But O'Keefe was not a man to be cowed by fear.

'Kate!' he said with a note of surprise. 'You calling my wife Kate makes me think you have feelings for her, Mister Tracy.'

Luke was hardly aware of the sudden silence around him. He was looking down a tunnel with O'Keefe at the other end. 'Your wife is the finest woman I have ever known,' he replied quietly. 'If killing you would help her, I wouldn't hesitate in doing it now. But she is too fine a woman to have even a goddamned son of a whore like you get her name related to a killin' in some scurvy pub. No. You get a second chance, O'Keefe.'

'You don't,' O'Keefe replied menacingly from the floor. 'If I ever hear you have been near her, Tracy, so help me God, I'll kill you.'

'You don't get a third chance, O'Keefe.' Luke snorted contemptuously with the revolver pointed steadily. 'If I hear that you have gone anywhere near Kate, I will kill you.'

'I believe you would,' O'Keefe replied with a puzzled frown as if finding it hard to come to grips with the fact that there was a man in Kate's life who was actually prepared to die for her. He knew he would not die for her. For that matter, no woman was worth dying for.

Luke carefully backed out of the hotel with his gun covering the patrons. Not that any of them appeared in the slightest bit interested in helping O'Keefe. Not even the girls who worked for him.

He untethered his horse from the hitching rail and eased himself up into the saddle. He had not gone far when he once again heard the screech of the fiddle belting out an Irish jig. Already the explosive confrontation between pimp and prospector was relegated to curious speculation among the hotel patrons who had witnessed the short but violent incident. The patrons had gone to the pub to drink and to drinking they returned.

Luke rode until he felt he was safely out of O'Keefe's possible attempts to follow him. Not that he thought that was probable. He remembered Kate's husband as a man more at home at a card table, or in another woman's bed, than in the bush.

And as he rode he thought about Kate. He had not seen her in five long years. Maybe it was time he went north to Rockhampton to tell her his feelings. He could now because he had money.

Overhead, the flying foxes flapped silently in a seemingly endless stream as they sought the wild fruits of the forests in the hills around Brisbane Town and Luke began to sing. At first softly, then more loudly.

I come from Alabama with a banjo on my knee.

It was a popular song from his homeland and it had crossed the Pacific with the Californians to the Ballarat goldfields in '54.

The implication of his momentous decision began to dawn on him and suddenly the night sounds of the Australian bush were as sweet as any sounds on earth. But first he had to visit a man he knew who owned the best thoroughbreds in the colony.

O, Susanna, O don't you cry for me ...

40

The room was dark although it was only mid-afternoon. The curtains were drawn for the woman who sat alone in the library of the immense house.

For David, Enid Macintosh had finally let flow the grief which she had withheld for the death of her first son. And now she sat alone, a gaunt and pale reflection of the woman she had once been.

The servants moved about the hallways of the mansion quietly so as not to disturb her, and the letters of condolence from friends and business acquaintances were piled high on the desk in the library where they lay unopened. Nor was Lady Enid accepting visitors to the Macintosh mansion. Strict instructions had been issued to the domestic staff that she was accepting only immediate family.

Throughout the day the grieving woman remained in the library where she took her meals. She only left the darkened library to sleep in her bedroom or attend to calls of nature.

The tragic news that her beloved David had been murdered in the Pacific islands by the savages had been more than any mother should bear in a lifetime. The news of his death had arrived by telegram, relayed over the telegraph line between Brisbane and Sydney. It was followed by a letter from Captain Mort expressing his condolences to the Macintosh family. His letter also contained a rambling and heroic account of how he had tried to fight his way back to recover David's body. But, alas! To no avail. Such was the ferocity of the natives.

Her dear boy was gone and no more would she see the loving and gentle smile of the man who preferred the pursuit of knowledge to the purchase of power. No more would she hear his laughter or his gently humorous and sometimes irreverent accounts of life in the hallowed halls of Oxford.

No matter what Captain Mort's report read, she knew that David had been murdered and why. If only she had insisted that David not take passage on the *Osprey*, he might be alive today, she thought in her grief. Mort may have carried out the execution but Granville had signed the warrant, she was sure. But she knew that to prove such a conspiracy was well beyond her for the moment. Her brooding thoughts were interrupted by Betsy, who had tapped softly on the library door to peer into the dark room.

'Lady Macintosh,' she called timidly around the door of the library. 'Your daughter, Missus White, is here to see you, if you please.'

'Send Missus White up, Betsy,' Enid replied in a tired voice. She was not surprised that her estranged daughter was calling on her. The death of her brother would at least warrant one official visit to express formal grief.

When Fiona entered the room, she saw her mother sitting in a large leather chair by the closed drapes and her pale face stood out starkly in the gloom. Fiona sat on a divan at the opposite side of the room, because she did not want to be near her mother.

'You know, Fiona, that your husband had David murdered,' Enid said in a flat voice by way of greeting her daughter. 'He . . . and Captain Mort.'

'Granville had nothing to do with David's death, Mother,' Fiona retorted in a shocked voice at the blunt accusation. 'You are obviously overwrought by events and have a need to blame someone. You cannot make him a scapegoat for your understandable grief,' she said.

Her mother sighed heavily. 'I know your husband was somehow behind David's death,' she replied bitterly. 'As surely as I know my son was murdered.' She fixed her daughter in the gloom and Fiona returned the hostile glare.

'You should know all about murder, Mother. Did you not arrange to have my son murdered?' she hissed with all the venom of the pent-up hate she felt for the stern woman who had ruled her life for so many years. 'Or was the so well-informed Enid Macintosh ignorant of the nature of baby farms?' she added savagely.

Enid glared at her daughter. Had they been torn this far apart that each accused the other of murder? It was true that she had given instructions for the baby to be disposed of at a baby farm, but Molly had not only betrayed Fiona, she had also betrayed her. It was only when she was long gone that Molly had sent a letter confessing the actual whereabouts of the baby boy. A letter which she had dictated to her parish priest, who had suggested it was best for Molly's peace of mind.

Enid had read the letter then destroyed it, as it did not matter to her that Molly had given the baby to the Duffy family to be raised. At least he was out of the way. One way or the other, Molly had satisfied the contract she had made with her and both had got what they wanted. But Enid had let her daughter believe that her baby had been sent to a baby farm and from that day to this Fiona had hated her mother, with no hope of reconciliation, for the perceived infanticide.

'You could never have married your husband', Enid spat back with venom equal to that of her daughter's, 'if you had kept the bastard of your lust . . . You were ruined goods.' Mother and daughter were like two cobras swaying for the fatal strike in the darkened room.

'There is so much pain when you lose a son, isn't there, Mother?' Fiona retaliated.

'David was also your brother,' Enid reminded her. 'Or have you forgotten that, Fiona?'

'No, Mother,' Fiona replied as her voice broke and the tears flowed. 'I have grieved for the dearest and gentlest man I have ever known.' She wiped her eyes angrily with a small handkerchief, as she had not wanted to show any weakness in front of her mother. 'But there is nothing more than grief that I can feel for David now,' Fiona continued. 'No one can bring him back. Besides, Mother, you taught us to be strong, no matter what. And I am strong, Mother. Stronger than you will ever know. I can thank you for knowing what duty is. Oh, and there is loyalty. You taught us the importance of loyalty. Well, I am loyal . . . to Granville. The Macintosh name will die now that David has gone. There are no other male heirs to inherit the name as all I seem to be able to bear are girls. And you know, I'm glad I have only girls, because the name will die when Father has passed on.'

Enid listened before interjecting quietly, 'And me, Fiona. You forget that I carry the Macintosh name and the name will be alive as long as I am.'

Fiona gave a short and bitter laugh at the irony.

'And I now carry the White name,' she replied. 'When my daughters come of age they will marry. And I swear that all memory of the Macintosh name will be erased forever. I swear that, Mother. The memory of Angus, you and Father, will be eradicated as if you never existed.'

Enid paled. Her daughter's talk was akin to sacrilege! 'If your father had heard what you have just said, he would cut you from his will,' she said in a trembling and emotionally charged whisper.

'You can tell him whatever you like,' Fiona retaliated. 'But who else is there left to leave the companies to? No, Father will at least leave me the companies as the only remaining person who carries his blood and my husband will ensure that they go on to bigger and better things in time. Without him, we are nothing. Father is only interested in Glen View since Angus was killed. And you, despite all your threats, will hope that some day I will see reason and do as you tell me and possibly leave my husband. Well, Mother, you will be hoping until hell freezes over.'

Oh, my daughter, you will never win against me,

Enid thought with savage determination. I know a secret that will one day bring you and that man you call a husband down.

'I think you have said enough, Fiona,' Enid answered quietly. She had regained control of her emotions and as far as she was concerned the conversation and her daughter's visit were at an end. 'I am sure you can make your own way out.'

Fiona stood to leave and there were tears of anger in her eyes. Anger for her mother not seeing the damage she had done over the years.

Fiona swept from the room, past the servants hovering downstairs, to her carriage waiting in the driveway. The coachman helped her through the open door.

'Miss Penelope White's house,' she ordered. The coachman flicked the short whip over the two perfectly matched greys and the coach wheels sprayed stones as they left the house of Fiona's birth. She did not look back.

Enid watched her daughter depart through the partly drawn curtains of the library. The pain for the loss of her son was also a pain for the loss of her daughter. She had always loved Fiona but she had never been able to tell her so. And now they were bitter enemies, locked in a contest of wills.

She felt her head swim. She had not eaten enough over the days since the arrival of the telegram and she slumped back into the comfort of the big leather chair which David had always sat in whenever he was in the library. How had the family come to this point? Where had it all started?

Vaguely the name Duffy, an obscure Irish family

of no social consequence, crept into her conscious thoughts. Had it all started with the death of the Irish teamster on Glen View? Or had the troubles begun with the now long-dead young Irishman who had sired Fiona's bastard? Had the diabolical twist of fate in the two diverse meetings brought about events that had a common factor of terrible destruction? Duffy and Macintosh! The names were linked forever in blood.

'Oh David, my beautiful boy, I have killed you,' Enid cried out as guilt burst like an infection from an angry red cyst. 'I have killed you, as surely as I have been blind to where my ambition would lead us all.'

She swooned and desperately groped for the long curtains draped on the wall by the window. Betsy heard the thump in the library just as she had heard the terrible cry of anguish from her mistress.

Penelope lay alone on her bed dressed only in a body-clinging silk chemise and she revelled in the wonderful feeling of freedom she had out of the constricting hooped dress that lay in an untidy pile on the floor. Bustles might be all the fashion but they were not a practical step towards female comfort. They were cumbersome and ridiculous in the Australian climate. She wondered idly at the mentality of those who designed such clothes. Why was it that women had to slavishly follow what people in faraway Europe dictated as fashion?

She ran her hand down her flat stomach and along her thighs and her fingers lingered tantalisingly between her legs. She felt a sense of pride in her body, which she knew aroused men with its sensuous curves.

The crunch of gravel in the driveway distracted her from her self-exploration. She had not expected visitors for the afternoon. With a languid sigh she padded across to the window where she drew aside the curtain and was surprised to see her cousin Fiona alight from her coach. Penelope could see that Fiona appeared visibly distressed. Had something happened between Fiona and her despicable brother, Granville? she questioned herself.

'Fiona! Up here,' she called down from the bedroom window. 'Tell the maid you are coming straight up!'

Fiona glanced up to see Penelope framed in the window with her long hair tumbling freely about her bare shoulders, trapping the rays of the late afternoon sun in a golden spray. The curtain at the window fell back and Penelope disappeared from view. Fiona made her greetings at the door and the maid led her up the staircase to her cousin's bedroom.

When she opened the door to Penelope's bedroom she was not surprised to see her cousin sitting brushing her hair and wearing only a silk chemise, as Penelope cared little for social inhibitions.

'You have been to see your mother,' Penelope said as she let the brush run through her hair. 'At first I thought my brother might have caused your obvious distress. But looking at you now, I know that only your mother could have caused that much distress to you.'

Fiona leant against the door, as she felt faint from the emotional trauma of the confrontation with her mother in the library.

'Penny, it was terrible,' she said in a voice on the verge of sobbing. 'She is saying that Granville killed David. She is out of her mind with anger and bitterness.'

Penelope rose from her chair and went to Fiona standing by the closed door.

'Do you think my brother had anything to do with David's death?' she asked as she touched Fiona on the cheek gently with her long fingers. Fiona shook her head and tried to look away from her cousin's full breasts exposed above the chemise. 'Then you should,' Penelope said softly and Fiona gasped and stared questioningly into Penelope's face.

'Granville was not even there,' Fiona countered. 'How could he have planned to have the natives kill David? How could you say something like that about your own brother?'

Penelope smiled as her fingers stroked Fiona's neck and she spoke softly with an edge of bitterness. 'Because I know my brother and he is capable of great evil. He is very good at destroying anything, and everyone. Granville loves only one thing in life and that is power. He sees all men as competitors . . . and women as a means of satisfying his rather unusual pleasures. But I think you know what I mean by that, Fiona. After all, you share his bed.'

Fiona could feel her cousin's fingers caress her throat with lingering strokes and her moist, sweet breath on her cheek. There was a strange almost glazed expression on her face that disturbed Fiona in a way that she found compelling enough to let Penny continue to do whatever she wanted with her.

Penelope leant forward and her lips brushed Fiona's throat while her tongue traced a thin and sensuous line up to her lips. The kiss was soft but strong. The pain Fiona was feeling dissolved and she was vaguely aware that her cousin's kiss was causing her confused and wonderfully forbidden feelings.

No words passed between them as Fiona let her hand be lifted by Penelope to touch her breasts under the chemise.

'Forget everything,' Penelope whispered hoarsely. 'Forget everything that is hurting you, my darling, and I will show you what you have always wanted. I will give you the pleasure that my brother cannot give you. I will give you the love we both crave.'

Penelope's words were soft and seductive and Fiona knew that she did not want to resist as her beautiful cousin guided her hand down between her thighs. With her free hand, Penelope lifted the hem of her short silk chemise and Fiona felt her hand guided between her cousin's legs.

Penelope closed her eyes and smiled with a soft sigh as she slid Fiona's fingers into her. Fiona caught her breath as the wet swelling yielded and opened as an invitation for her to probe her sensuality. Penelope shuddered as she felt her cousin's fingers willingly enter her.

'Let everything out of your mind,' she whispered in a husky voice as she gently led Fiona to the big double bed. 'Except that you and I are together alone in this room. Let your heart rule your head. And let that passion that I know you have had for me take you to my bed. What is between us can only be between women. The softness and sensitivity of true love that does not desire to dominate. Share the ecstasy of body and soul as one.'

Fiona was both frightened and fascinated at what was happening between them. Penelope was seducing her! And yet it felt so natural between them, she thought as her face and throat flushed hot and she felt her own desire rising as an irresistible force.

'Don't resist what you truly feel,' Penelope whispered hoarsely in her ear as she drew her down onto the bed and with practised hands began to strip away the clothes that separated their mutual desire. They knelt naked on the bed facing each other. 'I will show you things you never imagined could cause the exquisite pleasures of the body,' Penelope said as she leant forward to suckle one of her cousin's desire-swollen nipples and Fiona did not resist.

Daniel Duffy had stared at the letter many times. Was it a trick? The letter was real enough and the ornate letterhead confirmed the identity of the sender.

'No more appointments for today,' he called to the front office as he took his coat from a wooden peg at the back of his office door. 'I will be out for a while.'

It was chilly on the street outside his office as the first winds of autumn brought the cold heralding the coming winter. Daniel hailed a hansom cab and directed the driver to take him to the Botanic Gardens. He strolled around the gardens without taking in the collection of carefully selected trees and shrubs. His thoughts were on the meeting with the woman who had sent him the letter. Then he saw her.

She was alone as she had said she would be and she wore a black taffeta dress. She was bending slightly to examine a rosebush and she had the imperious air of one born to authority. She also had the delicate beauty of a woman who had never known physical labour. So this was Lady Enid Macintosh!

Daniel walked slowly towards her and tipped his hat out of habit.

'Lady Macintosh?'

'Mister Duffy?'

Enid's hands were enclosed in a fur muff and she appraised Daniel. So this was the enemy, he thought. But she was not as he would have imagined her. He had expected to see a stern straight-backed woman with a set jaw. Instead, she looked very frail. Daniel was not fooled by appearances, as Lady Enid Macintosh had a fearsome reputation in the world of high finance. It was said that she was the true ruler of the Macintosh companies and not her husband in faraway Queensland.

'I think we should walk and look at the gardens,' Enid said and Daniel knew that she had issued a command and not a request. 'Sadly, they are not at their best this time of year,' she sighed and continued, 'I suppose you are very curious as to why I should so urgently want to see you.'

'That I am, Lady Macintosh,' Daniel replied politely, despite his ingrained hatred for the Macintosh family. 'Your letter mentioned the

581

matter was of vital concern to both your family and mine.'

'I think, Mister Duffy,' she said as they walked slowly, feigning to examine the plants in the gardens, 'that when you have heard me out you will agree. I believe our meeting will prove to be fruitful for us both or, should I say, for both our families.'

Although he towered over the woman as they strolled, Daniel felt awkward beside her. She had a regal manner about her that both annoyed and impressed him.

'The damage your family has done mine is a poor start to any joint venture,' he said belligerently, 'if that is what you are proposing in some way. I think you must realise yourself that too much blood has been spilled between us.' Enid nodded her head and he could see that the woman was agreeing with him. How could she dare go any further with whatever she was going to propose or say, he wondered.

'I know what you are saying,' she answered calmly. 'But you must realise that my family has had its suffering. Even very recently with the death of my son, David.'

'Please accept my condolences for your son's death, Lady Macintosh,' Daniel replied with genuine sympathy. 'From what I have heard of your son, and to my knowledge, I don't think I could say my family had any argument with David. Only you, your husband and your son-in-law.'

'You are frank,' Enid replied without rancour. 'And you may have reason to believe what you are saying, Mister Duffy. I doubt anything I say will alter that. But believe me when I say I also damn my son-in-law to burn in hell and you might begin to see that we have enemies in common.'

Daniel tended to believe her when she said she condemned Granville White. Under the regal veneer, she appeared to be a woman who was very tired, almost beaten, and she was prepared to seek help anywhere. 'I believe what you say, Lady Macintosh,' he replied sympathetically. 'I think we should move on to why you wish to see me.'

Enid stopped walking and examined a pink rose before she turned and looked directly into Daniel's face. 'I arranged for us to meet to talk about Patrick Duffy,' she said quietly. 'I believe that is what Molly called Fiona's son.'

Daniel was aghast at the woman's mention of Patrick. How could she suddenly recognise Patrick, when she had done all within her power to dispose of him – even have him murdered! It was as if she were discussing a bank account and not the boy she had sent away five years earlier.

'You mean Michael's son, don't you?' he growled, but Enid disregarded his hostile retort.

'Michael is dead,' she replied calmly. 'That is the only reason I referred to Patrick as Fiona's son.'

'Michael would still be here and alive', Daniel reminded her, 'if your son-in-law had not set out to have him murdered by Jack Horton who I believe works for your company.'

Enid nodded. 'I know the facts, Mister Duffy,' she replied. 'But you as a practitioner of the law must be aware that knowing and proving are two totally different matters. In all the circumstances, nothing will bring Michael back. Oh, if I could go back in time, I would change everything. So many mistakes have occurred in the years past. I know I have caused my daughter to hate me. And in some way I have been instrumental in the death of my youngest son. You must believe that I would change things if I could, Mister Duffy.'

Daniel did not know whether to believe her or not. But, as a lawyer, he did understand facts. And the facts were as they stood. They were the matters of the present.

'So how does this meeting concern Patrick?' he asked and she looked him directly in the face. She did not want him to be in any doubt as to what she was about to propose.

'I want Patrick to inherit the Macintosh companies when he is twenty-one.'

A bomb could have exploded between them and it would have had less effect on Daniel than the woman's statement. He felt his head spin.

'Inherit the Macintosh wealth . . . !' he echoed. The bastard son of an Irish Catholic becoming part of the powerful and respectable Protestant empire of the Macintoshes. There was insanity in the woman.

'I am not surprised at your reaction, Mister Duffy,' Enid said, noting the utter shock in his expression. 'But I have very good reasons for Patrick to inherit the estates when Sir Donald and I have passed on. You see, he has Macintosh blood in him,' she uttered as simply as she could.

'And your daughter is not a Macintosh?' he asked, still reeling from Enid's simple but explosive statement.

'She has disowned her heritage,' Enid said

bitterly. 'And, as you are probably aware, there are no male heirs left alive – except Patrick. I doubt that my daughter will have any more children if she can help it. If the estate does not go to Patrick, then it will go to the man who, I believe in my heart, was responsible for the death of David. As I said, we have mutual enemies,' she replied with a frank and revealing explanation of the situation.

'You have proof that Granville White was responsible for the death of your son, Lady Macintosh?' Daniel asked and he felt a strange and fleeting empathy with the woman who was his sworn enemy.

'No. But do not underestimate a mother's intuition about such things,' she replied. 'I just know that Granville let my son die a horrible and lonely death.'

Daniel understood. Women's intuition was a strong trait in his own mother and particularly in his cousin Kate.

'You must realise, Lady Macintosh,' Daniel said in a flat voice, 'that Patrick has been baptised a Catholic and will die a Catholic and I doubt if this will be acceptable to your beliefs.'

Enid looked away, as the horrific thought of a Papist inheriting the Macintosh name was beyond even her. It was an abomination in the eyes of God!

'Do you believe that your Romanism is strong enough to stand up to the teachings of my faith, Mister Duffy?' she asked when she finally looked back. 'Or do you think your religion could flounder when compared to mine?'

'Once a Catholic, always a Catholic, Lady

Macintosh,' Daniel answered with quiet assuredness.

'I would ask that you give me the chance to teach Patrick my faith,' Enid said. 'And in time he could make up his own mind as to what path he should follow.'

'In what time are you talking?' Daniel asked.

'When Patrick has turned eleven years and one day,' she replied. 'Then you would release him to me and he will be given the opportunity for the best education the Macintosh wealth can buy. A chance to attend Oxford when he is ready and, when he is twenty-one, then let him choose between my faith and yours.'

'What if he should choose to remain a member of the True Church?' Daniel asked belligerently. 'Would he still inherit the Macintosh estate?'

Enid sighed. She had faith in the fact that Patrick would see the light and come over to her religion. It was worth the risk.

'Should he choose to remain a Roman Catholic, then I will accept his choice,' she answered.

'And his name? Would he be a Duffy or a Macintosh?'

'On this issue there is no debate. Patrick may keep his Irish name but his children must assume the Macintosh name as theirs,' she replied firmly. No, on this point there was no negotiation.

Daniel thought about the issue of name and conceded pragmatically that it was no great matter. What Lady Enid was offering were opportunities far beyond those he and Colleen could offer Patrick in the years to come.

As if sensing Daniel's thoughts, Enid said, 'At

least with my offer, Patrick would know who he truly is and would never have to wonder at his place in this world. Surely you must see that, Mister Duffy?'

'That is why I am considering what you are proposing.'

But it was not the only reason he knew he would accept the woman's offer. Here was a chance to take revenge on the family that had caused his so much grief. Patrick would always remain a Catholic, he was sure of that. And Patrick would control the estate over Granville White. Oh, it was so fitting. That a Duffy, the son of Michael and grandson of the first Patrick, should some day stand above the descendants of the Macintoshes.

'Patrick will be under your care,' Enid said. 'Until the day he turns eleven years and one day. We will draw up suitable documents concerning the matters we have discussed.'

Daniel pondered on all that she had said and finally replied, 'I think you should understand that Patrick's future welfare is of the greatest concern to myself and my family.'

'I understand your caution,' Enid said sympathetically. 'And I will arrange to have matters drawn up to protect us both, be assured of that. As it is, we need certain proof of Patrick's birth, and I have means of arranging that also, as it will be vital when the time comes.' Enid did not explain when this was, but already she was looking down the corridors of time. In September 1874, Patrick would turn eleven years of age.

As the matter between them required no further discussion, it would be passed into the hands of solicitors. Daniel walked with Enid towards the main entrance to the gardens.

'What sort of man was Patrick's father, Mister Duffy?' Enid unexpectedly asked and Daniel could see that the woman was even now thinking of Patrick as her grandson.

'Michael was a grand man,' he replied proudly. 'He was big, brave and strong and he had a gentle way about him. He dreamed of some day becoming a great artist and capturing the beauty he saw in this country. He wanted to show the world this country's soul in his paintings and his son is growing like him in every way.'

'He must have been an exceptional man', Enid sighed, 'for my daughter to have loved him so very much.' They parted, but not before she turned away briefly so he could not see the pain in her face. The tears would come later, when she was alone, for the terrible thing she had done to her daughter and to herself.

41

Hugh Darlington never tired of watching Kate dress herself.

She held no shame for her body and would wriggle into the tight corsets, exposing, for a short and erotic time, forbidden glimpses of milk-white flesh for his voyeuristic pleasure. As she wriggled into the uncomfortable and constraining corsets, she would often swear with unseemly and colourful words she had picked up from the bullockies in the bar and her use of profane language caused even the worldly-wise solicitor to wince.

Finally she buttoned her long dress and brushed it down before she sat on a chair to pull on the lace-up boots fashionable with the ladies in London and Rockhampton. Hugh lay against the brass bedhead and gazed admiringly at her.

'I will see you tomorrow, Kate?' he asked as thick smoke curled around his head from a cigar he puffed.

'No,' she replied as she gave an unladylike grunt and yanked at the laces. 'I have to make sure my new wagon is ready to leave for Tambo, so I shall be too busy to see you. It's Benjamin's first time out. I have a present for him which I have to pick up from the *Lady Mary*'s captain at the wharf.'

'I hope for your sake that one of those matters isn't an appointment at the bank about purchasing Glen View, Kate,' he said ominously and Kate froze in the act of tying the bootlace.

'What do you mean by that, Hugh?' she asked quietly.

'Just that I hear things in my business, as you full well know,' he replied. 'And there is a rumour you are going to try to buy Glen View from Sir Donald Macintosh.'

'Oh, he is a *sir* now,' Kate said bitterly and turned to Hugh. 'Although somehow that does not surprise me.'

Hugh took a long puff on his cigar and exhaled a stream of thick smoke before speaking. 'You have enough opportunities in your present position to capitalise other properties, Kate. So, as someone who cares for you, and as your solicitor, I would advise against stirring up things best left alone. Sir Donald is a powerful and, I suspect, a dangerous man to cross. I know of your vendetta against the Macintosh family – as it seems does most of the colony – for the alleged things you think they are responsible for. But you haven't any proof to be a one-woman nemesis. Although, it is rather apt that the word is derived from the Greek goddess of retribution,' he said, pleased with himself for his recall of the Greek classics.

Kate stared at him with an icy expression akin to hostility. 'Would you help me if I was trying to bring the man to justice?' she asked and he looked startled at both her question and its tone.

'It is not a question of helping you as much as a question of what is lawful,' he reflected. 'Of course I would help you if I thought you had solid grounds for your supposed suspicions. But you don't, Kate.'

She turned away from the man who only minutes earlier had held her in his arms and sworn his love to her. This was a different man virtually telling her that she was some kind of stupid and foolish woman infatuated with a hopeless cause. Damn him! Damn all men, she thought savagely as she rose to leave.

She knew there were others who would die for her. Men like the quiet and capable Luke Tracy. She turned back to Hugh before she left the room, snapping angrily, 'Never underestimate a woman, Mister Darlington. Especially a Duffy woman.'

His smile caught her unawares as he stretched lazily and shot at her, 'I never underestimate you, Kate O'Keefe. What man in his right mind would?'

She could not help smiling as he had a way of switching tactics and defusing her anger with his considerable charm. There were times she knew she could hate him for his smug male attitudes. But he had that way of making her want him. Damn you, Mister Darlington, I should leave your house and never return! But she knew full well that she would come back as the handsome and charming solicitor's magnetism was as strong as the candle's flame was to the moth.

Standing beside the massive wagon and bullock team, Benjamin Rosenblum felt embarrassed by his Aunt Judith's attention. She fussed over him as if she were his own mother. At fifteen years of age, Ben was a man. And men did not have women fussing over them like they were little boys.

The new wagon was loaded with the badly needed supplies for the trip west to the far-flung properties on the brigalow scrub plains beyond the Great Divide and the bullocks stood patiently waiting for the rifle-like crack of the whip over their heads.

Joe Hanrahan, the teamster Kate had employed to take the wagon west, had stopped at the appointed place at the edge of town to meet her for final instructions and the stopover gave the Cohens an opportunity to bid farewell to young Ben.

'Remember that we will always be thinking of you, Benjamin,' Judith said as she stepped back from the tall and gangling youth. 'And be always aware that you are a Rosenblum.'

Solomon stepped forward and gravely shook the young man's hand. At least his Uncle Solomon treated him like a man! Little Deborah was solemn when she handed her cousin a handful of wildflowers she had picked for him. The straggly bouquet was partly crushed in her chubby little hands but the childish and innocent gesture touched the young man. He accepted her gift with appropriate dignified gratitude and Deborah broke into a beaming smile of happiness.

Finally Kate took her turn to bid farewell to Ben. He blushed when his beautiful employer gave him a peck on the cheek and said, 'I have a present for you, Benjamin.' She thrust at him a finely polished wooden case with his name inscribed on a small brass plate affixed to the lid. He lifted the lid and gaped with stunned awe at the Colt revolver inside. It was the heavy navy model and came with powder flask, bullet mould, nipple key and a tin of percussion caps. Ben was lost for words as he stared at the magnanimous gift. All he could do was stammer, 'I, I . . .'

'It is the only insurance I can give you as an employee of the Eureka Company,' Kate said quietly to the young man. 'Joe will show you how to use it when you are on the track.'

Joe Hanrahan stood by Kate's team of oxen waiting patiently and the stocky teamster nodded to the boy while he uncoiled the stockwhip he held in his big hand. He made ready to move the wagon, which was one of the new four-wheeled giants that had replaced the two-wheeled drays on the frontier. It had the capacity to haul larger loads, which meant the teamsters were making good money per hundredweight of goods.

He nodded respectfully to Kate and, with a bellowed roar and crack of the long whip above the bullocks' backs, he set in motion the lumbering four-wheeled giant.

Ben tucked the case under his arm, gave a final wave, and followed in the wheel tracks of the creaking wagon.

Little Deborah clung to her mother's skirts and watched with wide-eyed awe the impressive demonstration of power, and she waved to her cousin trudging away from her in the rising dust raised by the hooves of the oxen.

Kate sighed as she watched her wagon slowly lumber down the track heading west for the mountains. She felt a touch of envy for young Ben, as she wished it was she who was walking beside the big wagon instead of Ben. For some strange reason, she had a fleeting memory of Luke who had once ridden with her along the same track that her wagon now journeyed.

Benjamin Rosenblum had travelled north from Sydney and had left behind his mother, who was Judith's sister, and his six sisters. On Judith's suggestion, his mother had agreed for him to travel to Queensland to take up work with the Eureka Company as an apprentice. She had grown concerned with her son's increasing connections with the sons of the always present underworld of hardened criminals who frequented the street corners of Woolloomooloo on the harbour front.

Ben was the eldest of her children and she had wanted to see him educated so that he could join the public service as a clerk for a secure lifelong job. But she also recognised the insidious reality of starvation for her family and the Cohens had offered to pay Ben's fare to Queensland.

Ben had arrived reluctantly in Rockhampton as a surly and gawky boy, resenting his exile from Sydney's bright lights and the flashy company of older youths involved in a life of petty crime that supported their hours of indolence. He'd commenced his apprenticeship with Kate O'Keefe, who needed a man to assist the taciturn and burly teamster Joe Hanrahan.

Like all boys his age from the sophisticated city, Ben was full of his own self-importance. But one night he came home severely bruised from a beating. He was a much chastened young man for his experience. Aunt Judith had shown no sympathy for her nephew and Ben had said nothing of the thrashing he had received from the teamster, whom he had pushed once too often with his advice and bad manners. Ben quickly learnt that not all the hard men lived on Sydney's street corners, boasting of their often exaggerated physical prowess. Some men like Joe Hanrahan just used their fists and said nothing of it.

And so Ben adjusted quickly, and painfully, to life in the Queensland colony while his Aunt Judith forwarded most of his wages to Sydney to his mother with letters describing how well young Ben was doing in his 'chosen' trade.

Joe Hanrahan had grudgingly admitted that the lad was turning out well after his unfortunate 'accident' of falling off the back of a dray. For the taciturn teamster to admit that much of a young man was praise in its own right.

When the ponderous wagon had creaked and groaned out of sight, Solomon turned to Kate. 'That was a fine thing, Kate,' he said gratefully. 'A fine gift for a man to have with him.'

Kate modestly dismissed the gratitude with a small wave of her hand. 'He is a fine young man, Solomon,' she said. 'And I know he will make you proud.'

Solomon smiled at her statement, as she was only six years older than Benjamin and yet she was talking like a woman much older than her tender years.

'Ben earned the gun,' Kate continued as she strolled with the Cohens back to their buggy. 'Joe told me he was an eager apprentice and has a good way about him when it comes to handling the beasts. He says Ben was born to be a bullocky.'

'It is good that he has employment with us,' Judith reflected. 'His mother will be proud to hear the things you have said about her son.'

Now that Ben walked beside the big wagon as a man, Solomon said a short prayer that God would look after him and Joe on the arduous and perilous journey west.

Judith wondered how Kate would react when she arrived back at the store with them to find a beautiful and expensive gift waiting for her. But her thoughts were also glum, as she knew of her friend's passionate affair with the handsome solicitor. Some things in life could not help bad timing. The gift waiting for her at the store was one such thing badly timed.

'Hello, Kate. You are as beautiful as the day you first came north,' Luke said with a broad smile on his bearded face as he stood in the paddock behind the Cohen's store. 'And this is Lady . . . She's yours.'

Kate did not know how to react as Luke stood holding the bridle of a magnificent mare. Sixteen hands, Kate thought. And the blackest coat she had seen on any horse, broken only by a single white blaze on her forehead. And the big brown eyes were the most intelligent for a horse she had ever seen.

The sudden and unexpected appearance of the American after so many years stunned Kate. She felt giddy with shock but forced herself to maintain a calm demeanour as she stepped forward to stroke the big animal's forehead.

'I can't accept such a beautiful horse, Luke,' she choked. 'She must have cost you a small fortune.'

Deborah danced around her mother with excited admiration for the most magnificent horse in the whole, wide world. 'Aunt Katie, Aunt Katie, take me for a ride on horse?' she squealed excitedly.

'I can't accept the horse,' Kate said gently to the little girl. 'She is far too beautiful and expensive for me to accept.' Luke passed the bridle to Kate, who protested feebly, 'I cannot take her.'

But her resolve crumbled when she felt the big finely chiselled nose of the mare nuzzle her. There were people who would literally kill to own such a fine horse, as Kate knew full well!

'I think I might look a bit out of place riding her side-saddle,' the American said with a grin, 'as is proper for ladies with the position I heard lately that you have around town.' Kate smiled as he had facetiously reminded her of a time when she defied custom by riding a horse as a man would. 'And besides, she doesn't like men very much. Lady has a habit of making men look foolish if they attempt to ride her.'

'But I presume you have ridden her?' Kate queried as she continued to stroke the horse's broad forehead. Lady nuzzled Kate's straw hat and they all laughed when the horse yanked it off her head. It snorted irritably as it attempted to chew the straw hat on the ground. Kate dropped the bridle and the horse was content to remain with the hat.

'Yeah. Well, Lady and I came to an agreement on the track up to Rockhampton,' the American drawled with a wry twinkle in his eyes. 'I told her I was the boss, but I promised her I would treat her right. And she figured the arrangement would do.' It had not been that easy, but Luke was a superb horseman and he had soon learnt to control her while leading his own mare.

Kate turned her attention to Luke, who was standing beside Solomon beaming with pleasure for his friend's extravagant gift to her. It had been over four years since she had last seen the American and he was still the same tall and ruggedly good-looking man she remembered from the trek west. Except now his hair and beard had a touch of grey and in his face were the signs of a fever not long gone. She could see that he moved his left arm with stiffer movements than his right.

'Lady was meant for you, Kate,' Luke said gently. 'You both have the same first name.' Kate felt his eyes on her filled with a tenderness that belied the bushman's tough way of life and she did not want to look into his gentle eyes. She knew that she would cry for the vulnerable sensitivity of the tall man who she knew, without any lingering doubts, loved her. She was hardly aware of his softly spoken words when he said, 'I remember you once gave me not one horse, but three. Let's say it is returning a favour . . . or something like that.'

'Accept Lady, Kate,' Judith urged gently. 'Luke has travelled a long way to give her to you.'

Kate fought back the tears welling in her eyes. She wanted to do something appropriate as a way of thanking Luke but she was still stunned by his unexpected appearance in her life.

She stood on her toes to kiss him on the cheek and she was startled by his sudden grasp of her arms as he held her and kissed her boldly on the lips. The kiss was strong and gentle and Kate felt confused. She was another man's woman now. Surely his kiss had come too late for them both . . .

Little Deborah watched puzzled and asked with childish curiosity, 'What is Uncle Luke doing to Aunt Kate?'

Judith smiled mysteriously and took her daughter's hand. 'Some day I will tell you,' she said as she led the little girl away and Solomon wisely followed his wife into the store.

Kate broke from Luke's embrace and stood back with an agonised expression on her face.

'Oh, why did you stay away for so long, Luke?' she said in her confusion. 'Time has changed so many things for you and me. I . . .' She could not find words to express her turbulent feelings and tears welled as she ran sobbing towards the store leaving Luke bewildered and alone.

'Time has changed so many things . . .' He felt miserable and foolish. But maybe that was it! Too many years had passed between them. After all, he had nothing to offer a woman, except a head full of dreams!

Alone that night in her bed, Kate did not sleep well. When she had last seen the American she had seen him through the eyes of a girl and even then he had been an attractive man. Now that she was able to see him through the eyes of a mature woman she knew she was still attracted to him.

But Hugh Darlington had come into her life. He was younger, financially well off, and socially acceptable in the best circles of frontier life. Luke on the other hand was older, always penniless and had no social standing, except with the tough frontiersmen to whom he had become something of a legend. She found herself comparing the two men as she tossed restlessly in her bed.

Luke was also brave, gentle and generous and for years he had always held a piece of her heart that she never dared admit to herself.

Every practical female instinct told her that the handsome and suave solicitor was the obvious choice between the two men, if she was to make a choice! But something kept Luke in her thoughts. It was that something that she could not give a name to that made the choice far from inevitable in Hugh Darlington's favour. If only Luke was the kind of man who could stay in one place there might be a hope for them. But the American was a man who she knew had a mistress. And that mistress had a name. Gold.

'Mister Darlington, I believe you are the solicitor acting for Missus Kate O'Keefe,' the tall man queried when Hugh ushered him into his office. The man was obviously an American from his accent, Hugh thought.

'That is correct, Mister . . . ah . . . Tracy,' he said as he sat down on a chair behind the desk which was cleared of all paper leaving only a silver ink stand and ivory pen. Luke eased himself into a chair and placed his hat on his lap.

'Solomon Cohen told me that Missus O'Keefe has her business registered through your office,' he said. 'And he told me she needs money for a matter of some importance to her. As her lawyer I figured you might be able to help me.'

Hugh entwined his fingers on the desk in front of him as was his habit when talking to clients and Luke could not help but notice how soft the man looked in comparison to the men he knew along the lonely tracks of Queensland's frontier.

The lawyer's pale skin was unblemished by the sun and nor were there any signs of scarring. His hands were delicate, like a woman's hands, and the clothes he wore were fashionable for even Sydney or Melbourne. In comparison, the American prospector felt drab, wearing his faded flannel shirt, moleskin trousers tucked into knee-length boots and a wide sash around his waist, less the practical adornment of the big Colt he normally wore. He did not carry his guns in Rockhampton any more as the town was getting civilised and not like the days, a mere five years earlier, when Rockhampton was truly on the frontier.

'How can I be of assistance to you?' Hugh asked as he leant back in the leather chair. 'And Missus O'Keefe's interests, Mister Tracy?'

'By investing this with Missus O'Keefe's company,' Luke replied as he dropped a canvas bag on the desk in front of the solicitor from which wads of banknotes spilled. Hugh almost fell off his chair.

'God almighty, man! How much is there?' he gasped in his surprise, leaning forward.

'Should be three thousand pounds,' Luke replied casually.

'Dare I ask where you got so large an amount, Mister Tracy?' the solicitor asked suspiciously, unable to take his eyes off the money.

'Put it this way, Mister Darlington,' Luke answered softly, 'I didn't rob or steal to get the money, but there are laws in this country about the exchange of gold for cash and, as a lawyer, I know you have to keep in confidence what I tell you.'

Hugh understood immediately. The Cohen connection! He guessed correctly that the American had used the Jewish storekeeper's contacts in the jewellery trade to make the exchange. If three thousand pounds was the result on the table, he thought, how much had the gold been worth? – a lot more! There were considerable 'fees' in such exchanges.

But it was also puzzling that the man had not declared a legitimate strike and exchanged the gold through lawful means. Very puzzling indeed. This was 'dirty money' and Hugh's first instinct was to dissociate himself from the American. But what connection was there to Kate?

His curiosity bettered his loyalty to the laws of the land. 'Just how do you know Missus O'Keefe, Mister Tracy, if I may ask?'

'The lady is a friend of mine,' Luke answered, cutting any other inquiry into his relationship with Kate. 'That is all you have to know, Mister Darlington.'

'I think I understand,' Hugh said enigmatically. The man was probably infatuated with Kate as half the single and married men in the district were. If Harry Hubner would leave his estate to

Kate, why shouldn't some fool of an American try to impress her with his money.

'I want the money to be invested in a way that Missus O'Keefe doesn't know about my involvement,' Luke continued and Hugh became very suspicious of the American's intentions. This was not what he had expected. He had anticipated the man was going to try to impress Kate with his contribution.

'So you want to be a silent partner,' Hugh said. 'To invest and take a share of the profits.'

'Not even that. I want Kate to use the money as she sees fit,' Luke replied, shaking his head. 'And after she is in a position to repay the money – she can return it to me through you.'

'At what percentage interest return for yourself,' the lawyer asked suspiciously.

'None.'

Hugh shook his head slowly and sneered, 'You aren't much of a businessman, Mister Tracy. You place a considerable amount of money on my desk and tell me you don't need to make it work for you. I am pleased you aren't my bank manager.'

Luke bridled at the sneering comment on his business acumen. He had not liked the man from the moment he had met him and even less now. He flushed angrily but fought down his urge to grab the man by the throat and drag him across the table.

'You just give me a receipt for the money,' he growled. 'Put it in Kate's account, and tell her any story you like as to how she has come by the money, Mister Darlington, and I will pay you well.'

Hugh sensed it was not wise to rile the grizzled American prospector. The scar on his face testified that the man was someone who was used to physical danger, whereas he had always had the luxury of sheltering behind the law. He had never faced any situation where his life was on the line and his only contact with danger had been a vicarious one through the legal association he sometimes had with one or two of his clients – men who lived outside the law.

'I think I can do that, Mister Tracy,' he said reasonably. 'If you will bear with me for a while I will prepare the necessary paperwork and the fee.'

Luke nodded and took out one of his evil-smelling cheroots to smoke. He sensed that the lawyer was not a man who would like the acrid smoke in his office.

When all matters had been settled, Luke left. The two men did not exchange a handshake on parting as a tacit agreement to dislike each other. Luke was not sure exactly why he disliked the solicitor but there was something about the man . . .

Hugh Darlington waited until Luke was out of sight before he closed the door to his office and walked quickly down to the police station. There was someone whom he had to see about an American who had contravened the gold laws of the colony. His motivations were not based on his responsibility to uphold the law, but the baser motivations based on a nagging jealousy and old-fashioned avarice.

42

The day started so well for Granville White.

He sat in the rather spartan office that had once been David's when he had temporarily controlled the companies and now he sat in the big leather chair that David had found so comfortable when he had so sanctimoniously passed judgement on his opinions. Opinions that, had they been put into practice, would have skyrocketed profits for the Macintosh companies, Granville brooded. But the pious David Macintosh had looked aghast at his ideas and thundered that if he didn't desist in his ideas he would be removed from the family business. At least David had shown a good grace in not mentioning the ideas outside the office walls, Granville reflected with a sense of relief.

He gazed around the office. The only adornments were a few sepia-like framed depictions of ships at anchor or moored to the city's wharves. Images captured by David on film and displayed with loving pride by him as frozen moments in time.

He smiled, leant back in the chair and clasped his hands behind his head as he considered his position in the Macintosh empire. He was to all intents and purposes the real power behind the future of the company. Of course Lady Enid, his aunt, was a minor obstacle in his future ambitions. He discounted Sir Donald as of little consequence because he was solely obsessed with turning Glen View into an Antipodean Eden. But Enid would not last forever and all he had to do was bide his time before he had total control through Fiona.

He had requested the shift to David's office as soon as he had been informed of his cousin's untimely death. His aunt had been so distressed by the news of her beloved son's death that she had not objected to his request and the symbolic act of occupying David's old office was seemingly overlooked by her.

Granville was acutely aware of her intense dislike for him but with no male heirs to inherit the family enterprises that left only Fiona to produce a male heir and he was certain he could do that, given time and his wife's compliance. Ahh . . . but some duties were not as irksome as dealing with bank managers and creditors.

To that extent he relished the idea of returning home that evening and inseminating his still beautiful and desirable wife. But first he would have to attend to the puzzling invitations that lay on his desk.

He unclasped his hands and leant forward to peruse the two delicately penned invitations on their respectively embossed letterheads. The first was from Lady Enid to call on her at 3 p.m. that day and the second was a note written in the bold hand of his sister, Penelope, to call on her at 7 p.m.

He frowned. He had not received any invitations from Aunt Enid since the dinner she had held supposedly for Penelope's farewell before Christmas. His sister was due to sail in two weeks and he supposed the invitation to call on her was merely a meeting to discuss any matters concerning her financial affairs.

He shook his head and sighed contentedly. The matters were of little importance in the overall scheme of things. After all, everything was going so well to plan and, when he reflected on the previous few years, he considered most of everything he'd plotted had turned out well in the end.

Before he called on his aunt, he would stop over at the Australia Club and take a port with Sir George Hartwell. Within the confines of the exclusive men's club, they could discuss the purchase of a block of tenement houses at Glebe. Sir George needed cash fast for his gambling debts and Granville could satisfy his need. Sir George had expressed his gratitude to him on a previous occasion when Granville had mentioned a generous sum he was prepared to offer for the block.

Granville's coach delivered him to the club, where he was greeted by the doorman, an old Waterloo veteran, who ushered him inside the tactfully plush bastion of colonial gentlemen. A polite murmur of male voices pervaded the club as did the pungent aroma of cigars and oiled leather. Here was a place where politics and financial power mixed as easily as the scotch and water served to the well-heeled moguls of the Australian colonies. The club was patronised by its exclusive clientele of wealthy squatters visiting from their properties, merchant bankers from their establishments and men like Granville whose controlling connections with the well-respected Macintosh companies assured him a place in the company of the colony's version of the aristocracy.

Granville glanced around the luxurious smoking room and saw Sir George sitting alone in one of the big leather chairs reading a newspaper while puffing contentedly on a fat cigar and toying with a tumbler of scotch. He looked up as Granville walked across the room towards him and put down his paper.

'Mister White, I see you are as punctual as ever,' he said without much of a welcoming smile. 'Have a seat, old chap.'

Granville plumped himself down in a dark leather chair opposite the knighted colonial, who was a man in his late forties and whose dissipated face reflected the story of his misspent life. Small streaks of alcohol-burst veins lined his nose and his hands trembled as he held the cigar in one hand and the tumbler of scotch in the other. At their first meeting, Sir George had expressed his surprise that Granville would want to purchase a property that teemed with nothing more than the riffraff of society: working-class people with large broods of brats and little money to pay rents.

'I would assume that your visit here is to confirm your desire to go ahead with the purchase,' Sir George said as he puffed on his cigar and lounged in his chair. 'But I am rather curious as to why you should still want to purchase a property that is not returning any rental profit of note.'

Granville's reply that his purchase was based on humanitarian grounds did not fool Sir George. His eyes narrowed and he stared at the younger man sitting opposite him, who toyed with a small goblet of port wine. The club stewards made a point of knowing what the members imbibed and they were alert to satisfy that need promptly upon a member's arrival.

'You are jeopardising the Macintosh name, old chap,' Sir George said quietly between puffs of his expensive cigar.

'I am sure you have the wrong idea, Sir George,' Granville responded in all innocence. 'My intentions are honourable.'

Sir George smiled contemptuously at the reply, as he suspected that the young lion of the Macintosh companies had more carnal aims in mind for the redevelopment of the tenements.

'I have heard a whisper that Lady Macintosh does not particularly like you,' Sir George said as he twirled the scotch in his glass before taking a sip from it. 'Should she learn of your . . . ah . . . business enterprise at Glebe I'm sure she would disinherit you from the companies.'

Granville fixed him with a smile. 'I am sure I do not know what you are talking about, Sir George,' he said in a way that indicated that the topic of conversation should wisely be dropped and, as Sir George did not want to jeopardise his opportunity to receive the cash deposit that would not appear in the purchase documents, he let the matter go. It was an under-the-table agreement which satisfied both parties.

For Granville, the purchase of the rundown

block of tiny tenements gave him an opportunity to exploit the lucrative vice of prostitution. Where there was poverty, women provided their bodies for the rent money and food for their children.

But it was not the mothers Granville was interested in so much as their prepubescent daughters. The fad for men to obtain their tiny bodies was all the rage in Victorian England and so-called virgins fetched good prices as a supposed cure for syphilis. The tenements promised fertile ground for Granville's recruiting campaign overseen by underworld thugs recruited from The Rocks. He would provide women for his brothels but it would be the financial return on the prepubescent girls which would swell his personal coffers through a maze of untraceable financial transactions. He had long plotted how certain monies could be skimmed from the Macintosh companies to be used in even more lucrative enterprises and the thought of having personal access to the young girls stirred him. He would remember young Jennifer's childish body when he went home to service his wife tonight and the exquisite thought caused him to squirm as his dark lust rose.

But first he had business to attend to, and with the discreet handing over of a thick envelope stuffed with paper currency of the colony to Sir George, he had ensured the first step in his depraved desire to sate his lust.

Sir George did not bother to examine the contents of the package. It was not the done thing to question a gentleman's honesty and he'd slipped the envelope inside his coat pocket without a word.

The transaction at the club had gone smoothly and Sir George had insisted on sealing their bargain with an excellent chilled French champagne, and so it was that Granville arrived in his carriage at his aunt's splendid residence overlooking the harbour feeling particularly mellow.

As Granville stood at the front door waiting to be invited inside, he had an idle thought that, in time, the magnificent house would most probably be his residence. Not that the house his in-laws had given his wife as a wedding present was anything less than a magnificent residence. It was just that the Macintosh residence symbolised a certain place in colonial society. Its existence had been a focal point in social functions for the colonial aristocracy over the years.

Betsy opened the door and ushered him inside. She took his top hat and cane as a matter of protocol and escorted him to the drawing room where he gazed around at the paintings on the walls and mused that the European art was already accumulating a good monetary value. Enid had been wise in purchasing them. He was surprised to see an Australian painting by Captain Forrest on the wall among the European landscapes, but he remembered how his aunt had once commented on how much the landscape of a mountain in Hobart reminded her of a European setting.

Enid was not present, as he had known she would not be. She had a habit of making people wait. She liked to remind her visitors that they were in her house, and she responded to her times, not theirs.

Enid entered the room and Granville turned

away from his perusal of the artwork to greet her with an icy smile. He was surprised to see how in control of her emotions she was, as he had expected her to be grief-stricken for the terrible loss of her favourite son. But the woman was the woman of old: cool and expressionless. She would have been an excellent gambler, he thought.

'Aunt Enid,' he said with just a slight and polite nod of his head. 'I am here as you requested in your kind invitation.'

She did not reply and for a moment Granville could feel the mellowness of the champagne evaporating, to be replaced by the unpleasant taste one gets after too much cheap port wine.

She sat herself gracefully on an elegant French-designed drawing room chair with ornately carved legs and placed her hands in her lap. Granville felt the power of her silence and retreated to a similar chair in the corner of the room as if to put a distance between himself and the forbidding woman.

'Are Fiona and my grand-daughters well?' she asked coldly and Granville immediately knew that their meeting would somehow ruin his day.

'You should see them more often, Aunt Enid,' he replied solicitously. 'They are, after all, your grandchildren.'

Enid's lips pursed as if she were considering something distasteful in his remark. 'And they have *your* blood,' she replied quietly. 'Although I suppose I cannot blame them for that.'

Granville blanched at her overt slur on his two daughters. 'Why did you ask me here?' he snapped as a way of showing her that he had no time for her insults.

'I wanted you to come here so that I could personally tell you that I know you were instrumental in David's death,' she replied calmly and Granville felt the blood drain from his face as she continued: 'And that I will not rest until you have paid the full price for his death.'

'Is that all?' he responded equally calmly, although he did not feel it. How could she know? he wondered. Mort was not likely to talk and even the police agreed that David was murdered by the savages.

He rose from the chair to indicate that the conversation was at an end. 'I will see my own way out,' he added but Enid had not finished with him.

'You well know I cannot prove your conspiracy in my son's brutal murder. But that does not matter because I will have my revenge and you will suffer as I have suffered.'

'Revenge, dear Aunt Enid?' Granville smiled smugly and challenged, 'And how will you have your revenge on an innocent man? What can you do to me, the husband of your daughter and the father of your grand-daughters? Would you have your revenge on a grandson when Fiona bears me a son? Oh no, dear Aunt, your obsession with the Macintosh name and its bloodline would never allow you to seek revenge against the father of your grandson. You might consider the idea of revenge while I only have daughters. But not if I am the father of your grandson.'

Enid listened impassively to his carefully delivered rebuke.

'My grandson will be my strong right arm to smite you down,' she said in a quiet and controlled voice. 'Just as the Lord smites the enemies of His people. Oh, and you can believe every word I say, when I tell you that it will be my grandson who will eventually destroy you and all you hold dear, if that is possible for a man as evil as you.'

Granville stood mesmerised by the burning green flame of the emerald eyes fixed on him and he had a terrible feeling that he was in the presence of some Old Testament prophet or a medieval witch casting a terrible curse on him. He shuddered and had a great need to be out of her presence.

Without a word he turned and hurried from the room, with her strange prediction echoing in his head. *My grandson will be my strong right arm to smite you down.* Logic told him that her statement was nothing more than the delusional ramblings of a grief-stricken woman. How could her grandson be used against him when Fiona had not borne him a son as yet?

Duffy!

The name came to him like some terrible ghost rising from the floor in front of him. A ghost of a tall and broad-shouldered young Irishman with thick dark curling hair and steel-grey eyes. And the ghost smiled, mocking his fear. But the bastard son of Fiona and Michael Duffy had been sent to a baby farm. He could not surely be alive. The woman was truly mad. And, as he reassured himself, the smile on the ghost's face faded to an agonised grimace of despair. Now it was Granville's turn to smile grimly at his own unfounded fears.

'Your hat and cane, Mister White?' Betsy asked with a curious expression on her pretty face. His brief moment of distress had obviously been noted by her when he had stumbled into the hallway to escape the witch in the drawing room.

'Yes, Betsy, you can fetch them,' he replied calmly as he regained control of himself. 'And you can inform my coachman to bring the carriage to the front door. I will wait outside.'

Granville had his coachman take him back to the club, where he drank alone and pondered his meeting with his aunt. No matter how much he attempted to persuade himself that the irrational fears she had conjured at the meeting had no substance, the drink did not drown them. Enid never made a threat without carrying it out, as he fully knew from past experience.

The Duffy bastard had to be dead if it was sent to a baby farm, he kept reassuring himself. And if he weren't, what hope did Enid ever have of finding him anyway? Around 6 p.m. the dinner gong was struck for the residents, reminding Granville that he had an obligation to call on his sister at her house.

He hefted himself unsteadily from the big leather chair and weaved towards the main entrance, where he was met by the doorman who greeted him politely and went to fetch his carriage driver waiting outside.

When the carriage arrived at Penelope's house, the driver gently prodded his employer awake. Irritably, Granville shook the sleep from his head and staggered to the front entrance. When he glanced at the well-kept hedges, he had a fleeting memory of his old gardener, Harris.

The door was opened by a maid Granville did not know. She was around sixteen years of age and rather pretty in a coarse sort of way. Probably a bit like the girls in his soon-to-be-acquired tenements at Glebe, he thought without a great deal of interest.

'You mus' be Mister White,' the girl said impertinently. 'Your sister said youse was to go straight up to her bedroom when youse got here.'

'Did you say her bedroom?' he mumbled as she held the door open for him to enter.

'That's what she said, Mister White,' she replied with a shrug of her shoulders. 'You is to go straight to her bedroom where she is expectin' youse.'

The invitation to his sister's bedroom was highly unusual, considering the old threat to kill him if he ever dared enter that sacred domain again.

Granville pushed past her and steadied himself as he climbed the stairs. The copious quantity of alcohol he had imbibed at the club had made his legs feel like gelatine, so he squared his shoulders and took a deep breath before preparing to enter the room.

He raised his hand to knock when he heard the sounds. He knew them well. They were the sounds of a woman in the throes of sexual ecstasy and he smiled to himself. In his alcohol-befuddled mind, he guessed that his sister had some perverse need for him to witness her in the act of enjoying the carnal embraces of another man and his hopes soared. Was it that she had missed his attentions when they had been young and now wanted him to join in her lust? He did not knock but eased the bedroom door open to step inside.

616

It took some moments for his eyes to adjust to the flickering light of the many candles placed around the room. Golden soft shadows danced around the two naked bodies writhing on the white silk sheets in an embrace that made them oblivious to everything except their mutual ecstasy.

Granville blinked, adjusting to the candlelight. He gaped at the two sets of well-rounded buttocks and he was confused as he tried to reconcile what he was seeing. He watched as his naked sister pulled herself up to prop herself against the brass bedhead, where she gripped the corner-posts. Her eyes were closed to near slits and the flickering candlelight caught her expression of sensual rapture with a golden glow while her ecstasy flowed like fire through the room to burn an absolute dawning comprehension in Granville's horror-stricken mind.

His sister's sexual partner slid down the sheets where her long raven hair flowed over Penelope's legs spread lasciviously to receive her partner's attentions.

Slowly Penelope's eyes opened and turned to stare into his. The normally beautiful blue eyes were black and limpid pools of an evil akin to his own dark soul and were aware of his presence as they taunted him with the reality of the present.

Penelope arched her back and her hands came down to entwine her fingers in the long raven hair between her legs, forcing the head deeper into her as if that part of her body could swallow the beautiful creature giving her so much sensual pleasure. She moaned her pleasure and her legs slowly folded over Fiona to hold her in the embrace as if forever.

Granville felt the nausea rising in his throat and fought the urge to vomit up the afternoon's alcohol and bitterness. He was barely aware that the name of his wife came to his lips as a strangled hiss as he backed away from the door.

He stumbled from the room and down the stairs to buckle and vomit his despair on the floor of the landing. And as he vomited, he realised that his sister had carefully planned for him to witness her power over him.

She had plotted a revenge so subtle that only a woman could have understood the implications it had to his self-esteem as a man. She had taken her cousin, his wife, from him with the very sexual forces he had so long ago brutally unleashed in his sister.

He now knew why his wife had made excuses to move to another room away from him. She had, in fact, moved to his sister's bed.

For Granville White, the subtle strength of women would never again be dismissed as something of no consequence. Now the two people who most frightened him were both women: one Lady Enid Macintosh and the other his own sister.

Fiona had not been aware of her husband's brief presence in the bedroom as her whole existence had narrowed to the erotic pleasure that Penelope's body, with its soft curves and smooth flesh, provided for her.

So absorbed was she in drinking the sweetness of her cousin's body that she was unaware of the tension that came as a momentary wave to flow through Penelope's ecstatic pleasure. All that she was aware of was that that same forbidden pleasure was also her own. And she knew with each time they made love that she would always be a slave to the unimagined joys she had learnt in the arms of her beautiful cousin.

When they were both spent, Penelope held Fiona in her arms and they lay together in a deep and mutual embrace, caressing each other with lingering words of love.

Later in her own bed, Fiona could not be sure whether she had dreamed her cousin's words, or if they were real. But it did not matter, as they were words she would always treasure when she had heard them drift to her on the golden glow of the flickering candles. 'Granville will never hurt you again, my love. You and I will always be together, no matter who else is in our lives. I promise you that for always.'

When Fiona returned to her home she was confronted by her uncharacteristically distraught husband.

'Have you no shame?' he wailed as his wife stood defiantly in her bedroom. He stared at Fiona's huge bed. 'Have you ...?' he could not bring himself to ask and she laughed bitterly before replying, 'That is no longer any business of yours.' So he knew, she thought. How he knew, she did not care. 'What is between Penelope and me is very special.'

'It is unnatural. An abomination in the eyes of God,' he exploded, gathering the bombastic remnants of his old self, and Fiona's face flushed with rage.

But when she spoke it was in a clearly controlled voice. 'Is making a twelve-year-old girl pregnant,' she said, 'then discarding her as if she were nothing but rubbish, less an abomination? Is your plan to buy the Glebe tenements from Sir George to be used for prostitution not an abomination?' Fiona noticed the stricken expression on her husband's face as she revealed all that Penelope had told her of his activities. 'You need not ask me how I know all these things, and more, because it is not important. What is important for you to know is that I will live with you in this house. But you and I will never share the same bed again. We will be, as far as everyone is concerned, including my mother, a married couple. Oh, I will be a good wife for you, and a good mother to our daughters, but that is all. From now on, we live separate lives and I don't have to warn you that any attempt to break those conditions will cause me to inform the relevant people of your secrets. Of how you are embezzling the family business to finance criminal activities. And of your peculiar desire for young girls. And your possible links to an unsavoury character by the name of Jack Horton. Yes, I know how you hired Mister Horton to kill Michael Duffy.'

Granville stared at the beautiful young woman who had once been so compliant to his every whim and desire. His self-esteem had taken a terrible mauling and this confrontation was the death blow to his power over her. He realised for the first time just how much his wife had inherited of her mother's characteristics. She was strong like her mother and she had displayed a form of ruthlessness like her mother. It seemed only one person had power over Fiona and that was his hated sister. In the world of the Macintosh and White families, Penelope had emerged as an adversary to be reckoned with.

As he stared at his wife, he felt a surge of desire for her. But it was a desire for something he knew he could never have again and, without comment, he turned on his heel and walked away.

Fiona stood defiantly in the centre of the room watching him leave. When he slammed the door and she could hear his footsteps in the hallway, the uncontrollable trembling came to her. She broke down in tears and cursed herself for her weakness. It was then that she was suddenly aware of how much like her mother she really was. And in recognising how much she resembled her mother, she felt a terrible and despairing loss for the grief that the rift between them had caused.

Of all the people she most wanted to be close to now, it was that stern and ever-present entity in her life. 'Mother,' she whispered through her tears. 'Oh, Mother.' But her mother had taught her well. And one thing that she had been taught was pride. It was that very characteristic, she knew, that would forever keep them apart as bitter enemies.

43

The hammering on his hotel room door snapped Luke from his sleep.

He rolled from the bed and was immediately on his feet, blinking away the last shreds of his stupor like a battered fighter in the corner of a boxing ring.

'Luke, are you in there? It's Solomon.'

He heard the voice call to him through the door. 'Wait a moment, Sol,' he answered groggily as he slipped on his trousers. Downstairs in the hotel, he could hear the rowdy sounds of men in the bar swilling down last drinks before closing time. He crossed the dark and sweltering room, opened the door warily and saw his friend standing in the dimly lit hallway.

'You have to get out of Rockhampton, Luke,' Solomon said as he pushed past him. 'The traps are after you.'

'Goddamn!' Luke swore. 'What in the hell for, Sol? Why do they want me?'

Solomon went across to the window and peered out cautiously as if expecting to find a lurking police officer on the other side.

'They seem to know about you making an exchange of gold for money,' he said, turning away from the window, 'and they suspect me as well.'

'Goddamn Darlington!' Luke snarled. 'The bastard must have gone to the traps after I saw him this afternoon.'

'Mister Darlington . . . Kate's solicitor . . . You went to see him . . . Why?' Solomon queried as he could not think of any good reason for Luke to see Kate's solicitor.

'It doesn't matter, Sol. What matters right now is that my going to see him might put you and Judith in a bad position if I stay around,' Luke said as he quickly recovered his clothes and few personal possessions in the near darkness of the hotel room. 'Tell me what happened. Have the traps spoken to you yet?'

Solomon placed himself by the door, which he held ajar to watch for anyone who might approach down the hallway.

'A Constable Richards came down to the store and asked to talk to me,' Solomon said. 'He didn't beat around the bush. He said that he had information that you and I had been involved in an unlawful gold transaction. He said that he wanted to know where you were staying and I naturally said I didn't know. He got angry and started making threats, in front of Judith and Deborah, that he would lock me up when he caught you.'

Luke knew Solomon was very worried and he knew the little man's fear was not for himself. He gripped his friend's shoulder to reassure him.

'The traps aren't about to catch me, Sol,' he said as he thrust his Colt into the belt of his trousers.

'So he won't be able to carry out his threat, I will be out of here before you reach the front door.'

'I'm not frightened for myself,' Solomon replied. 'But I'm frightened for Judith and Deborah. Oi. This Constable Richards is a bad type. I hear he is not a straight policeman.'

'My horse is at the back of the hotel,' Luke said as he hoisted his saddle onto his shoulder along with his bed-roll and rifle. 'It won't take me long to hit the track south. By morning, I should be thirty miles from here.'

'Where are you going? New South Wales?' Solomon asked.

Luke shook his head and replied thoughtfully, 'I think it is time I went home to see the sequoias, old partner. And it is better you know nothing else.' He hesitated and Solomon could sense that his friend was struggling to say something important. Finally he continued, 'Could you tell Katie I will be back again some day. Tell her I love her.'

'I will. God go with you, Luke,' Solomon said as he grasped Luke's callused hand in both of his and then grabbed Luke in a short bearhug, patting him on the back. 'Be careful, my friend.'

Luke slipped through the bedroom window and onto the verandah. He suspected that Solomon might have been followed by the police, who could be waiting in the hotel for him to come down.

Making his way cautiously, he came to the end of the hotel where there was a dark alley beside the building. Luke slung his saddle into the alley beside the hotel before climbing down a verandah post.

He had guessed that the police would expect

him to come out the back way after Solomon had made his visit to warn him. A couple of drunken patrons leaving the hotel saw the American slide down to the street.

'Can't pay the bill, matey?' one of them said with a laugh.

'Something like that,' Luke grinned back as he picked up his saddle and strolled as casually as possible down the laneway between the hotel and a butcher's shop. The smell of sweltering meat was strong in his nostrils as he left the laneway and entered the backyard of the hotel, treading warily in the shadows cast by the building.

He was extremely aware that he was most vulnerable now if the traps had followed Solomon and he half expected to hear the police command him to 'Stand in the Queen's name!' But no challenge came.

In the stables, he steadied his mare and threw the cloth over her back as she stood patiently waiting to be saddled. Poor work by the traps, Luke thought. They only had to follow Solomon to find me.

But Luke was wrong.

Constable Richards crouched in the shadows at the rear of the hotel where he was concealed by a dray and he observed the American saddle his horse. He smiled grimly to himself and was satisfied that the man he was watching was unaware of his presence.

Richards raised his revolver to take an aim on the American fugitive as Luke led his horse across the yard. But the policeman was frustrated by the lack of light as he followed the vague shapes of man and horse down the sights of his pistol until Luke stepped momentarily into a pool of light cast from a hotel window above the yard. The policeman had a clear shot and he knew that he could not miss, so close was the American to him.

Slowly Richards lowered his pistol.

Luke swung himself into the saddle and carefully picked his way into the alley beside the hotel. The constable smiled as the bushman rode cautiously out of the yard. Probably heading for Brisbane, he ventured as a guess. Or maybe even further south. It didn't matter where he was going, so long as it was a long way from Rockhampton.

Constable Richards had earned his money. A large amount for such a simple job, he thought. Darlington must have a lot at stake to pay fifty quid. All he had to do now was report back to the solicitor and tell him that the American had left town.

By sunrise, Luke was twenty-five miles closer to California. And as he rode with the rising sun at his elbow he carried the memory of a single kiss and a love that could never be.

By the time he had reached the Brisbane River days later, Hugh Darlington had presented Kate with one thousand pounds to invest in her company. The young woman was overwhelmed by his magnanimous generosity and he made a point that he did not expect Kate to repay him until she was ready. He also added that no interest was required on the capital, as the money was a token of his love for her.

Solomon felt very uneasy lying to Kate and the

young woman's expression seemed to melt away, exposing the pain of confusion and despair for the feelings she could never reveal to the world, let alone herself, for the American. 'He loves you very much, Kate,' Solomon mumbled as he shifted uneasily in the cool shadows of his store.

Kate turned and stared at the rectangular patch of burning bright light that marked the doorway to the building. There were words that could be said but Kate bit back on her lip. It was obvious Solomon knew more than he was prepared to say about the mysterious and sudden disappearance of Luke. But to press him would only cause her friend more pain in divided loyalties.

Without a further word, she walked towards the rectangular patch of light and out onto the street. The American was gone from her life for good and it was probably meant to be. Men like Luke Tracy were not to be confined by the definitions of streets and houses. They were men born with a wild spirit that took them to the desolate places others called hell.

She fought back the tears as she walked towards her office. No, he was gone. And she had a business to run. There was a visit to Townsville scheduled and an inspection of the estates old Harry had left her in his will.

She lifted her chin and her steps took on a purpose as she continued to walk along the dusty street of the frontier town. Besides, she told herself, Luke was just a very good friend whom she held in particular esteem . . . nothing more. The thought echoed with an unconvincing ring in her heart.

Luke stood on the wharf gazing at the flotilla of small coastal steamers and sailing ships anchored in the channel of the muddy tidal river.

The remaining money from the gold transaction had purchased him a ticket for a sea voyage to San Francisco and he was going home to walk once again among the majestic sequoia trees and smell the heavy scent of pine. But he knew part of him would remember the pungent antiseptic scent of eucalyptus and be lost forever on the vast brigalow plains beyond Queensland's frontier.

A coastal steamer with big paddlewheels, slime-streaked sides and a tall funnel blowing plumes of black smoke edged towards the wooden wharf. Luke watched the ship arriving from Sydney with little interest, as his thoughts were lonely in a way that made his world seem small. The one thing worth fighting and dying for in his life he would never have.

He sighed and watched the gangplanks rattle down the sides of the ship when it docked. And he watched, without seeing, the passengers disembark with their meagre luggage gripped tightly in their hands. Around him people waiting for friends and relatives surged forward to hug, cry, babble and laugh as they met their loved ones.

The American stood back and hefted his bed-roll and saddle onto his shoulders. The ship would soon be cleared for the round trip to Sydney when it had taken aboard coal for the boilers and rations for the passengers. As Luke had nowhere to stay in Brisbane, he decided to board the ship early.

When it appeared the last of the passengers had

disembarked, he pulled his ticket from his trouser pocket and strode towards the gangplank. An old man, in company with a young and pretty girl nursing a baby, stood looking pathetically lost at the foot of the gangway.

Luke took little notice of them until he was close enough for the man to say, 'Excuse me, sir, but do you know of any good lodgin's in Brisbane Town?'

Luke broke his stride and dropped the saddle and bedroll at his feet. A sudden whiff of lavender caught his attention and he realised that the young girl with the large strawberry birthmark on one side of her face must be wearing the perfumed water.

'I'm sorry, pardner,' he replied politely and his attention went to the young girl nursing the baby. She must be about twelve, he thought idly, and he guessed that the baby was her younger brother or sister as it lay asleep in a soiled swaddling cloth. 'I don't come from around these parts.' Luke also noticed the signs of advanced consumption in the man. Its debilitating effects had aged him beyond his years.

'Thank you anyway, sir,' the man replied with a weak smile for the tall American's courteous reply. 'I suppose someone will know a place for me an' my daughter that don't cost too much.'

For some strange and inexplicable reason, Luke suddenly felt a surge of pity for the pathetic trio. He sensed that some terrible tragedy had caused them to uproot and travel north. Was it that he remembered his own young wife and daughter who had so tragically died in Brisbane of the fever many years earlier? Or was it that the scent of lavender water reminded him of Kate and her tragic trip to the colony of Queensland? For whatever reason, he found himself impulsively reaching into his pocket to retrieve the last of his pound notes, which he thrust towards the old man.

'This will get you a decent place to stay until you get things sorted out,' he said gruffly. 'Call it a loan until I see you again.'

The man stared at the crumpled pound note in amazement. Then he glanced up into the eyes of the tall stranger, who he guessed was a Yank from his accent.

'I doan know what to say, sir,' he choked. 'I never know'd such generosity in all me life.' Although Harris carried the money Granville White had given him for his silence, he was shrewd enough to know it would not go far in supporting his daughter and grandson. The one pound given to him by the Yank was a lot of money.

'Nothin' to say,' Luke replied. 'Just make sure you get a good place for your young 'uns for a while.'

The man took the proffered pound note and tears came to his rheumy eyes. 'Me name's Harris, sir . . . an' this is me daughter, Jennifer. An' this 'ere is her young 'un Willy,' he said, offering his hand. 'Mebbe one day I can do a good turn fer you.'

Luke nodded, but he doubted that he would ever see the trio again and excused himself so that he would not have to suffer a profusion of gratitude from the man with consumption. He hefted the saddle and bed-roll onto his shoulder and brushed past them to board the coastal steamer for Sydney.

44

The shimmering heat distorted Tom Duffy's vision as he propped his rifle against the rough bark of a gnarled tree and set his sights on a scrawny steer. The steer stood oblivious to the fact that within a split second of hearing a sound like summer lightning, it would feel the deadly thud of a heavy lead bullet tear through its shoulder to rupture its big heart.

Tom took a deep breath and exhaled slowly. The blade sight settled in the V notch and squarely on the point of aim on the steer. The beast was about a hundred yards away and Tom silently cursed the oppressive heat haze rising off the plain for causing the glimmering shine on the metal foresight.

Fifty paces or so behind him, Wallarie stood in the sparse shade of the spindly brigalow trees holding the reins of their two horses. But as he waited patiently, he was acutely alert to the subtle nuances of the bush around him. They were at the southern extremity of the Gulf Country that bordered the territory of the fierce and dreaded Kalkadoon tribesmen, whose traditional lands lay just a little further south in the ancient and eroded mineral-rich hills near the tiny frontier outpost of Cloncurry. The huge warriors were an ever-present threat to white settlers and foreign Aboriginals like himself.

The stillness of the late afternoon exploded.

The steer buckled at the knees and slumped forward, collapsing in the red dust where it rolled on its side, kicking feebly as its ruptured heart pumped blood into the cavity of its broad chest.

Tom grinned behind his bushy black beard and hefted the smoking Snider rifle on his shoulder. 'Good tucker tonight, Wallarie,' he said as the Aboriginal bushranger led the horses forward.

'You bloody too slow to kill 'im cow,' he said with a cheeky grin on his bearded black face. 'Bloody cow grow too old to eat 'im now. Waitin' you to kill 'im.' The Irishman took a playful swipe at his friend with his free hand but Wallarie ducked and danced away, causing the two mounts he led to skitter nervously.

'Bloody ungrateful blackfella,' Tom chuckled as he turned to stride towards the steer now lying dead in the red dust. 'You couldn't have done any better.' Even as he made his statement, Tom knew that the Aboriginal, who had once been a renowned young hunter among his people, was probably a better shot with both rifle and pistol than he.

He had taught him well and the Aboriginal hunter's instincts had done the rest. Wallarie was highly intelligent and, without his knowledge of the bush, Tom fully appreciated that he would have been long dead from either a trooper's bullet or as a victim of an unforgiving land. In a sense the two men had taught each other their respective ways and that had made their unusual partnership a force to be reckoned with.

It had been the Aboriginal's keen tracking skills that had brought them to the steer and Tom's European rifle had ensured their prey would provide a pleasant change from kangaroo meat in the cooking fire.

For nearly five years they had lived off the land with occasional raids on isolated homesteads, ambushes on travellers and even the rare trip into a tiny frontier town to purchase the highly sought supplies of tea, sugar, tobacco and flour with the money taken in the raids and ambushes. Tom would go alone to the towns so as not to draw attention to himself by travelling with his Aboriginal companion.

And in those five years Tom Duffy had fathered three children to Mondo.

The birth of the children had taken his little group from three to six and the beef they were about to take would ensure his babies would not have distended bellies from hunger.

There had been times in the years past that he had found himself reflecting on what he had lost – a life as a European, his family and any certainty of a future. Life was now living from day to day with nature. His Garden of Eden was a strange place where his Eve was black and the devil tempted him with memories of his life before he had crossed the line. With a wry smile he thought about his Eden and wondered what he would choose if given the chance to once again inhabit the European world of his youth. His answer was in the present memory of his children and the woman who loved him. What he needed from his European world he took anyway by force of arms. He answered to no man. Unlike Adam he had not been exiled from Eden – he would always be a part of the red earth and silent spaces.

Tom slid the lethal Bowie knife from the side of his knee-length riding boot and knelt in the dust beside the dead steer. He wondered if he should thank the spirit of the steer that had strayed in the bush. The fleeting thought made him smile, but he did not have a chance to reflect any further on his Aboriginal-acquired spirituality.

'Get out of here, bloody quick,' Wallarie hissed as he flung himself into the saddle of his mount. Tom did not hesitate. He slid the knife back in the side of his boot and snatched the rifle lying beside him.

Astride his horse, he turned to Wallarie.

'Bloody horses comin' this way,' Wallarie growled as he flung his arm to the south. 'Many bloody horses comin' quick.'

Tom swung around in his saddle and glimpsed a thin pall of dust rising low over the scrub. He knew that Wallarie's exceptional hearing abilities had picked up the horses long before he saw the dust that their hooves raised. Troopers . . . stockmen . . . it did not matter. All men on the frontier were enemies to the bushrangers.

He spurred after Wallarie.

Overhead, billowing towers of thunderhead clouds massed as a herald to the coming of the monsoonal wet season. If the rain came it would give them a temporary respite from their pursuers as it turned creeks into rivers and rivers into raging seas to cover the plains.

Five horsemen reined to a halt beside the carcass of the dead steer.

'Bastards!' One of the men swore as he swung himself from the saddle and examined the bullet wound that had attracted a cloud of flies. 'White man did this. Too good a shot for a blackfella.'

The attention of the one black horseman was not on the dead beast but the hoof marks a short distance away. He squinted and frowned as his eyes fell on the footprints near the dead steer.

As a station stockman and sometime tracker, his keen eyes were already providing his mind with a clear picture of who had been the killers of the stray animal. 'One blackfella, boss,' he said softly from astride his horse, and the man standing over the carcass looked up at him.

'What?'

'One blackfella, one whitefella ride 'im away quick time. Ride 'im away that way.' The Aboriginal stockman pointed to the south-east and the dismounted man grabbed the reins of his horse to swing himself back into the saddle. The three European stockmen looked to him for a decision as he sat staring towards the east.

'A blackfella and a whitefella riding together,' he mused. 'Must be that bloody Irish bushwhacker Duffy and his myall mate.'

'We go after them, Charlie?' one of the stockmen asked. 'Or we tell the traps in Burketown?' Charlie scratched at the stubble on his chin irritably as he pondered his decision. They had finally closed in on whoever had been butchering the station's strays. Some of the strays had been speared by hungry Aboriginal hunters roving the plains, but he had not expected to come so close to the infamous and reputedly very dangerous pair of bushrangers who were wanted the length and breadth of the colony. In the past, whenever they had found what was left of other dead cattle, the state of the stripped carcasses had left no trace of how they had died. Nor any tracks to indicate who had killed them. Now they knew why. But the knowledge did not cheer him. Even with his four armed companions, Charlie did not underestimate the wanted men. It was said that Tom Duffy had already killed three men without the slightest sign of mercy.

Charlie took off his broad-brimmed hat and stared up at the gathering storm clouds billowing over the parched plains. 'Where would you go when the wet time came?' he asked the Aboriginal stockman as he continued to gaze at the purple-hued sky streaked with flashes of lightning.

'Go big rock ground, boss,' he replied without hesitation. 'Plenty good place when wet come.'

'That's what I thought,' Charlie said as he pulled his hat low over his eyes and pulled down on the reins. 'We go north to Burketown. Let the Native Mounted go after them. That's what they get paid for.'

Tom and Wallarie rode hard until they could feel their mounts tiring under them. Then they slowed to a canter and finally brought the horses to a walk.

Wallarie signalled a stop as he slid from the saddle and walked a short distance from his horse, which stood sweating and exhausted with its head down. Tom did not have to ask Wallarie what he was doing. He knew he was scanning the horizon for a sign that only his acute eyesight would see. He stood very still and Tom knew he was also listening.

Overhead a deep rumble rolled in the sky and heavy, fat raindrops spattered the dusty earth like a hail of lazy bullets. Wallarie turned and walked back to his horse, which had lifted its head and snorted with equine pleasure for the wonderful rich and fecund scent of newly wet earth.

'Not following us,' he said with a grunt and swung into the saddle. 'They go that way,' he added and pointed to the north.

'It doesn't matter now anyway, you black bastard,' Tom whooped. 'The wet might be late this year, but it's sure as Hades going to stop anyone ever tracking us. Let's go home.'

Wallarie glanced to the north as Tom kicked his mount forward. The riders appeared to have gone north, but this did not make him easier in spirit. It was most likely that the party had an Aboriginal tracker with them and he would have seen their tracks near the dead steer. Wallarie had a bad feeling.

He shook his head when he glanced across at Tom, who was grinning from ear to ear as they rode east. Maybe Tom was right about the rain causing any pursuit of them to be abandoned for some time.

The late afternoon was turning to a premature

early evening as the rain settled into a steady downpour drenching man and beast to the bone. The horses slowed to a miserable plodding pace but Tom felt his spirits rise as the rocky outcrop of low hills came into sight. They had reached the place of the big rocks – and the place of their sanctuary – where Mondo and his three children waited for him with stoic patience.

45

Emma James knew the sounds well: the shouts of men bawling orders, the jangle of saddlery metal and the whinny of horses, who seemed to know when they were going on patrol. The sounds drifted to her small cottage a short distance from the Mounted Police barracks at Burketown.

She went to the back door of her timber-and-iron-clad home and gazed across the rain-soaked paddock where she watched her husband approaching with his distinctive limping stride. Even at a distance, she could see the grim expression set on his face.

She turned away to go to the latticed food chest to take out a loaf of bread, a jar of melon jam and a tin of tea leaves. She would prepare her husband a thick-sliced jam sandwich and a mug of tea. It was a simple tradition that had evolved in the years of their marriage whenever he had to leave on one of the patrols into the vast and lonely bush of the colony. Sometimes he would be gone for a few days. At other times, weeks and even months. But such was the life of a mounted policeman on the frontier and the life of the women they left behind to raise families.

Long lonely days and nights living in one of the most isolated places on earth, it was a far cry for the young woman who had spent most of her life in the crowded and noisy tenements of an English industrial city. In England, human-created sounds were taken for granted. On the frontier the sounds were primitive: the screech of a hawk in the azure sky, the lazy murmur of the Mounted Police laughing and talking in the single men's barracks at the back of the police station, and the comforting babble of her son, Gordon, toddling around the house or playing contentedly in the yard in the ever-present red dust of the Gulf Country.

And regularly each year, the rain came to roar a pounding tattoo on the iron roof, deafening all other sounds from existence as it had all night when she had lain beside her husband in their big double bed, listening to the rain while holding each other. She loved her big burly bear of a man with an almost childish awe for his strong spirit as much as his hard body. He was to her the epitome of masculinity: tough but gentle, courageous yet sensitive to her feelings and needs. In his arms she felt protected and desired.

The privations of living in the isolated outpost of Burketown mattered little. When they were together, the bed became their universe – as the great Elizabethan poet, John Donne, had once written. Had the bed been located in the finest of homes in the finest of cities, it would have made no difference to her. That it was located in a tiny timber cottage on the flat lands around Burketown, under an oppressive tropical sky, was irrelevant to her when she was in the arms of her husband. But now she was afraid that the one thing that made her life bearable on the frontier was going to be taken from her. Henry was going on patrol.

He scraped his boots on the back step and wiped the rain from his face with his hand while Emma poured boiling water from the soot-blackened kettle into a china teapot that had been a belated wedding gift from Kate O'Keefe. She glanced up at her husband's face and her intuitions were confirmed. Whatever he was about to do was worrying him.

'What is it, Henry?' she asked as she sat at the table and rotated the teapot to stir the leaves with the hot water.

'We have been called to duty to go out after Tom Duffy,' he replied in a flat voice. 'Mister Uhr has intelligence from a party that got through from Lily Pond station. They think he is holed up with Wallarie in a place they call the Big Rocks.'

Emma ceased rotating the teapot and stared at her husband. 'Do you think they are right? Do you think that Tom is hiding out in the district?' she asked.

The big police sergeant slumped down onto a chair at the table and placed his hands on its rough wood surface. 'I think Tom has run out of places to hide,' he reflected miserably and Emma gently took his hands in hers.

'You do not want to go on this patrol, do you?' she asked softly and he shook his head with a miserable forlorn look.

'Mister Uhr is the best policeman in the colony,' Henry answered. 'I don't think Tom has much of a chance. When Mister Uhr goes after a man he does not give up, and I think Tom has finally met his match.'

'You don't want to be there . . . when Mister Uhr finds Tom,' Emma said, voicing her husband's troubled thoughts.

He glanced down at the table to avoid letting her see his fears and mumbled, 'It's not only Tom, but the blackfella, Wallarie.' He did not have to explain what he meant, as Emma had long known of her husband's guilt for the years he had hunted and dispersed the tribes of central-west Queensland. She suspected that her husband's guilt would be further deepened if he felt responsible for the death of the last warrior of the Nerambura clan. It was something very deep – almost a primitive superstition. She had grown to realise it existed in the soul of her gentle giant of a man, whose life had been scarred by war and the brutalities of policing the frontier.

'I cannot see why Mister Uhr would risk going out in this weather,' she said, squeezing his hands hopefully. 'Surely he would not risk being cut off by the floods when they come.'

Henry glanced up at his wife miserably. 'Mister Uhr knows that when the floods recede, Tom and Wallarie will move on. They have always kept on the move to avoid being trapped. He suspects that Tom thinks he will be safe for the very reason that the floods will provide him with a kind of barrier to our movement. But Mister Uhr is prepared to take the risk. The Big Rocks are only a few days' ride from here and we leave within the hour.'

He stared grimly at the teapot and his thoughts

drifted to that time when he lay helpless, staring up into the barrel of the rifle Wallarie had aimed at him. He remembered the dark eyes, devoid of pity, and how Tom had stopped the Nerambura bushranger from killing him. And he also remembered how Tom Duffy had risked his freedom by getting him back to the grog shanty for medical help. Tom Duffy was not only the brother of Kate O'Keefe, who had grown to be one of Emma's best friends, but he was also a man capable of great compassion. And now it seemed that Henry would repay the debt of gratitude for his life by being part of a mission to capture – or kill – him.

He knew his duty to the oath that he had sworn years earlier, to obey orders and uphold the law regardless of personal feeling. But this was very different. He instinctively knew that Tom Duffy would never allow himself to be captured and, if cornered, he would go down fighting. He would most probably take a few of the police with him to hell. Maybe even himself.

One way or the other, he knew that one of them was fated to die.

Emma released her hands from his and poured the tea into a big enamel mug to which she added a generous spoonful of sugar. 'I am surprised Mister Uhr does not leave you behind', she said, stirring the tea, 'to take charge of the station while he leads the patrol after Tom.'

'He realises that he needs every man available,' Henry replied as he wrapped his fingers through the handle of the mug. 'He does not underestimate Tom in any way. He has all intentions of taking him alive but ... if that is not possible ...' His voice trailed away and he sipped at the sweetened black tea.

Emma gazed at her husband's face. She could see the agony there and, for the first time, she realised that she might never again have his strong arms hold her in their bed or feel his bushy beard against her face. Nor would Gordon grow up in the protective shadow of his big gentle father. Frontier policing was dangerous at the best of times, but it was even more dangerous when the patrol was going out after two men like Tom and Wallarie.

She fought back the tears which she knew would come when he was gone and pushed her chair away from the table. 'I will make you a sandwich,' she said in a controlled and calm voice with her back to him. She did not want him to see her distress. 'You will need something to eat before you go.'

He nodded vacantly, as his thoughts were elsewhere. He was going over in his mind the supplies and kit he would need to ensure were taken on the patrol. Ammunition was at the top of his list and he hoped there was enough in the police storeroom for the confrontation. Despite his personal feelings concerning the mission, he was also concerned for the men he rode with. Their safety took priority over Tom Duffy's life. Even his own . . .

Emma stood in the red mud in the backyard of their cottage and watched the blue-uniformed police ride out of the barracks in single file with their bodies hunched against the drizzling rain. Little Gordon James stood holding her hand and sucking his thumb as she waved to the big man

644

who rode at the rear of the file. He turned and raised his hand. Henry flashed a smile which Emma felt rather than saw from the distance, and she did not care that the rain was soaking through the cotton dress clinging to her slim body.

She remained watching the patrol until it disappeared in a line of scrub trees on the horizon. Only then did she turn and walk slowly back to the cottage to sit at the table where her husband had been minutes earlier. He had not touched the jam sandwich she had made for him. It lay on the enamel plate forlornly, like part of him left behind. The sight of the uneaten sandwich triggered great racking sobs.

She bent her head and the emotions, which she had so carefully controlled for her husband, flowed as if without any hope. In her grief, she had a fleeting guilty thought that wrenched her with its utter selfishness. She hoped that when Henry and Tom met again, it would be Kate O'Keefe who would be crying her tears of grief. It was a terrible thought for the woman whom she considered almost as close as a sister.

Little Gordon James stared wide-eyed at his mother sobbing inconsolably at the kitchen table. Although the toddler did not know of such things as the existence of death, he did understand sorrow. And he knew there was nothing he could do for the woman in his life. Except share her sorrow.

Little Gordon James hugged his mother's legs and howled his distress. It was beyond his childish comprehension that the big and gentle male creature might not be a permanent fixture in his life.

46

After a short sea trip on a coastal steamer from
Rockhampton to Townsville and a round of meetings with stock and station agents, Kate was driven
by a jolly middle-aged agent to inspect Harry's
residence, now hers. As they drew close to the
house, she immediately fell in love with it.

It was a high-set rambling timber house with a
wide verandah. Tall eucalypts provided shade and
Harry had planted a grove of mango trees whose
thick and spreading foliage gave a coolness in the
tropical heat.

The journey to Townsville had been prompted
by a need to consolidate the estates old Harry
Hubner had left her in his will. She had forgotten
the oath she had sworn after learning of the old
teamster's generous gift to her. And to honour his
memory she wanted to bring his Townsville home
alive with her presence.

Kate alighted and strolled around the building,
examining its structure with the eye of a professional. The house had not fallen into disrepair.
The agent told her that Harry had lived the last
days of his life here. She smiled and promised the

old teamster's spirit that in his home she would one day provide the laughter of children and the voices of a happy family and friends.

Oh, there was work to be done to make the house the place she imagined for the future. But time and money would easily do that. And the money would be there as her transport business flourished under her astute business management. She may have come to the new colony to build a hotel, but her dreams went further even than that now. One day she would be the richest woman in the colony . . . nay . . . the richest woman in Australia! Her dreams might be grander than her means at the moment, but she had youth, capital and ambition on her side. She was a Duffy, she reminded herself. And the Duffys had overcome greater adversities than merely acquiring a fortune.

For a brief moment she felt a kind of uninvited bittersweet sadness intrude on her thoughts as if, somehow, the ghosts of her father and Old Billy were there with her. Curiously, she could not feel her beloved brother Michael's spirit. Was it that she would feel his presence under other circumstances? she wondered. Would he come to her in some time of need?

How could it be that she had so much good fortune when the men in her family had suffered so much? Michael dead in far-off New Zealand. Her father buried in central-west Queensland and her brother Tom living life where a bullet from a police trooper or a hangman's noose always shadowed his life.

The ghosts faded from her thoughts and she turned to the agent. 'I think we should inspect inside, Mister Cafe,' she said lightly and followed him up the broad wooden steps with their ornate timber supports. With a critical eye, she was already redesigning the house: a wall out there to give more room to the rather small dining room, a new polish to the teak floor, and paint to replace the peeling wallpaper which had suffered from the constant heat of Townsville.

'The house has six bedrooms, Missus O'Keefe,' the agent said as he stood in the room that was obviously designed as a place to dine. It appeared the old teamster had grandiose ideas for his retirement, but he had lacked a woman's fertile imagination for style. His functionalism tended to compartmentalise the house into practical areas.

'Big enough to start a family . . .' the agent bit his tongue as he remembered the tragic stories he had heard about the beautiful young woman, deserted by a worthless husband years earlier. Being a staunch Catholic himself, he realised that Missus O'Keefe probably considered herself still married, regardless of the long separation, and as such unable to remarry. Divorce was out of the question under the circumstances.

He coughed to hide his embarrassment and Kate realised that the kindly man was uncomfortable. She said, 'Enough room for friends and relatives to stay over when they visit me in Townsville, Mister Cafe.'

He nodded. He liked the young woman very much, which was not hard as she seemed to carry an aura of someone very special. An aura much older than her twenty-three years on earth.

On the trip back to town Kate babbled happily to

648

the stock and station agent of how she proposed to renovate the house. He listened with an eagerness that was infectious and he could easily understand how she impressed people in her business dealings. In a short time they reached his office, which was a pleasant stone building with wide verandahs.

It was noticeably cooler inside, where a heavy but clean scent of leather perfumed the air. A big clock on the wall made a lazy tick-tocking sound, matched by the noise of a scribbling pen wielded by a young gawky clerk sitting at a desk in the corner of the room. The clerk was fifteen years old and had aspirations to become a stock and station agent one day. He glanced up as his boss entered the office with Missus O'Keefe at his elbow. The clerk's eyes swivelled to indicate that a stranger was present in the room.

Mister Cafe followed the young man's glance and noticed a short but dapper man standing with his hands clasped behind his back. The stranger wore a dark three-piece suit and looked as fresh as if he were standing in cooler climes. Kate guessed he was in his mid-forties and she had the impression that the man was a foreigner to Australian shores. There was something alien about his whole demeanour.

'Ah, Fraulein O'Keefe, I presume,' the dapper little man said stiffly.

'I'm afraid I must correct you, sir. I am Missus O'Keefe.' Everyone in the room was stunned when Kate replied in excellent German. The stranger smiled warmly, extending his hand.

'Your grasp of my language is excellent, Missus O'Keefe,' he said as Kate met his light handshake. 'I did not realise you spoke German.'

She laughed lightly and replied in German, 'It is almost impossible not to learn German when one grows up with an "uncle" who could hardly speak English. But, I'm afraid, my first words in German as a little girl are hardly fitting to repeat now.'

The dapper little German who had appeared so stiff on first impression burst into laughter and his eyes twinkled.

'Was he your real uncle?' he asked with a chuckle.

'Uncle Max was a seaman from Hamburg who jumped ship in Melbourne', Kate replied, 'to try his luck on the goldfields back in '54 . . . And somehow, since then, he has been part of my family.'

'Ahh . . . yes,' the German said in a more serious tone. 'I believe you are Irish and, like your people, we are not exactly the best friends with the English.'

Kate glanced at the clerk and Mister Cafe who had followed the conversation, which had alternated between English and German, with a certain amount of awe. She was a most interesting young woman and the younger man was obviously smitten by her beautiful looks as he sat staring with unabashed admiration for her. Kate felt a touch of unease at the German's reference to international animosities. Australia was far from European intrigue, as if the continent were a planet unto itself, floating in a space of the Indian and Pacific oceans. The German detected her unease and tactfully changed the subject. He switched to his excellent English.

'I am afraid I have been very rude in not introducing myself to you all ... I am Herr Jurgen Rubenstein.' He held out his hand to Cafe, who replied with his own introduction and a hearty handshake. 'I have travelled a long way to find you, Missus O'Keefe,' the German said, turning to Kate. 'All the way from Sydney. We have much to talk about. But', he said looking at the stock and station agent, 'I must apologise to Mister Cafe that our conversation should be in private.'

Cafe rumbled his understanding and kindly offered them the privacy of his office. 'Come on, young Harry,' he said to his clerk. 'Let's go and see what's on for lunch down at the pub.'

Rubenstein thanked Cafe. When the men had left, he gestured to Kate to take a chair. She did so wondering who the mysterious German was. But she did not have to ask. He promptly explained who he was and why he had sought her out.

'I represent commercial interests in my country, who have sent me to prepare a report on the feasibility of establishing a meatworks here. My company gave me the name of a Mister Isaac Levi, who is a partner with a firm of solicitors, Levi & Sullivan ...'

Daniel! Kate suddenly thought. That was the firm her cousin Daniel worked for!

As if reading her thoughts, he smiled and said, 'I had the good fortune of meeting a close relative of yours while I was there. Daniel Duffy is an impressive young man, Missus O'Keefe.'

'You are Jewish,' Kate stated without the prejudice that might have been apparent in anyone else. 'That is why you contacted Mister Levi.'

He stared briefly into her eyes as if to detect a covert bigotry, but found none. 'That is correct, Missus O'Keefe. I am a Jew. There are many people like me in Germany who put our country before our ancient beliefs. God forbid . . . as the English would say. I dare say as you would put your country before your religion.'

Kate thought about that and realised the man was right. She would rather fight to retain land than religion. Were we not from the earth? And to the earth – one day – we would return, she thought.

'But matters of high intellectualism are not the reason why I have sought you out. My mission is to discuss with you the purchase of a cattle property in the Rockhampton district. I have spoken to a Mister Solomon Cohen. He told me that you have already discussed the idea of establishing a meatworks at Rockhampton, and you plan to supply it with beef from properties west of that town.'

Kate raised her eyebrows in surprise as she sat with her hands in her lap.

'I presume that Mister Levi recommended that you speak to Mister Cohen,' she said, to clarify the chain of contacts.

But he smiled at her presumption and replied, 'No . . . Mister Daniel Duffy did. It seems you and he have been in correspondence with each other.' Kate felt a little foolish at her words and she blushed lightly at her mistake. She had written many letters to her family and Daniel and she had carried on a lengthy correspondence concerning any means they could find to continue the fight against the Macintoshes.

Jurgen continued. 'He has told me that you have identified a property called Glen View which seems to be suffering cash-flow difficulties because of the current low price for beef. And it seems that Glen View may suit our needs admirably.'

'I would assume, Herr Rubenstein,' Kate said shrewdly, 'that you have a rather substantial means for backing my purchase.'

He nodded. 'We have, Frau O'Keefe,' he replied. 'But I am also led to believe that you are able to finance part of the purchase.'

'Why do you need me if . . . as I can only guess . . . you are in a position to purchase Glen View outright? Why approach me?'

He paused and she could see that he was most probably searching for a way to explain his position without telling her too much.

'We are a German company, *mein Frau*. As such, we have reasons not to publicise our financial interests in an English colony. I had hoped that you would be satisfied with that alone as an explanation.'

Kate was quick to anticipate his meaning.

'You wish my Eureka Company to be the purchasing agent while your company retains a silent share – albeit a majority – in the purchase?'

'That is correct,' he confirmed with a gentle hint of a sigh. 'I think you will agree . . . when we consider the . . . how do you say it . . . the sentimental value Glen View has to you and your family.'

Better to share the property with a foreign interest than not be able to have the property at all, Kate thought. After all, she would have access to those places that had become so significant in her life: the grave of her father, and the sacred place of the Nerambura people. The oath that she had sworn all those years earlier when she and Luke Tracy had confronted Donald Macintosh on his land was now within grasp of realisation. She was close to honouring her vow of taking the land he held so dear from him and placing it in Duffy hands . . . with the Germans.

'I think we can do it, Herr Rubenstein,' she said quietly and this time he appeared relaxed.

He smiled and helped her to her feet with his hand. 'Then all we need is a lawyer you consider can be discreet in such a matter to prepare the papers. And may I be so presumptuous as to invite you to share dinner with me at my hotel so that we can clarify any other matters that you may consider need attention . . . I should point out at this stage that the management of Glen View will be completely under your control. All we need is a financial interest in the property with exclusive terms to the beef for our meatworks. I am sure the arrangement will prove very profitable for us both. And now . . . can you recommend a lawyer?'

'Without hesitation I would recommend Mister Darlington from the Rockhampton firm of Darlington & Darlington,' Kate said confidently. 'They are a reputable firm with excellent credentials, Herr Rubenstein.'

'If you have absolute trust in them, then that is good enough for me,' he said as he escorted Kate to the door. 'So until tonight I shall bid you good afternoon, Frau O'Keefe.' And with a gallant Teutonic click of the heels, he left her at the front door of the stock and station office to stride across the dusty street.

Kate watched him walk away and wondered a little uneasily why the German should go to such secretive lengths to enter into a conspiracy with her. Conspiracy, she snorted. There was no conspiracy in wresting Glen View from the Macintoshes. Whatever the reasons the Germans had, they were no concern of hers. If it was something adverse to English interests, then all the better.

47

Four days later Kate O'Keefe sat in Hugh Darlington's Rockhampton office with her hands in her lap waiting for him to make a comment.

He made little humming noises which Kate found appealing. He flipped through the papers on his desk, finally closed the folder in front of him and looked up at her. 'Are you sure you are doing the right thing in this matter, Kate?' he asked and rubbed his forehead with his hand as if attempting to wipe away a troublesome thought.

'You know how much it means to me . . . to secure Glen View,' she said quietly. 'It probably means more than I can find words for.'

He stared for a brief moment into her serious grey eyes and felt the spell of her spirit cast its magic over him. How could he steer her away from the purchase of the Macintosh property? he thought miserably. How could he sabotage her efforts to wrest the land that both Macintosh and Duffy blood had fertilised years earlier? He was fully aware of the tragic events that had occurred on the property west of Rockhampton.

'You realise, of course, that your percentage

interest in Glen View will be significantly smaller than that of your partners' in this enterprise,' he ventured, hoping to appeal to the businesswoman in her rather than the emotional female obsessed with revenge. 'And that is not a sound financial investment in anyone's books.'

'I know,' Kate replied simply. 'But my partners have clearly set out that I have first option to buy them out in the future, should that situation arise. You have that in writing,' she added, tapping the folder on Hugh's desk with her finger.

'I know that,' he replied shortly and regretted his minor display of irritability. 'I was only thinking of you.'

'If you mean what you say, then you will do everything within your power to ensure that the purchase goes through,' Kate said, fixing him with her eyes. 'And I believe you will, because you have proved your love for me with the thousand pounds you so readily invested in my business. I do not know of any other man who would have done that for me when I am considered by most as nothing more than a silly young girl with grandiose ideas well beyond her capabilities.'

Hugh glanced down at the folder in front of him and flipped it open. He stared unseeingly at the copperplate writing on the pages and hoped she did not see the guilt in his face. He looked up from the folder and cleared his throat.

'You know that I love you, Kate . . . and would do anything for you.' Kate had a fleeting and disturbing feeling that his words rang just a little hollow. But she dismissed the thought as a misinterpretation by her highly strung emotions at a time when she was so near to realising her dream.

'I know that,' Kate said reassuringly. But she was not quite sure whom she was reassuring and she deliberately let the thought go from her mind. And to affirm her feelings for him she added, 'I have an appointment today to see Father Murlay about the annulment of my marriage.' Her announcement brought a wan smile to his face.

Kate rose from her chair and bade farewell as she left his office. As she did, she found herself reflecting on their meeting with an uneasy and unexplainable feeling of doubt about the expressions of love that had passed between them. There was something about Hugh's whole demeanour that did not feel right to her. Something intangible that passed between people without a need for words, but just as strong in its communication of emotions. That intangible something she could only think of as a woman's intuition. And intuition had no scientific basis – so she had been often told by men. But it was late in the day and she was weary from the busy schedule she had undertaken. All she felt was a dire need for a good night's sleep and hopefully in the morning to wake to a new and promising day.

48

They came under the cover of a thunderstorm.
Horses' heads drooped and tails tucked against
the driving rain while the troopers shivered as the
water drenched them. Although it was only late
afternoon, it felt more like early evening as the
storm had drowned the sun and extinguished its
light. Men and horses felt miserably exposed on
the scrubby plain and the numbed thoughts of the
drenched troopers were mostly on the comforts of
their barracks many long miles behind them.

Soon the land would be green and alive in the
Gulf Country. The lagoons would be covered in
flowering waterlilies and countless water birds
such as the black and white magpie geese, ducks,
herons and long-beaked ibis would flock to the
banks of the water holes. The tall and graceful
brolgas would dance with graceful leaps. It would
be a time of plenty.

But now it was the transitional period before the
dry season crept once again upon the land to bake
the earth and turn the water holes into places of
death, even for the undisputed master of the Gulf's
waterways, the giant estuarine crocodile. The

Rainbow Serpent had not yet reached His own lagoon and it could be seen in the last of the storms that rent the tropical sky electric blue and drenched the earth below with each heavy downpour of rain.

Lieutenant Wentworth Uhr's thoughts were on the small range of hills somewhere to the south of the police patrol. As miserable as the day was, it was only one such day, typical of life in the Native Mounted Police. The long-ranging patrols had often lived with the vagaries of the weather. Tomorrow would probably be oppressively humid and the police would be plagued by the myriad of insects that rose off the lush green grass to bite and sting them. The troopers would grumble irritably and yearn for the rain to return and drive away the pests.

Behind Uhr rode Sergeant Henry James, whose thoughts were decidedly mixed. In all probability this would be the second time he would meet the infamous bushranger. He secretly hoped that Tom would not be in the hills.

Lieutenant Uhr brought the mounted column to a halt as his Aboriginal tracker, who had been sent ahead on foot to reconnoitre the hills, stood silently on the trail waiting for the patrol to catch up to him. He jogged back to Uhr and stood by the stirrup of the police officer's mount.

'Big-fella hill there, Mahmy,' he said, pointing into the wall of rain to the south. 'One man blackfella, one man whitefella, one fella gin got camp.'

'Good man,' Uhr said and twisted in the saddle to address his sergeant. 'Sergeant James, we will split up here,' he said. 'You take two of the troopers of your choosing and I will keep the other five with me.'

Henry did not have to ask any questions of his boss. The plan had been worked out the night before at their last camp site. He turned to the column, choosing two Aboriginal troopers whom he knew well. They were men who had served with him at Rockhampton and both troopers were now the most experienced and reliable in the patrol. Uhr respected his sergeant's choice of men. What he lacked in numbers, he made up for in years of experience with his choice.

Henry gave the order to his two troopers to move out with him and the three policemen wheeled away from the troop to ride south. The plan was for them to take up a position on the reverse side of the hills and act as a cut-off should Duffy attempt to retreat from the advance of the main body of police.

When the rain had swallowed Henry and his two troopers, Uhr contemplated the weather. The damned rain was a nuisance! But it did provide concealment to the patrol advancing on the wanted men. He had anticipated that the bush-ranger would never expect a police patrol to be dogging him under such atrocious conditions.

'Dismount!'

The lieutenant's order to the remaining troopers was welcome, as they had a need to stretch their legs that had stiffened from the long ride and soaking cold rain. Although they would not be able to find shelter, they could at least huddle by a tree while they waited for Sergeant James to get closer to the hill.

They waited an hour until Uhr gave the order to his men to prepare to advance on foot. The horses were left hobbled and the troopers gripped carbines as they followed their officer towards the rocky slopes of the hill.

The bushrangers' camp was protected by a convenient rock overhang which gave them shelter. At the same time, it allowed for the camp fire smoke to disperse without choking them. Tom had selected the site because it was a naturally protected position with a commanding view of the sparse tree plains below. But the panoramic view only existed when it was not raining.

Mondo slapped at young Peter's hand as he snatched greedily at the flat bread damper in the hot ashes. Peter was the elder of the two boys. He was dark like his mother but he had his father's grey eyes. At five years of age, he was already learning the ways of the bush from Mondo and Wallarie. From his father, he had become relatively fluent in the English language. Tim, at four years of age, was lighter in colour than his older brother and it was evident that he would take after his father in appearance, except that his eyes were brown like Mondo's. And finally there was Sarah. Just over two years old, she had the lightest colouring of the three children. She was chubby and a spoiled favourite of her father.

'Hot!' Mondo said to her greedy son in English, but he had already learnt the lesson. He sucked at his fingers and glared at the damper while his father laughed at his son's discomfort.

'That will teach you, boy,' he said as he ruffled

his elder son's curly mop of dark hair.

Mondo smiled as she watched her man give the boy a couple of playful punches. Tom was a good man! And she was grateful that he had turned out to be a provider for his growing family. There would be a fourth child, as was evident from the swelling of her belly. To provide was all-important and a good hunter made the difference of whether a man's sons would grow strong like their father and be able to provide for their generations of families. Although her children had at first looked strange to Mondo, she had long forgotten the physical differences with her own people. She knew that, whatever they were – white or Darambal – they would grow strong.

Little Sarah sucked her thumb with one chubby arm on her mother's shoulders as Mondo sat by the fire baking the damper. They also had the delicious sweet jam that Tom had taken in a raid on a property and tea that Mondo had acquired a taste for. She was very content during the time the Rainbow Serpent was away from His lagoon. It was a time when Tom and Wallarie stayed close to their hills. A time when game was plentiful, which left the two men time to sit cross-legged and talk for hours in a smatter of English and Nerambura dialect around the camp fire. They were as close as brothers and Mondo knew this was good because, between the two men, they were able to use the best of their skills – black and white – to stay ahead of the troopers.

The storm rolled around them and the echoes of thunder bounced off the cliff faces of the ancient hills. The big bearded bushranger was laughing and keeping young Peter playfully at an arm's length as he tried to grapple with his father. Tom glanced across the fire and saw his wife staring at him with the strangest of expressions. Her big dark eyes were opened wide and she had an odd look that gave her an expression of wonder and bewilderment. He could see that she was trying to tell him something, then blood erupted from her mouth as she pitched forward into the fire.

Tom snatched Peter under his arm as the child stood stunned, staring down at his mother lying face down in the camp fire. He had not heard the killing shot of the police carbine as it had been muffled by the thunder. His father's reactions were fast. He flung the boy on the ground, knocking the air from the child's lungs.

'*Wallarie!*' Tom screamed as he made a leap to push Sarah away from the body of her dead mother. The little girl stood with her thumb in her mouth, staring wide-eyed at the body on the fire. She could not understand why her mother's head was in the flames. Her mother had always told her that fire was hot. Tim saw his father push Sarah away from the light of the fire and knew that something was terribly wrong. The little boy stood and bawled with fear until Wallarie scooped him up and dropped him behind a rock.

Tom spun and hurled himself across the open space to the body of his wife where he reached with a frantic effort for her ankles to drag her from the fire. But a vicious volley of shots rang out, sending spurts of wet earth to spatter his face and pluck at his boot, wrenching his ankle painfully sideways.

Illuminated by the light from the camp fire, he knew he was the perfect target for the marksman hidden in the rocks below. Tom was not even aware that he was screaming his frustration. He made a last desperate tug at Mondo's ankles and fell back, feeling the sting of a grazing shot across his hand.

'Leave the woman!' Wallarie screamed as he slithered across the clearing around the fire and slammed into Tom. 'Leave her now! She is dead!'

Tom felt Wallarie grasp his hair and shake him savagely. He realised that his friend was risking his own life by exposing himself in the clearing beside him. He cast Wallarie an imploring look but only received an answering plea in the warrior's smoky eyes. Death had already come to Mondo. The fire could do no more to her.

A bullet exploded a spout of earth between them only inches from both men's faces. Tom rolled away from the fire while Wallarie slid across the clearing to the protection of the rocks and the Snider rifles that were close at hand. As well as the Sniders, both men usually carried three Colts each. But now they were some feet away, wrapped in blankets to keep them dry.

The crash of rifles echoed in the hills and the whine of ricocheting bullets left shattered fragments of rock showering down on the two men and the three children, who could smell the pungent aroma of burning flesh as the red-hot coals of the fire cooked away Mondo's face.

Peter watched horrified from behind the protection of the rocks as his mother's upper body began to sizzle. He wanted to scream at her to get out of the fire because it was hot. But no words came to him and, instead, he shut his eyes as tightly as possible to make the sight of his dead mother's body go away. He could hear his father screaming at him to stay behind the rocks and keep Sarah and Tim safe. And he could feel Sarah and Tim clinging to him like the koala or possum young clung to their mothers.

On the slope in the cover of the rocks, Lieutenant Uhr roared angrily at the trooper who had fired the shot that killed Mondo. 'You bloody stupid man. I said no shooting unless fired on.'

The trooper grinned sheepishly back at his boss. 'Me tink Duffy see me, boss. Me shoot. But miss Duffy. Gettim his gin,' came the reply from the trooper and Uhr cursed him to hell. He had hoped to use the storm and the gathering night to get closer and take both Duffy and the Aboriginal by surprise . . . and alive. Now the patrol was committed to a pitched battle in the rocks and the police officer did not underestimate his opponents. They had not stayed ahead of the best of the Native Police for so long without reason.

The two shots that came from the hill were uncomfortably close to Uhr and the trooper whom he'd chastised for firing without orders. The well-aimed shots told him that the men on the hill had not panicked. They were carefully selecting their targets. It was going to be a long night.

Tom flipped open the breech of the Snider and slipped a cartridge into the chamber of the rifle. He closed the breech and pulled back the hammer. The weapon had the advantage of range to keep the police at bay while Wallarie crawled across the

666

space to where the revolvers were wrapped in a blanket and then crawled back with them to Tom. Now they had the means to deliver a rapid fire on any foolishly attempted rush by the police troopers. Neither bushranger had any intention of being taken alive.

The Irishman glanced across at the rocks a few feet away where his children were huddled. He hissed at Peter to make sure that he kept his brother and sister with him, safe between two rocks, while he and Wallarie lay on their bellies with their rifles tucked into their shoulders.

When they had fired, they would crawl away to take up a new position and their shots were always answered with a volley from down the slope. Some of the stray police rounds plucked at Mondo's smouldering body and the impact of the heavy rounds caused her to jerk as if she were still alive.

Peter saw the body twitch with each impacting round and wondered why his mother refused to get up and get out of the fire. Her death was a concept the young boy could not come to grips with, even though he knew of death. He had helped his father and Wallarie hunt and he had hunted for lizards and small game by himself. But the idea that his mother could be dead was beyond the boy's thinking.

During a lull in the shooting, Uhr had called on the bushrangers to surrender in the Queen's name. He received a chip of shattered rock in his face for his effort. He realised that by speaking he had identified his position to the men above him and Tom's next round almost found its mark. He crouched as the bullet whined away into the night and guessed that surrender was out of the question for the bushranger. Wisely, he did not attempt to call on him again.

Slowly – and very cautiously – the police troopers advanced up the hill in a leapfrogging manoeuvre as they gave each other covering fire while dodging from position to position behind the cover of the rocky slope. Each stop was just a little closer to the summit where Tom and Wallarie held them at bay.

Tom knew it was only a matter of time before the troopers would be in a position to either rush them or pin them down, without any hope of escape. So far all the firing had come from their front. He suspected there might be another party of police quietly flanking their position while they were engaged by the troopers who fired on them from below. It was the thought of the flanking tactic that worried Tom most. If it was successful, then they would be surely trapped, cut off from escape on the other side of the hill.

'Wallarie,' he called softly to his friend a few feet away, 'I want you to take the children and head down the hill behind us while I will lay on as much fire as I can and you make the break for the plains. I will keep the traps occupied here.' Tom had spoken in the Nerambura dialect in case there were troopers within hearing.

'No, Tom,' Wallarie hissed back over the space between them. 'They are your children and you must take them. I will stay for a while and fire at the black crows, because I am better than you at getting away on my own.'

He knew Wallarie was right and he reached out

668

to pat his friend on the shoulder. Wallarie was naked and he was naturally camouflaged by the night. Tom's European clothes made it harder for him to move unseen in the darkness.

'I will go when I tell you I am ready,' Tom whispered. There was no time to argue as both men had heard the sound of a small avalanche of rocks from only a few yards out, where one of the advancing troopers had carelessly dislodged them.

Tom crawled on his belly to his children and gave them short instructions on what to do. He scooped up his little daughter with one arm and held his rifle in the other hand. 'Going now!' he called softly to Wallarie in the Nerambura language. Immediately Wallarie used two of his pistols to blast away at the unseen troopers lower down on the rocky slope. When the guns were empty he rolled away from his position and fired his third pistol into the dark. The troopers instinctively kept their heads down as the bullets cracked and whined around the slope.

And it was while Wallarie was blasting away with the pistols that Tom made his break. The heavy rain may have provided concealment for the troopers, but it was a dual-edged weapon. The troopers did not know that the voice that chatted in a conversational tone on the hill was engaged in a monologue.

Wallarie kept up the one-sided conversation as he expertly reloaded his revolvers. He knew that while he held the summit, the troopers dared not expose themselves to his deadly, rapid fire. But he also knew the delaying tactic could not work forever. A bluff was a bluff in any man's language.

49

Kate's every instinct screamed. She was in dire peril for her life and lay in her bed praying that the silence of the crickets would end. She needed to once again hear their reassuring chirping in the night and know she was alone. She was not able to explain why the feeling of dread had come on her, except that something was not right. Had Luke taught her too well . . . to listen even when she was asleep?

There was an uncanny silence outside her house and she thought she had heard the dull thud of heavy footsteps on the wood plank verandah. Dear God, let it be her imagination, she prayed. As she pulled the sheet up to her chin, she remembered the little pepperbox pistol Judith had given her as a gift for her journey west with the American. Where did she leave it? Yes, in a drawer beside the bed.

Kate eased herself up and placed her feet gently on the floor. But the bedsprings squeaked with the loudness of a steam train braking to an emergency halt, and she gritted her teeth in a futile gesture to make the noise go away. Then she heard the distinctive and sinister sound of a rusty hinge as the front door to the house was slowly pushed open. Could it be Hugh come to surprise her with a visit? But her instincts echoed a hollow *no!*

Very carefully she slid the drawer open in the small wooden bedside table and fumbled for the pistol. She was rewarded with the feel of its solid frame at her fingertips. She gripped the compact multi-barrelled pistol in her hand and placed the gun on the bed as she reached for a kerosene lantern and fumbled for a wax match from a tin. But the unlit match fell from her hand as the door to the bedroom crashed open and the dark room was filled with the odour of whisky and sweat.

Kate's cry was stifled by the voice that snarled from the doorway.

'Don't scream, Missus O'Keefe.'

She flung herself on the mattress to crouch against the brass bedhead with her legs tucked under her long nightdress and she groped for the pistol jammed uncomfortably beneath her.

'I'm not come here to hurt you,' the voice said with a drunken slur. 'Just to warn you that you will never get Glen View while I'm alive. Or even after I'm dead.'

Kate was acutely aware of who the unseen and threatening intruder was.

'Mister Macintosh,' she hissed through clenched teeth. She had recognised the Scottish squatter's voice despite all the years that had passed since he had last confronted her on Glen View. Luke had protected her then. But Luke was not with her now. She realised with rising terror that she was alone facing the man who she knew in her heart had been responsible for the murder of her father and the deaths of so many innocent men, women and children of the Darambal people.

'Sir Donald to you, lassie,' he growled. 'Only my betters call me by my old title. And you aren't one of them by any long shot.'

Kate could vaguely make out the squatter sliding down her wall to sit on the floor beside the bedroom door. She considered fleeing but cautiously decided that attempting to dodge past the burly man might put her in greater danger. Instead she fought to keep down her panic and play for time. She had another option, and that was to fight. Slowly Kate eased her hand down to the pistol under her hip.

'What do you want here, Sir Donald?' she asked and tried to sound calm, although her heart pounded uncontrollably like a hammer in her breast. 'Why have you come to my house uninvited at this time of the night?'

The squatter snorted at her question.

'I've just come to tell you that I'm on my way south for my younger son's memorial service,' he replied. 'And that I know about your very foolish attempt to buy up my lease. Well, I've got news for you, lassie, and that is: it's not going to happen, because I've just got a loan to refinance Glen View.'

'Now that you have told me what you said you came to do, you can leave my house,' Kate said in a firm and unwavering voice. She was answered by a menacing chuckle from the squatter sitting in the dark.

'I'll go when I'm ready,' he said, 'and not when

you tell me. I want you to know some things about your family . . . and mine . . . Missus O'Keefe.'

'What things, Sir Donald?' she asked and heard him sigh heavily before he answered.

'Things like the fact that there is a curse on us, Missus O'Keefe. On us. And you. Oh yes, a curse that has taken two of my sons and has taken your brother. Damned if I can think of his name.'

'Michael,' Kate whispered. And his name was picked up by the man who sat across the room from her.

'Michael. Yes, Michael Duffy. It seems the bloody curse has taken my two sons, and if it all goes to course, then it will take one of your family next. Maybe your murdering bushranging brother. The Native Mounted Police will get him sooner or later.'

Kate flared and spat back angrily, 'They will never catch Tom to hang him,' she said. 'He is a Duffy. He is like my father whom your English soldiers hunted in Ireland and tried to murder at the Eureka Stockade. He stayed alive, despite their best efforts.'

'Until he came to Glen View,' Donald cut across her savagely. 'Where he was foolish enough to try to step between me and the murdering black bastard who killed my elder son. And he paid with his worthless life for doing so.'

Kate listened with cold hatred to the next best thing to a confession of guilt from the squatter and she wrapped her hand around the butt of the pepperbox pistol as her finger curled on the trigger. Fear and rage came together as a deadly combination.

'You killed my father, you bastard!' she hissed in the dark with a cold and calculating fury.

Donald laughed softly.

'I never said that, lassie,' he replied. 'And I wouldn't be putting it around that I did if I were you, either. We have laws about such things in the colonies. No, I can say with all honesty, I didn't kill your father. Let us say that I agreed with what did happen to him in the end.'

Kate raised the pistol.

'I am going to kill you, Sir Donald,' she said calmly. 'I have a pistol and it's aimed at you.'

'Then shoot, lassie,' Donald said softly. 'You could do no worse to me. It is possible that both you and I are the intended sacrifices to the myall curse because, if you kill me, you will also surely hang and dance with me in hell. Go ahead and shoot. Let me join my sons. Or are the Duffys only capable of bushwhacking their victims?'

He laughed and laughed until the laughter became almost a sobbing cry, while Kate fought to keep calm. She knew the squatter was taunting her. She would remain calm, because she wanted the man to suffer for a lot longer yet. Until she found a way of hurting him.

A dead man feels no more pain and she wanted him to be alive to feel the pain she would eventually bring him in a way that he would know had come from her. The death of his second son was *his* pain now. Even she could not make it worse and if she did kill him, she knew that would be an act of mercy. She suddenly experienced a feeling akin to sympathy for the man who she could sense was hurting as much as any human could. But regardless of her unspoken acknowledgement for his grief, she knew he was responsible for much suffering to her own family and for that he would eventually have to account.

As she pondered the strange situation being played out in her bedroom, she heard his boots scrape on the floor as he heaved himself to his feet and lurched out the door without further comment.

Kate remained huddled on the bed for some time after the squatter had left the house and she was vaguely aware that she was trembling. Whether it was through fear for the short but emotionally violent intrusion of the squatter, or the anger she felt at her own sympathy for the man's grief, she was not sure. But she knew the man had said something that had always haunted her. Was there a curse on the two families? She found her thoughts drifting to her brother Tom, whom she had not seen since she was a little girl in Sydney, a time when Tom had stood beside her father and waved as he bade her farewell. Oh, how she had missed Tom. He had always been good to her. First she had lost Michael, and now Tom was a man hunted like some wild and savage animal in the colony's wilderness.

She listened to the return of the reassuring crickets' chirp in the quiet and solitary hours of the morning. A dog barked from somewhere in town and further in the distance she could hear the mournful cry of the curlews. A cold shiver went through her as they seemed to be calling to her . . . or someone in her family!

And she experienced another fear that she did not want to admit that had come from something Sir Donald had said in his drunken and rambling discourse. How did he know about her attempt to buy his lease?

50

As Tom picked his way down the other side of the
hill, his thoughts were of Mondo. But he knew that
he could not dwell on her death. To do so would
distract him from his primary task of getting their
three children to safety. Mondo would have
wanted that. She had been born of a people whose
dictates were practical and, in their often harsh
world, the survival of the young mattered to the
countless generations of women of the Nerambura
people.

The distant carbine and revolver fire continued
spasmodically from atop the hill as a seemingly
harmless popping sound. Tom made his way with
the children to a site at the base of the hills where
weapons and food were cached for such an
emergency. The horses that had been left hobbled
and grazing on the plain might have attracted the
attention of the troopers who could be lying in
ambush waiting for him to make an attempt at
riding out. He knew he would not be able to use
them in his escape.

When he finally reached the bottom of the hill at
the edge of the long grassed plain, everything went

terribly wrong. First the rain ceased and then the clouds parted to allow the moon to shine through.

Tom was also acutely aware of the frightening silence that now came from the top of the craggy hill where Wallarie had been holding the troopers at bay. He knew that he could not have run out of ammunition as they had stocked a good supply of powder and ball.

The pale light from the half moon revealed a sea of dripping grass as high as a man, beyond which were the thinly scattered trees of the plain. Tom hefted Sarah off his shoulders and placed her gently down, and he gripped the Snider in both hands as he quickly surveyed the horizon to his front. At least to cross the moonlit plain would allow the tall grass to swallow them as surely as the sea rolls over a drowning man. But using the grass-covered plain would also make it easy to track him and the three children.

'Stand in the Queen's name!'

Tom froze. The bastards had ambushed him! The command came from his right and the voice was vaguely familiar. He could see that he was only twenty paces from the long grass and the concealment that beckoned to him. But the bloody moon had lit them up as surely as a lantern in a public bar.

'Sergeant James! That you?' Tom called into the night warily. He sensed that he was at the end of a rifle sight, as the voice had been very close. Twenty, maybe thirty yards, he guessed. He still held his rifle as he desperately sought about for cover. Peter clung to his belt and would not let go. Sarah now held Tim's hand and was crying softly as she trembled with fear for the strange events of the night.

'It's me, Tom,' Henry called back. 'Throw down your gun. I'm not alone this time.'

Henry knew that if the moon went behind the clouds he would lose sight of the bushranger. And had it not been for the rain stopping and the moon suddenly appearing, Tom could easily have slipped past his flimsy cordon. The police sergeant knew that the bushranger was stalling for time, waiting for the moon to disappear, then he would try to make a dash to the taller grasses of the plains.

'I have my kids with me, Sergeant James,' Tom called. 'Tell your troopers to be careful about where their trigger fingers are.'

Henry could see the big man silhouetted against the night sky, but he could not see the children. Then he saw the slight movement of Peter's head next to Tom's waist. He swore. He did not know Tom had kids. If things went bad, the children could be caught in a lethal crossfire.

'How many?' he called to Tom.

'Three . . . two boys and a girl.' The clouds were too far apart. The time was running out for him to make a break for the concealment of the long grass.

'Then for the sake of your kids you had better throw down your gun, Tom,' Henry pleaded. 'I don't want their blood on my hands. Nor do you.'

The Irish bushranger knew the police sergeant was right. To try to make a break meant that Henry and his troopers would be forced to shoot, and in the dark bullets did not discriminate between the innocent or the guilty. Although he was prepared to take the chance in making a dash for the long grass, it would mean putting his children's lives at risk.

The moon was only seconds from a cloud which now drifted across the sky to swallow the half circle of light. The frogs croaked in a deafening cacophony of sound as he watched the two troopers rise out of the long grass with their carbines pointed at him. They were advancing on him, taking advantage of the last seconds of light. Although Tom knew there was a slim chance, young Peter still had hold of his belt. Little Sarah sobbed while Tim was silent. He was too frightened to make a sound.

Tom sighed. He might have a chance. But his kids were all that he had. The rifle dropped from his hands and he raised them above his head.

'It's done!' he called to Henry, who rose from the grass with his rifle levelled.

The night exploded and a bullet took Tom in the back, flinging him forwards.

Henry looked up and could see the line of troopers on the hill with rifles raised to their shoulders. Smoke drifted like an evil mist around them as the echo of the volley of shots shattered the night. There had been a terrible mistake!

'Christ, no!' Henry screamed as he sprinted forward to drop on his knees beside the critically wounded bushranger. He ripped a scarf from around his own throat and tried desperately to stem the flow of blood, although he knew it was hopeless.

The three children stared wide-eyed at the big white man who cradled their father's head.

'You once said you knew Kate, Sergeant James,' Tom said, clutching his chest, and Henry nodded. 'I'm not going to see the sun rise . . . I know that. But I want you to promise me that you will get my kids to Kate, wherever she is,' Tom said, fighting back the darkness that came on him in waves. There were things to be said before he died. Urgent things.

'I can do that for you, Tom,' Henry said gently. 'Kate is living in Townsville and I promise you that I will get them to her. I owe you that much. What happened here tonight wasn't personal.'

'I know that, Sergeant James,' the dying bushranger said with a pain-twisted grin. 'Peter is my oldest,' Tom continued. 'That's Tim over there holding onto Sarah's hand,' he said, turning his head. 'They are a bit wild and Kate will have to be firm with 'em. Look at that! The bloody moon is finally gone and I'm lying here in the arms of some bloody trap. It's not a decent thing, Sergeant James,' he said with an attempt at a laugh, then began to choke on his own blood.

Henry knew Tom was almost gone when he had made his observation of the moon's disappearance behind the clouds. The moon had not disappeared. The evening sky was clearing and the stars, washed clean, sparkled overhead. Tom stiffened and with a long sad sigh, he relaxed.

Henry rose slowly to his feet. 'He's dead,' he said in a flat voice and the children stared wide-eyed at the police sergeant, although they did not understand what the white man had said.

Henry looked at the three children huddled and trembling together, and wished he knew what he should do next. But his troubled thoughts were distracted by the sound of the remaining troopers picking their way down the track from the hill with Lieutenant Uhr leading the way. When they reached him, they cast the children curious looks while the police lieutenant squatted on his haunches to examine the body of the dead man at Henry's feet.

'Tom Duffy, sir. These are his kids. He surrendered without a fight . . .' Henry began angrily, but knew that, in the circumstances, it was really no one's fault. 'Just one of those things.'

Lieutenant Uhr rubbed his face wearily. 'Well,' he said with a sigh, 'at least we got one of them. The blackfella got away on us. Damned well slipped past us when we were right on him,' he said. 'I suppose we should be grateful we didn't suffer any casualties.' He stood and stared in the direction of the Duffy children. 'We will have to take them back to Burketown and let the authorities figure out what they are going to do with them. We'll camp on the hill and bury the gin in the morning. Duffy's body goes back with us. You can organise the men to bed down for the night, as I doubt if we will find the blackfella now he is on his own. At least not for a while.'

'Sir!' Henry acknowledged. He would talk to Mister Uhr in the morning about the fate of the Duffy children. For now it was a matter of consolidating their position for the night. They were all weary and the tension of the events of the past hour had taken a toll on their spirits. Henry knew he would somehow get the children to Kate. What happened after that was up to her. But he also

682

knew that she would not allow the sons and daughter of her brother to be cast aside. They were, after all, her kin.

The rain was gone and the clouds had drifted away. In the distance, the curlews called to the spirit of Tom Duffy. Wallarie also heard the cry of the curlews and knew his friend was dead. How? He could not tell. But he knew he would never see him again. Except in the world beyond the Dreaming.

The Aboriginal warrior cast away his rifle and revolver. They were things of the white man's world and their possession would mark him to the white men who would always hunt him. Naked and without the guns, he was as much a part of the land as were his ancestors. Ancestors he would avenge, as the warrior of the cave had called to him for vengeance.

While he walked with the sounds of the bush and the light of the shimmering stars above, he knew it was time to return to the old ways. He gazed up at the heavens, seeking the spirits that would guide him on his journey. And when he found the spirits he sought, he commenced the long journey south to the traditional lands of the Darambal people.

As the last full-blooded Nerambura tribesman, he would sing the death chant for his white friend whose spirit he knew was now sleeping, one with that of the sacred hill.

Hugh Darlington shrank from her fury as Kate stood quivering in her rage in the doorway of his office.

'You told him about the purchase,' she said with a venom in her voice to match the fire in her grey eyes that were like flints throwing off sparks. 'You told Sir Donald, even though you swore your love for me. Why? I cannot understand why you would do that.' Her last statement trailed away as a plea, a desperate attempt to allow him to explain the impossible.

'I cannot tell you my reasons, Kate,' he replied in a choked voice as he sat behind his desk. For a second Kate felt almost a twinge of sympathy for him. He looked so pathetic as he sat slumped in his chair and he no longer appeared in her eyes as the strong and decisive man she had loved. He was like a snivelling, goddamned son of a bitch, Kate thought, and she wondered how the strong language of the American prospector had crept into her thoughts so easily. She shook her head, turned her back and slammed the door as she walked out of his life.

The only two men she had given herself to had betrayed her, she thought savagely. But she refused to allow her sense of loss to overwhelm her in maudlin sentimentality. And all the men who had truly loved her – her father, brothers and Luke Tracy – had been taken from her life in one way or another.

As Kate swept across the dusty street striding purposefully to her office, she held her head high and had a set expression of determination on her pretty face. A few bystanders stared curiously at the beautiful young woman who marched past them without acknowledging their greetings. Anger was an emotion easily felt and none dared ask the fiery Kate O'Keefe what was wrong. The expression on her face did not invite questions.

In her office, she leant on the closed door and burst into deep racking sobs.

Kate cried not for the betrayal of a worthless man who had used her for his own carnal needs, but for the men she knew she would never see again. The men who had truly loved her in their quiet and gentle ways.

51

Kate heard the rattle of the wagon outside her house and she felt her panic rise as it came to a stop. It had to be Sergeant James bringing them to her, she thought, as she steadied herself. He had said in his telegram that he had expected to arrive with them today. Who else could it be?

With a brief glimpse in the mirror she patted her hair and took a deep breath. Then she went to the door with a rustle of her best satin dress and a confident demeanour. But when she opened the door, her confidence evaporated.

The three children stood on the wide verandah with frightened and confused expressions on their faces. They were dressed in ill-fitting and ragged European clothes that Henry had been able to scrounge in Burketown. They looked like trapped animals before the tall and solid frame of their captor, Sergeant Henry James.

'Good afternoon to you, Missus O'Keefe,' Henry said solemnly, dusting down his trousers with his hat. 'I have them safe and sound, as you can see. They weren't much trouble. Still trying to come to grips with their situation, I suppose.'

'Would you like to come in and have some tea?' Kate offered as her eyes scanned the three little faces.

The sergeant nodded. 'That would be nice,' he said. 'It's been a long trip.'

'I'm sure it has,' Kate replied politely as he gently herded the three children through the door.

Kate poured the tea from a well-used and blackened kettle into fine china teacups set on the table and added a spoon of sugar to each. Henry accepted his cup with a mumbled thanks while the children gazed curiously around the kitchen, taking in its plain clean decor. Newly painted and unadorned wood plank walls were marked by sooty smoke stains from the small wrought-iron combustible stove.

Kate had moved into the house a few days earlier, after she had received the telegram from the police sergeant informing her that her brother was dead and that Tom had bequeathed his three children to her care.

The move to Townsville had been very much her way of leaving behind a place that held few happy memories for her. She would miss the many friends that she had left behind in Rockhampton, but Judith Cohen had quietly reassured her that she and Solomon would go about the transfer of her business interests while she started to make a home for Tom's children. Kate had thanked her with tears and hugs.

Kate placed slabs of freshly buttered bread on a plate and offered it to the children, who accepted the meal with shy and apprehensive gratitude.

They ate the bread smearing butter on their little faces. Kate noticed the eldest boy catch her eye with some defiance as she passed him the buttered bread. It was then that she felt a twinge of guilty regret for accepting the responsibility of rearing her brother's offspring. Would she prove adequate for the daunting task ahead?

Henry sipped his tea in a rather delicate manner for such a big man.

'They were no trouble on the trip over from Burketown,' he said, by way of conversation. 'Poor little buggers don't know what they're in for, I suppose.'

'They will be suitably cared for, Sergeant James,' Kate replied quickly as if the policeman had somehow read her guilty thoughts. 'I expect they will need time to settle in.'

'They've been roaming the bush with your brother and his gin,' Henry said tactlessly and he realised the error of his thoughtless statement. 'I'm sorry, Missus O'Keefe. I didn't mean it that way.'

'I understand,' Kate replied. 'And I agree that they have been living a wild and nomadic life. But I'm sure they will adapt to life with me.'

'I'm sure,' he echoed awkwardly and he sipped his tea while Kate sat down at the table to drink hers.

'Was Tom given a decent funeral?' she asked softly and Henry bowed his head.

'We buried him as a Christian. I made sure of that. Least I could do for him. He was a good man, despite him being a bushranger,' he said with faltering words. He still had trouble finding means to express his mixed feelings for the man he had hunted over the years.

'And what of the mother of these children?' she asked, glancing at them. 'Did she get a decent funeral?'

A pained expression clouded the sergeant's bearded face. 'She weren't a Christian,' he replied with an edge of embarrassment in his voice. 'We left her in the hills where she died. Figure that was the blackfella way. The way she would have wanted.'

'You could be right,' Kate reflected. 'She was a woman of the plains and bush and it is probably fitting that her soul remain with the land that was her home.' She paused and stared at an empty place beyond the sergeant. 'It's just that . . . I think my brother would have liked the mother of his children to be with him in the eternal sleep.'

Henry did not have an answer. He was a man who had seen much death in his lifetime, from the bloody battlefields of the Crimea to the terrible dispersals of the colony. Death was death! It was time to make his departure and return to his wife and son waiting for him at Burketown.

'If you are right with the kids, then I will be best getting back to the missus,' he said awkwardly. 'She sends her regards and says that if you need any help, you only have to ask.'

'Please thank Emma for her offer,' Kate answered with a warm smile. 'You can tell her that I will visit as soon as I have the children settled in. Or she should visit me whenever she has the time.'

Kate saw him to the door and waved goodbye as he hauled himself up onto the seat of the wagon. The draught-horse snorted and pulled the wagon away with a bump and a rattle down the dusty road.

She returned to the kitchen where the children stood looking at her with dark eyes. The boys watched her with suspicion while young Sarah followed her with the growing curiosity peculiar to toddlers. Kate stared back at them with tears welling in her eyes. This was all that was left of her brother – three mixed-race children. Three children caught between two worlds, she thought with growing despair. But her despair turned to hope when little Sarah toddled towards her with her chubby arms held out.

It was then that Kate knew that she would overcome all that life could cruelly thrust upon her.

52

No one was quite sure where the stories had started. But the old shepherds told them to the young stockmen. And they told the stories so convincingly that the younger stockmen did not scoff at their conviction in the telling. It was said that the land around the ancient volcanic outcrop on Glen View was a cursed area. A *baal* place! A place where eerie balls of fire had been seen rolling aimlessly along the plains on hot and prickly nights. A place the Aboriginal station hands avoided with the inherent knowledge that the hills were a sacred site to be respected by the living.

Sir Donald dismissed the stories as superstitious nonsense. He lived alone in his newly built homestead. It was a grand place of mudbrick and wide cool verandahs. It had many rooms and should have been the home where Angus brought his bride. A woman who would have borne the sons for the Macintosh name to continue. But it was an empty place, where Donald sat alone on the verandahs in the evenings, gazing bleakly out across the stockyards and stockmen's quarters. And from the verandah he was able to view the grave of Angus nestled under the shadows of a big old gum tree.

Six years had passed since his son's death at the hands of the Darambal warrior. Sir Donald rode on an annual pilgrimage to the place where his son had been slain.

In the dusty depths of the brigalow scrub, not far from the old camp site of the Nerambura clan who once lived on the creek, Sir Donald was able to remember a living son. Here he was truly able to mourn as he sat astride his horse and talked to Angus as if he were a living entity in the scrub. He talked to him of the past season. He talked about the land and how he would forge Glen View into a place Angus would have been proud of . . . had he lived. And when his words no longer came, he cried bitter tears for all that had been lost to him at the end of a Darambal spear.

At sundown, Sir Donald spurred his mount forward to ride to the water holes where the few remaining bones of the Nerambura people could still be seen scattered in the dust and dry grass.

He dismounted and knelt to scoop water with his cupped hands from the gently flowing stream. Soon the continuing dry season would slow the water to a sluggish and eventually stagnant halt. He sighed when he had finished drinking, and waited patiently until his mount had finished taking her fill. As he stood there, he idly scanned the surrounding bush hushed with the first approach of evening. It was a peaceful time when the land lost its harshness to take on an exhausted serenity cloaked in the soft pastel colours of the setting sun.

He turned his attention to the west where the

long shadows of the small range of hills spread slowly across the dry scrub and dusty plains, and he shaded his eyes as he gazed up at the summit of the sacred hill.

With a sudden and explosive fear, he realised he was not alone!

Against the setting sun was a distinctly ominous silhouette. A tall and naked warrior stood watching him. Sir Donald did not have to see the man's face. He instinctively knew who he was.

'You!' he hissed as he rose slowly from the ground, reaching for the pistol in his belt. There was a blur of movement in the orange glow of the setting sun and the squatter felt his body plucked backwards as the long wooden spear buried itself deep in his chest.

Wallarie squatted impassively in the dust watching the white man die. The flight of the spear had been true. The man who had ordered the dispersal of Wallarie's people lay on his back, clutching the spear as he glared with hate-filled and despairing eyes up at his executioner. Sir Donald Macintosh died with a final strangled cry of Gaelic words that Wallarie did not understand.

When the man was dead, Wallarie rose and walked towards the sacred hill.

One day he would come.

Wallarie did not know when. All he knew was that the warrior of the cave was real. Even now Wallarie was being called from beyond the grave to hunt and kill the devil with the pale blue eyes and black heart.

Although he did not know when the warrior's

spirit would rise from the grave, he did know the white men of Glen View would eventually find the squatter's body and they would recognise the Nerambura spear.

It was important that the white men knew it was the spear of the last surviving warrior of the Nerambura clan. The last of his tribe.

EPILOGUE

Across the great river dividing Mexico from the United States of America lay El Paso and Fort Bliss. And from Fort Bliss to El Paso's sister town of El Paso del Norte rode Major Alfred A. Lees of the United States Army in company with a man known by all as Maori Jack.

They crossed the broad and sluggishly flowing river under a blazing sun, wearing the clothes of western drifters. Their mission into Mexican territory was of a sensitive nature and the sight of military uniforms was not conducive to their meeting with the man Maori Jack had identified weeks earlier while carousing in a Mexican brothel.

The two men came armed, although their big Colt revolvers were concealed from view. This was a place where a gringo could end up with his throat cut for the price of his boots. But, despite their disguise as drifters, both men exuded an air of two men whose boots were best left on their feet. Major Lees had the hard look of a man acquainted with war and the solidly built man who rode beside him had the scarred look of a man used to violence.

In the Mexican town, they reined their horses at a cantina and hitched them before warily stepping inside the drinking establishment. For a moment, the cool gloom of the place caused them to hesitate as they searched the corners for the man Maori Jack had assured the major would be there. Maori Jack nodded his head and steered the major towards a trestle-like wooden table in one corner where a tall and broad-shouldered young man sat facing the door watching them with his one good eye. Over the other eye, a black leather patch indicated the extent of his disability.

'I brought the major,' Maori Jack said as he stood at the edge of the table, looking down on the young man whose single grey eye appraised the two visitors with calculated interest. 'He's gonna talk to you 'bout sumthin' that's no business of mine.'

'Thanks, Jack,' the young man said without rising. 'Get yourself a drink at the bar while the major and I talk.' He produced a silver dollar and slid it across the rough plank table to Maori Jack, who grinned as he picked it up.

'Reckon I will,' Maori Jack replied and he turned to walk to the bar where a big man of Spanish–Indian blood stood watching the two strangers from behind dark eyes. The place was empty with the exception of the three gringos, and the barman was grateful for the patronage.

'I believe your name is Michael Duffy,' the major said as he sat himself down at the table. 'And that you are looking for employment.'

Michael nodded and pushed a glass and a bottle of clear and fiery liquid towards the major, who he

696

guessed to be in his mid-thirties. From the way the major spoke, it was obvious to Michael that the man was probably a West Pointer.

'That's right, Major,' Michael said, filling his own glass. 'Kind of got myself unemployed after Señor Pablo Juarez was elected president of Mexico.'

The major filled his glass and took a delicate sip of the fiery local brew.

'You have an interesting history, Mister Duffy,' the major said as his eyes watered from the effects of the drink. 'Not only did you fight for the Union forces in the war, but you also fought under Count Ferdinand von Tempsky in the Maori Wars in New Zealand. And lately with Juarez's forces against the French in Mexico . . . a man with considerable military experience considering your age. How old are you? Twenty-five, thirty?'

'Twenty-seven,' Michael replied bluntly. 'That got anything to do with the possibility of me working for you?'

'Not particularly,' Lees replied with just the hint of a smile. 'Just that you are pretty goddamned resourceful for a man of your limited years. Maori Jack told me about your supposed death in New Zealand before you came over here to join up and fight. Got the Congressional Medal of Honour as a captain, didn't you,' he said rather than asked.

Michael scowled. 'Cost me my bloody eye,' he said quietly. 'Rather have the eye than the medal. The change to my face didn't help much in hiding me from my past.'

'Maori Jack told me how you and he fought together in New Zealand,' Lees said. 'It may be your good luck that he recognised you after all those years, as you seem to have the qualities I am looking for ... for the work I do.'

'What work would that be, Major?' Michael asked with a glint of challenge in his good eye. 'Spying?'

The major frowned and leant forward on the table towards Michael.

'It's called intelligence,' he said softly. 'And it wins wars where stupid commanders would necessarily lose them if they weren't told what their counterparts were thinking. Like knowing that you are wanted for murder back in your home town of Sydney in New South Wales. I believe they hang men for murder in Australia, like we do here.' He was pleased to see that his intimate knowledge of Michael Duffy's history had wiped any expression of haughtiness from the Irishman's face.

The knowledge had come easily, as Maori Jack was familiar with the events surrounding the young man's reasons for faking his death after his true identity had been exposed in the '63 Waikato campaign. Maori Jack and Michael had served together under the legendary Prussian adventurer Count von Tempsky, in one of his guerilla units fighting the Maoris. And it had been Maori Jack who had aided Michael in his escape from the law in New Zealand, only to meet again by chance, thousands of miles away in a Mexican brothel.

'I need work,' Michael said, chastened by the major's coolness. 'And it seems that the only work I know now is what I've done since New Zealand. If you have that kind of work, then I am your man without question.'

'I think you are, Mister Duffy,' Lees replied. 'And you have a job, as soon as I get permission from my superiors in Washington to hire you. So you can come home to the States and leave this Mexican shit behind.'

'Home for me, Major, is a long way from the States,' Michael replied quietly. 'Home for me is a place on the other side of the world across the Pacific.'

'Yeah, I forgot,' the major said, bravely taking a gulp of the drink from his glass. 'You're a Paddy.'

Michael stared briefly into the eyes of the American sitting across the table from him and replied, 'I was once an Australian. But now I'm a man who fights for anyone who can afford me.'

'Maybe you'll get home one day,' the major said as he rose from the table and caught Maori Jack's eye. 'Meet me at Fort Bliss headquarters next week and I'll confirm you are with us for a job down in South America. Maori Jack tells me you speak passable Spanish.'

Michael watched the two men depart the cantina and walk into the sun-baked dusty street outside. He sat and stared at the rectangle of brilliant light marking the place of their exit and he wondered on a place he had not thought about for many years. Just staying alive had kept his thoughts on the places he had been, rather than where he had come from. His life had changed so dramatically in a mere six years. All he had known, since that fateful night in a Sydney back-street, had been war. But now the American major's words echoed in his mind. 'Maybe you'll get home one day.'

If he ever did then he knew he must return as another man. But that would not be hard. War had made him another man and the skills, which were once gentle and creative, had been blasted out of him on the battlefields. He was no longer the aspiring painter. Now he was a soldier of fortune. Maybe he would return home one day, he thought. If he did there would be many scores to settle.

THE END

AUTHOR'S NOTE

In the tradition of the historical saga, fact and fiction have been woven together to produce the tapestry of this story's setting. All Aboriginal tribes mentioned are fictional with the exception of references to the Darambal people, who inhabited the Fitzroy basin region of Queensland, and the Kalkadoon tribe. I have used upper case when making reference to the entity of the Rainbow Serpent although this usage may not be considered grammatically correct. This was not done out of a need for political correctness but motivated by my personal perception of the sanctity of other people's spiritual beliefs.

The use of the police dispersals (a euphemism for genocide) is well documented, although it was not legitimised by the laws of the time. In defence of the Native Mounted Police, it should be noted that not all commanding officers abused their power as portrayed in the character of Lieutenant Morrison Mort. One officer who did was the infamous Frederick Wheeler, who was eventually captured by the authorities. He, however, was never brought to trial, and disappeared. Some say he escaped to the Americas. Aboriginal folklore says that in his escape from European law he met with Aboriginal law and was duly punished.

Lieutenant Wentworth D'Arcy Uhr is a real character. In 1866, at the age of twenty-one, he was appointed to command the Native Mounted Police at Burketown. Alone, his real life exploits could be used as the basis of an action adventure novel. I have used literary licence to place him in the hunt for Tom Duffy as the arduous and dangerous trek was typical of his nature.

Port Denison as it was once known is today called Bowen. Burke's Land is today known as the Gulf Country and Burketown its tiny capital – a town with a wild and colourful frontier history and a place well worth a visit for the adventurous traveller.

Readers of this novel may draw interesting comparisons to what we call today America's Wild West. The comparisons are valid. The Colt revolver and Snider rifle were companions to the settlers as the Colt and Winchester were in the Americas; their impact on indigenous people was just as deadly.

The age of the blackbirders in our history had parallels with slavery in the Americas before their bloody Civil War. But it should be noted that not all recruiting methods were as barbaric as those employed by the character of Mort. Many of the recruits were more than willing to leave impoverished islands for a chance to earn European goods in the far-off colony of Queensland.

The 'baby farms' referred to in the novel actually existed and are a dark and infamous chapter of Australia's colourful history. The practice of handing over unwanted infants to private concerns was finally addressed in the 1886 *Select Committee on Registration of Births, Deaths and Marriages* and 1892 saw the passing of a Children's Protection Act. In 1893 a John Makin was hanged for numerous acts of infanticide and his wife sentenced to life imprisonment. For years they had been burying the bodies of babies in various Sydney backyards and at least fifteen of these have since been located. How many more backyards conceal these tiny bones may never be known . . .

But all this and more is best described by the two authors of historical works I used as a basis for the story. Glenville Pike and Hector Holthouse have written extensively on the events of the Queensland frontier and I thoroughly recommend their works to anyone interested in learning more about Australia's own wild north of the nineteenth century.

A SELECTED LIST OF FINE WRITING
AVAILABLE FROM CORGI BOOKS

14168 2	JIGSAW	Campbell Armstrong	£5.99
14169 0	HEAT	Campbell Armstrong	£5.99
14496 7	SILENCER	Campbell Armstrong	£5.99
14497 5	BLACKOUT	Campbell Armstrong	£5.99
14645 5	KINGDOM OF THE BLIND	Alan Blackwood	£5.99
14646 3	PLAGUE OF ANGELS	Alan Blackwood	£5.99
14586 6	SHADOW DANCER	Tom Bradby	£5.99
14578 5	THE MIRACLE STRAIN	Michael Cordy	£5.99
14654 4	THE HORSE WHISPERER	Nicholas Evans	£5.99
14495 9	THE LOOP	Nicholas Evans	£5.99
13823 1	THE DECEIVER	Frederick Forsyth	£5.99
12140 1	NO COMEBACKS	Frederick Forsyth	£5.99
13990 4	THE FIST OF GOD	Frederick Forsyth	£5.99
13991 2	ICON	Frederick Forsyth	£5.99
14224 7	OUT OF THE SUN	Robert Goddard	£5.99
54593 7	INTO THE BLUE	Robert Goddard	£5.99
14225 5	BEYOND RECALL	Robert Goddard	£5.99
14597 1	CAUGHT IN THE LIGHT	Robert Goddard	£5.99
14376 6	DETECTIVE	Arthur Hailey	£5.99
13691 3	WHEELS	Arthur Hailey	£5.99
13699 9	HOTEL	Arthur Hailey	£5.99
13697 2	AIRPORT	Arthur Hailey	£5.99
54535 X	KILLING GROUND	Gerald Seymour	£5.99
14605 6	THE WAITING TIME	Gerald Seymour	£5.99
14682 X	A LINE IN THE SAND	Gerald Seymour	£5.99
14722 2	HARRY'S GAME	Gerald Seymour	£5.99
14391 X	A SIMPLE PLAN	Scott Smith	£5.99
10565 1	TRINITY	Leon Uris	£6.99
14047 3	UNHOLY ALLIANCE	David Yallop	£5.99